DISCARD

181804

REUNION

A novel by Michael B. Oren

MacAdam/Cage Publishing
155 Sansome Street, Suite 550
San Francisco, CA 94104
www.macadamcage.com

Library of Congress Cataloging-in-Publication Data

Oren, Michael.
Reunion : a novel / by Michael Oren.
p. cm.
ISBN 1-931561-26-5 (alk. paper)
1. World War, 1939-1945—Veterans—Fiction. 2. Americans—Belgium—Fiction. 3. Reunions—Fiction. 4. Belgium—Fiction. I. Title.
PS3615.R46 R48 2003
813'.6—dc21

2002153580

Manufactured in the United States of America
10 9 8 7 6 5 4 3 2 1

Book design by Dorothy Carico Smith.

Publisher's Note: This is a work of fiction. Names, characters, places, and incidents either are the product of the author's imagination or are used fictitiously. Any resemblance to actual events, locales, or persons, living or dead, is entirely coincidental.

REUNION

A novel by Michael B. Oren

MacAdam/Cage

For My Father

Between the shadow and the ghost,
Between the white and the red,
Between the bullet and the lies,
Where would you hide your head?

Your name and your deeds were forgotten
Before your bones were dry,
And the lie that slew you is buried
Under a deeper lie;

But the thing that I saw in your face
No power can disinherit;
No bomb that ever burst
Shatters the crystal spirit.

—*George Orwell*

☆ ☆ ☆

Who else is going to hold still and listen to us talk? We're as obsolete as dinosaurs. We're the old fools who saved the world.

—*Gwyn Liddell*, veteran of Iwo Jima,
quoted in the *New Jersey Star Ledger*, Feb. 27, 2001.

PROLOGUE

The old man bore his sack through the forest. He was a large man, his back, gnarled and brawny as an ox-yoke, broadened by a greatcoat of some dark but indeterminate color. His head—sloping brow, swollen nose, an immense, low-slung jaw—was ox-like as well, and topped with a moth-eaten hat of a style last seen in the '50s. The oilskin sack was stuffed to bursting, thick and nearly as long as the old man himself, and cumbersome. Yet he wielded it indifferently, gripping the sack with a pair of iron pincers that he balanced across his shoulder. He tramped, this old big man in a greatcoat and a hat, lugging his sack through the evergreen wilds of the Ardennes.

The branches were frost-laden, the temperature flirted with zero. Early morning fog, dense and resinous, clung to the earth, the tree trunks, and the cuffs of the old man's galoshes. Weather made little difference to him. He'd taken this trip so often, and always his pace was the same, and his path, headlong through the trees. Snowbirds ceased warbling whenever he approached and foraging varmints scampered. The forest, he felt, was his.

He plodded, and a brownish liquid seeped where the pincers pierced the sack. Blood. It trickled along the tails of his greatcoat and down into his galoshes' heels. The old man ignored it, though. Neither wetness nor weather, distances nor burdens affected him. His numb strength was legendary in this corner of the Ardennes, an area not wanting for legends. Many attributed it to his hearty diet or to his lifestyle, solitary as a monk's. For most, though, he was merely a simpleton, too weak in the head to distinguish between light and heavy, wet or dry, heat or the cold. *Le crétin*, they called him, *der Trottel*—the fool. Didn't even know he was old, they said.

He was aware of the rumors about him, and recalling them now, he smiled. Gaping, drooling: an idiot's smile, and yet he flourished it regally. The trees seemed to arch back in awe. He was a man with a secret, and a secret, he knew, was power. It made him strong, enabled him to lift a fully grown sow or solid blocks of ice, kept him fit while others withered. Freed him from needs—running water, electric lights, or even a dog's companionship. A man with a secret was self-sufficient, he believed, and more perhaps—immortal. He marched through the branches that slapped his shoulders, as though the forest itself were congratulating him.

In time, the woods gave way to a clearing. Sunlight bored through the fog, through the moth holes in the brim of his hat. In the misty glaze, he could imagine the meadow that once flourished here—feather grass and fescue, lavender and rye—before it became a battlefield. Here the soldiers had fought, six days and six nights, with their aerial bombs and incendiary rounds, their mortar shells and potato mashers. The soldiers had ravaged the meadow; the grass had never grown back. The earth, still barren, crackled beneath the old man's galoshes as he climbed a craggy hill.

He climbed to the top, a ridge, tipped up his hat and wiped his sweating forehead. In the ground around him were shallow pits, half-filled with needles now but once deep enough to hide a man, to fight from during the battle.

The battle had been fiercest on the ridge, hand-to-hand. Wave after wave of Germans attacked only to be beaten back by the Americans. But the Germans kept coming and at last the defenders gave in. Like ghosts they rose, hands raised, and hobbled down to the meadow.

The battle had harmed him as well. It destroyed the cottage where he and his father lived, and blew his father to bits. That winter, half-starved, he was reduced to scavenging the forest for bullet-casings and helmets, canteens and shells, all to sell for scrap. But in the spring he made his fortune, not in metal this time, but meat.

Bodies: the forest was rife with them. Sprawled on the ridge, coiled in gullies where the wounded had crawled off to die. How had he known to collect them, to stuff them in his sack and haul them back to the cold house? Could he really be the fool they claimed he was, knowing the Americans would come?

And come they did. An officer and his assistant, the two of them sent to find and tag those bodies and to ship them home for burial. He paid well, that officer, twenty dollars for every corpse, fifteen for sundry remains.

With the money he earned he rebuilt the cottage and revived his father's business, delivering freshly killed meat from the farms to the villages, to Houffalize and Saint-Vith. And so he had thrived for fifty years or more—he never counted—alone and content with his secret.

The old man tugged down his hat. He hitched up his sack and skidded down the ridge, back into the trackless forest. There he encountered rows of concrete obstacles—dragons' teeth, they called them, though he couldn't remember whose teeth they were, the Americans' or Germans'. He slalomed through them, hustling now through an aura of his own steam. Twenty paces onward and already he could see his yard.

Arriving, he paused and peered for any sign of trespassers, for the children who sometimes spied on him, on the fool and his oilskin sack. But all was as he'd left it: the yard, the cottage. The cold house snug in its hollow.

Squat and oblong, sagging in the beam, the cold house had been built by his father—the father who rarely spoke to him but beat him like another beast—out of stone so thick not even the bombs could jar it. Inside, on hooks, the carcasses hung, seemingly adrift in darkness. Inside was the ice that preserved them all; that held the stones the officer hid, and kept his secret forever.

The officer had come for the stones, he said, but what he really wanted was the secret. Touching, groping him to get at it. But he hadn't succeeded; the pincers had seen to that. Bleeding, the officer ran, and since then no stranger had entered the cold house. All remained as it had been back then: unchanged and unchanging, divine.

The old man let the sack slip to the ground, flexed and curled his fingers. Already he could see himself relaxing that night, galoshes off, enjoying a smoke by the fire. But first there was work to do. The hog to be quartered and cleaned and readied for the Hotel Ardennes, whose proprietor still cared about quality. Who'd given him a key to the kitchen door, so that he could deliver his meat directly.

The old man hated the village, hated the Americans who stayed there to relive their days in the war. Drinking in Saint-Vith, or in Houffalize, dancing all night with the ladies. Loud and brash, weak and sentimental, he avoided them all, the louts.

But would they avoid *him*, the old man wondered as he descended to the cold house door, fiddled with its rusted padlock. Would someday that officer return, more desperate than ever to reclaim what had never been his? If so, the old man was ready for him. He had his strength still, his pincers. No one—no foreigner certainly—could steal his secret and live.

The padlock dropped open, and the door, lightly pushed, creaked inward. Stooping under a lintel so low that even as a child he'd had to dip under it, the old man dragged his sack over the threshold, across the floor slickly lacquered with blood. The door swung shut, but he paid it no notice. Backward he stepped, threading through the meat, deep into frozen darkness.

Book One

ROLL CALL

ONE

Buddy Hill was getting anxious. He didn't like airports, didn't like ports, period. An inveterate homebody, he'd only been overseas once in his life and that was hardly out of volition. His idea of a vacation was an afternoon lolling in his favorite armchair, with his beer and the Game of the Week. Come Christmas time, when other folks his age with sufficient cash and brain cells rushed south, sunward, he insisted on staying in the frigid north, fast by the tree and in the company of his only grandchild. Yet here he was, a retired bank manager from Rutherford, Iowa, thrust into the chaos of New York's Kennedy International Airport. Disoriented, cut loose from the home he loved, he felt his anxiety rising. His temperature, too. For Buddy Hill was sick, very sick. The man who'd spent his entire adult life reviewing and approving other people's loans was himself living on borrowed time.

Kaye could almost feel her husband's discomfort, but there was little she could do about it. The irony of the situation struck her that after years of trying to entice him with eye-snatching brochures, with secondhand reports of their neighbors' trips abroad, that they should be embarking for the dullest part of Europe, in December. "Travel is nothing but trouble," had always been his answer, and he would repeat it at every opportunity, like one of the aphorisms he'd coin for his clients at the bank. Clever Buddy Hill, affable, ever so dependable. Dimples like parentheses around a smile that said "trust me." If he weren't so ill right now she'd murder him.

"Travel is trouble," Kaye grunted, just loud enough for Buddy to hear.

"You can say that again." He scowled at the brash, confetti-colored lights, at the plastic Santas and holly wreaths garishly marring the walls. Yuletide Muzak thrummed. "Damn loudspeakers. My head is splitting."

"Time for another pill, then."

Kaye, herself feeling wobbly in the knees, deigned to loop her arm around his elbow. What could she do? Here was her husband, the man she'd lived with and loved, her best friend and confidante, since she was eighteen. Of course he could be bullheaded at times, was prone to picking his nose at restaurants and missing the toilet at home, but otherwise he was a good man, faithful and aboveboard, a churchgoer. But then this same man had decided to leave her now, suddenly, a widow in her old age.

She pointed her cane at a bench. "You ought to sit down," she said flatly. "You look pale." Buddy flexed his arm slightly, subtly squeezing hers. "No problem," he lied. "I'm fine."

He felt God-awful. Beads of cold sweat dappled his forehead. His head swam and his bones ached, and a dogged little man with a jackhammer—so he imagined him—was drilling into the base of his spine. He wasn't going to complain, though, especially not to Kaye. He hardly thought she'd sympathize.

☆ ☆ ☆

It was all Sorgenson's fault. Plump, bald, and doughy-skinned, Dr. Sorgenson looked a bit like a tumor himself, especially as he pinned up Buddy's X-rays. Then in a voice muted to instill calm, the doctor dealt him the blow. But Buddy wasn't shocked, wasn't even perturbed. He'd long sensed something was wrong with him, *really* wrong. Aches where they shouldn't be, night sweats, and then this unshakable exhaustion. Duly, he asked some questions—*What kind of pain we talking about, Doc? What's my time-frame?*—and received the standard replies. A man of his age, he'd seen these things often. He knew what more or less to expect.

But then Sorgenson started in on this newfangled treatment he'd been tinkering with, wheeling out an arsenal of terms none of which

Buddy had ever heard of or understood with the exclusion of one, "radical surgery," and that was enough. The rest of it was just wasted breath, the business about the 50-50 survival rate, the impotence and incontinence, the danger of paralysis, partial or total. Buddy had already made his decision. Period. He promised Sorgenson that he'd get back to him promptly—anything to shut him up—but in turn wanted the doctor to keep this matter between them and not tell anyone, especially not his wife.

Especially not my wife. The reason for the request seemed so clear to him then, noble and selfless. Eminently the right thing to do. Kaye was not going to squander her golden years tending to some incapacitated eunuch, no way. Their relationship had been too solid, too *right*, to end ignominiously. No, he'd go out pretty much the way he was now, if not in his prime then at least still able to eat and shit for himself, the way he'd want people—her—to remember him.

And she might have, if Sorgenson had kept his word. If he hadn't tried persuading his patient through his patient's wife so that now, in addition to being mortally ill, Buddy was also in trouble. Loose lips had sunk his ship but good. He came home from running errands one evening to find his supper uncooked and Kaye in his armchair, stewing.

"No glorified lumberjack's going to cut me down," Buddy, without waiting for her to say anything, declared. "I was born with these balls and I'll die with 'em."

From then on Kaye was on the warpath, a state he'd learned to dread. The times in their marriage when she was boiling, steam-out-of-the-ears mad at him—a few slipped birthdays, a school recital he'd plum forgotten about, working late at the bank—could be counted on his fingers, but then oh how those fingers would shake. A perdition's worth of anger could be fired up inside that little white-haired lady with the double hip replacement and a cane. She barely uttered a word to him that night nor any night or day thereafter for two weeks running. His condition worsened, but so, too, did her wrath.

Coping with that fury, in any condition, was Herculean enough—the last thing he needed was that phone call. What he did need was a quiet

Sunday afternoon after church, enthroned on his armchair with the game about to start, with an opened bottle of beer that he hadn't the stomach to drink but enjoyed the presence of anyway. He needed just to sit and feel normal again, as if maybe nothing had changed, but then the phone started ringing—once, twice—and the sickening feeling returned.

Buddy just stared at it. Probably some salesman: all-weather lawn chairs, time-sharing in Vermont. "Call me after the Super Bowl," was how he'd usually greet them, or with another aphorism—"To supply is saintly, to solicit, profane"—just before hanging up.

The third ring, the fourth. The message recorder only came on after the sixth—Kaye needed that many to reach a receiver—but then he'd be safe. Off the hook, as it were.

"You can answer that, Edwin," Kaye chided him from their bedroom upstairs, where she'd gone to change into house clothes. "*That* won't kill you."

He'd groaned, "I got it. I got it" like some lackadaisical outfielder, and finally reached for the phone. "Hill."

There was no response at first, only the crackle of a long-distance line. For a moment Buddy assumed that this was his daughter Allison, calling from Long Island. She phoned dutifully every week and always with the same questions: "Have you been keeping busy, Dad? How's Mom getting around?" And he'd answer them, equally dutifully, all the while waiting for the moment that she'd hand the phone over to *her* daughter—his granddaughter—a person with whom he could really hold a conversation. Thrilled by that prospect, he almost spoke her name.

"Ain't no 'o' at the end of that Hill?" a voice on the other end snorted. "Shit, Buddy, where's your manners?"

A taut, twangy voice, menacingly edged, like razor wire. He'd recognize it anywhere—on the phone, in a foxhole, over the shriek of incoming rounds.

Buddy sunk into his chair. "Major."

"Major," the voice mimicked Buddy's response. "Pathetic. What say we try that again? Major!" The receiver blared in his ear. "Why, I haven't seen you in a calf's ass! How the blazes are you?" The Major answered himself. "Not bad, Buddy, not bad t'all, given them vital statistics. Signing autographs left and right. Folks still takin' me for Clint Eastwood."

Buddy didn't say a word, didn't have to. Christened something-or-other Walker (nobody seemed to remember his real name or where he was from, exactly: somewhere in Texas), he'd made his rank in World War II and kept it ever since. Inherited a fortune and doubled it, a combination rancher and oilman. The Major: hawk-nosed and bow-legged, rascality in his eyes and a shit-eating grin. An authentic pain in the butt.

"Clint Eastwood or Brad Pitt, whoever the fuck *he* is," the Major drawled on, and then, without so much as a breath: "And you?"

"Fine. Fine. A little slower, I guess."

"Slower, hell, I'm still waitin' for you to get your butt back on that ridge."

Buddy frowned. He rolled his eyes and wondered if the Major could sense them rolling.

He'd seen him a handful of times over the years, and the memories were equally lurid. The Major in Boston yakking up a storm, relentlessly extolling his exploits, military and carnal. The Major "just passing through" Rutherford with a girl about Allison's age who disturbingly referred to him as "Daddy." The Major, drunk and pinching asses, nearly getting himself killed by those asses' escorts, in a Chicago convention hall where Buddy hoped he'd recognize no one. There was something child-like about the Major, as if he were moving in the opposite direction from the rest of their contemporaries, getting younger while others aged. Any day now, Buddy mused, the man could be sporting diapers.

"Suppose you know why I'm callin'."

"If you're planning to be anywhere near these parts, Kaye and I would surely..."

"You didn't get it, did you?"

"Get what?" Buddy asked. "What didn't I get?"

"The invitation, damn it." The Major enunciated the next word carefully, majestically almost, accenting the first syllable—*Re*—and slurring the last two: *yunyun*.

"You're not serious…"

The Major laughed his hacking, smart-ass laugh. "Yeah, well, I *do* have that reputation." This reunion would be different, he explained. This one would be held in Saint-Vith, on the ridge, six days of touring topped by an unveiling ceremony, a stone commemorating their battle. "All that and maybe even a night in Houffalize, dancing with the ladies. Leave it to Label," the Major said.

The reference was to Leonard Perlmutter, the world-class historian who started out as B Company's lowly clerk and after the war acted as the veterans' corresponding secretary, sending out Christmas cards and birth and death notices, and once every some-odd years, organizing reunions. Professor Perlmutter. Label.

"To Label," Buddy repeated. "But, shoot, Major, I don't know… Christmas and all. And I haven't been feeling my best lately. What I'd give to be seventy again…"

"Don't you pull that crap with me, Buddy Hill," the Major shouted, so loud that even Buddy with his blunted hearing had to take his ear from the phone. "Once was enough." Buddy was waiting for this, the guilt-trip. That "once" referred to the time that he, Lt. Hill, had left his men on the ridge and never again returned.

The Major went on, shifting gears. "We're talking duty here, Hill. *Solemn* duty. Fact is, I need you there."

"You need…" Buddy audibly gulped. "Me?"

"We're takin' our bows here, Buddy, and it's got to be honorable. You know what I mean. Nothing can happen…" the Major paused and practically whispered. "*Unbecoming*."

"No. You're right. Nothing."

"This time 'round, Lieutenant, we win."

The dial tone wailed like a siren. He didn't notice it, though, nor the ruckus on TV as Houston ran an interception eighty yards to the goal. Only when Kaye eased her way down the stairs—left foot first, followed by the cane, then the right—and asked "Who was it?" did he finally snap out of it.

"Don't know," he lied again. "Some crank."

He couldn't watch the game anymore, couldn't concentrate. Short of halftime, he found himself wandering over to the bookcase, kneeling imprudently to the bottom shelf. There, jammed between a never-consulted Cajun cookbook and Allison's piano scores, he found the album. Brought it back to his armchair and blew the dust from its cover. The pages inside were fragile—the borders came off in his hands—and the photographs, yellowed, as if they'd been taken not fifty but a hundred years ago, back in some mythic past.

Mythic. The word kept hounding him as he browsed. Pictures of gutted buildings, of troops on the march and of pretty young girls toasting the photographer with wine. Paris, Leipzig, Berlin. Vistas of the Rhine looking placid, after it had run with blood. Belgium before the battle... He viewed them all as if they were part of somebody else's life—he felt that far from them. *Youth is but the dream of old age, a fantasy*, he found himself thinking. Another aphorism.

Buddy came to the last page. He fumbled in his blazer for his reading glasses and brought the book close to his face. There, beneath the final photograph, he recognized his early, cursive script. *B Company, 133rd Infantry Battalion. Saint-Vith. December 14, 1944.*

Some wore their helmets, others held them like great steel studs on their chests. In light waist-length jackets that were soon to prove laughably inadequate, several of them even sporting sunglasses, they looked like a fraternity out for a Sunday brunch. Except for the fact that they were armed: M-1 Garand rifles and bandoliers of .30 caliber clips, hand grenades and bayonets, a Thompson submachine gun or two. And yet they seemed totally at ease, laid-back, as though all this armament was merely an accessory, as if nothing in the world could go wrong.

The Major was the easiest to identify, even then. A thumbs-on-his web-belt type of man, rangy and tough. There was goofy Spagnola, a round-faced lug with glasses and a paunch that he'd managed to maintain, even on battle rations. Towering over Spagnola was a boy they called Sweet—was that his real name?—with a face as long and flat as a plowshare, a farm boy. There was Pringle and Croker and Pfc. Tommy Vorhees, otherwise known as the Vicar. And there was Sgt. Joseph Papino, *Pappy*, the hardened veteran of North Africa and Sicily who'd taken one very green lieutenant and taught him what he needed to survive.

He saw that lieutenant now, strapping and broad-shouldered, with the high cheekbones and narrow eyes of his mixed Scottish and Blackfoot blood, and a smirk on his face that seemed to say 'take your best shot, I can handle it.' The rugged youth who'd moved to town after his parents' farm folded, who'd grown up poor, the object of derision at school because of his patched-up overalls and hand-me-down shoes, but who'd showed everybody by becoming a star running back and captain of his team. Who'd then been drafted, donned a different uniform, different helmet, and was commissioned an officer. The kind of young man who, just by the looks of him, was likely to return home and marry the prettiest little girl from up the street, to settle down and get a respectable job, an officer now of the bank. A man who'd take life and its ample joys—a honeymoon, picnics, promotions—in stride, as he would its one great tragedy: the death of his only son. Who'd retire at the honorable age of 70 (the bank practically begged him to stay on) to the home he'd built, to a bottle of beer and the Game of the Week, to spend the rest of his days with the only woman he'd ever loved, who happened to be his wife.

Buddy Hill hardly recognized himself. He tried to imagine being back in that lithe, robust body, gazing out through the brightness of those eyes—at himself, a very old man with a fatal disease whose wife was barely talking to him, a man estranged from his youth.

He was about to shut the album when another figure caught his eye. Standing apart from the others in the photo, posing with his movie star's face—sleek-featured, square-jawed—and his crest of hair that Buddy remembered as red, was a private, maybe nineteen years old. He stared down at the camera with a mixture of amusement and contempt, hand on jutted hip as if to convey his coolness. "Featherstone," Buddy muttered out loud. "Dean Featherstone."

A week after the phone call, the invitation finally arrived. Rag paper, black embossing, with the unit's snake and sword emblazoned on the crest—Label always did things right. The text was terse, though, like a battle order:

THE MEN OF B COMPANY
OF THE 133RD INFANTRY BATTALION
REQUEST YOUR PRESENCE
AT A REUNION
TO BE HELD IN
SAINT-VITH, BELGIUM, DECEMBER 16 – 22
RSVP, PROF. (CPL.) L. PERLMUTTER

And as though he'd really received an order, he knew he had to obey. For all his attempts to forget what the Major had told him, denying it to himself, even lying about it to Kaye, he realized there'd be no getting around it. Not this time. Some obligations are just like that, Buddy concluded, inescapable.

"A reunion? The problem's not in your balls, Edwin, it's your brain."

Buddy took cover in his armchair, practically coiled into it. A bear of a man, even now, well into his eighth decade, he could still be an intimidating presence when he needed to be. Amazing, then, how instantly that veneer could contract when confronted with his own folly.

"It's not as if it's the first one. I've gone to 'em before—when was that, five, six years ago?"

"I remember, all right. Remember you saying, 'Kitty, next time they invite me to one of these things, remind me to saw my foot off!'" Her tone had become emphatic, her cane, stiffly planted, an exclamation point. "And three days was one thing, but this, six, and in..." She whipped the invitation up to her eyes and grimaced. "Whatsitmacalled."

Of course she was right: Boston had been a fiasco. Thanksgiving at Allison's in Long Island with the reunion just a few hours' drive up the pike. How could he have refused? Or so he'd justified it to Kaye—justified it to himself as well, when in truth it was merely an impulse. Call it curiosity, wanting to see how the men would react to him after all these years. But few of the men had shown, deterred by an early snow, and so it was three days at the bar mostly, in the Major's garrulous grip. A disaster, in short, and yet here he was selling it to Kaye again, telling her this time was different.

"Saint-Vith. The town's called Saint-Vith, and it isn't Boston. It's..." He paused, swallowed hard, and changed course. "I have to go. I know it sounds nuts, but they're depending on me."

"And what about *me*? Who the hell do *I* depend on?"

"Aw, Kitty, we're talking apples and oranges here. Apples and oranges." Buddy shifted to the edge of the armchair, preparatory, it appeared, to kneeling. His voice mellowed with candor. "The men want me there. There aren't going to *be* any more reunions after this one. It's the last. They're old now, not just *getting* old, *old*."

He was sputtering, he knew, clawing his way out of the hole he'd dug himself. Not that it would've helped. Never in their forty-eight years together had he ever seen his wife this mad.

But she was more than mad. She was incredulous and frustrated and scared, but most of all hurt, wounded in a way she hadn't been since the death of their son, Robert—Bobby—from polio. Buddy talked of obligations, but only one obligation mattered to her—the one that bound married people to stay together, to stay alive, at least. Now that bond was being broken. Trampled on, ripped. Now, on top of it, her husband was proposing to squander his last holiday season in some godforsaken village, drinking too much and rehashing shaggy war stories. And the cruelest thing was: he probably expected her to join him.

Two months later, sure enough, there was Kaye packing for them both. Grousing about how bullheaded he was, knowing how much he hated traveling, especially in his present condition. Yet, *how would he make it alone?* she asked herself. *How could she let him?*

Call her old-fashioned, but forty-eight years after vowing to, she intended to stick with her promise, to stand by him through health and sickness, whatever. The whole rigmarole, she still bought into it and was too old a woman to change. Call her a fool, but she still loved her husband, Buddy Hill.

☆ ☆ ☆

On his tiptoes, Buddy strained. A tall man, at least for his generation, a six-footer, he struggled to get a glimpse of the crowd. The motion was excruciating; that little man was at it again, boring with his jackhammer through Buddy's spine. Yet he refused to sit until he found them.

"A reunion, at Christmas time, of all things," Kaye grumbled. "Who would choose such a time?"

"The Germans," Buddy responded, but only half-attentively. His search was growing frantic as their boarding time approached, as the danger loomed that he might not get to see them—see *her*: his granddaughter—at all.

"Edwin, would you *please* sit down!"

He wouldn't, of course, and Kaye knew there was little use trying to persuade him. He was in his dependable mode, that same bent of character that had been his success in life. Dependability in the war, at the bank. Dependability in searching for Allison, who had supposedly come to Kennedy, along with her husband and daughter, to see her parents off.

Allison, a bright but distant person, frail in a way reminiscent of Kaye, but Kaye at seventy, not as a middle-aged woman. Giving birth to her in the wake of Robert's death, when she wasn't even sure she wanted another child, Kaye doted on her, pampered and championed her. But Buddy, the lovingest father to his son while he lived, matched his daughter's distance precisely. He paid for her ballet and piano lessons, attended her recitals, and finally sent her off to Mount Holyoke, a chemistry major preparing for med school. He'd done his duty toward her, that much was certain, and when she met Paul Butrospolus, an Amherst grad, and married him, it was Buddy who'd helped the boy through law school. Loans for the house, for a car; he was always there when they needed him. The couple settled in Marblehead, Massachusetts, Paul's hometown—Iowa was out of the question—where Allison set up house, promptly forgot about medicine, and instead found work in pharmaceuticals.

To Allison, he was a dutiful father, but to her daughter, Melissa, he was much more, something else entirely. She'd come into the world when everybody, Buddy included, had given up hope; after Allison had tried every treatment in the book, was nearing forty and had already reconciled herself to barrenness. And then, out of nowhere, Melissa. A miracle, an ineffably generous gift.

Buddy couldn't explain it exactly, the intensity of his attachment to her. Outwardly, there was nothing all that special, a rather homely girl with her mother's thin face, broad nose, her father's Mediterranean complexion. Yet she was unlike any other child he'd ever met, any person, period. Or maybe being with her made *him* feel different—relaxed, uninterested in appearances or having to seem strong: himself. And though he rarely saw her more than once a year, at Christmas, he made the most of those times, reading to her, playing cards, dolls, anything just so long as it was with her. He'd ignore Kaye's insinuations that he was spoiling the child, or Allison suggesting, "Say, Dad, maybe you could use a rest."

He could certainly have used one now, could've sprawled down right there on the airport floor, he was that exhausted. But he wasn't going to rest, not for a single second, until he found her. He searched, but all he could see were gift-laden people rushing for flights, people of hues and getups rarely seen in his parts.

In the holiday tide he stood, tilted slightly in his herringbone coat, pylon-like. Stood with his thick salt-and-pepper hair, his eyes a strong tempered blue and his teeth entirely his own. Dressed in his cardigan, corduroys and loafers, he could still project that country squire look, careless, as if the years had merely glanced him. But not Kaye. Of that petite, pretty girl he'd married, the once-avid golfer and Ladies' Club devotee, scarcely a glimmer remained. In her place was this wizened woman in sneakers and baggy pantsuit, her fingers crooked on a cane. Seeing her reminded him of the injustices of life—and the ironies. The old cripple might well make it to one hundred, while her husband was unlikely to live out the year.

"That's it, I'm sitting down," Kaye announced finally. "You want to give yourself a heart attack, good. Either way…"

"Kitty, hold on," he called as she clutched her purse and worked her cane, paddling toward a row of chairs.

Buddy was all set to follow—next thing you know she'd be lost, too—when he heard it. The call was faint at first, drowned out by the PA system on its *n*th rendition of "Jingle Bell Rock," and for a second he thought it was his own ears ringing as they tended to ever since the war. But then it reached him again, the cry: "Dad! Hey Dad! Over here…"

He turned this way and that, totally flustered.

"What? What is it?" Kaye asked from the chair. He looked like he was gasping for breath.

"Nothing. I heard something, that's all. Allison, I thought."

The confusion continued until he finally felt a tap on his back, a two-fingered rap that was probably meant to be gentle but sliced up his neck like a blade.

"Jesus, Dad, didn't you hear us?"

He managed to show her a smile. "There you are. Your mother and me, we were worried." He motioned toward the chair where Kaye was waiting, motioned her to stay where she was; *they* would come to *her*.

"We were looking and looking and looking," Allison said in her nasal, slightly simpering way. She placed a kiss on his cheek and Buddy cupped her shoulders, noticing how scrawny they felt beneath her coat. Allison, too thin and long-faced, her skin and hair that same washed-out color, bleached, he imagined, by the fluorescent lights of her lab.

"You had *us* worried," said Paul. He shook his father-in-law's hand, a conscientiously firm shake, and Buddy matched the pressure, marveling as he always did what a strange couple they made—pale Allison and her plump, swarthy husband, shorter than she by a head. And yet together they'd produced Melissa, as perfect a being as he'd ever in his life encountered.

The three of them drifted over to Kaye; Allison insisted she sit. Kisses were exchanged, then pleasantries—*How was your flight in? Do you believe this holiday traffic?*—while Buddy remained oblivious. He was looking around again, as frantic as ever, though trying not to show it.

Melissa was nowhere in sight.

Was she sick? Busy with other things—birthday parties, girl scouts? He couldn't bring himself to ask. But just then, like a jack-'n-the-box, she sprung up from behind the bench. Braid and tongue flailing, "Gotcha!" she shrieked.

Allison clutched the front of her coat. "Melissa, will you *please* not do that. I told you..."

"You've already been punished once today," Paul put in.

Her parents scolded her but her grandfather only laughed. One of his rare but memorable belly laughs, and for a moment the others—Allison, Paul, and Kaye—just stared at him. Melissa, meanwhile, scrambled over the bench, in her red skirt, black tights and bulky brown sweater: a calico comet. She caught him at midsection and with such a thrust that he nearly lost his balance—his consciousness, too, with the sudden jolt to his bones. But he hugged her back, relishing the heat of her face, her hair's prickly tickle, the tang of bubblegum.

"Oh my, that's quite a hug there. Best I've had in—how long's it been, Kitty?" But Kaye didn't answer.

"My Granapple," Melissa sang, using the name for him she'd coined as a toddler and kept, a special endearment, though she was nearly eight.

"Melissa..."

She pulled away from him, finger wagging in his face. "Missy."

"Oh, yes, I'm sorry," Buddy pouted, "Missy," then stooped with puckered lips. Melissa giggled and puckered her lips as well, moved them toward his but before they met, blew a bubble that instantly burgeoned and burst.

"Melissa!" boomed her parents in unison. But Buddy and his granddaughter were too busy laughing, picking the gum off from one another's faces, and laughing even harder. Hardly noticing the battery of expressions—Kaye's impatience, Paul's disapproval, a captious envy on Allison—aimed at them.

"Go kiss your grandma," Buddy instructed her, and after rolling her eyes, Melissa skipped over to Kaye, who refused to be kissed until she'd reached into her purse for a tissue and wiped the little girl's face. Melissa then turned back to Buddy with arched brows—*Was that okay?* they asked—and Buddy looked up at his family, sighing, "I think we'd better get moving."

They joined the procession of passengers heading for the departure gates. Allison and Paul escorted Kaye while in front of them, in their own cloistered world, an old man and his granddaughter bantered.

"You like drawings?" Melissa was asking.

"You mean do I like looking at drawings or drawing drawings?"

She turned up a nostril, lowered a tawny brow. "Don't play dumb with me," she warned.

"Okay, okay. I *did* like drawing once. Horses especially. Only I wasn't very good at it. Just the tails."

"Tails are easy," Melissa agreed. "Hooves are hard."

"Hooves are downright impossible."

Try as he did not to, he was staring at her—at her pert, pursed mouth reddened by bubblegum, her defiant chin, and the kinky black hair that was not so much tied back as battened. She seemed to him life in its essence, life reduced to a brazen, mega-potent drop. Walking with her, he could think of nothing else—not illnesses, not reunions—nor wanted to.

"I was never much of an artist," Buddy admitted. "More of the practical type. Mortgages, CDs, money market accounts. Boring stuff."

Melissa sneered, "pl-*lease*," hands clapped over her ears. "But before all that boring stuff you were a soldier, right? Very handsome—Grandma told me. Mommy, too. Very brave."

"Well, handsome maybe..."

"They gave you medals!"

"Medals aren't everything. Anybody can get medals."

He took the liberty of stroking her hair, the part of her person she was always fussiest about. She let him. Her mind was on other things, he could see, assessing incompatible data, probing the quirky universe of adults.

"And that's why you're going back there," she suddenly deduced, "to prove you *are* brave."

He chortled, "Kind of late in the game for that."

"Then why are you going, Granapple? I don't get it..."

He chortled on for a moment longer before realizing that Melissa wasn't chortling with him. She was crying. A real tear cut down her cheek—wrung, so it felt, from his heart.

"Oh, don't be sad." Buddy stopped and knelt on one knee—screw the pain. He held her quavering shoulders. "Please..."

"You're going far away and you can't spend Christmas with me at your house."

"It's not true. Who told you that?"

"I did."

Buddy looked up. Allison and Paul had caught up with him, the two of them like brackets around Kaye, at once supporting and restraining her.

"Me, I told Allison." She fixed her husband squarely. "We're getting back on the 23rd. It would've been too much for you."

Kaye was talking sense, of course, but sense wasn't her purpose. More like vengeance. Buddy could see that right away, and he wondered if Allison had noticed it too.

"Nonsense, Kitty, I can handle it." He made a show of springing up from his crouch, a costly demonstration. "Your husband's as fit as a bull."

"Pity the bull," mumbled Kaye.

"Really, Dad, Mom's right," Allison cut in. "You don't seem yourself, I'm sorry. Maybe this whole trip is too much. It's not too late to cancel."

"You aren't getting any younger, you know," Paul offered.

Buddy felt a tug on his sleeve. "You could always come to our house," Melissa whimpered. She had tears in both eyes now, a double-barreled cry that almost had him crying too.

"Hey, that's a grand idea."

Kaye sighed, "We'll see, Melissa," and taking their cue from her, exchanging fretful glances, Paul and Allison agreed: "We'll see."

They walked in silence now, Buddy and Melissa, holding hands. Her hand felt weightless, febrile yet powerful, giving and extracting as it squeezed. And he returned those squeezes, meekly.

They arrived at the security check and the sign that warned TICKETED PASSENGERS ONLY BEYOND THIS POINT. A woman's voice broke into "White Christmas" to announce that the flight to Brussels would begin boarding.

"I guess this is it," Buddy exclaimed, trying his best to sound upbeat, but all the same feeling foolish. Seeing himself as Paul and Allison saw him—a sappy old geezer struggling to recapture his youth—or, worse, as Kaye and Melissa did: a huge disappointment, a cad.

That moment it dawned on him: the connection between his granddaughter and his wife. Two females, one nearing the end of her life and the other just starting, jilted by the same selfish man. The man who had pledged to them, each in their own way, to remain steadfast and true—at the very least alive. Now he was breaking that pledge.

The point was hammered in by the look that Kaye gave him as he again knelt to receive Melissa's hug, as he felt her tears on his cheeks and heard her voice in his ear whispering, "You *are* coming back. You have to promise."

He embraced her, hard as he dared without hurting either of them. "I promise. Of course I promise, cross my heart." His chin lay on her shoulder, but his eyes were locked with Kaye's. Her eyes were calling him *liar*.

Good-byes were said all around. Buddy received another peck from Allison and another studied handshake from Paul. Kaye kissed all three of them, and then, after a slight hesitation, accepted her husband's elbow.

"Have a great time, folks, enjoy yourselves," Allison called after them.

"Take care," said Paul.

"You, too," Buddy replied, then twisted for a final glimpse. "You be good, Melissa."

The little girl whipped a sleeve across her eyes and under her nose in a single peevish sweep. "Missy," she sniffed.

He had thought his decision courageous at first, the manly thing to do. The *moral* thing, for hadn't he led a full life until now, so why be greedy for more? And even if the surgery succeeded, at best he'd be half a man and maybe less, a vegetable.

But then, helping his wife down the ramp, he remembered, too, how heroic he'd felt on the ridge, volunteering to take Sgt. Papino with his frostbitten feet back to the aid station, straight through enemy lines. A regular Sergeant York. But after delivering Pappy, Lt. Hill never returned to the ridge. He remained in Saint-Vith while the men of B Company, the men who'd depended on him, fell prisoner.

Heroism. Dependability. Cowardice. Neglect. Where was the thick black line that used to separate them, Buddy wondered. Everything seemed so fuzzy, particularly now, with his medication wearing off. Here was Kaye's arm on his, at once distant and needy, and on his cheek, the sting of dried tears and gum. But then there was the ache in his bones, the fatigue, and that spot on his spine where the man with the jack-hammer was drilling. An eagle-nosed man with a shit-eating grin who, it occurred to him suddenly, bore a nagging resemblance to the Major.

To the accompaniment of babies wailing, they entered the plane, to a teenage chorus of "hun'red bottles of beer on the wall," raucous and off-key. There was pushing in the aisles, and scattered arguments about seats—all of which reminded Buddy, in case he'd forgotten, what trouble travel really was. That he despised all kinds of ports, and airports especially. How he hated that word, terminal.

TWO

"First the alarm goes off—*woo, woo, woo.* Just like that. Then, sure as you're sitting here, some smart-ass cop or security guard comes swooping down and arrests me. *Me.*"

Spagnola paused and looked around the group—squinted, rather, through the hazy-thick lenses of his trifocals. He always began with the alarm going off and mimicked the sound loudly, making sure that the members were listening. They were, of course; that was their job, to listen. They *came* to listen, every Wednesday night from eight to ten-thirty. They knew Spagnola's stories by heart, as he knew theirs, but repetition was what the therapy was all about, reliving the traumas again and again until they became trivial, sufferable. And so the same stories were told, Wednesday after Wednesday, and Spagnola's was by far the longest.

"There's a logical explanation, of course. I got it all figured." He pinched the brim of his Caterpillar cap and hitched up his trousers, shifted his ample bulk from one flank to the other of his bowling jacket. "There's this top-secret file, see, this manual. Law enforcement types get it, and inside there're these mug shots of most-wanted criminals. Counterfeiters, ax murderers." Spagnola shrugged, "I guess I just *look* guilty."

Wherever he went it seemed—to football games, into banks, down the street for a beer—he was always getting detained, body-searched and interrogated. He'd even been tackled by a federal agent, once, during a visit of Pope John Paul II.

"Can you imagine that, an old fart like me? Fat, half-blind, half-*dead*, and a practicing Catholic to boot. Imagine me takin' out the Holy Father?"

The members of the support group went on nodding, as instructed. They never spoke during these "testimonies" as they were called, never offered advice or encouragement. They never laughed, certainly, though Spagnola liked making people laugh. It was the one sure thing he was good at.

Only the group leader could make comments, that was the rule, and the group leader—the rule-maker—was Captain Carruthers. He, too, had been a POW. Seven years he'd wasted in a Vietcong gulag, tortured and diseased, only to emerge and find his life a shambles, his wife shacked up with some other guy and his own kids strangers to him. And yet he'd managed to rebuild himself, sliver by sliver, relying on that same balls-to-the-wall grit that had kept him alive, kept him sane, in captivity.

"Of course you're not a threat, Francis," Carruthers spoke now. "It's just a coincidence, probably all in your mind." He perched on the edge of a high stool (the others sat on folding chairs) a spare, severe-looking man whose features seemed to have stripped down for survival—thin lips, tapered cheeks, no more nose than was necessary. His eyes and hair were the same color—steel gray—and his accent either Southern or Western, anything but Northern New Jersey. He pointed officiously at Spagnola. "But *you* have the power to get beyond that. All of us do."

By "us" Carruthers meant not only the members present but all those who had sat in those same chairs before them; all who, throughout Warfare, had suffered the indignity of capture. It was a category of men that had dwindled radically over the years. Though the group was always eager to accept new members, none of the nation's more recent engagements—not Panama or Granada or even the Gulf—had produced so much as a single released POW. Now, all that remained were five veterans of Korea and two from Vietnam, late-middle-aged, solidly middle class men whose ghosts were manageable, especially if let out once a week and aired. And then there was Spagnola, the oldest of the bunch, from World War II and practically a specter himself.

He'd always been faithful in attending the sessions, fanatical even, squeezing them in between Tuesday night bowling and Thursday's meetings of the Kearny chapter of the Knights of Columbus. He liked the veterans' company, he said, that camaraderie, and was unabashed in his worship of Carruthers. He welcomed the chance to get out. Yet there was also a deeper need. It wasn't just the ordeal of having been captured by the Nazis, marched clear across Germany in the snow, degraded, battered, and starved—enough to drive anybody into therapy—but the more terrifying realization that he'd never really been free, not even before the war. That he'd practically been born a prisoner.

☆ ☆ ☆

The problem began, Spagnola told the group, like so many problems of this sort, with his father. Tough guy, busted nose, few teeth, a hard-drinking dockhand working the night shift in Hoboken—"not whatcha call the bonding type." Spagnola Senior rarely saw his son, never shot the bull with him about sports or the facts of life, never shagged him fungoes in the park. But he did beat him regularly for the slightest infraction, viciously. However drunk or bushed from his nightshift, he always had it in him to thrash what he called "that filthy, sissy, good-for-nothing kid of mine," using his studded belt.

"Quite an arm on him, my old man," Spagnola observed. "Coulda pitched in the majors."

His home, in Jersey City, was a rickety affair, porous to rain and the noxious smells of the docks. But inside it was spotless. "You could eat off them floors. We *did*," Spagnola swore, and it was all thanks to his mother, the saint. A woman on her knees, or so he still pictured her, a lumpy form bent over a scrub bucket. Laboring all day, her nights spent mostly alone, and yet she managed to bring seven little Spagnolas into the world, to wash their clothes and wipe their butts and noses. But their souls were another matter, too precious for a working-class woman like her. Their souls she consigned to the Church.

That was his second home, the Church, or more accurately his real home, since he passed so much of his time there. Weekdays it was Our Lady of the Assumption, a grim, brown-brick building, bland and echoing inside, where the canings of the nuns were a very close second to his father's. Yet he received other things as well—catechism, faith, awe and communion. And guilt. Above all guilt, though for what, precisely, he was never entirely sure. The way he understood it, the mere act of living was a crime and a mortal one at that. This was the knowledge drummed into him every weekday at Our Lady, and on Sundays, during mass. Born in sin, you're pretty much bound to die in sin as well, and spend all of eternity paying for it. Francis grew up convinced he was on probation—worse: that he was behind bars already, already accused and presumed derelict, pending trial.

When not at Church, Francis Vincent Spagnola—it was always Francis, never Frank—spent most of his time indoors. Always pudgy, even as a kid, uninterested in sports, he remained in his room shunning the neighborhood stickball games, the high school mixers, his brothers and sisters. He collected parakeets, at one time amassing as many as nine of them, each bird named for a saint. But then his father got rid of the bunch—the chirping awakened him mornings—and after that there were no other hobbies, no interests. Francis listened to radio shows, "Jack Benny" and "The Shadow" being his favorites, and occasionally struggled with his homework. Often he prayed, if for no other reason than to kill time, and wondered if anybody was listening.

So passed his youth with few changes and fewer expectations of changes to come. After graduation, he'd most likely take a job in some store (not on the docks; he hadn't his father's muscle), marry a homely local girl, raise a Spagnola or two. He'd keep going to church on Sundays, there to be reminded of the crime he'd committed by merely drawing breath, and of the punishment awaiting him when he stopped.

Then, one such Sunday, word came of the Japanese attack on Pearl Harbor, and the world suddenly changed for Spagnola. Suddenly war was everywhere—in North Africa and the 350, in France and Italy and the Philippines, places out of storybooks, out of the movies. While the priest offered prayers for deliverance, Spagnola saw himself aboard battleships, on oceans startlingly blue. He flew circles around mountains in silver fighter planes and trekked jungles where the parakeets, fabulously plumed, flew wild.

"I know I should have been ashamed of myself," Spagnola admitted to the group, "what with Guam and Bataan, with Anzio. All them fine young boys getting killed. But I couldn't help myself. I was almost eighteen and the war was my ticket out."

If his life had been a prison, the war had created a breech, a shining glimpse of freedom. But only a glimpse. Francis was called up soon enough, and soon enough discovered that the Army was no different from what he'd known before, another jail. He had merely changed uniforms, substituted his priests and nuns for officers and noncoms, crucifixes for crossed carbines on his shirt. Only hell no longer waited for him in the next life, it was right here roiling in this. It pounced on him each morning at reveille and pursued him throughout the day with blisters and mud and abuse. It cursed him to sleep at night and, for a few fitful hours, tortured his dreams as well.

Spagnola hated the Army. He hated the smell of bleach in the barracks and of cordite on the firing range, hated the lack of privacy. Not only his body but also his soul, he felt, had been reduced to a number, to a pair of boots and dogtags, all of them Government Issue.

He might have made the ideal orderly or, better, a chaplain's assistant, but the Army needed infantrymen and Spagnola had all the qualifications. On paper, that is, for no sooner had he arrived at the 133rd than he proved himself a catastrophe. Never robust, he found he wasn't much for discipline, either, found he couldn't march straight or keep his leggings hitched or his field kit in order. The skills of basic soldiering eluded him. Then there was the matter of killing. Grenades, Bangalore torpedoes—all were beyond his competence. His eyes impulsively shut whenever he shot his M-1 or, more perilously, the .30 caliber Browning. Firing, Spagnola was a hazard to his company. The men instinctively ducked.

Sgt. Papino refused to give up on him, though. He vowed to make Francis into a soldier even if it killed him. And it nearly did. During mess or after taps, Pappy drove Spagnola back to the obstacle course, made him run it over and over again in full battle gear, booting him when he fell, or out to the firing range, there to shoot until his molars rang and his shoulder felt ready to fall off. But the targets remained virginal—Maggie Draws, the soldiers inexplicably called them—and the obstacle course uncowed. "You're a disgrace to that fuckin' uniform," the sergeant berated him, hawking cigar juice in his face.

Prospects were hardly looking bright for him, but then Spagnola discovered something, a secret he'd never suspected. A talent. The former recluse, the kid who'd been afraid to make so much as a peep in class, in the Army became a gregarious wise-ass, the company clown. He learned to make light of his own incompetence, of his buddies' habits and their commanders' quirks, of the myriad absurdities of Army life. There was Spagnola prancing around the barracks in nothing but his skivvies and helmet. Spagnola eating creamed beef—SOS: Shit on a Shingle—with an entrenching tool. He collected jokes, dirty jokes, stupid jokes, could always boast that he had a million of them, though few would've raised a chuckle in peacetime. Yet the men adored them, relished that momentary break from routine.

Laughter: his sole contribution to the war effort. But there *was* a war on and the 133rd eventually reached it. The 12th of June 1944—D-Day Plus Six—found Spagnola at the front of the LST ramp, bowing low with one arm sweeping toward the beach. "After you. *Please*. No, I *insist*."

Most of the carnage on Omaha Beach had already been cleaned up by then, and the Germans pushed inland. Still, the men were antsy, seasick and confused. They couldn't tell whether the plangent thuds they heard—a sound like heavy iron doors slamming shut—were made by the surf or by howitzers; whether that persistent rattling was bulldozers working or small-arms fire.

It was then, while waiting for orders, that Major Walker—the Major—proposed a patrol of the silenced German gun emplacements on the bluff. A little sightseeing tour, he said, on the house—"someday they'll charge you admission."

Spagnola snooped around the machine gun nests, the ramparts and pillboxes. There was nothing much to see apart from spent cartridges and bullet holes—that and the ubiquitous shit piles with which the waves of GIs before theirs had left their mark. But then, under a stack of singed blankets he found something. In mint condition, a freshly oiled machine pistol, a Schmeiser.

"What did I know about Jerry guns?" Spagnola shrugged at the semicircle of former POWs. "Christ, I didn't even know it was loaded."

Arriving late at the rendezvous point, he brandished his find in the air. "Hey, guys, looky what I got!" he called, and almost out of reflex, in relief, the men started laughing. The Schmeiser, too. EHEHEHEHEHEH, it sniggered, and suddenly the men weren't laughing anymore but diving onto the beach, crawling and clawing sand. EHEHEHEHEHEH. The bullets sprayed in wild arcs through the air, an entire magazine-full. Finally, only Francis was left standing. He gawked at the smoke-entwined muzzle.

A better soldier might have been court-martialed, but with horseplay generally expected of him, the incident merely earned a nickname—Spa-a-a-a-gnola. He would've preferred the stockade, frankly, especially once the real shooting started.

And started it did in the hedgerow country beyond the beach, and from there it rarely stopped. Unlike the rest of his outfit, country boys like Lt. Hill and "Sweet" Martinson, who seemed to enjoy a scrabble, Spagnola couldn't bring himself to fire, couldn't hit anything if he tried. Instead, with the first whiff of combat, he'd roll himself into a human ball, hands tossed over his helmet, face between his knees. He gagged at the sight of bodies—Germans first, truncated and green, but then GI bodies, fellows he knew, buddies he had once made laugh.

Three months later and the men had changed. They were listless now, shorn of all but two instincts: to survive and to kill. Impervious to jokes, inimical to cowards, they'd lost their stomach for Spagnola.

A persona non grata, a pariah, so he remained until the beginning of December. By then the war was winding down. The Nazis would surrender soon, the scuttlebutt ran; Americans might be home again by Christmas. Bivouacked in Belgium, in the Ardennes forest near the

German border, the men of the 133rd unwound. There, in spite of the cold, their iciness to Spagnola thawed. He still had his one-liners from boot camp, his imitations of officers, living and dead. On leave in Houffalize, a friendly, French-speaking town, he'd put on mime shows for the children in the street, and in the café, delighted the ladies who came there to dance. Forgetting the terrors of the previous months, he began to dream again—not of oceans and jungles anymore, but of stages, even movie screens.

"The Costello of Company B, they called me," he boasted to the group. "I was good at that comedy stuff."

Day and night he was at it, dashing from platoon to platoon and performing his bit, getting paid with cigarettes and chocolate rations. Except for Sundays. Early Sunday mornings he would slip off to Saint-Vith—"Sandpit," the GIs called it—the village closest to their camp. A hostile place, stripped from Germany after World War I but its people still loyal to their Fatherland. A picturesque town: gable roofs, cobblestone streets, a scene out of *Hansel and Gretel.* There were several churches, but one that Spagnola liked best. A peasant's church, crude and simple, with gargoyles perched on the roof.

Spagnola kept to himself, away from the parishioners' glances, waiting for the mass to end. Only later, when even the priest had left, did he approach the altar and pray.

He prayed as he hadn't since before the war, at home alone in his room. A prayer for the men in his outfit, even for Pappy, and for his mother, cleaning other people's houses now that his father had taken sick. He fingered his rosaries, tried to concentrate, but his mind kept wandering to comedy, to cooking up new jokes, ways of improving his act. In the end, guilt-ridden, he gave up praying altogether. He sat staring at the nave and the barrel vaults, and at the stained-glass image of Christ.

A Christ unlike any he'd ever seen: gaunt and ugly, coarsely clad in a loincloth. In the window above the altar He hung, His face contorted, body writhing as if in an effort to break free. Wounds as real as any he'd receive in battle. And yet there was also munificence. Here was a man sorely in need of saving himself but who was ready to save humanity, to embrace it, His arms and hands outstretched. He gazed at the window and its colors—blue, red, deathly white—washed across the walls of the church. Spagnola felt bathed by them.

The window burst apart. In a myriad scintillating shards Jesus flew at him. Spagnola's hands jerked up to his face, but not before his cheeks were lacerated. Horrendous ripping sounds, whistles, then deafening explosions. The church seemed to rise for an instant and drop as stones fell from the ceiling and altarpieces clattered across the floor. When he next opened his eyes, confirmed that he still *had* eyes, the first thing he saw was one of the gargoyles akimbo on the pew next to him—a buck-toothed griffin, laughing.

Saint-Vith was being bombarded. "I never seen anything like it." Spagnola recalled for the group. "Not in France, nowhere. Big, big stuff—88s. Size of garbage cans."

His first thought was to stay inside the church, but then, after a few more close hits, when the entire structure seemed near to collapsing, he was ready to take his chances outside. He grabbed his gun, his helmet, and stumbled down the aisle through the smoke toward where he reckoned the portal might be. He made it through, and stood teetering at the top of the church steps, gulping. All he could see was smoke and bomb flashes, fragments of houses in flight. But suddenly he spotted someone—a soldier, a GI, sprinting down the street. The man was helmetless, jacketless, and his uniform looked wet. His hair seemed wet as well, and red.

Spagnola called after him and started down the steps, but didn't get far. A sniper's bullet hissed past his head and smacked into the archway behind him. A triplet of shells tore into the town, diced the street with shrapnel. Spagnola froze for an instant, then scurried back into the church.

Crouched in a niche behind a headless Virgin Mary, he shook while the bombing raged. An hour passed, perhaps two—he never thought to look at his watch—until it seemed inconceivable that the Germans had more rounds to fire or that Saint-Vith wasn't already flattened. Then, just as unexpectedly as they'd opened up, the guns fell silent.

On rubbery legs he rose and again staggered outside. The air was still, unruffled except for the crack of flames and a single dog howling. Though nearly dusk, he could see the village around him was devastated.

"They shot up their own kin, the Jerries," Spagnola shrugged at the group. "Suppose they figured it was worth it, you know, sort of clear the lanes for their attack."

But this was more than a mere attack. It was the opening of a colossal offensive, Germany's last of the war. Tiger tanks, virtually unstoppable, and crack Wehrmacht troops broke through the complacent Allies' lines in what some illustrative mind would someday call the Bulge.

Spagnola had no way of knowing that, though. He didn't know that enemy armor and infantry were closing in on the village, an important road junction with access routes leading straight across Belgium, to Antwerp and the Atlantic coast. He knew only that he was frightened out of his wits, freezing cold—a light snow had started falling—and lost. Praying out loud now, he stumbled through the debris to the outskirts of the village, where the cobblestones met the forest.

Through the trees he blundered. The sun had set and the only lights were the flares and tracer bullets streaking overhead. Branches slashed his face, roots tripped him, and yet somehow he made it back to the bivouac without getting himself lost or shot or both. But the place was empty. Huts, pickets—all deserted. Spagnola slumped onto the ground, put his head in his hands and cried.

"Goddammit," somebody growled behind him. He felt himself being lifted up by the collar, raised to the point where his face met the mean yet blessed mug of Sgt. Papino. "For Christ's fucking sake, get your butt up on that ridge. Find Lt. Hill—he needs every man. Even you."

A stony spine lying parallel to the village, the ridge formed an ideal defense line against any force approaching Saint-Vith through the forest. Which was just what the Germans, their tanks stalled by resistance pockets along the road, were planning. But Spagnola had no way of knowing that. He hadn't an inkling, in fact, what the 133rd was doing on that ridge in the first place—why they hadn't gotten the hell out of there when the offensive began and saved their asses.

"You should've seen 'em on that ridge. Talk about guts." In this, as in every session, he had gone through the entire litany of his life, even the painful parts about his father, matter-of-factly, even jocularly. But the battle was still an ordeal. He paused to hitch up his trousers again and shift his paunch. Though they didn't need cleaning, he blew on the lenses of his trifocals and rubbed them along his sleeve. "They fought like wolves, every one of them," he choked finally. "Everyone 'cept me."

There were just flares at first, filtering down over the forest, illuminating the men in their foxholes. Then mortar rounds burst in the treetops, and machine gun fire, fiery tines of it, raked the ridge. Late in digging his hole, Spagnola burrowed furiously, hacked with spade and clawed with his nails until his fingers were frozen and raw. He was digging still when the firing suddenly stopped and a silence set in, as heavy as the fog on the meadow beneath the ridge.

"Here they come, ladies. Show 'em what you got!"

That was the Major hollering, but Spagnola chose not to hear. Tried not to hear the ridge erupting with all of the unit's weapons—rifles, grease guns, B.A.R.s—but his. His M-1 lay in his hole, locked, while its owner imitated a curlicue.

Men died, the first of them Captain Toth. B Company's commander, from Louisiana, sandy-haired and dimpled—a boy's face on a man's body—soft-spoken and strong, with none of the Major's bluster. Shot in the groin in that first wave, he hung on an hour or more, but the medics couldn't reach him; the firing was too intense. Above Toth's foxhole Spagnola watched the breath steam rise, billows at first, then tendrils and strands, then…nothing.

Toth's breath was the last thing Spagnola saw. After that he never raised his head again, scarcely moved, even to take a crap. By the second day, most of the outfit had even forgotten that he was there. But not Sgt.

Papino. His hole wasn't far from Francis's, and with every fresh assault, Pappy's voice could be heard yelping, "Goddamn faggot, Spagnola, get the fuck up here and fight!" But such exhortations were wasted on him, only made him hug his knees tighter and scrape more furiously at the earth. He squirmed in his own filth, without blankets or gloves, shivering as the din of the battle passed over him, and the screams of dying men.

On the third day, Sgt. Papino came down with frostbite—Hill volunteered to evacuate him—and for all purposes Spagnola disappeared. The Jerries, though, kept coming, and every fresh wave gained ground. By the sixth night they had crossed the meadow and had reached the base of the ridge, close enough to lob potato mashers up and into the foxholes. And the only question was: whose sector would they break through first?

Company B's seemed the likeliest, what with Hill and Pappy gone and others as well—Featherstone, the company machine gunner, who'd been sent out on some errand before the battle began, and the two guys dispatched to find him, Tully and Sweet. There were men too badly wounded to fight, dead men, and there was Spagnola, who wasn't wounded *or* dead, but useless nevertheless.

"Hold 'em now, boys! Hold 'em!" The Major shouted as he hustled the length of the ridge, doubled-over. "Every goddamn inch—make 'em pay!"

He brought fresh belts of ammunition to Ronald Barkin, Featherstone's replacement on the .50, in the foxhole closest to Spagnola's. Barkin did his best, firing in short, well-concentrated bursts, conserving his rounds. Must have killed twenty or thirty of them. But then a grenade landed smack in his lap. "Oh, shit," Spagnola heard him gasp just before the explosion, before pieces of Barkin, hot and gooey, came raining.

"Medic!" Francis cried, the first words he'd uttered in days. "Medic!" as if any amount of bandaging could make Barkin whole again. But the only answer he got was, "Shaddup and get the fuck on that gun!"

Did they really mean him? Spagnola couldn't believe it, yet his was the closest hole; nobody else could reach it. This was his test but a test of what—courage? Faith? Without knowing how, he managed to slither out of his hole. Bullets sluiced the air over his head and chopped the dirt around him.

"The *gun*! You chickenshit sonofabitch..."

Francis crawled and whimpered. His feet and hands were numb, his uniform stiff with squalor. He prayed, racing through every prayer he'd ever been made to memorize, until all at once he was over Barkin's position, his chin hooked over its lip. The .50 cal was there, loaded, operational. All he had to do was tumble down and pull the trigger. The only problem was Barkin himself. Barkin's steaming innards and Barkin's brains. An eyeball that stared out of a sinewy red mess, straight at him, as if to say, *Jesus, look what they did to me.*

He couldn't. Just couldn't. Spagnola remembered, "I lied there for a couple of minutes, I guess, with everybody yelling at me to get on that gun, and the Jerries getting closer, right under us. And then, the next thing I know is I got this Mauser crammed in my ear and somebody's barking at me in Kraut."

Then, and only then, did he rise and put his hands in the air, high, as if it were the most natural thing in the world for him to do. As though he'd been rehearsing it for years. He turned to his captors and treated them to his favorite Stan Laurel grin—never failed to get a laugh—thinking, *hell, they're just like us really, small-town guys. Christians. White.* Then a rifle butt plowed into his groin and another one clipped him across the jaw, cracking two of his teeth.

"Not in a laughing mood, I guess," Spagnola said and contrived a chuckle himself. Only now it came out as a sigh. He fell silent then, and lowered his head.

If the story of the battle was hard to tell, the next chapter was almost unbearable. The chronicle of his months in the camp. Cruelty, starvation, the relentless scorching cold. At the end—April it was, only a couple of weeks before V-E Day—after their guards had marched them clear across Germany and all the way to the Czech border, one crisp spring morning Spagnola and five other GIs in a work detail suddenly found themselves alone on a dirt road with not a single Jerry in sight. Liberated.

"Liberated my ass," Francis repeated with a bitterness that might seem ungracious to any but the members of his group. They understood the guilt he felt, surviving while others died, and for failing to man that machine gun. They knew the anger at whoever it was—the brass—who had put him in the infantry to begin with. Who'd stuck him on that ridge where his foibles were exposed, and left him a prisoner forever.

He reached into the pocket of his bowling jacket and extracted a Marlboro. Smoking was not allowed in the group—Carruthers loathed it—but with Spagnola they made an exception, especially at this point in his talk. He'd started smoking during the war, thinking it made him look older, and kept it up later, trying to feel young. *Smoke 'em if you got 'em*—the only Army expression he ever liked. He lit up and dragged deeply, held the smoke and exhaled at last with a groan.

He'd wanted to go on telling them his story. About his return to Jersey City at the end of '45, about his father's death and then his mother's, an old woman already at 50. About his marriage to one Harriet Poltowski, a plain, far from brilliant girl, a real bitch, whose one asset—gigantic knockers—Spagnola would praise with hands cupped in front of his chest. Such prizes would have been denied him surely if he hadn't come back a hero. "That's right, a hero." The same neighborhood that had never given him a second thought before the war suddenly revered him. "*I* had showed gallantry under fire," Spagnola chortled. "*I* had survived the stalag."

He lived with that lie and lived with Harriet who put out just enough to give him two sons, both of whom would leave the house as soon as they could, heading out West from where they called once in a blue moon, mostly when they needed money. He wanted to summarize his 30 years' employment in his father-in-law's demolition business, bound literally to ball and chain, leveling other people's walls. He could have entertained them with the story of how that single asset of Harriet's eventually did her in, with a little help from the booze and the pills, ten years ago, and how the wrecking business eventually wrecked itself, leaving him a pension and a house in working-class Kearny. "Aluminum siding—you know. Lawns with elves and Madonnas."

Things weren't all that bad, though, what with bowling and the Knights of Columbus and these Wednesday night sessions, his favorite. He'd gone back to raising parakeets, and rarely missed Sunday mass and confession. Everything would be okay, he'd conclude, if not for his health, and if not for that manual. The manual with his photograph in it that always made him a suspect in crimes he didn't commit.

Tears welled up in his eyes and fogged the blur of his trifocals. He wept, Francis Spagnola, a fat man in a Caterpillar hat and a Knights of Columbus bowling jacket, a pack-and-a-half-a-day man who also drank too much and suffered from a half-dozen chronic disabilities—high blood pressure, hardening of the arteries, phlebitis, arrhythmia—any one of which could have killed him. A man who should have been thankful just being alive, sobbed like a child deprived of that one thing he wants, freedom.

"I think it's best we wrap it up for now, Francis,"Carruthers said, descending from his stool. He strode over to Spagnola and clasped a hand on his shoulder. "It's good you got it out, though, the way you did. You don't often get this far. I'm proud of you." He pinched the cigarette from Spagnola's hand, dropped it and crushed it with his shoe.

Spagnola looked up at him. Captain Carruthers with his eyes like frozen ponds—Alpine eyes—his helmet-shaped hair, recalled the German soldier to whom Spagnola had surrendered in the war, and surrendered still, every Wednesday night.

His photo appeared in some manual—that's why they arrested him at airports and ballgames and rallies. Or maybe there was no photo but only his face and the guilt that burnt through it. Guilt for the sins he'd committed since birth. Guilt, above all, for the war.

"No," Francis blurted out and with a conviction that surprised everyone, himself included. "There's one more thing."

He fumbled in his jacket pockets again, churning up used tissues and old lottery tickets, tobacco and lint, until he had exhumed a compacted rectangle of paper. Spagnola unfolded it and held it up to his glasses, as if to read, as if he hadn't learned its contents by heart.

"It's an invitation," he said, sniffing. "Seems Company B's having a reunion. In Belgium, the very place we got licked."

Carruthers seemed unimpressed. "Nothing unusual about that, is there, Francis? Lots of outfits have them." He seemed impatient now, anxious to get on to the next testimony. But Spagnola would not sit down.

"It's the last, y'see," he explained. "Won't be no more after this."

"If you're thinking of going, Francis—if that's what you're saying—I can't say I'd recommend it. Not right now, just when you've made such progress."

With a shred of tissue, he wiped the tears from his bell-shaped cheeks, and blew his fat clapper of a nose. He folded and unfolded the invitation. "I don't know..."

Then, suddenly, from someone in the group—one of the Vietnam vets, a black man who worked in television—came the call: "Do it, man."

"Go," said another, a Teaneck physician, captured north of the Yalu. "Go. Confront it. It'll do you good."

Carruthers tried to contain them—"Let's hold on here..."—but they'd already begun stamping their feet.

"Go! Go! Go!"

Spagnola gaped at them, at the men who sat listening to him week after week, whose faces, blurred, he'd often imagined were those of his old Army buddies, judging him.

"Gee, I don't know..." he shrugged. And he didn't. Why had he brought the invitation to begin with? So that Carruthers could tell him that he shouldn't feel compelled to attend, that the reunion could do him harm? Or was it for this: for the men who were always yearning for *closure*—whatever that meant—and their need to make peace with their past?

The members surrounded him now, slapped the back of his bowling jacket and tugged down the brim of his cap.

"As you were," Carruthers snapped, but Spagnola was already imagining what it'd be like to walk up to another group of onetime POWs—the survivors of the 133rd—and greet them without remorse. Without shame, chewing the fat, reminiscing. He wondered how remarkable it would be to shake their hands and then take leave of them, for once in his life, a free man.

THREE

The stairs groaned under his feet. The boards seemed more fragile lately, more plaintive than he remembered, descending them each dawn for the past fifty years. And no wonder. A big man himself, his two hundred pounds alone might have been enough to crack the entire staircase. But then there was the weight of the stone.

Slabs of it, monoliths—granite, whitestone, domestic strains of marble—roughly hewn in shapes that did not always conform to his basement's door. Some so heavy it took four strong men to maneuver them down those stairs and coax them onto his workbench. Between grunts, they'd ask him whether he ever considered moving his shop to another location—the abandoned barn behind his house or, better yet, into town. No, he'd tell them, he preferred the basement, even with all the headaches involved. You could say it had sentimental value for him. It was down here that he'd first started with headstones, cutting and inscribing them, just after the War, and here he'd been thriving at it ever since.

There was comfort in the cold and the dark, Pieter Martinson thought as he took another step, heard the groan, and paused. No distractions, none of those sudden shifts of light and temperature that could divert his chisel a single millimeter this way or that and so ruin the entire block. An atmosphere in which he could view the product of his labors as he imagined his customers would, on a gray, raw March morning. A melancholy thought, perhaps, but then again he wasn't exactly in the party favors business. Headstones were about death—the downside—but they were about other things as well: respect, dignity, legacy, remembrance. That's where the art came in. *His* art, for any hacker could whack away at a stone, machines did it twice as fast, but only he, working with his hands, with time-tried tools some of them as delicate as a dentist's, could sense the image *inside* the stone—like Michelangelo, though he'd never admit to the comparison—could reach inside and release it.

That was the rock on which his reputation had been built, the certainty that his markers were not merely carved but created, that he put his heart into every one, no matter how modest. Throughout the state of Wisconsin and into Eastern Minnesota, south to Illinois, a Martinson Memorial was a sign of the deceased's final worth and of a family's caring, a status symbol of sorts that was less like a Rolls-Royce than a well-stocked library. And anybody could get one, whether they'd been a schoolteacher or the governor, a business tycoon or a traffic cop. It was an article of faith with Pieter that no one should be deprived of his skills for lack of resources. He was poor once himself, and alone, and knew what vast comfort might be found in even the simplest kindness.

Pieter hazarded another step. Perhaps it wasn't the stairs at all, he mused, but his own bones creaking, giving out after all those years of abuse. A bad back threatened to give on him, whether he was upright or supine—the result of a wrestling injury he'd suffered in high school. He lied about it then and lied about it again when he went into the service. There they gave him the Browning Automatic Rifle—B.A.R.—a hefty weapon of 24 lbs., along with bandoliers of magazines, belts of .50 cal. ammunition, mines, C-ration kits—anything they could pile on, saying "he can take it, the guy's a fuckin' bulldozer." And so his back problem became chronic, painful but not paralyzing, the lesser of his wartime scars.

☆ ☆ ☆

He had never been a complainer. Nor did he brag, a modest man in spite of the many letters of praise he'd received from former customers—letters displayed, modestly enough, on a corkboard over his bench.

Silence was a quality he'd come by naturally, his legacy as the only child of older parents, immigrant farmers from Sweden, strict Lutherans who believed in laboring hard and never griping about it. Every dawn from the time he was eight he rose, through scorching summers and those ruthless Wisconsin winters, to help his father with the planting and the baling, the shoveling of manure and the no end of fences to mend. It never tired him, though, a big kid, a full head above the rest of his class. He was the type that women in the movies were always falling for: tall, hardy, taciturn. But Pieter Martinson was anything but a heartthrob. A square-shouldered hulk with hands dangling down to his knees, long-faced and mouse-eared, a divot of loamy hair on his head, he had every reason to be shy around people, around girls his age especially.

Except for this one girl named Meg. Daughter to a dirt-poor family in the feed business, Meg Housen lived on the same country lane as Pieter, shared his view of boundless cornfields. She, too, was painfully shy and nothing much to look at, frizzy-haired and bespectacled, a short, frail girl who in an earlier generation might not have survived her infancy. Similar backgrounds, similar blessings or lack of them, they also shared something else, abstract and indefinable—a wavelength.

Though they rarely spoke, they were constantly bantering, relying not on words but on gestures—arched brows, curled lips, an assortment of nods and winces. Their subtle, secret code. Through it they'd exchange opinions about happenings at school, teachers and classmates, and then the future, about jobs, a home and in it, a family. More complex feelings would somehow be communicated—*imparted*—almost telepathically. Anyone following them down that country lane (and children often did, just for the sport of it) could witness the strangest scene: a burly giant and a four-eyed gnome walking side by side, heads bent, silently but deeply conversing.

Meg loved him, though the word "love" was just one of many that never passed her lips. She loved him for his strength and for the gentleness with which he wielded it, for the uncrackable kernel of goodness in his heart.

Afternoons, she'd wait for him outside their high school gym, in a knee-length pleated skirt and oversized sweater, a beret afloat on her hair. With a build like Pieter's it was only natural that he play some kind of sport, though he proved too slow a runner for football, too tender a soul. He preferred his violence constrained. And so he took up wrestling. A heavyweight, he went nearly undefeated his sophomore and junior years, then led his team to the state championship.

Meg never missed a match. In the uppermost bleachers she sat hugging her knees and biting her lower lip. She never cheered, never even gasped, not even during the finals when she was sure—she *felt* it—he'd been injured. Later, after the victory celebration, she would point her chin in the direction of his lower back and so let him know that she knew. Pieter merely shrugged.

Friends since early childhood, they had watched each other's bodies grow, and sensed the changes within them. Yet they never slept together, never engaged in "heavy petting" as it was called or even kissed much, unsure of what to do with their tongues. It wasn't because of the discrepancy in their sizes, nor for lack of opportunity or private space. They yearned to explore but they didn't. Virtue? Propriety? Such values were deeply embedded back then, and in those parts particularly. But with Pieter it was something more—fear. Meg seemed so frail, so breakable, as if the merest hug might crush her. Caring and fearing for her both, it was enough for him just to lift up her tortoiseshell glasses and stare and stare into her eyes—hazel eyes, speckled with russet and flax. Nothing could be more intimate.

Content with Meg, hoarding their solitude, Pieter shunned the popularity his wrestling abilities might have brought him. Though there was talk of a sports scholarship to Madison, of a career in one of the professions, he had no plans other than to remain where he was, marrying and settling down. *What* he'd be in life seemed secondary to the *way* he'd live it: a family man, surrounded by the few people who mattered. His future might have its challenges, its inevitable ups and downs, but otherwise no surprises. A linear life, its days aligned like furrows, the years like fields, ripe and fallow.

Then the war broke out, impossibly remote at first, with battles fought in places they could hardly pronounce—Guadalcanal, Kasserine, El Katar—much less locate on a map. It was hard to imagine that any of the black-and-white horrors hinted at by the newsreels could somehow attain color and taint them there, on their country lane leading home. But then, late one June afternoon, rushing to a rehearsal for their graduation ceremony, trying to beat out a brewing storm, Pieter and Meg were approached by a boy. One of the brats who sometimes followed them on their walks, taunting them, only this time he wasn't laughing. "D'ja hear the news?" he gasped, "Herbert Shank's been kilt. His ma got the telegram this morning. Jap torpedo," and scampered off to spread the word.

Pieter stopped in his tracks, the wind knocked out of him. Herbert Shanks had been a wrestler as well, a lightweight, one year ahead of him, who'd joined the Navy right out of school. Little turtle-faced Shanks, pimply and none too hygienic but always volunteering to post the scores or stack the mats, anything for the team, a good man, now lay unburied at the bottom of the Pacific Ocean. Pieter gazed at the sky, at the black fists of clouds and the pulse of lightning above him. Then, exhaling brusquely, willfully as if to work out a cramp, he walked on. Meg walked with him, and the silence between them was real.

He reached the bottom of the stairs and the sound of groaning stopped. It *was* his bones after all, Pieter concluded. He drew in a breath, sampling the pungent brew of turpentine and linseed oil, industrial glues and paint. Then, sighing, he approached the workbench. Solid oak half a foot thick, the bench bore the nicks and gouges of five decades' carving. Marble dust, white, pink and purple, sparkled in the grooves. Pieter was richly notched as well, his hands scarred, nails split—a collaborative effort of time and his own occasional clumsiness. In the same khaki pants and frayed flannel shirt he wore to work each day, he bore an air of age and dissolution around him. His face had grown longer over the years, his cheeks hollowed, teeth clenched behind leathered lips. Hairs like caper weeds sprouted from his ears and nostrils. Not a happy man, Martinson, but not a sad one either; more like numb, a bit of a rock himself. Hard like one, too, for he never missed a day on the job, not even when his back was killing him.

He stood there for a moment, palms on the oak, remembering Herbert Shanks. Not Shanks the young man but Shanks the memorial. His had been a simple affair, a rounded stone of low-quality granite, unbeveled, and the inscription brief—too brief, with just his name, birth and death date. He deserved more, Pieter remembered thinking, and in later years, had often made a mental note to himself to devote some spare time to carving a better one. But there had never been any spare time, no vacations, and the dream of making that memorial remained that—a dream, a winsome one. Though many more men he'd known would die in the war, men he'd liked far better and sorely missed, Herbert Shanks' death remained the most painful, perhaps because of all that died along with him.

The memorial service for Herbert Shanks had taken place some weeks after the news of his death, at the school, and later, he walked Meg home as usual. Pieter's house was the closest—the custom was to pass it en route to hers, with Pieter doubling back—but fifty yards short of the drive, Meg broke into a run. She ran fast, shedding her books, frenzied. It took a moment for Pieter, with his 20-20 vision, to see what Meg with her myopia had spied first. The mailbox. A miniature Quonset hut, vaguely military in form, its little tin flag hung at half-mast.

Meg sprinted up to the mailbox, flung it open and reached in to extract a bland, olive green envelope, ripped its seal and pinched out the letter inside. Breath held, she read the salutation: *Greetings.*

"How long?" was all he said when he finally caught up to her.

"One month."

"Time enough. Maybe we should…"

Meg shook her head. "I can wait."

It never occurred to him that she wouldn't. But what about him? This was war, not a wrestling match, and Pieter, morosely inclined even then, was not like other youths, convinced of their own immortality. Big as he was, he knew that it would only take one bullet, a piece of metal as small as his thumbnail, to kill him. The sudden thought of her weeping over his grave, or more dreadful still, marrying someone else, terrified him. He found himself imagining her as he hadn't dared to before—naked—and in bed with another man, the other man touching her, entering her…

Panic seized him, shot up from the depths where it had lain dormant and undetected, until suddenly tapped by the war.

"You all right?"

Pieter gripped the mailbox, as if for support. "Nothing," he said. "Let's walk."

Meg Housen, reticent in the extreme, over the course of the next month unexpectedly found her voice. A full and sonorous voice, as it turned out, bigger than her size would suggest. It had been drawn out by the matter of his back, or rather by his refusal to face up to it and apply for a medical exemption.

"How are you going to carry things? Packs, guns? You're in constant pain as it is."

It startled him, the sudden power of her tone. Yet the sound of his own voice, usually heard from the inside only, was no less surprising, deep-pitched and plodding, a bumpkin's voice. "I'll just work it through like always," he explained, then lowered his head toward hers. "Besides," he said, "I have to."

Of course he had to. It wasn't only that he had no way of proving his problem—it wouldn't show up on an X-ray—or that he had to go before a medical board and swear to it, an otherwise healthy eighteen-year-old and wrestling champion. Beyond all that there was the matter of honor, *ära* in Swedish, a concept his parents had drubbed into him, or rather *vanära*, dishonor: the need for the immigrants' son to show that he was no different than the rest of the boys in his class, all of whom were signing up and marching off to serve their country. To show his coach and teammates that their pride in him hadn't been misplaced. His back, his fears about Meg and the future, would have to remain hidden within.

Over the next month, Meg and Pieter exchanged more words than they had in the previous six years, but at the end of it, there she was waving to him as he and twenty other inductees boarded a bus for basic training. Not the scene the movies had led them to expect—no flags, no brass bands and streamers. No tears, not even kisses; theirs was a stoical stock. But at the last minute, Pieter, soon to be Pvt. Martinson, B.A.R. bearer of 1st Platoon, B Company, 133rd Infantry of the United States Army, called out her name. Jamming his block of a torso through the window, he called it once, loud and painfully. Its echo seemed to remain, swirling with the dust, long after the bus pulled away.

Tough, team player that he was, Pieter made one hell of a soldier. A natural. Not only a good shot, a dead-eye, but also a good sport, the kind of buddy every boy dreamed of making in the service: quiet, friendly, there when you needed him. And they needed him. Whenever there were loads to be carried—and when weren't there: spools of wire, ammo crates?—the call would go up for him. "Swede!" they'd cry, "Gimme the friggin' Swede!" Complacently, he accepted the nickname dubbed on every GI over six feet tall, blondish and of Scandinavian extraction, and accepted again when, over the course of basic training and in recognition of the unshakable tenderness he showed, the name got altered to "Sweet."

"Good work, Sweet," Lt. Hill would compliment him during maneuvers as the sturdy Pfc—soon to be corporal—Martinson bore a designated wounded man across his shoulders. The way he worked that B.A.R., swinging it scythe-like from his hip, could almost make Sgt. Papino smile. "Sweet, fuckin' A," he'd cackle.

"Sweet!" the cry resounded, more urgently, in battle. "Ammo, Sweet! Stretcher, Sweet!" The enemy and the wounds were real, yet still he came running. He learned the craft—warcraft—well, learned to distinguish between incoming and outgoing, when to dig in and when not to bother. He weighed his chances in action, calculated the risks and took them. The men in his outfit figured him fearless. There was Sweet putting down suppressing fire while his squad crossed a hedgerow; Sweet sticking his fist into McGonigal's neck wound, blood spurting, until the medics arrived. And though McGonigal died, Lt. Hill put him in for a

Bronze Star—"For selfless gallantry, providing effective cover with his weapon and so enabling his unit to escape an enfilading ambush." Bets were he'd chalk up a Silver Star as well, or even the Big One: a Medal of Honor. The war seemed made for brave, unassuming farm boys like Martinson.

Only he was scared shitless. It wasn't the threat of pain that got to him or of being maimed or even of losing his life per se, but rather of losing her. Meg. If he died, she'd marry someone else eventually, make love and have kids with him. Soon he, Pieter, would become a memory, and a faint one at that. Death for him meant Meglessness, and the thought of it tormented him. It haunted him at night, on patrol, and in the morning while he cleaned his gun. Like the pain in his back, the slightest aggravation—a distant shelling, the shake on the arm that aroused him for guard duty—could ignite it.

His only respite came in combat itself, when other men got hit, men smaller and more cautious than he was, and he suddenly became focused and calm. It was almost as if he welcomed a good skirmish, as if he were just waiting for that cry of "Sweet! Over here, Sweet!" He counted on it.

December 1944. The 133rd wintered in the Ardennes, waited for Christmas, in their lean-tos like multiple crèches. Days were spent toppling trees for corduroy tank paths that tanks would never take—the war would be over in weeks, they reckoned—or fortifying a ridge that would never have to be defended. Nights passed bullshitting around the bivouac or, on furlough, dancing with the ladies' club in Houffalize. But Pieter kept mostly to himself. When he wasn't cleaning the B.A.R., a two-hour process, he wrote to Meg. One, sometimes two letters a day; letters that described every detail of his Army life—the dull food, the preference for Lucky Strikes over Camels, various men in his outfit, the weather. But not a word about his feelings, his fears. As once he revealed them without talking, so, too, he supposed, she'd sense them behind his words.

He was already writing his next letter, mentally, outside his hut where his B.A.R. was disassembled, the morning that Sgt. Papino found him.

"My butt should be so clean," Pappy snorted. His boot tip tapped the automatic rifle's stock, smudging it.

"Never doubted it wasn't." With his rag, Pieter wiped the stock.

"Yeah, well, get *your* ass and your weapon together, Sweet," said Pappy. He spat through sullied teeth. "I got a little job."

Pieter glanced up at him, at that face that looked like it had seen a hundred fights and lost half of them. Ancient by battalion standards—twenty-seven—Pappy affected a pencil mustache and a cravat looped around his neck, a .45 automatic on his hip, and beneath his pants leg (rumor had it) a Bowie knife. The only GI in the entire Army who had no known hometown, no past or parents or girl, Pappy cared passionately about his squad, though he often had a hard time expressing it.

"We got a missing man, Featherstone of all the sonofabitches. Hiked down to Sandpit and nobody's seen 'im since."

Pieter peered down the length of his gun barrel, blew some dust from the muzzle. "Went off, just like that?"

"*Sent* off. Some shit-for-brains errand."

"An errand, you say. What kind of errand?"

"Don't ask—you wouldn't believe it anyway." Pappy snorted, "Rifesnider's fuckin' idea," then changed the subject. "Go and look for him, you. And take Tully."

Pieter admitted a frown. A stroll around Sandpit—Saint-Vith, a less-than-friendly town—was not relished, especially with a goldbrick like Tully. "Nobody else around? Morgan? Croker?"

"Up on the ridge, all of 'em, digging in." Pappy's lips stretched around his stogie—his trademark smirk. "The Major and his goddamn ridge."

That was it. Pappy said no more, didn't have to; he knew his Sweet. And sure enough, without another word, Pieter reconstructed his gun and went off searching for Tully.

He found him writhing on the floor of his hut, wrestling unsuccessfully with a hangover.

"Let's go, Tully, we're going down to Sandpit. Featherstone's missing and we got to find him." Pieter had begun gently enough, showing mercy.

"Shit, Sweet, can't you see I'm dyin'," Tully moaned, clutching himself as if he'd been gut-shot. Pea-eyed, purportedly pea-brained as well, he was a stringy kid from somewhere in Maryland, with acne-scarred skin and teeth so bucked they could—so they said—eat corn cobs through a picket fence.

Pieter, a person of near illimitable patience, was quickly getting irked. "On your feet. Now, private! That's an order."

But shouting also proved useless, and though he hated to, Pieter resorted to his boot. It connected once, hard, with Tully's rump, to be followed by a succession of lighter punts assuring that the soldier got belted up, armed and helmeted. Pieter hiked behind him, shoving, as they cut through the forest toward Saint-Vith.

The afternoon, a Sunday, was exceptionally quiet, even for the pine-hushed Ardennes. No growl of jeeps or tanks, no planes abuzz or even birds warbling in the branches. The sky, gray and distended with snow, drooped to the very treetops. Pieter released the safety catch on his B.A.R. He had a bad feeling about this assignment, had had them before—in France, for instance, that day they were ambushed in Saint Lô—and he knew to take them seriously. He hoisted his weapon to chest level, easing the stress on his back, and tried not to think of Meg.

The journey took twice as long as he'd estimated. Tully kept stopping to retch, dropping to one knee to hack up some vile-smelling goop while his helmet pitched into the dirt. And each time Pieter picked up the helmet and tossed it back to him, cursed and scolded him, reminding him that Sandpit was not a place to be poking around in after dark.

They arrived, finally, in the late afternoon, and began their search. Even by Belgian standards, Saint-Vith was a small village, but big enough to conceal a single soldier who might not want to be found. Pieter hadn't known Featherstone very well—nobody in the outfit did, it seemed, a standoffish guy, a little too proud of his good looks and swagger. A favorite of Col. Rifesnider, another prima donna, who couldn't be bothered with the day-to-day running of the battalion and pretty much left it to the Major. Through Rifesnider, Featherstone was always getting the first pick of the new fatigues when they arrived, the choicest billets, even weekend passes to Paris. Such favoritism invariably gave rise to questions—what was it between the private and the colonel that didn't quite jibe with the war effort?—and resentment.

But then Featherstone was not without merit. An ace with the .50 cal., as cool under fire as he was sauntering around camp, he'd already been decorated for bravery during the hedgerow campaign. More than a few of the men owed him their lives. Pieter didn't have much feeling for him either way, neither disgust nor envy or awe. Only the desire to find him as quickly as possible, and get the hell out of Saint-Vith.

He began in the town square. Nothing. The shops were all closed—it was Sunday—and the windows above them tightly shuttered. He traced the dark, medieval alleyways, advanced quietly as he might on patrol. The effect, though, was lost on Tully, still retching, still fumbling after his helmet as it clattered onto the cobblestones. And still not a sign of Featherstone. No sign of people, either, as though the imminence of snow had sent them all hibernating.

Pieter's anxiety climbed. He hated the idea of coming back empty-handed, of disappointing Pappy, and yet something felt wrong here. Terribly wrong. The same wavelength he'd shared with Meg had homed into a discordant frequency, a danger. Inside him, anger grappled with fear. He could die in this place, die and lose Meg forever, and all because of that goddamned dandy Featherstone. He found himself muttering—Pieter, who rarely cussed—*Fuck the colonel and fuck his errand, too.*

By the time they'd finished combing the village and returned to the square, dusk had fallen. The sun, a smudge on the tarnished sky, had all but vanished. The temperature had fallen, along with a flurrying snow. Stay much longer and they were just as likely to freeze to death as get shot at, Pieter reckoned. He decided to call it quits. Pappy or no Pappy, disappointing or not, Featherstone would remain unfound.

He thumped Tully on the shoulder—"Let's move"—and motioned in the direction of the forest. He turned, and in turning took one last look around. That's when he saw it. At the far end of the square, a house, slightly bigger than the others, fancier: gables and spires and such. Amber light poured from its open shutters, and the front door hung ajar. A sign above it told him that this was the Hotel Ardennes.

He had to have a look inside, if for no other reason than his own sense of diligence, to honestly tell Pappy he'd searched for Featherstone everywhere. "Stay close," Pieter told Tully. "And try not to puke on me."

Pieter covered half of the distance to the hotel, some twenty yards, before halting when he heard the sound. A deafening rasp over the rooftops…

"Incoming!" he hollered, spun, and tackled Tully to the ground.

The shell's explosion singed the back of their coats. Tully tried to get up but Pieter yanked him down again, jammed the helmet onto his head and pushed his face into the cobblestones. Another round crashed. "Move when I tell you, asshole!"

The shells blasted, tearing up houses and streets. But Pieter was frozen, unable to budge. Until a chunk of shrapnel came whizzing across the cobblestones, whirling in white-hot circles, and suddenly there was no choice.

"Up! Up! Go!"

Pieter wrenched Tully to his feet and hauled him toward the Hotel Ardennes. It was still standing, miraculously—the adjacent houses were ablaze—and its lights were on and flickering.

Shells smashed behind and beside them, yet somehow they barreled through the door.

"Mother of God. Mother of fuckin' God," Tully wept as he coiled around his knees in a corner.

Pieter let him go. The building shook; it swarmed with smoke and dust. Even if not directly hit, the roof was likely to come down. He had to find shelter quickly.

Groping, stumbling like a Keystone Kop as the lights pulsed off and on, he made it to a staircase. Between the whistles and the blasts, he heard a strange bumping noise on the landing above him, and then a stranger one still. *Splashing*.

Pieter Martinson was never the impulsive type, and yet he climbed up those stairs. Why? What drew him? These were questions that he'd later ask himself, each time drawing a blank. All he knew was that he started ascending, up through the swaths of smoke.

He heard the splashing again, louder now, and the bumps. They seemed to be coming from behind a rectangle of light—a door—glimmering at the head of the stairs.

He reached for the knob but just then the door burst open. Steam billowed out, entwined with the smoke, and blinded him. Pieter stumbled backward and felt something, somebody pushing past. He only caught a glimpse of him from behind: a red-haired soldier, running without his helmet, no gun, his uniform sopping wet.

Pieter had neither the time nor breath to call after him. He regained his footing, peered through the door, picking out what looked like towel racks, a tiled floor, and flush against the farthest wall, a bathtub. One of those old-fashioned tubs, porcelain-coated with elaborate copper taps. There was still water inside, hot water, and it occurred to Pieter that the soldier had been bathing himself, luxuriating when bombing started. He'd thrown on his clothes and bolted down the stairs, Pieter concluded, and concluded that he and Tully should be bolting as well before the building collapsed.

"Tully!" Pieter managed to shout before an 88 slammed into the roof. His legs bowled out and he fell, careening into the wall and back onto the banister, uprooting the newel before landing smack on his coccyx. Pain impaled him, sliced him from scrotum to neck. *I'm hit. I'm fucking cut in half.*

Fire blazed through the hotel's second floor; smoke rolled down the stairs. But Pieter didn't budge, wouldn't, imagining that the slightest movement would kill him. He felt detached suddenly, watching his predicament from afar and thinking *Poor Pieter*. But then someone was tugging on his coat and screaming at him.

"Get up, Sweet! Get up!"

"Leave me alone."

"No! Come on!"

Too tired to resist, Pieter offered up his hand and Tully heaved him, howling as he rose.

"I'm hurt..."

"Where? I don't see nothin'..."

"My back."

Bent, grunting, he tottered toward the entrance. Outside, the bombardment had shifted out of the village and toward the forest. The square, strewn with smoldering debris, seemed safe enough to cross.

"I'll go first this time," Tully said and if it weren't for the pain, Pieter would have laughed at him. But there was Tully, the creep whose first name few in the outfit had bothered to learn, wheeling his rifle this way and that as he inched out of the hotel and into the square, soldier-like. "All clear," he hissed, and waved for Pieter to follow.

But then Tully's boot caught on a crooked cobblestone. He stumbled, lost his grip on his gun and, lunging for it, again sent his helmet tumbling. "Shit," he spat and was just reaching for the helmet when a bullet punched through his forehead and blew off the back of his skull.

Forgetting his back, Pieter threw himself flat against the door. Another two rounds whizzed by, cleaving the air with the sound of well-oiled zippers. The reports came next, poignant crackles. Pieter was trapped. The burning hotel was behind him and in front, somewhere off the square, sat the sniper. His choice was to burn to death or end up like Tully, with his brains spewed over the street.

Half an hour passed. Pieter was lucky. Though it nearly choked him, the fire was slow-burning, producing more smoke than flames. And cover. At dusk, he felt he could chance a dash across the square. Only he couldn't dash anymore, at best hobble, advancing sideways in a simian hop that bore him to the nearest alleyway. From there the way was clear to the fringes of the town and the outer reaches of the forest.

By then a full-blown battle was on. The forest bed quavered with shellfire and the grumbling treads of tanks. Flares spangled the sky. Pieter struggled toward where the bivouac might be, uncertain of his exact direction. He staggered until, in the shimmering flarelight, he thought he spied some footprints.

Striated toes, horseshoe heels—GI footprints, he saw, fresh in the unblemished snow. Pieter followed them, through yet another thicket of trees, zigzagging between rows of dragons' teeth, until he emerged into a clearing that he mistook for the meadow near the ridge. In fact, this clearing was smaller, scruffier and littered with the remains of what until recently had been a cottage and the farmer who owned it. But there were the footprints again, leading away from the ruins and back to the rear of the yard, to a hollow and inside it, a primitive stone structure. The footprints ended at its door.

The door—a hatch, really, barely big enough for a child—was open. Pieter bent as low as he could, stifling his groan, and pushed his way inside.

The darkness within was thicker than the forest's, and the air palpably colder. A strange odor hovered, mawkish and rank. Pieter hesitated for a moment, squinting, sniffing. Here was another point at which he might have decided differently, might have turned and headed back to the forest, found his outfit and fought. But Pieter did not turn around, did not fight. Instead, he stepped deeper into a blackness in which he was the only living presence—or so he sensed, and yet he wasn't alone.

His shoulder knocked against something hard, but which yielded to his shoulder and swayed. Pieter reached into his breast pocket and extracted a box of matches, lit one and gasped.

Animal carcasses, from the looks of them freshly slaughtered, hung from hooks in the rafters. Thick blocks of ice lined the walls on either side. For a moment, Pieter imagined that if his back were up to it he just might help himself to a side or two of beef. Why not? The farmer wasn't in any position to object. He saw himself charging into battle as the cries went up "Sweet! Over here, Sweet!" to deliver not ammo or bandages but a week's supply of steak. He pictured the expression on the men's faces, the open mouths and ogling eyes, and started to laugh.

Wantonly he laughed, as loud as he could, in a most un-Martinson way. He didn't care. He was injured, true, nerve-frayed and lost, but he had survived. Against all odds alive and still in possession of his future, of Meg. Drunk with relief, he bellowed, ignored the pain as he heaved back and forth, twisted about and found himself staring into a pair of glassy blue eyes and a smirk hideously frozen.

If he screamed, Pieter didn't remember it. His first waking thought was of the cold, a blunted sensation of wandering through the dark, through branches, and around some kind of town. Explosions and light and screaming. As if he were dreaming, detached and watching himself, an unmoored soul, from afar. The dreaminess left him gradually and he came to on a stony floor, amid the moans and cries of an improvised field hospital. He was in the old church in Saint-Vith, down in the crypt with the artillery thundering above.

Pieter had no idea how he'd gotten there. He hadn't been hit as far as he could tell, his body free of the third-degree burns, the sucking chest wounds and mangled limbs he witnessed all around him. And yet he couldn't move, no matter how hard he struggled, and couldn't stop sobbing like a toddler.

"Somebody shut that bastard up!" barked a doctor, wrist-deep in some lieutenant's guts.

It took a second for Pieter to realize that that bastard was him, but he kept on crying anyway. He cried for Meg, howled out her name. On the flagstones he lay, in darkness, until a face suddenly appeared above him, moonlike, effulgent.

"Rest yourself, soldier, you're gonna be okay." Caring smile, soothing voice. The nurturing aroma of woman-ness.

"I'm not going to die?"

"'Course not. Just had a little scare, that's all. Happens."

Her cheeks were freckled—he could almost swear it—richly freckled, and the hair beneath her helmet was frizzy.

He whispered, "Meg?"

"Whoever you want, honey," the face replied and the smile warmed from caring to affection. "Meg."

And then there were only scraps. The evacuation in the snow, under fire, his hospitalization in Antwerp. There, too, he kept to himself, but without much choice in the matter. The other patients, those who had been honorably wounded, all but ignored him, and even the doctors remained distant.

Though no longer considered a crime by the military, tantamount to desertion, battle fatigue was still a far cry from getting your jaw shot off or losing a foot or an eye. The Army still viewed it with skepticism, deeply frowned on it and deplored it. For all intents, Pieter was a marked man and the mark was a bright red C for "cowardice." He still remembered nothing about what had happened to him in the cold house, could tell the Army psychiatrists little, even under hypnosis. His was a hard case. There were no witnesses to the event that had made him snap, no records. And the men who might have vouched for him—his buddies in Company B—had either been captured or killed.

He stayed in Antwerp for six more months, often sedated, alone. Days were spent wandering the corridors or perched on his bed before a blank block of paper, gnawing on a pen. Every day he started a letter to Meg, but he rarely got past "Dear." The mere sight of her name afflicted him; writing it was torture. He tore up his letters and scattered the pieces. He tore up her letters as well, or placed them on the bed next to his, on the chest of a comatose man in a body cast. Once an orderly, not knowing any better, read them aloud to the man. Pieter moved out of earshot.

☆ ☆ ☆

Awls, gimlets, gouges, files. Leaning onto his workbench, Pieter surveyed his tools. Scoops, emery wheels, assorted steel brushes and subtle gradients of sandpaper. A custom-made diamond-edged saw. With these he worked the stone, trimmed and fashioned it, gave it new and everlasting life as enduring testaments to the dead. Large stones for adults and invariably small ones for children. This is where he beveled the borders, filigreed his cornices, engraved his crosses and stars. Here, epitaphs by the thousands were etched.

Pieter learned all there was to know of his craft; he was a master. But standards had changed. Nowadays machines did most of the masonry and headstones were mass-produced. No more art, no more integrity. Even death was different. Once sacred and a source of awe, it had become unsightly, a stigma. No matter how loved you'd been in life, once dead, folks wanted nothing more than to stick you in the ground, slap some dirt and a rock over you, and be done with it as soon as doable. People were everywhere on the go, in a rush. No one had time for eternity.

He bent under the workbench—gingerly, one hand propped into the small of his back—and extracted an old black leather valise, of the sort doctors once toted on house calls. He zipped it open and blew out the dust inside. Then, like a duelist selecting his weapons, one by one, he chose his tools. Levels, chisels, hawks—he lifted them from their hooks on the wall and laid them inside the valise.

He could hardly believe he was doing this, a man of his age and condition, after all these years. After all he'd been through. *I ought to have my head examined,* he'd rebuked himself more than once since the invitation arrived. But how could he refuse? The Pieter Martinson who devoted his skills to poor and rich alike, impartially; who had once acceded to the request of an Eagle River man sentenced to hang for multiple rape and murder, a final request for a proper Christian burial—how could he turn his back on these people, the survivors of Company B?

He looked up at the corkboard. There, tacked over strata of thank you notes from grateful customers, hung the invitation. No different than similar invitations he'd received over the years, the same embossed lettering, the sword-and-snake emblem, that no-bullshit tone—*the men request your presence...* As usual, there was the note from Leonard Perlmutter, the company secretary, Label, telling him how good it would be to see him again. Pieter had never responded—until now. In this invitation, Label went straight for his weak spot, zeroing in on it the way folks sometimes did in this region, knowing that he couldn't say no.

The men would be deeply honored if you would carve their memorial, the testament to their sacrifice and heroism. I will take care of all the details—the purchase and delivery of the stone to the ridge in Saint-Vith—all you need bring is your tools. Though I know there are great demands on your prodigious talent, please, please, say yes.

Label had been lavish in his compliments, and Pieter was flattered, certainly, but also appalled. Revisiting that particular place, seeing those people... But then there was *plikt*, another notion he'd inherited from his parents, the highest principle of all. Duty. *Plikt* and *ära*, his sense of honor, assured that he wouldn't reject the invitation out of hand. Whatever his weaknesses, however deep his fears, at the very least he would think about it.

With his finger, Pieter lifted the invitation from the board, lifted the thank you card behind it from those poor bereaved parents in Drummond. Beneath them all was a photograph. Overexposed when taken and fading ever since, the image still seemed crisp to him, as familiar as any of his tools. The girl in the denim pants and checkered cardigan, whose tortoiseshell frames had been replaced by stainless steel, her hair tightly tamed in a bun.

This was Meg about the last time he saw her. A Meg who'd spent the war years at college, finishing her degree and getting ready to go on for another, in economics, out East. The same hopelessly shy girl for whom the mere uttering of words was an impertinence, who'd talked with him rarely and then only in code, had blossomed into a feisty, assertive woman. And Pieter? If he'd been quiet before the war, he'd come back hermetic. Silence like a crust enveloped him, and inside it was lonely but safe.

Pieter placed a mallet in the valise and spare batteries for his electric sander, his one concession to modernity, an indulgence to his back. He packed his high-powered flashlight as well, in case he had to work after dark.

Such was his stonecraft, a matter of commitment, of pride. So it had been for over fifty years, a life of dedication, of solitude unbroken except by business transactions and the occasional tryst—widows mostly—in the years when he needed such things. Little change, no surprises, and now, out of nowhere, this. Belgium. A reunion. Saint-Vith.

Yes, he'd replied to Label, *it'd be an honor*, deciding then and there to stop thinking about that event—whatever it was—that had altered his life irrevocably. That ran beneath his consciousness like a fault. *Yes, I will come and yes, I will carve your monument.*

He zipped the valise and took up the twin cord handles, lifting tentatively, testing its weight. Hefty, to say the least, the mass of his tools had outgrown that of his muscles to carry them. His back was nearly buckling. Yet he bore it, grunting as he hauled the bag from the work-bench to the base of the stairs.

He climbed. Well into his seventies, Pieter Martinson was still a strong man, a seemingly hale man who never missed a day of work. But when he heard it—not a sigh or a groan this time, but a yawning, crescendoing whine—he realized how vulnerable he was. The steps could snap and he'd go crashing, he and his bulky valise. Bust his head in half, no doubt. But it'd serve him right for failing to fix those stairs, for blaming their creak on his bones. Like so many other things he'd never got done, no matter how many times he'd sworn to—making that memorial for Herbert Shanks, for example. Or even one for himself.

He made another mental note as he huffed up the remaining steps and emerged from the basement safely. Once back from the reunion, he would carve Shanks an elaborate stone—eagles, flags, boldly engraved with the pertinent dates and *Gave His Life for His Country*, or some such—in pink Sudanese marble. Any visitor to the cemetery would see it, and nobody would ever forget.

Pieter's own monument, though, would be humble. Local granite, broad and stunted in a way that he'd never been, at least not in stature. Set in the midst of a cornfield where someday somebody might chance upon it, lovers perhaps. They'd stare at it and try to imagine the life led by the person beneath, a life affirmed by the simplest of inscriptions—by one word, in fact: *Sweet.*

FOUR

Darkness buries the sky. A darkness so thick and smooth, rippled and swirling, it almost looks liquid. Or perhaps it *is* liquid, and this isn't the sky he's gazing into but the river below him, slipping. The silence is total. It's sublime. *Don't move*, he says to himself, *don't you so much as breathe*. But then, all at once, there's this sharp popping noise, like a bottle uncorking, and a moment later, light. A searing, blinding flash gouges into his eyes. The darkness is shattered; the silence is fissured by screams. His mind's on fire, body numb, and the only sensation comes from his arm, from someone tugging on his sleeve.

"Leave me..."

"We've landed, Edwin," Kaye informed him, "We have to get up now."

Buddy Hill shook himself awake, or tried to. The extra dose of painkiller he'd taken shortly after take-off had certainly done its trick—that and the two glasses of champagne he'd chugged back to back. He'd splurged on the tickets, gone business class ("Hey, how often do we fly?"), hoping to assuage his wife, to relax and cuddle up with her like they used to, picnicking on the shore of Lake Konseegan. But no sooner had he downed that second glass than he was out cold and snoring, as good as a cadaver already.

He was scarcely awake now as the cabin lights blazed and the stewardesses—so Buddy still insisted on calling them—collected headsets. A pilot's voice announced the local time and the temperature outside—

three degrees Celsius, whatever that meant—and welcomed them all to Brussels.

None of it quite sunk in. The dream he'd been dreaming seemed more tangible than the plane around him, the river deeply black and powerful, the light hellish, the screams… It was only when he reached up to the overhead bin to retrieve their coats, as the pain burned a path through his fog, that he finally awakened to the fact that they had indeed arrived in Europe.

"Thank you," Kaye said, rather formally, after he'd helped her to her feet and cane. Unlike her husband, she hadn't so much as dozed during the flight but had watched some inane disaster movie with the volume turned off, trying to sort things out. She hadn't been very successful.

Her initial anger at Buddy was waning, just as she knew it would, dispelled by her own chins-up nature and hardscrabble grit—her family's traits since frontier days. It had gotten her over some mighty rough turf—the arthritis, the fractured hips, putting her first-born child in the ground—and was bearing her through this as well, telling her, *heck, in his place I'd probably do likewise.*

But in its wake, anger had left something worse: emptiness, a vacuum lined with uncertainty. Once widowed, she wondered, just what was she supposed to do, find fresh interests—poetry, perhaps, ceramics—join another club? Cultivate grace or grow bitter? She had no answers, nor was she sure of the questions, as Buddy helped her into her coat and made sure she remembered her purse.

"Thank you," she repeated with similar stiffness and said—said, not asked, "You all right."

Buddy nodded. "You?"

"All right."

And so, lying, the Hills laconically deplaned.

The trek to the arrivals area seemed interminable, up escalators, down ramps, past advertisements for products they'd never buy, in languages they didn't understand. If Buddy had disliked airports before, he instantly hated this one—too clean, too precious. Foreign.

At customs, with their stiff shiny passports in hand, Buddy and Kaye inched forward until at last they reached a glass booth. The uniformed young woman inside it barely acknowledged their presence.

Buddy grinned, "Hi. How are you today?" jacking up the charm the way he used to with rookie tellers at the bank, refugees from broken families and hearts—it wouldn't take him long to melt down their defenses, get them trusting in him and laughing. "Lots of travelers on the holidays, huh," he said to this woman, with the pressed lips and indifferent expression, her hair lashed back with barrettes. "Got your work cut out for you, I'd say."

But all he got for his trouble was a smack and a thud as his passport was stamped and pushed back to him, as the woman looked past him at the person behind him in line. "You have a good day, ma'am," he managed to say as Kaye steered him clear of the booth.

The woman's coldness left Buddy sulking, shuffling toward baggage claim and wondering whether it wasn't too late, whether he could still turn around and catch the very next plane back to New York, tell the Major to go screw. He could still see Melissa for Christmas…

A jolt of pain coursed through his pelvis. He managed, barely, to ride it through and keep up his pace, and Kaye was none the wiser. But exhausted again, Buddy could think only of resting. He glanced at the floor, a far sight cleaner than Kennedy's, and imagined how good it'd be to stretch himself out on it, to sleep and never get up.

All at once alarms started clanging, a siren wailed. As if on cue, the other passengers abandoned their bags and scattered, and the Hills suddenly found themselves alone.

"My God," Kaye panicked, "Terrorists…"

"Take it easy. Take it easy," Buddy kept telling her while searching for the source of the commotion. "It's probably just a drill."

Men came running, in camouflage fatigues, armed with black submachine guns. They converged on the glass booth that the Hills had just passed, on a man with his hands in the air. Buddy made out a parka of some sort, Irish green, and a cap of the kind worn by truck drivers. He could hear somebody snuffling in English: "S'not me. No kiddin'. I just look like the guy."

Kaye was yanking on his coat. "Hurry. Into one of the stores..." But Buddy ignored her, and lingered for a moment, squinting. Without quite knowing why, he started back toward the booth.

"Edwin, where are you going? *Edwin!*"

Every step he took brought another feature into view: the paunch, the glasses. Years peeled away with proximity. He began remembering a much younger man—chubby, ungainly, too frightened to do anything but joke. Ignoring Kaye's pleas behind him, Buddy gasped, "Well I'll be damned..." and nearly broke into a run.

He knew the routine. Hands up, legs spread. Protest your innocence to the high heavens if you want, demand to see a lawyer—none of it'll do any good. When they had you they had you and the best you could do was to let the guards play rough for a while, let them get their kicks and bully you until the truth left them looking like jerks. That's what Carruthers had taught him, and he usually took the advice. Only this time was different. This time he was an entire ocean away from home and not facing cops or even federal agents. These guys were soldiers, armed to the teeth and jabbering away in a lingo he couldn't make heads or tails of. Their machine guns were pointed at his heart.

"I'm just a tourist. One week and I'm outta here. Promise."

They were searching him, a full-body shakedown right there in the terminal. Cold hard hands slapped his thighs, his armpits that were already streaming. Sweat fogged his glasses; his knees had started to shake. This was all one colossal error, his coming to Belgium. What an idiot he'd been allowing himself to get talked into it, to leaving Kearny, his weekly routine and the support group. Maybe it *was* a kind of prison, but even prison was better than the jam he faced now, about to get brutalized, or worse, thousands of miles from home.

One of the soldiers, an officer by the looks of him—stripes on his epaulettes, sidearm in provocative display—stepped up and began rifling Spagnola's pockets. He removed the used tissues and the crumpled cigarette pack, and finally the invitation, still folded in a tiny square.

"Open it. Read it!" Spagnola pleaded, but the officer ignored him. He kept looking at the photo in the passport and then at his suspect's face, his own face a frozen belligerence. Then he reached inside the bowling jacket and pulled out a St. Christopher's medal—a communion gift from Spagnola's mother—inspected it and weighed it on his palm.

"Leave that!" Spagnola burst out and, without thinking, snatched the medal back. The soldiers pounced, machine guns first, the officer hollered, and Spagnola broke into sobs. "Don't!" he cried and crossed his arms over his face.

"Get away from that man!"

One by one the soldiers retreated, leapt backwards in what looked to Spagnola like an almost preternatural trick. It took him a moment to realize that they weren't leaping at all, but being lifted practically off of their feet and pulled by someone behind them.

"You heard me, back off!"

The officer was hollering still, ranting, though no longer at Spagnola but at whoever it was roughhousing his men.

"This is the way you treat guests in your country?" that man was ranting in return—in English, Spagnola realized. "You call this hospitality?"

He couldn't see who his savior was—too much confusion, his lenses still fogged—but he could hear the argument escalating, the officer's *jzejzejze* in French, and the American's "Don't give me any of your guff." And then the strangest thing yet, from someplace across the terminal a woman's voice pleading over and over, "Edwin, Edwin listen to me," and shouting finally, "Buddy Hill, goddammit!"

"Lieutenant?"

Spagnola whipped off his glasses, rubbed them as quickly and as best he could on his jacket's hem. "Lieutenant Hill?"

The sight he saw when again bespectacled startled him. A silver-haired man, manifestly fit and almost as handsome as the youth he remembered. Lieutenant Hill: good officer, a good guy, always there when you needed him. Willing to put up with the company clown, even when there was nothing to clown about.

"Just Buddy, please," Buddy told Spagnola, and in the same breath berated the officer. "You ungrateful little...do you have any idea what this man *did* for your country?" *This man*, Spagnola gathered from the direction of Hill's finger, was him, though he was hard-pressed to recall what he'd done for any country, much less for this one. "You have any idea, long before you were even *born*?"

Buddy was enjoying himself, he had to admit. Once the initial fear had passed, once he realized that the officer was little more than a runt, oily-haired and pasty, and wearing, of all things, *cologne*. He simply plucked the passport out of the officer's hand, said "thank you" and strode through the phalanx of machine guns now trained on his chest. Buddy marched up to Spagnola and asked, "you okay?"

"Yeah. Sort of. Little shaky, maybe. But Jesus, Lieutenant, what'll we do now?"

Buddy winked at him. "Nothing. Follow me."

He took a fistful of Spagnola's jacket, pulled him close and led him away. "Don't even look at 'em," Buddy whispered and Spagnola obeyed. They kept their eyes straight ahead, walking purposefully until they'd emerged from the cluster of soldiers and into the open terminal. If the officer was furious, if he was nonplused or ashamed, they didn't turn back to see. Their only view was of Kaye leaning hard over her cane and fuming.

"Damned stupidest thing I ever saw," she upbraided them, "Complete foolishness—could've gotten the both of you shot."

"He was terrific, ma'am," Spagnola insisted. "You shoulda seen 'im, a hero."

"A dead hero, you mean, almost."

Buddy released one of his deep belly laughs. "Kaye Hill, meet... what's your first name again?"

"Francis."

"Francis? Not Frank?"

"Never mind," Spagnola said and held out his hand to Kaye. "Spagnola'll do. Great to meet you, Kaye."

He shook the bony hand of a woman who seemed considerably older than her husband. Apologizing for the dampness of his palm, he tried drying it on one of his crumpled tissues. Spagnola offered the tissue to Kaye.

"No need, thank you," she recoiled. Rarely had she met so unattractive a figure—repulsive with his paunch and multiple chins, his cheap, wrinkled pants and bowling jacket. Her horror only deepened as he lit up a cigarette without even asking, and treated Buddy to a faceful of secondary smoke.

Buddy didn't seem to care, though; on the contrary, he just kept on prattling, "Spa-a-a-a-gnola, we called him. You'll never guess why, Kitty," as if nothing were remotely amiss.

☆ ☆ ☆

They found their luggage—the Hills', a salmon-colored Samsonite set ordered specially for the trip, and Spagnola's green plastic suitcase, secured with a length of rope. Kaye gave Buddy a poignant look while Buddy shrugged, as if to say, *hey, what can you do?*

He was feeling better, Buddy, still flushed from his showdown with the soldiers. He'd forgotten about the woman at passport control, about the myriad troubles of traveling. The exhaustion had dissipated suddenly, his pain humbled to a tolerable ache. For the moment, he was almost looking forward to this reunion.

Spagnola, too, was bubbling. He'd met his first hurdle—an officer of the 133rd—and vaulted it. Here was Buddy Hill joking and smiling as if he, Spagnola, hadn't fucked up royally in the war. As if the two of them had really been friends.

"And *now*?" asked Kaye.

Spagnola replied, "We wait for reinforcements."

"We wait, it says here..." Buddy shifted through the papers attached to his invitation. "For a driver. Label arranged it."

He exchanged a nod with Spagnola. Label, they knew, would not leave them stranded in Brussels. Leonard Perlmutter, still taunted by the combat soldiers with the name they'd heard his mother call him once, when she'd traveled two thousand miles to Colorado to bring him socks and a big jar of chopped liver—Label—had always been known for thoroughness. They waited, ten, fifteen minutes, watching the doors, their shoe tips. Spagnola treated the Hills to the story of his life—the abbreviated Wednesday night version—with emphasis on its post-war chapters.

Buddy tried to look interested. "A wrecker, you don't say?"

"Kind of gets you down,'" Spagnola winked at him and elbowed him. "Ruins your whole day."

Kaye, glancing the other way so her husband wouldn't see, frowned and rolled her eyes. The men continued to banter, about the war now, about some grizzled sergeant named Pappy and Colonel some-such-or-other, whom they'd both like to get their hands on. She didn't want to listen to it, couldn't understand how Buddy could, a man who never once talked about his experiences in battle. Tuning them out, Kaye concentrated on searching for the driver. She imagined a young male in a dark coat, a cap perhaps, and a service-minded disposition. But nobody fit that description, anywhere. All she found was one rather quirky individual stationed in the far corner of the lobby. An ashen-faced man, marmoreal—for a moment Kaye wondered whether he was human at all and not one of those real-life statues that kept popping up in town squares and shopping malls. In his formless, dun-colored parka, clutching a black valise, he had the look of an old-fashioned country doctor who suddenly lost his country.

"See anything, Kitty?" Buddy called out to her, then assured Spagnola, "Eyes like an eagle, that woman."

"No, nothing dear," she replied. "Only that person there," and pointed with her cane. "Maybe that's your Mr. Perlmutter?"

Spagnola laughed. "He's twice Label's height."

"Probably half Label's brain," chortled Buddy. But then both of them fell silent.

"You don't suppose?"

"Nah. Can't be."

"Couldn't it?"

"Jesus..."

He didn't see them coming. He didn't see much of anything except colors and forms passing around him, all of them alien. Aware of how strange he, Pieter, must have looked in his parka, construction boots and khakis—like someone who'd gotten off on the wrong stop to Wichita—with his hair sticking straight up in the air.

The flight, his first across an ocean, had been torturous, six hours in a seat too small for him by a third, contorted in the worst possible position for his back. Pieter had emerged bent and bewildered and totally unsure about what he was supposed to do next. Somehow, he'd managed to get this far, lugging his valise through passport control and locating his suitcase. But from here on was anybody's guess and least of all his.

He remembered vaguely some mention of a driver, something about Label and arrangements taken care of, yet beyond that—confusion. It was like being in the battle all over again: waking up in a strange place with no sense of where he was or how he'd gotten there. Pieter wished to God he was back in his basement, back behind his workbench with its marble dust and glues and the yellowed photograph on his corkboard. He was wishing he had never left Wisconsin when he finally caught sight of the two men.

How strange they looked, both of them elderly, but one very fat and the other slender, careering toward him. Pieter fully expected them to barrel past, assumed that their objective was someone or somewhere else. He poked a finger at his chest and shrugged at them.

"Yes, you!" the two mouthed back, nodding frantically.

Now Pieter really wanted out, not merely wishing himself home but actually running for the nearest exit. He might have, too, if not for the valise and the sudden realization that he hadn't really run, sprinted, in decades.

And then they arrived. Halting a few feet from him as if in a last-second check of their own enthusiasm, gasping like fish on a dock.

"Sweet," the first one, the thin one, succeeded in choking. "Sweet..." and then turned to his portly sidekick. "Help me out, will you?"

That sidekick seemed in the worse shape of the two. His face was wattled and sweaty, chest heaving. Yet he managed to smile and even to supply the answer. "Martinson. I'll-be-goddamned, it's Martinson."

Pieter just stared at them, still contemplating that sprint for the door, still wishing the two of them into nonexistence. He wasn't ready for this. Sure, he knew that it would have to happen eventually—it *was* a reunion, remember—but not so soon, in the airport before he had got his bearings straight. A person devoid of spontaneity, a craftsman who never rushed, he hadn't had time to prepare. And yet there he was confronting two outstretched hands like spades stabbing at his midsection. What else could he do but shake them?

"How the hell are ya?" the fat man was saying, and then Pieter heard himself answer, "Fine. Very well, thank you. Spagnola, isn't it?"

"You got it. Spagnola, that's what they call me. Right. And this guy, you remember him?"

Pieter took the man's hand and squeezed it warmly, even as the rest of his body went cold. Spagnola had been a lousy soldier, Pieter remembered, but this other man had been something else entirely—an officer Pieter once looked up to and admired. A man who still might judge him.

"You haven't changed, Lieutenant," Pieter mumbled.

Buddy shrugged off the compliment. "These days it's Senior Citizen Hill." His hand gave Pieter's an extra, vigorous shake. "Or just Buddy."

"Spagnola. Buddy." Pieter repeated the names, warmed to them as he took their hands again, this time in both of his. "Sweet. Gosh, nobody's called me that since...whoa." Wrinkles and crow's feet splayed around his face, splintered like well-struck stone. "Sweet," he repeated as his lips curved unaccustomedly. "I like it."

They rejoined Kaye where they'd left her. She hadn't budged, hadn't changed the sardonic smile she'd foisted on Spagnola earlier. She had expected this new man to be equally unimpressive, but meeting him, Kaye knew she was mistaken. If Spagnola were a character out of a tragicomedy, Pieter was merely tragic. The hooded, downcast eyes, the slouch in his shoulders, his entire weary cast told her that here was a person who had suffered greatly but could never have laughed it off. She shook his hand, a strong shake stiff with reined-in power, and felt its clefts and calluses. Hardly the hand of a person introduced to her as Sweet.

"One of the great soldiers of all time," Buddy was saying. "A demon with the B.A.R."

"The B.A.R., you don't say?" She hadn't the foggiest what that meant, though it was difficult to imagine him demonic with anything, the man seemed so harmless.

"And a mason. A master. He's going to cut us a memorial stone, with his own hands."

Unused to face-to-face compliments, Pieter blushed and to a depth he wouldn't have thought himself capable. He held up his valise. "My tools."

"A memorial," Kaye remarked and let her eyes drift toward her husband. "You don't say?"

With that the conversation died, in spite of Buddy's struggles to revive it. He inquired about children, to which Pieter nodded "no" and Spagnola responded, "Two boys. Somewhere." He asked about their health next. "Fine," said Pieter and Spagnola smirked, "*What* health?" After that, Buddy simply gave up, surrendering to an uneasy silence.

They were still waiting for Label's driver to arrive and ferry them all to Saint-Vith. Buddy was beginning to feel foolish, entirely at a loss as to what to do next. Some officer indeed! He could see frustration in the faces of his friend. He didn't dare glance at Kaye's.

Just when he thought that they'd better find out about a cab, another man approached. A slight, dark-skinned man in a gray trench coat and a mountaineer's hat complete with feathered brim. He paused for a moment to consult a clipboard he was carrying before continuing in a beeline for Buddy. He presented himself directly in front of him, straightened his back and said, "Mr. Spagnola."

Kaye sunk two sets of fingernails deep into her husband's arm. The man's face was gaunt, stripped of excess flesh, and hairless. A jagged scar cut diagonally from the right forehead, across a brow and the bridge of the man's nose, to just below his left jaw. The mere sight of the face terrified her.

Spagnola tapped the man's shoulder. "That's me you want. Over here." The man hardly reacted but again consulted his clipboard. "Mr. Hill, then. And Mrs. Hill." He bowed slightly to Kaye.

"That's right," Buddy acknowledged, barely suppressing a scowl. He didn't like the looks of this man—too bizarre, too non-American—and didn't like that bowing stuff either. "I'm Hill and this…"

Pieter volunteered, "Mr. Martinson."

"My name is Kuhlmann," the man informed them. "I am your driver."

Spagnola huffed, "*You* are our *driver?*"

Kuhlmann was unruffled. "*Jah,*" he repeated, more deliberately this time. "I am your driver. I will take you to your hotel in Saint-Vith."

"Right, then," Kaye hurried to say. "Let's go."

Kuhlmann shook his head. He held up the clipboard as if any of them could see what was written on it. "There is one more. A person by the name of…" He squinted at the roster. "Wheatty."

"Wheatty?" Buddy echoed. He looked at Sweet and Spagnola, both of whose expressions were blank. "There wasn't any Wheatty."

"It says we must wait for Wheatty," the driver insisted, and rapped his bony fingers on the clipboard.

They went back to waiting, the five of them now, to shuffling. Only Spagnola perked up once, seemingly thinking out loud, "Don't remember no Wheatty person. No sir."

☆ ☆ ☆

The face in the mirror was not as she preferred, paler and more deeply lined than the last time she powdered her nose, before boarding the plane from Los Angeles.

It had been a long flight, direct to London and with little time to freshen up before making the connection to Brussels. Alma writhed the whole way, unable to sleep, though the journey was hardly unfamiliar to her. Nerves. The flutters she'd experienced surprised her. After all, she was an old hand at this, a veteran of three wars and of a great many reunions. And if those reunions had become scarcer in recent years, the attendees fewer and frailer; if they were harder to hear about through the grapevine (the vine, itself, had withered) and wrangle herself an invitation, so what? Alma played this role so often in the past, played it to the hilt, that even after a break of several years she could still perform it flawlessly.

Which was precisely how she thought of it, a performance. The airport was her stage and here she was waiting in the wings and applying her makeup. There was her audience: three old men and an even older looking woman, utterly unaware of the show they were about to enjoy. *I almost envy them*, Alma thought as she pancaked her chin and dabbed her teeth with a tissue.

The face was rather plain, she knew. Lackluster eyes, a beanball nose and a mouth that was much more business than pleasure. A face like hundreds you'd see passing in an airport like this and scarcely take notice. And yet that very plainness was also its advantage, the key to its allure. If airports were stages her face was a screen for projecting images of others—a mother or a girlfriend or a wife. Alma could be any of them at any time, but especially when it mattered most. When men would give anything, their very last breath, to see the woman they loved.

She turned her head and fluffed her hair, aligned her mother-of-pearl studs. All was ready, as put together as the old gal was going to get. She lifted her suitcase—no porters or trolleys; she'd show them her strength, show them her bust and her defense-busting smile. Prepared finally, in character, Alma closed her compact case and strode forward, into the concourse lights.

"Get a load of this one," Spagnola sniggered when he first caught sight of the buxom woman in heels, skirt, and cowl-neck sweater. An older woman, clearly, but generally well-preserved. The skirt and sweater were a daring chartreuse and more than suggestively tight-fitting. Her hair was permed and streaked. She was stepping in their general direction, en route no doubt to some other destination, an airport bar or

Aruba. Buddy ogled her as well—Kaye noted, disapprovingly—and Pieter. But then, one by one, their leers fell away, to be replaced by gawks of befuddlement.

"Hiya, boys," the woman sang, "waitin' long?" She nodded at Kaye. "Ma'am."

"You're…" Spagnola choked, "Wheatty?"

"Yeah, Wheatty, you got it. Like the cereal, only singular. Captain, U.S. Army Medical Corps," she trumpeted then added, *sotto voce*, "Retired."

"A *nurse?*" Buddy wondered.

She patted his cheek and winked at the others, "You can always tell the college boys."

Spagnola stammered, "You were there? At Saint-Vith?"

"Bet your sweet A I was." She aimed a honed, cherry-colored fingernail at his heart—"Just like you were there"—and then at Buddy's. "You were there, too, a patient of mine. I never forget a face. Frostbite, wasn't it?"

"Not me," Buddy stammered. "My sergeant, maybe."

Her scrutiny then turned on Pieter, and her voice altered suddenly, from hard-baked to dulcet. "And you…"

Pieter merely blushed again, purpler. He wished now that the floor would open up and swallow him, that he could squirm into his own valise and zipper it.

"You'd had a case of…" But then the woman checked herself, frowned and shook her head. "A good memory is a terrible thing. Like an attic where nothing gets thrown away." Her hand shot out at Pieter. "Name's Alma. What's yours, soldier?"

"Martinson," he said, and tentatively accepted her grip. "Pieter Martinson."

"Call him Sweet, we all do," Buddy interposed, "and I'm Buddy Hill, and this is Francis Spagnola."

"Just Spagnola."

"Our driver—Mr. Kolberg is it?"

"Kuhl*mann*," the driver snapped, then bowed.

"And, oh heck, forgive me, my wife, Kitty."

"Kaye," Kaye said. She hadn't decided if this woman was for real or not, her brazenness. Part cowgirl, part moll, her larynx lined with gravel. But Kaye, for one, wasn't going to fall for it. She put out her hand before Alma could, let go of her cane and lost her balance. But Alma managed to catch her, to clasp her arm as if in greeting and save her any embarrassment.

"Well, that's all of us." Buddy clapped. "What do you say Mr. Kuhlmann?"

"I say that you must follow me to the bus."

They followed him, luggage in tow, across the lobby and through the glass doors, out into an afternoon so cold the air itself seemed frozen. Unbreathable. Buddy felt it searing through his coat and his cardigan, and the toes in his loafers grew numb. He tried to put his arm around Kaye, to give her what little warmth he had, but she wanted to move quickly, not cuddle, and merely shooed him away.

"Christ, was it *this* cold?" Spagnola asked but never received an answer.

It had been, of course; they all knew it. Knew that in this same weather they'd spent entire days and nights cramped in foxholes, had fought and eaten and shat. But they were so much younger then and resilient. Fifty-five years of age, of pampering, of rich food and central heating separated that time from now. Exposed to these same elements today, they wouldn't last an hour.

"Hurry, will ya." Spagnola shivered in his bowling jacket, all he had, as Kuhlmann fumbled with his keys. He found the right one and opened the door to a Mercedes minibus. They bustled in, shivering, first Alma and then Spagnola and Sweet. Buddy assisted his wife onto the first step, then resisted the urge to push her up the remaining two so that he could get into the warmth. Inside, they fell into the nearest seats and there they sat huddled and hushed.

The minibus pulled out onto a busy highway but soon afterward exited onto a side road that was virtually empty of traffic. The landscape was bleak, gray beneath an even grizzlier sky. Abandoned lots, piles of rusting oil drums, service stations servicing no one. Where, the veterans wondered, were the rolling fields interspersed with sleepy, steepled hamlets? Where was that picturesque countryside each of them singularly remembered?

Buddy watched it all from his window. No sooner had they hit the road than Kaye fell asleep on his shoulder, the poor girl all tuckered out. She purred there in the soft, affecting manner he had relished ever since they were married. He was thoroughly exhausted himself and yet he couldn't nap. Too much excitement, he reckoned, and too much fear as well. The fear of meeting up with the men he'd known in his youth, who'd depended on him when the chips were down. The fear of something going wrong at the reunion, of conduct—how had the Major put it?—unbecoming.

He didn't sleep, nor did he join in as Spagnola told Sweet and Alma all about his rescue by Buddy at the airport, about the manual of most-wanted men that he was sure existed and that contained an exact description of him. Instead, Buddy gazed at the old man gazing back at him in his window and tried to remember what it was like to be nineteen again—nineteen and imagining what he'd look like someday at seventy.

☆ ☆ ☆

He doubted he would make it to twenty, during the war. Seasoned soldier though he was, Buddy had witnessed too much to think himself invincible, had seen too many soldiers more experienced than him take a bullet in the brain or, hit by a mortar round, simply vanish. He knew what it was to die young. Even with the war's end in sight, his future was at best uncertain. The odds were pretty much even, he figured, for getting home in one piece as they were for remaining in Europe eternally, interred under foreign grass.

Those were the odds he was banking on, the night of the crossing of the Rhine March, 1945, three months after the Bulge, after the battle in which all of his men had been wounded, captured or killed. But now Buddy had a new unit—Label had seen to that, the company clerk who'd also escaped Saint-Vith. A new unit and new men. Men? Green replacements, fidgety kids who'd never seen a day of combat. He didn't even know their names, and yet he was assigned to lead them, rowing, across the midnight Rhine.

A holiday cruise, his commanders said. A barrage would be laid on the enemy bank and, once the boats were launched, there would be smokescreen across the water. *A piece of cake*, they promised. But Buddy did not buy it. The moon was full and the night too quiet, and the water had a sinister sheen. Sure enough, the opening bombardment crashed not on the opposite shore but on their own. German 88s screamed in bursting with a vacuous *badoom* that sucked the guts up his throat.

"Move out! Move it!" he had heard himself shouting. He ran, laden with pack and gun and a large wooden paddle. The boat, an oaken, ancient vessel such as the Apostles might have rowed, had to be shoved to the water. Shells exploded and men cried. Splinters, clods of mud, pieces of God-knows-what pelted him. He no longer cared. He had reached that place he had known several times in the past, beyond fear, a place so confined as to admit none but the singular thought of survival. And to survive—the lunacy!—he had to get out on that river.

They made it to the bank, he and twelve of his men, heaving the boat. "In! In!" But they just stood there, shitting and pissing themselves, frozen with fear. He had to push them inside. "You over there. You and you, here, down." Like a schoolmarm, he got them seated, then waded thigh-deep into the flow. "Shove off!"

The boat jerked forward. Its hull growled on the shoal, lifted suddenly, then flowed. Buddy followed it out until the water numbed his sternum, then heaved himself over the bow.

"Row," he rasped, and the soldiers reacted, those with paddles paddling frantically, others using their gunbutts, into the current's embrace. And then they were sailing, steadily, rhythmically, and not alone; other boats were visible both starboard and port. The cannon fire had ceased, and while the promised smokescreen never materialized, he didn't seem to mind. It was so damn peaceful on that river. The tinkle of water on the gunwales. The moon, opalescent, admiring itself on the waves. Tranquil.

Pock.

He heard it well before it went off. You always did. Perhaps his men, being green, didn't know yet what a magnesium flare sounded like bursting. "Get down," he waved to them urgently, as if they were still on dry land, in foxholes. As if they understood a word of what he was hissing at them.

The flare opened, brightened, blazed. Icicles of light descended from the sky and melted across the water. The boats on either side of his were now ghost ships cast in an eerie relief, adrift on ether. "Aw shit," he heard someone groan. Someone who knew as well as he did what in another semisecond would happen.

The tracers pulsed. Streams of them like scorching necklaces. The first bursts hit wide, whacking into icy water, churning up cascades. A gasp ran through his boat—he could feel it in the keel—half-shock, half-gratitude. They were still alive. But an instant later one of the other boats was hit, a boat so close Buddy could see the expressions on the faces of the men inside, their pop-eyed, yawping-mouthed terror as chunks of hot metal gashed through them.

"Row! Row!"

He was shouting again, the voice sounding stranger than ever; somebody else's voice. He heard it hollering beneath the din of screams and drumming machine gun fire. "Row you motherfuckers for God's fuckin' goddamn sake row!"

He rowed. Paddled, actually, but he didn't know the difference, had never been afloat in anything but a Liberty Ship, and yet he stroked liked a pro, his life literally depending on it, pausing only once and that was to snatch a soldier who passed thrashing beside the prow. Buddy caught him by the bandolier and tried to lift him, but then saw that the lower part of his face had been shot away, his entire jaw and nose, and that only a pair of eyes remained, darting wildly. He lifted anyway but as he did the thrashing stopped; the eyes went still, and Buddy released his grip. Mechanically, he went back to rowing.

When, how, did he land? He couldn't remember exactly, only some fuzzy image of the surprise of it all, the boat grinding onto rocks a few yards short of the bank. The soldiers just sitting there, stunned.

"Go! Go!"

He'd had to shake a few and slap them, practically toss them out of the boat into the knee-high freezing water. One private refused to move altogether and it took Buddy a second or so to realize that the boy had been shot in his upper arm; another second to find the exit wound on the other shoulder, the bullet having passed through his chest. "Tell 'em to wait for me, Lieutenant" the private burbled as Buddy held him, "I don't want to stay here."

He didn't want to stay either. He wanted to fight. For the first time in the war Buddy felt hatred, a hatred so thick and bilious he could gag on it. He wanted to kill, if possible with his bare hands. Gently, he laid the boy down in the boat, and waited until he was gone. Only then did Buddy drop into the water, unlock and bolt his gun. He only got as far as the shore. No sooner had he stepped on dry land than tracers flashed directly at his head, ricocheted off his helmet, denting it. Buddy fell onto his knees first, trying to keep a grip on his consciousness, and then flat onto his belly and face. The ground was stony and cold. Drifting, he heard echoes from the hills above:

Nein! Nein!

Shaddap, you sonofabitch!

BRRRRUUPPP—a Thompson's rattle, followed a high, undulating howl.

☆ ☆ ☆

The garbage dumps and gas stations had fallen away, somewhere, Buddy wasn't sure when, to be replaced by verdant pines. A virtual wall of them lined each side of the road. *This is where it happened*, he thought to himself. *Right here*. The Ardennes: dark and seemingly impenetrable.

The minibus braked at the crest of the hill. Lights like granules of sugar glistened in the bowl-shaped valley below. Alma had been going on about her career in the service—"two tours in Korea, three in 'Nam, and then that..." halted in midsentence and nobody asked her why, not

Spagnola, not Pieter. Buddy felt his body stiffen, as if it had come to attention.

"Robbie, no!" Kaye scolded in her sleep, and startled herself awake. "Where are we?"

"We are here, Mrs. Hill," came the reply from the driver's seat—Kuhlmann, who'd passed the entire journey in silence. Kaye saw him now in his rearview mirror, his jack-o'-lantern grin illuminated by the dashboard. "Here," he pointed over the rim of his steering wheel, at the village winking back at them. "Saint-Vith."

FIVE

He had not gotten over the thrill. The idea that he could just push through the office door and saunter inside; plop down in that high-backed leather chair and swivel and belch if he wanted to, smack his Doc Martens on top of the massive walnut desk that had once been altar-like in its sanctity. He could open any of its drawers, select any book from the bookshelves, or admire one of the many diplomas and awards framed and displayed on the walls. Or he could unhinge those frames, smash them and dance a jig on the glass as he overturned the shelves and dumped the drawers on the floor. Then he could select a pipe—the Merchsham, the professor's favorite—ease back and light up and enshroud himself in smoke the aromatic trails of which would wind through the keyhole when he, Richard, was a child, and the office was strictly off-limits.

Richard could do all that—anything—as the house was technically, if not yet legally, his. He could, but he wouldn't. Instead he took pains to to be as orderly as possible, quiet and respectful, as was only fitting, for a man was dying upstairs.

ALS: the disease that took you piece by piece, function by function, endowing the merest tasks with indignity. The mind that had brought that man so much—fame, wealth, women—was now all he had left. The internationally esteemed scholar to whom students once flocked and colleagues deferred was now alone and unvenerated—unwiped, if it weren't for Richard.

Richard had stayed with him, cared for him when the professor declined to be taken to the hospice. When he insisted on remaining in his own bed while a research assistant recited proofs of what was incontestably his last book (an analysis of Abolitionist morality), taping terse responses with his index finger—his sole, still movable digit—onto his laptop. It was Richard who exercised his limbs, changed his sheets, emptied and cleaned the bedpans. Who but an only son would check and recheck the respirator that kept his father breathing? Who would read to him the entire de Bernieres trilogy, late into the night, until his voice was hoarse and faint?

And who would see to the reunion—to the invitations, the reservations and logistics—so that not just his father but his friends who'd fought the battle could close that chapter honorably?

Richard had always been curious about the reunions, since he was never allowed to attend them. None of them had, neither he nor his older sister, or even their mother. Nor were they permitted to help with the voluminous paperwork, the old man's burden as corresponding secretary, busy as he was. Whether certain things were said at those reunions, painful recollections that the professor preferred they not hear, his family could only speculate; they never dared ask. The war was yet another realm of the professor's life entirely sealed off to his family.

Which was why Richard positively beamed when the request appeared on the laptop.

Would you do it for me?

The task was formidable: RSVPs to record, bookings confirmed, a stone to order for the unit's memorial. A plethora of details confronted him with the reunion only a few weeks away. But the prospect of it was enough to make Richard's stomach flutter, as it hadn't since he was a kid, alone in the house and stealing into his father's office.

"No problem, Pop," he replied. "My pleasure."

It wasn't as if he had anything better to do. He'd been looking for jobs for some time now—"between them" was the euphemism of choice—and had pretty much given up on finding a college position anywhere, even Podunk. There wasn't much market for middle-aged historians with New Age ideas, for suckers who still believed in the truth.

Leaning forward, Richard reached under the desk to a small and hidden cabinet whose lock he had easily picked. Inside were trim manila files, each one marked with a tab. If the office was the professor's temple, its altar the desk, then this cabinet was the holy of holies. The repository of his dimmest, his most intimate secrets.

Richard paused for a breath. There were traces of his father's tobacco in the air, he imagined, and the warm, dusty smell of his suits. And something else, sweeter, perfume-like. A stillness seemed to grip the office suddenly and he became aware of sounds—the tick of an antique clock (Gift of the Class of '59), the respirator on the floor above, soughing.

Richard's fingertips trotted the tabs, searching for the one he sought. Invariably they got detoured, though, and delved into other files—a file named "Students" for example. Inside were papers relating to a certain Tina Beauvallet, master's candidate in social history, interested in gender issues and race. A handwritten memo to him, dated November 1979, expressed her desire to write on Victorian women's cooperatives, and to assist him editing his work. Professional enough, yet there were nuances in the language, her tone, that suggested a more casual collaboration. With his keen eye for documents, Richard could detect a love note.

The thought that his father had slept with this girl hardly shocked Richard. He had been in similar situations himself. Those spherically-assed, turgid-breasted students who made eyes at him during lectures and who invariably showed up after class, after office hours, lubriciously dressed and asking nonsensical questions.

Smart, ambitious girls, confident of their ability to please—he'd married two of them only to discover how swiftly that classroom magic, once removed to the bedroom and beyond—to kitchens and toilets—dispersed. Then there he'd be, physically spent and bored out of his wits, and his poor wife stuck with a man nearly old enough to be her father but with none of his father's professional prospects.

A snapshot of Tina showed her to be thirty-ish, dark and fine-featured, West Indian perhaps, boasting a ganglion of dreadlocks. A woman not much younger than he was, a contemporary almost—a colleague.

How had his father managed to break her heart and yet keep her quiet, Richard wondered? Certainly his wife, Richard's mother, hadn't an inkling of it, or if she had, she never let on. Confrontations were not in her Puritan programming, nor in her interests materially.

A biology wiz at Wesleyan, en route to a Princeton Ph.D., rich and pretty to boot, she'd given it all up to marry the *wunderkind* from Columbia. The Dorchester geek who taught himself German and French during the war, later Italian, who'd taken to pipe smoking and patching his corduroy elbows. She'd fallen for him, for the optimism that survived all the horrors he had seen, for his keen, supple mind and his ambitions to alter the world.

And the image, of course—for that, too, she fell. The Tudor house in Newton, faculty parties and summer retreats, conferences in Aspen and Aix. The life of a woman married to the head of one of the nation's leading departments was an engaging yet safeguarded life. Why give up all that for one silly peccadillo, or even two? Why eschew appearances even when her teenage son gets busted for anti-war activities, or when her daughter runs off to a Colorado commune and remains there, incommunicado, ever since?

She kept guard, Richard's mother, stood sentry by that office door and refused to let a soul inside who wasn't summoned, or to let anything out, however slight, threatening scandal. Even after the mastectomy, she kept vigilant for as long as she could, until the cancer metastasized and took her in a matter of weeks. Still, sometimes it seemed her ghost was lingering; that she was watching her son as he rifled through her husband's papers and scolding him, *Richard, how many times have I told you?*

Richard's fingers ventured on, deeper into the cabinet. Another file—"Publications"—with correspondence from Mr. Thomas Freiling, a very angry young man. Seems the professor was accused of "borrowing" a chunk of Freiling's research on Reconstruction, or so the writer maintained. Other letters followed—from lawyers, publishers, and a sworn deposition from the professor himself asserting his incontestable rights. Richard remembered the book and how it had been hailed as ingenious, a modern classic. But this Freiling insisted it was his.

Richard played with his ponytail. He removed his gold-rimmed glasses and ruminatively chewed on a stem. History writing was only so much luck, he reminded himself, hitting on the right subject at just the right time, gauging the waves just before they crested. Knowing what and when to steal from other historians, and the chances of getting away with it.

Richard had never been much for stealing. Few ideas, other than his own, seemed worth it. His timing was hopeless, too. His theories had always been too avant-garde, too far out in front. Take his theory about Europe's conquest of the New World (the result not of Western technology but of Native American exposure to smallpox), about the causes of World War I (capitalism) and Lincoln's investments in the slave trade. His colleagues scoffed at his findings—that is, until years later when they claimed them all for themselves. Artless, uncunning, Richard could never quite play the game, never knew with whom to hobnob or how to dress, with his long graying hair and motorcycle jacket. Tenure consistently eluded him.

All in the timing, Richard thought as he pushed his glasses onto his nose, as he laid his fingers back on the files and again set them probing.

Files marked "Vacations" and "Readers' Responses." A "Miscellaneous" file with receipts for monthly payments made in the late forties, to some provincial bank in Belgium. Letters in French and German...Richard didn't dwell on them. He was anxious now, impatient to reach his goal.

He came to it, finally: the section he had read so often he almost knew it by heart. But still he couldn't help feeling that he'd missed something, some crucial, elemental fact. He removed the files and stacked them on the desk before him. Each was tabbed with a single number—133—along with a proper name: Pringle, for example. Croker and Spagnola.

He felt he knew these men personally. Through the data of résumés and paper clippings, Christmas cards and service records, he had become thoroughly acquainted with them. Edwin Hill, for example, the former lieutenant and bank manager; Richard had always idealized him, picturing him tall and broad-shouldered, a natural leader of men. Or the Walker character, the Texan who preferred to be called the Major—a character out of an old Jack Palance flick. There was Joseph Papino, Richard's favorite, *Pappy*, who remained in Paris, slumming it, while the others lived their American dreams. There were miners and wreckers and high school teachers. A man named Martinson, a mason, who of all things carved tombstones.

Most intriguing, though, was the file of Adrian Rifesnider. *Dr.* Rifesnider: colonel and former commander of the 133rd. A graduate of Choate, of Dartmouth College and Yale, and then headmaster at a succession of prestigious prep schools. His CV boasted of awards for best educator, for citizenship and volunteerism. Yet his last place of employment, this Harper's Academy, appeared to have dropped him abruptly. A newspaper article from some time after that intimated the existence of certain "improprieties" between the headmaster and several of the school's tenth grade students—an accusation, merely, but enough to get him sacked. Rifesnider was said to have returned to Virginia, his home state, holing up against an onslaught of civil suits stemming from the episode at Harper's as well as from several earlier, murkier incidents that subsequently came to light.

The article's photograph showed an elderly, intelligent-looking man, a mite too dapper for Richard's tastes, yet he couldn't help feeling sorry for him. He knew how it felt to be hounded by the system, to find yourself excluded and alone. Hardly a just reward for a man who had not only served honorably during the war but after it, returning to Saint-Vith for a full half a year as an officer with Graves Registration.

He was looking for corpses, Richard deduced, for the men who had died in the battle but were still listed officially as missing. Rifesnider had volunteered for the search but the only bodies he found, unfortunately, were German. Men with names like Augsberger and Beck, Engelbrecht and Dreiser, and the usual sprinkling of Vons. Troops of the Waffen SS, officers (Hauptsturmführer, Brigadefuhrer, Generalmajor), Nazis. The very people who had defeated the GIs on the ridge, and taken the survivors prisoner. Rifesnider could easily have incinerated the remains, but instead he wrote affidavits on each—the state in which they were found, their personal effects—all in a fastidious hand.

A noble job, yet it was quickly forgotten with the scandal at Harper's. Even his old Army friends had scorned him, it seemed, for Rifesnider had not been invited to the reunion. But Richard had rectified that, overnighting an invitation to the headmaster's Virginia address. Invitations had also gone out to a Mrs. Alma Wheatty, USAMC (retired), who'd written to him about the reunion, and to Pappy, at his last known residence in Paris. There were invitations, too, for Tully, for Ronald Barkin and Rhys—all the men who appeared in the files but for some reason had gone unnoticed. An invitation for a Mr. Dean Featherstone, of Warsaw, Indiana, the last of the septuagenarian lot.

Richard shut the Rifesnider file and turned to the next, the last and possibly the thinnest. Inside was an abridged résumé (the full version, complete with publication list, ran nearly twenty pages), with the relevant dates: Born February 23, 1924, in Dorchester, Mass.; inducted, U.S. Army, March 1942 and assigned to B Company, 133rd Infantry Battalion, Camp Carson, Colorado. A succession of campaigns—Normandy, Brest, the Bulge. Discharged, November 1945.

An impressive record, all in all, for a man who had served as a clerk. Yet he had that clerkish look about him, even in uniform. A photo from the period seemed to accentuate his prominent forehead, the domineering nose and the mouth, thin and pursed, cringing under them. Though he was old enough to be father to the soldier in the picture, Richard could easily recognize himself. The likeness was startling, down to the hair, raisin-colored with a tendency to wave. Down to the gold-rimmed glasses Richard had affected in the Sixties, when his father switched to synthetic frames.

The file held other photos as well—of a stone cottage or farmhouse, perhaps in Europe somewhere, and of another young woman, rather plain and pinched-nosed, in one of those poodle-esque hairstyles of the '40s—no Tina Beauvallet, certainly. Richard restored them all to his father's file, and the file to the hidden cabinet.

He marveled at the splendid order of it all, the precise and purposeful script in which each of the files had been labeled. "Label," the veterans' nickname for his father—it still appeared in their correspondence—seemed rather fitting for a company clerk, Richard always thought. That same orderliness was evident throughout the office—in the books aligned alphabetically by author, in the desk drawers replete with paper-clips and staplers, all in symmetrical rows. It was a mystery to Richard how a man so retentive, so afraid to let loose, had risen so very far. And mysterious why he, more audacious and free, was still, in his mid-40s, a guest in his father's house.

Perfunctorily, he closed the cabinet. The rush he first experienced entering the office had peaked, and Richard felt drained suddenly, crashing. He regretted that he couldn't attend the reunion himself, to meet them finally—the Martinsons and the Majors and the Hills—to shake their hands and stand them a drink and to try out his own theory about the battle, why they had fought it and lost. Someday he hoped to write a book about it, how the industrial-military elites orchestrated an entire campaign just to serve their capitalist interests—a best-seller, Richard believed. The same universities that had denied him a post would beg to get him on board.

But attending the reunion was out of the question for Richard, with his father needing round-the-clock care. No, Company B would return to Saint-Vith while Richard remained here, with his files and his theories, the bedpans and the pills, attending its dying clerk.

Richard rose and brushed off the lap of his jeans. He repatriated the Merchsham to the pipe rack and straightened the high-backed chair, righted the little American flag that his father, the first-generation patriot, always kept on his desk. The office was just as the professor left it—sacrosanct, immaculate—and as Richard had kept it since. He exited, and locked the door behind him.

Time to check on the patient. Richard mounted a winding staircase, past the post-impressionist paintings, the niches backlit with busts. He climbed, tweaked again by the sense that he'd missed something in the files, a fact so glaring and in-your-face huge it'd somehow managed to elude him. The handwriting on Rifesnider's affidavits—it seemed familiar to him. The farmhouse photo, those payments to a Belgian bank… The questions nagged him as they often did in his research, and even more frequently in life.

Short of the second floor, he already smelled the medicines, the fetidness; he could hear the respirator whir. Why, Richard wondered, why was he nursing his father? It was a question he kept asking himself and yet, unlike issues of history, there seemed no simple explanation. For all the times that his father stepped back so as not to get muddied by his son's messy failures, for all the years he shut him out of his room, his life and affection—what did Richard owe him? Nothing, of course. And yet, in his illness, the professor appeared to have changed. Only the day before, while changing the sheets, did Richard notice that his father's laptop was on and the words *Forgive Me* had been typed on the screen.

"Forgive you? What for?"

Bad things.

"I forgive you, okay Pop? Now I got to get this stuff in the laundry."

He gathered the soiled sheets to his chest while the old man gazed at him with a face—lipless, almost skinless—no longer capable of expression. Still his finger rose and fell, rose and fell, typing.

You are a good son.

The words continued to burn in Richard, long after they vanished from the screen. Bad things, good son: they seemed to upset his take on things, the ways he divided the world.

Since then Richard had trouble focusing—on the files, for instance, the questions he had about Rifesnider's affidavits, the dates of his father's discharge. He considered posing them to his father casually, while he flexed his atrophied limbs. He wondered whether the professor would know that his office, his cabinet, had been violated. He wondered if different words would then appear on the screen.

Richard deliberated as he strode down the hallway, past the Dürer prints and the Venetian watercolors, to open the bedroom door.

He knew it immediately; there was no need to take a pulse. Something in the air, or rather the absence of something. True, the chest still swelled as the respirator worked, the IV dripped, but the pallor in the face—the peace—was permanent. Richard remained at the threshold and stared at his father, at the ellipsis that his finger, dead on the keyboard, dispatched.

He stood there and trembled. "Daddy," Richard cried in a voice aggrieved and abandoned, of the child locked out for good.

SIX

Nothing was recognizable. Even in the dark, the place looked entirely different. The narrow winding alleys had all been replaced by boulevards; the houses, once picture-book, by uniform banalities of brick. The cobblestones, too, had vanished, pried up and paved over, a memory beneath the macadam.

Saint-Vith—Sandpit, the GIs called it, a derisive play on the village's name, or rather on its local pronunciation. A means of contrasting it with friendly towns like Houffalize where the soldiers were feted by clubs of welcoming ladies, like local USOs. In Saint-Vith, though, they were cold-shouldered; in Saint-Vith they were snubbed. And yet, strangely, the rebuilt Saint-Vith seemed even less hospitable than the original. Icy. There was a Burger King, there was KFC and McDonald's. Traffic lights disciplined the cars. Gazing out of his window, Buddy Hill could scarcely believe the coldness, the blight. *Thank God I didn't die here*, he thought.

He was thinking, too, about the hotel, about seeing the other men after so much time, about the Major. He was thinking about how he longed to do nothing more than sink into bed, down a shot of bourbon and a pair of his mightiest painkillers. But it wouldn't be that easy, Buddy knew. He had responsibilities—small talk to make, ensuring that everyone was settled in comfortably. Though it felt like midnight, his watch said the local time was only 7 with a relentlessly long evening ahead. *You have to become the officer again*, Buddy told himself. Become the manager again, dependable.

Pieter's fears were not that far from Buddy's. Twisted in his seat with one knee drawn up—the only position that eased his back—gazing out at the nondescript houses that reminded him of absolutely nothing, he dreaded the encounters ahead. More old men snapping their fingers as they struggled to dredge up his identity, to summon some detail they almost recalled yet couldn't quite get a handle on. Until finally they gave up and asked him outright: *so what did you do in the battle?* Leaving him to smirk or to mutter some lie or, knowing himself, to tell them the disreputable truth.

Yet what use was it worrying about it now? He'd given his word, had boarded a plane and now this bus. He was duty- and honor-bound, *plikt* and *ära,* and there was no turning back. The bus negotiated the streets while Pieter watched and clutched the valise resting in his lap. His tools rattled restlessly inside.

They stopped at an intersection, waited as a group of teenage boys passed in front of them. Local toughs, crew-cuts and studded leather jackets, they halted and gestured obscenely at the bus. Then they just stood there sniggering.

Bastards, Spagnola thought. He'd been craning his neck for a sign of anything familiar—an alleyway, the church—squinting hard through his glasses, but the very search was disorienting. And now these smart-asses. No respect for guests or elders, not even here in Europe. If only he were a young man again, he'd get off the bus and stomp right up to them and teach them a lesson or two. That's what he'd do, Spagnola swore before admitting to himself that it just wasn't true and never had been. He was always the bullied one, in the Army by Pappy and then as a POW—he'd never stood up for anyone, least of all himself. He hadn't interceded for Eisenhower.

Spagnola squirmed in his seat. The name itself unsettled him. He rarely thought it, much less said it out loud. The members of his therapy group had never heard it, not even Carruthers. Eisenhower: not the Commander-in-Chief, of course, but a private of the same name, an easy source of humor when jokes had grown scarce, in the Stalag. *Ike, about my transfer,* Spagnola would jeer him during work details, *Help you with that latrine, sir,* he'd say. He couldn't remember if the kid ever answered him, couldn't recall him talking at all, a shy, slight, pimply boy from somewhere like Delaware, a green replacement captured his first day on the line. Eisenhower. What if the veterans asked about him? What if they remembered the day the two of them left on a work detail, and only Spagnola came back alive? What if they started asking, *Say, what ever happened to that quiet little guy you went off with...whatshisname...Patton? Bradley? Eisenhower! Why didn't he ever return?*

Outside the bus, the teenagers gestured obscenely before cackling their way across the road. Spagnola imagined himself running after them, snatching them by their studded collars and shaking them out of their bones. He imagined standing up for himself—for the others on the bus as well—while in his seat he remained stupefied, neither moving nor uttering a sound. The light turned green, and the driver stepped on the gas.

One pair of eyes still followed the boys, though, for as long as they could as the bus accelerated. Alma's eyes. Nasty as they were, she couldn't help liking their impudence, their spunk. It was one of the best things about being an Army nurse. No matter how old she got, the boys were always the same age—nineteen, twenty, most of them. A feisty age, an age of passion, but also of need. Sure they could get it up seven times a day, especially the not-so-seriously-wounded, but at the end of that day they were still just kids, really, and what they each needed most was mothering.

Young men at her beckoning, at her mercy: a serious professional perk. An ethical dilemma? She thought about it sometimes, wondered how she'd feel if things were the other way around, a horny middle-aged doctor tending to a ward of girls? But it was never just the physicality for her; there was also the caring. To tend to them, that was her real desire; to truly heal and not just through skin and viscera but in the heart, the part of them most grievously injured.

Here was the truth, unsavory as it sounded: in war, amid death, that's when she felt most alive. She had understood that truth back in '44, before the battle, as she dispiritedly decorated the unit's tree. The saddest holiday she could remember, believing that the war would soon be over and that they'd all be going home. But then the bombardment began. Then the tanks came crashing, forcing them first into the church, then down to the crypt. The wounded dribbled in, the wounded streamed and flooded, and Alma, though half-dead herself, blossomed.

But the war did end eventually, and five years followed until the next one. Five dull, unmemorable years before Vance arrived to enliven them. A Tennessee boy, considerably younger than Alma only twenty-two, yet Vance Wheatty had already served as a jet pilot in Korea. Shot down, he was left with a five-inch plate in his skull and reduced to an infant and an old man at once, prone to temper tantrums and long bouts of depression, insomnia and zero attention span. Who would have him after that? What woman would tend to him and put up with him, even with his swanky good looks and his Old Faithful virility? Who, but her, would love him thoroughly, knowing from the start he was doomed?

Compassion could justify her marriage to Vance, back then when she was still under thirty. What could sanction her behavior now, with seventy well behind her? Was she fucking out of her mind? Perhaps, but the thought of that had never stopped her from going to reunions in the past, nor had it given her pause in securing an invitation to this one, possibly the last. It wasn't relationships she was after anymore, not affairs or one-night flings. Rather, she came for the camaraderie, to recapture, however scantily, a feeling once rare and vital. Not just for the old men who, like those desperately wounded boys, so needed nursing, but now for a touch of that same treatment, for someone to care for *her*.

Alma fiddled with her compact, failed, and tried buffeting up her hair. The three other veterans—Hill, Spagnola, the man they called Sweet—sat cached in silence, bereft of small talk, fidgeting.

Kaye, too, was antsy. Having slept most of the way from the airport, she was wide awake now and ferociously hungry. One of the advantages of aging, as far as she was concerned: the reduction of life to small but vehement urges. Increasingly infant-like, the older she became the more readily she slept when she needed to, peed, broke wind simply as the impetus arose. "You think they'll have dinner waiting when we get there?" she elbowed her husband.

Buddy didn't answer her. He was too busy coping with his pain, corralling it into some corner of his mind where it might be better subdued.

Kaye continued, nonetheless. "Do you think Belgian food is like French food? Snails? Grasshoppers?"

She'd gobble up spiders if they served them, she swore as the bus turned onto a broad, piazza-type space—the town square. They traced its perimeter, past tourist boutiques and souvenir shops with names like Battlefield, Inc. and Rommel's Revenge, in neon. Until, rather suddenly, the bus braked and pitched all five of them forward.

"Hey..." Buddy started, knocked out of his reverie and straight into his dependable mode. "Breakable cargo back here!"

He was about to reproach the driver again, but then he saw the sign outside. Lit up by a brace of arc lamps, stenciled with the frill-less script of sulfa packs and ammo crates, was a sign for the Hotel Ardennes—Buddy saw it and knew that they had finally arrived.

Pieter slapped a hand over his mouth and muttered "pardon," making as if he'd hiccuped. The sight of that sign had startled him. The Hotel Ardennes—how hadn't he noticed it on the itinerary?—the same Hotel Ardennes where he and Tully took shelter during the battle, where he'd tripped and nearly busted his back and Tully caught a bullet through the head. The same hotel and yet in no way similar. No gables or spires, but only more of that pedestrian brick he'd seen everywhere in the town, the stonemason's nightmare. Apart from the name, there was nothing to confirm that this was indeed the place where things began to go wrong for him, where his neatly woven life started unraveling.

"We are here," Kuhlmann announced. Mannequin-like throughout the trip, steering with what seemed like an iron purpose, he bound out of his seat and began shooing the passengers, as if he'd already had his fill of them. "Proceed inside. Quickly. I will take your bags."

"Hotdiggity," Alma applauded, standing already and making her way down the aisle. Kaye was close behind her, trundling. But Buddy remained seated for a moment, straining to muster his strength. "I guess this is it, boys," he said to Pieter and Spagnola.

They stood and held their breath, much as they had on the landing craft churning toward the Normandy beach, not knowing what dangers, what glories and horrors and deviations of fate awaited them on the beaches ahead. "And keep your muzzles dry," Buddy added as the doors to the minibus hissed open.

SEVEN

"Excuse me," Buddy said softly, as if reluctant to startle the boy. "Son?"

But the kid didn't budge, didn't lift his cheek from the desk where it rested. The jazz blasting in the headphones on his ears was so loud even Buddy could hear it.

He tapped the counter bell. "Excuse me? Guests?"

"Oh, Jesus," grumbled Kaye.

But then Alma butted in. She hip-shoved Buddy aside, slammed the bell and rapped on the desk, and when that failed to work, she leaned over and whisked the earphones away. "Morning, kiddo. Customers."

The boy bolted out his chair. "Forgive me. Forgive me. It will not happen again." He straightened the flaps of his red livery vest and swept spikes of richly moussed hair from his eyes. A gangling boy, spotty, yet with that wide-eyed, pug-nosed innocence that came with the age—eighteen, nineteen at most—that the veterans had come to celebrate.

"I cannot tell you what an honor it is to have you here in Saint-Vith," the boy exclaimed, redeeming himself. Then, with a flair that might have been rehearsed or even obligatory, he announced, "We owe you all our freedom."

Buddy and Pieter traded glances, Alma and Spagnola, shrugs. They could not tell whether the boy was earnest or merely following orders.

The boy introduced himself as Waldemar, though he preferred that they call him Miles. "Like Miles Davis. You know, the great jazz musician. I can play the trumpet myself."

"Miles it is," conceded Buddy who, while the others signed the register, quietly inspected the lobby. There was not that much to inspect—a cramped, uninviting space with faux walnut paneling, fluorescent chandeliers, and a fireplace fashioned from plaster. Made up to look like an old rustic lodge, the hotel was basically a fleabag. Even the Christmas tree blinking wearily in one corner was artificial—artificial, here in the Ardennes, home to a million pines.

Feeding into the lobby on either side were broad staircases, the stairs sheathed in carpeting so thick as to muffle the plod of heavy shoes descending. Buddy looked up to see a stubby old man tackling the steps one at a time, sideways. He reached the lobby, drew a breath, and waddled over to the desk.

"Supper time yet?" he hollered, seemingly at nobody in particular.

Miles answered—"A few more minutes, Mr...."—and glanced at his registry, "Morgan."

The man turned to Pieter. "What'd he say?"

"A few more minutes!"

"Morgan...Morgan..." Buddy snapped his fingers and said, "*Stan* Morgan?"

"What he say?"

Spagnola's turn to shout: "Stan Morgan!"

"Yeah, that's me," the man admitted, "Morgan." Lusterless in his limp gray suit, in his stainless steel glasses and bow tie, his only distinction was the shape of his head—remarkably rounded—and its wispy nimbus of hair. "Stan Morgan," he repeated and pulled on his lapels, as if to lay claim to himself. "Do I know you?"

"It's me, Morgan. Spagnola."

"Spagnola, yeah, yeah..." He rubbed what had once been a chin. "Funny guy. Screwup. And you're..."

"Martinson."

His watery eyes, washed-out blue, settled on Pieter. "Martinson...right. What was that we called you? Sven?"

"Sweet, Stan!" Buddy corrected him loudly, "We called him Sweet!"

Morgan again tugged on his lapels, each with its constellation of pins—veterans' and community groups, the United Postal Workers, the Evanstown Community Church. "Sweet. Well I'll be..."

He had just turned back to Buddy Hill, to figure out who the heck *he* was, when more plods were heard on the stairs. Creaks and shuffles and grunts. In seconds, the lobby was swarming. Men, mostly, but also a smattering of women, all of a generation. All of them guessing at the newcomers' identities—like guests at a costume party, the faces behind their masks.

"Spagnola, isn't it? Don't you recognize me?"

He didn't, not at first. A slender man, too slender, with a long, pointy nose and a flat-top haircut—anvil-headed. "It's me, Croker. *Harry* Croker."

Spagnola felt his hand being seized, squeezed and jostled. He was looking at Croker and trying to picture him without the crevice-like lines sectioning off his face. "Croker...Jeez...yeah..."

"Spagnola *and* Lieutenant Hill," said another man, as stout as Croker was thin, who presented himself as Pringle. Maurice Pringle, bearded with a yachting jacket—crossed oars and cravat—and a look of permanent pique. "And you, your name's..."

"It's Sweet," Morgan informed him, puffing up his chest. "I knew him first thing."

"Sweet?...*Sweet!*" Pringle swiveled toward the others. "You hear that fellas? Sweet's here."

They stepped forward, hesitantly at first and then in a sudden rush. Hollister and McCloski and Jimmy Rob. They converged, pumping hands and shaking shoulders. Roger Gimpel with a dolled-up younger woman, and Phil Conforti and his wife. Harold Billings on a walker. They surrounded the three men, and practically smothered them.

Pieter stood speechless, motionless, as the blows fell on his back. Never had blows felt more heartening. Even Spagnola was tongue-tied, reveling in the sound of his name being called affectionately. Only Buddy was garrulous—atypically so—introducing his wife, introducing Alma, thrilled that this part of the reunion, the hardest, he reckoned, was over.

They shook hands, they hugged, but then all at once the crowd fell silent. The circle around them parted, and Buddy, Spagnola and Pieter found themselves confronting a tall pale man with a sterling corona of hair. His glasses were dark and so was his suit, except for the clerical collar. A woman led him forward.

"What's this I hear about replacements arriving?" the man inquired. "Lieutenant Hill?"

"Say, you're lookin' fine, Vicar. Terrific," Buddy greeted him.

"I know," Tommy Vorhees agreed, his voice soft and high, almost effeminate. Long fingers alighted on Buddy's cheek. "You're pretty chipper yourself."

The woman added, "He always speaks so fondly of you. You were his favorite officer, I think," the woman—Tommy's wife, Genie—said. Hers was a heart-shaped face, framed in frosted curls, a Valentine face, tilted in empathy. "Kind of like a father figure."

"And look who's the father now," Tommy laughed and Buddy joined him—they all did. Laughing for the Vicar, blinded on the battle's first day, and for themselves, the remnants of Company B. Their laughter reverberated around the lobby, but then the lobby started to rise—or so Buddy thought. He felt his feet lift off the floor, felt the wind whoosh from his chest and the pain exploding in his spine. The room began to darken…

"Goddamn, I knew you'd make it!" he heard from someplace distant, and then another voice, higher, frantic:

"Let him down! You'll kill him!"

His body fell back to earth, his mind to consciousness. Buddy was in the lobby again and gasping.

"Are you crazy?" Kaye shouted, but the Major seemed unperturbed.

He stood with thumbs in his jeans' pockets, in cowboy boots and vest and string tie. Leaner than the last time Buddy saw him, leathern, like something you'd find dangling in a tackle shop. But the face was the same—hawk nose, button-hole eyes—and so was the grin, arrogant and impish.

"I'm fine, Kitty, really," Buddy choked. "No harm done."

"Didn't know you broke so easy, Hill, big country boy like you," the Major huffed. He turned away from Buddy and strode toward Pieter. "Mr. Martinson, I believe."

Pieter stiffened. It was one thing meeting the others, ex-soldiers like himself, even Lieutenant Hill, but this was the deputy battalion commander. This was serious brass. "Sir…"

"Y'hear that, boys? He called me Sir. Kinda like that." The Major saluted him, and then with the same hand grabbed Pieter's. "Good to have you back, son."

"Son" was also what he called Spagnola, welcoming both him and his humor—"We'll be needin' it, too, what with this sorry bunch of grunts."

With Alma it was "pleased to meet you, Ma'am," delivered with a click of his boot heels and a doffed imaginary hat. But he never asked her name or what she was doing in Saint-Vith. Kaye he simply ignored.

"Well," he applauded finally, pivoting this way and that. "We can stay here gabbin' in the lobby or we can get down to some heavy-duty reunionin'."

"What's he saying?" Stan Morgan inquired with a tug on the nearest sleeve—Hollister's.

A native Kentuckian, long in both face and drawl, Hollister pointed to a sign on the wall—Bastogne Bar—with one of his remaining fingers. "He wants to buy us a drink."

"Next round's on Hill," the rancher from Texas announced. He was already making for the bar, and without further word, obediently, the entire entourage followed him. All except for Kaye. She held back, resisting Buddy's efforts to urge her.

"I'm not sure I like that man," she grumbled.

"He's the Major," her husband explained. "You're not supposed to."

☆ ☆ ☆

"To the men of the 133rd. Tried in battle from Brest to the Bulge, who sent a shitload of Jerries to their Maker. To us who made it this far and to the good men that didn't…"

"To us!" Croker shouted, responding to the Major's toast.

"Here! Here!"

The men downed their liquor, Scotch mostly. Buddy was having a double, and Kaye watched in horror as he chugged it.

"Easy, Edwin, you're in no shape."

"Oh, I'm in shape all right," he grunted, "ship-shape," and pounding his glass on the bar top, requested another.

Named for the Bulge's most famous battle, the Bastogne was a dingy, stale-smelling lounge where green-tinted lights turned a bleach blonde barmaid iridescent. She'd been chatting with her only customer, a man in a motorcycle jacket, when the veterans trooped in and boisterously ordered their drinks.

More toasts followed—to the neighboring town of Houffalize where as soldiers they had once spent their leaves, and to the ladies there who danced with them. McCloski, a retired Pennsylvania miner, a chunky man in whose mitts the shot glass looked thimble-like, raised that glass to Camp Carson, scene of their brutal basic training, and to the Liberty Ship, the S.S. *Monticello*, that just as brutally bore them home. C-rations, A and B bags, dogtags, leggings—all were extolled and drunk to, and even Spagnola was emboldened to speak up. "To Omaha Beach," he bellowed, and scattered bleats of "Spa-a-a-a-gnola" followed. But it didn't bother him—no, in the haze of booze and brotherhood, he took it as a kind of compliment.

The veterans were still laughing when Buddy stood, shaking off Kaye's restraining hand, and said: "To Sergeant Papino."

Not just glasses but all of the men rose. For the man who made most of them soldiers, who turned down a Purple Heart because his wound—a shell splinter in the thumb—was only superficial, and a Silver Star, because other guys deserved it more—for him they could do no less.

"The best," said Buddy. "The bravest." And a dozen voices repeated each word. "To Pappy," he concluded, and downed another drink.

The toasting might have ended there, somberly, but then someone proposed a salute to Col. Rifesnider—a joke, but the men hardly took it that way.

"Over my dead body," Billings swore and Phil Conforti snorted, "Screw him." The mood was only saved by the Major stepping in and quipping, "I'll drink to *that*!" and after a short, derisive silence, they did.

They were well on to their third or fourth round when Waldemar from the front desk—Miles—burst in, sans headphones, and announced that dinner was now being served. He didn't need to repeat it. Promptly, if more unsteadily, the guests barged back into the lobby and then through another door, to the dining room.

The Major brought up the rear this time, but not before leaving a generous tip and pinching the barmaid's cheek. "Darlin'," he said to her and "ev'nin'" to the lone customer in the motorcycle jacket, in the incongruously long hair and granny glasses, who'd been sitting there quietly, watching. Then, wiping the rouge from his fingertips, with a pull on his studded cuffs, the Major teetered out.

☆ ☆ ☆

The Bayonet Hall: linoleum floors, Formica tables, a bland, chilly room ruthlessly lit with fluorescence. Yet here and there were attempts at decor, in the antiquities hung on the walls—rifles and helmets and of course bayonets—and the banner proclaiming *Welcome Company B*. Lavish, by comparison, was the food itself, the dense platters of meat and poultry, salads overflowing their bowls. There was beer in sweating pitchers, and racks of local wine. The veterans could hardly complain; they scarcely spoke as they filled up their plates and shuffled toward the tables, dropping into the nearest seats.

"I'll never forget the time you stuck two carrots in your helmet net and went hopping and squealing at Tully on guard duty."

They had only started eating and already Billings was starting in. The stories had begun and Spagnola knew where they'd lead.

"I was sure he was going to shoot you, poor bastard."

"Or the time on the ridge," Phil Conforti, seated opposite, continued. "With you down in your foxhole, for good, and Pappy calling, 'yoohoo, Spagnola, you can come out now, dear!'"

Spagnola responded by stuffing a wedge of bratwurst into his mouth, chewing and mumbling, "Mmpphph."

Billings sighed. "Yeah, but we were a helluva lot younger then. None of the crap we got to put up with today." A beetle-browed man with flared nostrils, a shrunken, concave mouth—Spagnola recalled him, a sourpuss even in the war. His one source of brightness had been his hair, a thick, honey-hued bouffant lovingly brushed each morning with a stiff wire brush, back and forth and this side to that, according to a calibrated formula. But now even that hair was gone, reduced to tufts like atolls in a milky sea, and his face was sourer than ever.

"I feel like one of them Jerry cities we used to ride through," Billings said. "Bombed-out." He launched into a litany of bodily ailments that began with angina and osteoporosis and worked its way through a series of "cerebral events," the last of which had bequeathed him his walker. He sighed again and asked, "And how's it with you?"

Spagnola saw his chance and leapt at it. Swallowed hard and nodded, "Just awful. High blood pressure. Phlebitis. Arteries like the goddamned pavement."

"You think you've got problems," Phil hastened in. Phil the Pill, they'd called him: short and vaguely rhomboid, purple bags like bunting under his eyes. But there were glimmers in those eyes still, remnants of the days when he'd croon "Stardust" in his tent, in the most ineffable tenor, and the men would gather outside.

"Let me tell you about my prostate," Phil said, and proceeded to in detail while Billings and Spagnola ate. While Phil's wife, Mary, plucked both the salt and pepper shakers from the table and deposited them inside her purse.

An Irish beauty, Mary, white skin against hair dyed its original black, long-necked with a face like some delicate frond. The kind of woman who'd make you wonder, even now, what-in-heaven's-name she'd seen in her husband. Perhaps it was his dexterity, the way he reached into the purse and extracted the shakers, or the tenderness with which he then took her hand—all without missing a beat of his story: the scalpel, the scars, the incontinence.

"He likes complaining, my husband," Mary said rather suddenly, smiling.

"I *like* complaining," he agreed, and explained how complaining had been part of their act—*Phil and Mary*: light comedy, song-and-dance. Weddings, bar mitzvahs, small-time stuff, the Poconos mostly. "It came naturally to me. Hey, complaining is what we soldiers are all about, am I right?"

Her smile became a pout. "And I thought it was courage."

"I'll give you courage. Try a proctological exam." Phil's finger corkscrewed the air. "I got medals," he said.

Billings reached for the beer pitcher. He filled his glass and Spagnola's too. "To complaining," he proposed.

"To complaining," drank Spagnola. "Goddammit."

The banter at Spagnola's table reached Pieter Martinson's, but failed to improve the mood. Pieter blamed himself, his stiffness and lack of animation, which was hardly conducive to small talk.

"Let me get this straight," Hollister was saying. "You cut *tombstones?*"

Pieter nodded. "Monuments."

Pringle, with a mouthful of cole slaw, tried not to spit. "People just dying for your business..."

"Rest in Peace, Post No Bills, that kind of thing?" Hollister pried.

"Whatever you want, provided it's tasteful."

Pringle managed to swallow. He'd put on many pounds since the war, grown a beard whiter than the tablecloth. His eyebrows were miniature mustaches. In his cravat and yachting jacket, he looked like some off-season Santa. "You were the bravest sonofagun I'd ever seen," he told Pieter. "Fearless, wasn't he, Greg?"

"Fearless," Hollister agreed.

"I can still see you running out under fire, carrying ammunition—where was that, Saint-Lô, we were all pinned down."

Hollister nodded, "Saint-Lô."

"We were pinned down, could hardly lift our heads up, and there suddenly I hear, 'Jesus Christ, will you look at that! It's Sweet!'"

"Sweet! Sweet! I remember somebody shouting it. Everybody."

"Damn bravest sonofagun ever," Pringle shook his head and lowered it, opened his mouth for another forkful of slaw, but then hesitated. "Until..."

The conversation died, precipitously. Pieter stared into his plate and fumbled for some alibi, an excuse for leaving the table.

Then Hollister mulled, "Tasteful you say, hmm?" and tweaked an owly brow with two of his remaining fingers. "Like I could have, 'Here Lies Greg Hollister—minus a digit or two?'"

"If you prefer," said Pieter.

"How about: 'Now Do You Believe I Was Sick?'"

"No problem."

They were ribbing him, Pieter knew, and it came as colossal relief. He allowed himself to eat, finally, if only furtive nibbles.

"He's making us one of his monuments, you know," Hollister informed Pringle.

"So I heard. What's it going to say, Sweet?" He blocked off the words in the air. "To the men of the 133rd. They held their ground and fought like hell until their Social Security ran out."

"*And* their Viagra," sighed Hollister.

"Social Security, Viagra..." Pieter, drinking, smiled inside his glass. "Yes, I think that's possible."

"*Impossible*," Willa Gimpel was saying. "Impossible I tell myself when I look around and think: these men actually *fought* in World War II."

Kaye nodded. Ravenous, she was entirely too busy eating to do much more than that, and even if she weren't, didn't have much to say. She'd taken an instant disliking to Willa, a big-boned woman with large, platinum hair and jewelry of similar hues and proportions. Horsy or piggy-looking, Kaye wasn't sure which, but with a definite twenty-year advantage over any other woman present.

"When I get into bed with him, with Roger, I can't help thinking to myself that here I am in bed with a man born when Herbert Hoover was President." She popped a mushroom in her mouth and then nearly spit it out laughing—braying. "Imagine!"

Piggy, Kaye decided. "Actually, I think it was Calvin Coolidge," she said, and glared at her husband across the table. He wasn't eating, she noticed, not even after all that Scotch. Instead he sat listening to Roger's account of how he and Willa met—on a fishing trip up in Maine, in Millinocket.

"Dry flies, live bait, she's quite the *anglah*," Roger boasted in the accent of his native Portland, where his paper products plant once thrived. Meeting Willa had changed his whole life, he said, as his face turned unnaturally florid and his paunch strained the buttons of his shirt. He had all the signs of an older man striving to look younger—ID bracelet, mahogany toupee—and he swore he'd never felt better, "not since the *waa*, not since the *aamy*." Roger pursed his lips at her and she touched them with her napkin, removing an errant crumb.

From the topic of Willa, Roger veered off into politics, into Congressional corruption and overspending, into Wall Street and then back to Willa again. Buddy made a show of listening. Allied, the liquor and the pills he'd swallowed were together assaulting his brain. His attention wavered, his eyes meandered the room. Such strange faces, he might've passed any one of them on the street back in Rutherford and never so much as blinked.

One face, though, would have stuck out anywhere, back home or here in Belgium. Prominent nose, prodigious forehead—a face that broadcast intelligence, a sage, discriminating face. Where, Buddy wondered, when the reunion was well underway, where was Leonard Perlmutter?

Which was precisely the question the Major kept asking himself, whenever he gave himself a minute to pause. But the Major rarely paused. One minute he was talking about the battle—"Show 'em what you got ladies! that's what I said first night they come at us out of the fog"—and the next about fluctuating oil prices, about grazing rights, with gestures as grand as the plains. An audience had gathered around his table—Rob and Croker, Tommy Vorhees and his wife—hanging on his words, unable to get their own in edgewise.

"Surrendering? The toughest thing I ever had to do. There you are colder than a witch's tit—pardon me, Genie—with no food left, no bandages. Almost out of ammo. I got dead—Toth, you remember him, Rhys, Barkin. I got wounded like you, Vicar, who I got to get down from the ridge. We're surrounded. And somebody's got to decide. Sure as hell's not going to be the Colonel, who's off doin' shit-what in his hole. Somebody's got to decide but there ain't much time left. One more assault and the Krauts are on top of us."

The Major's voice, wave-like, swept over the other conversations around the hall, and one by one drowned them. Soon all the veterans were listening to him, and none more raptly than Alma. Relieved to be free of Ralph McCloski, his personal history in strip-mines, she turned her chair to face the Major, at an angle that practically forced him to face her.

The Major rose from the table to his brief but compact height. "So I decided, and I told you men, I told you. Said I'd gone down first. Only I ain't got no white flag—nothing's white anymore, least of all my skivvies. All I got is my hands, and I put 'em up like this." Arms, hands elevated over his head and its scrubby strands of hair.

"I'm coming down and I'm thinking 'don't shoot! Don't shoot, you Nazi bastards!' Thinking I'm going to get one, sure 'nough, right between the eyes. But they don't shoot me. Bastards too damned shocked themselves. I go down and some Kraut privates take me—shit, weren't no more'n kids. Take my watch, my cigarettes, then they bring me to this officer of theirs, this SS sleaze with a skull 'n' crossbones on his cap. Thinks he's Long John Silver, only he's speaking English better'n I do. Tells me I'm a prisoner of war, like I don't know this, and says we'll be treated according to the Geneva Convention. Only that was a crock, and you men know it, 'cause they beat us and they starved us and they marched and worked us to death."

The Major stopped. His hands drooped, his head, too, and when he next looked up, his eyes had reddened and watered. You could hear the lump in his throat. "I read somewhere recently that they found some British pilots from the war, RAF guys, frozen solid. In Iceland, I think it was; their plane had crashed. Found 'em sittin' in the ice like nothin' had ever happened. Like they were waitin' for their next orders to come through. I read that and I thought, 'Hell, that's what I woulda liked. Frozen in my foxhole, fifty years or more, 'til somebody come along and find me. Anything been better than makin' that decision I made. The hardest thing ever."

A stark tense quiet filled the hall. Buddy stared at the Major but the Major was gazing distantly, scratching the bridge of his nose. The old men glanced at one another, and an awkwardness began to congeal. Then, suddenly, with a squeal of a chair, Alma rose with her glass. "A toast!" she declared.

Another clumsy moment passed, while no one joined in her gesture. No one looked at her except for the Major, and with an expression slightly confused. "Miss?"

"Wheatty. Alma Wheatty. Mrs. We met before. The nurse, remember?"

"Ah, yes, Miss Wheatty," he said, and the spark rekindled in his eyes. He, too, raised his glass. "A toast, then. But to what? Pappy? The 133rd? Hell, we've done it all..."

"To you, of course," Alma replied and aimed her glass straight at him. "To the Major!" she exclaimed, and the men—those still cogent—echoed her:

"The Major!"

The dinner broke up finally, close to midnight. Singly or in couples, the veterans pried themselves from the tables and peeled off to bed. Roger took the trouble of waking Stan Morgan, slavering with his mouth agape, snoring, while Croker and Rob each took an arm of McCloski, who'd gone rather heavily on the beer. Spagnola limped, his phlebitis acting up, and Pieter rushed, anxious to get a few hours' sleep before his work began, anxious, too, about his valise, that the desk boy—Waldemar or Miles or whatever—had assured him would be delivered to his room. Only the Major held out. He went strong, elaborating on the pros and cons of force-feeding, while Alma still listened to him with her chin in her hands. But her head kept slipping through her palms and soon she, too, excused herself.

On the staircase, Buddy and Kaye cautiously began their ascent.

"Here, let me…" He offered his arm as a banister.

"Better get a grip yourself, Edwin. With all that whiskey you drank. I swear. Medication on top of it."

"I felt good, though. I felt nothing."

"Yes, well, it's a feeling you might want to get used to."

They paused and stared at one another, silent, until Kaye at last spoke. "I'm sorry. Really…I've been trying so hard. First, at the airport, what with you almost getting yourself shot, and then tonight, the Major and that awful Gimpel woman. I…sometimes it just comes out."

She was as close to crying as Buddy had seen her in many years—he was the sentimental type, not her—and he was helpless as to how to react. He patted her arm, assuring her, "It's all right, Kitty," when what he really wanted to do was hug her. "I understand."

"You understand but you don't understand. How can you?" Kaye caught herself. She stiffened and sniffed back the tears that might have formed. "I have an idea." She hooked her cane over her forearm and offered him her hand. "Truce. I won't be nasty anymore and you won't do anything stupid. No more heroics, no more booze."

Buddy smiled and pinched the air.

"Well…a sip here and there," Kaye conceded, "but no more. I'll be watching."

And with that they shook on it and continued their climb, this time with her hand laid on Buddy's.

They had almost reached their door when Kaye stopped short. "My purse…"

"You sure you had it with you?"

"Sure I'm sure. The one with the gold sequins—It's my favorite. My makeup. Pictures of the kids. My wallet...Oh, no..."

"It's got to be downstairs somewhere. Where we ate. You go to the room, settle in. I'll be right back."

He started to turn, but Kaye held on to his wrist. "Promise?"

Buddy's eyebrows fluttered. "Don't call me dependable for nothin'."

☆ ☆ ☆

In the so-called Bayonet Hall he found a lady's comb and a bottle of pills with a prescription he couldn't read, but no sign of any purse. His head was still fuzzy, numbed sufficiently to deaden the pain but also to hinder any attempt to reconstruct his whereabouts that evening. Buddy was about to head back to the lobby, to wake up that Miles kid and have him look for the purse as well, when he suddenly remembered the bar.

He located it without much difficulty, following a cardboard sign in the shape of a Sherman tank. *Bayonet Hall, Bastogne Bar, they've got to be kidding*, Buddy thought as he reentered the musty darkness. It took him a moment to readjust to the light, the lack of it, but then he saw that nothing had changed. The same slatternly barmaid, the same solitary customer, the two of them mulling over cocktails. They stopped talking the second he entered, though, and the woman sauntered over.

"You are looking for something?" She smiled at him, showed him a face—painted lips, painted brows—considerably older than her body suggested.

"For this, I think." She reached under the bar and came up with Kaye's purse.

"Yes, thank you very much," Buddy stammered. He accepted the purse and cradled it, football-like. He reminded himself that it wouldn't be polite to open it and check its contents right there in front of her, but should wait until he returned to the room.

"My wife will be very relieved," he said, and instead reached for his wallet, thinking a sawbuck should do.

"That won't be necessary," someone said—not the woman, Buddy took a moment realizing, for the voice was masculine, deep and distinctively American. "Tip's on me."

It was the customer at the other end of the bar. Buddy glared at him, but the man held back in the shadows, a silhouette with shoulder-length hair and the faintest glint of eyeglasses.

"Well, then thank *you*," Buddy told him. At home, his inclination would have been to introduce himself to the stranger, offer to buy him a drink, but this wasn't home and Buddy's only inclination was bed. He nodded in the silhouette's direction, then turned to leave the bar.

"You're Mr. Hill, aren't you?"

Buddy stopped, reversed, and squinted. "Excuse me?"

"*Lieutenant* Hill—I'm sorry. I think they call you Buddy."

"Do I know you?" Buddy stepped toward him, impatiently at first then cautiously as one by one his features came into view: the prominent forehead and nose, the mouth contrastingly small. "You look familiar..."

"Never captured. Decorated for crossing the Rhine under fire," the man recounted, barely pausing for breath. "By the way, did you know why Patton had you crossing there? Because he wanted to beat Montgomery to Berlin. It was all a race, you see, an ego thing..."

Buddy had his hands up, ready to physically stop him. "Slow, slow down, pal. We've never even *met*."

The man halted, frowned and struck his forehead. "Geez, I'm sorry. I just got so excited. I can explain, though." He pulled out an empty stool. "Please. Sit."

Buddy was bushed—worse than bushed, out of it—and Kaye was no doubt worrying, but what could he do? Here was another invitation he couldn't refuse. He sat stiffly, and gave the stranger his best bank-manager-to-solicitor stare, straight in the eyes.

"A drink?"

Buddy shook his head no.

The man wagged his finger at his empty glass. There was no need to get the barmaid's attention; her gaze had never left him. She hustled over to replenish his vodka martini, then retreated to the far end of the bar.

"Name's Richard." He wiped his hand on the front of his jacket and offered it.

Buddy, with a hesitation, took it.

"Richard Perlmutter."

"Perlmutter..." Buddy's hand went from shaking to holding. "Leonard's..."

"Son."

"*Son?*" Buddy's stare had changed as well, was no longer penetrating, but puzzled.

"He's dead, Mr. Hill, of ALS, only a few weeks ago."

"Label..."

"One of his last wishes was that I take care of all the arrangements for this reunion, and it was my pleasure, really. An honor."

"But you knew my name..."

"Guessed it, really, and I've seen some old photos. I think you were a kind of hero for him."

"A hero..."

"Well, yeah...kind of for me as well. And since he couldn't be here of course, and since I wasn't doing anything special, I thought: why not come to the reunion myself? Lend a hand, maybe. I'm a history professor, too, you see and I've been studying your battle. I have this theory..."

"Label's son," Buddy interrupted him. "Gosh, it's good to have you aboard." The initial shock had passed soon enough, as it did these days, whenever he heard about death. The hand that was still holding Richard's went back to shaking it again, fervently. "Why didn't you introduce yourself earlier?" He motioned at the vodka martini Richard just then downed, practically in a gulp. "We could've stood you some of those."

"Well, you know, I didn't want to spoil things, sad news and all. Besides, I was just enjoying myself looking at you men, figuring out who was who. I picked you out more or less, and that Major, of course—how could I miss? Pringle, Rob, some of the others."

Richard's finger trawled his glass for the olive. He popped it in his mouth, sucking, while he reached into one of his jacket's many pockets and extracted a dog-eared list.

"But I *was* wondering about the guys who I think *didn't* come," Richard swallowed. "Take this Toth. Captain, company commander.

Good-looking guy in the war, sort of like Tyrone Power. I was surprised that he didn't show up. Or Barkin..."

"Hold it, just hold on," Buddy found himself saying again. The man had had a few too many, it seemed, had spun off talking nonsense. Buddy pointed at the list, asking, "Could I see that, please," and reaching into his own pocket for reading glasses.

"Be my guest."

Buddy held the list at arm's length, obliquely to catch some light. "And you invited all of these people? Rhys? Tully?"

Richard nodded and Buddy clicked his tongue, "Waste of postage, I'm afraid."

Richard glared at him, guileless.

Buddy tried to explain: "These men—how can I put this...They're in the same place your father is, only they got there earlier. A *lot* earlier."

"Whoa." Richard gasped. He looked into his empty cocktail glass, as if he regretted emptying it. "Are you telling me these people are all...dead?"

"*Long* dead. KIA."

"But that can't be. My father's files had them as living. Had their addresses, too."

Buddy seemed not to listen for a second, seemed distracted. "And this one, here"—he pointed to the last name on the list—"You invited him as well?"

Richard squinted, nodded. "But he wasn't dead, Mr. Hill. He even RSVP'd. Phoned me. A very refined voice—you know, New England gentleman-like. He asked me about my dad?"

"And?"

"And I told him. Then, when I said the reunion was still on, that I was handling it now, he confirmed. That's all. Only I haven't seen him around yet, have you?"

Buddy sighed, "pray for rain, damned with downpours."

"I'm sorry?"

"Nothing. Something I say." Buddy refolded the list. "Mind if I keep this?"

"Sure. But can you tell me what's going on?"

The retired banker shook his head as he once would, amicably, turning down a loan. It was late, he apologized; he was practically dead on his feet. He'd be happy to see Richard in the morning, though, "I'll introduce you around—guys'll love you." Muttering goodnights, he started away from the bar only to return a half-second later; he took Kaye's purse and left.

Richard could only watch him depart. He raised his glass to Buddy's back, and then to the barmaid, jiggling the olive inside. Hips swinging, she hurried toward him, snatching the bottle en route.

Buddy made straight for the reception desk—toward the Major who'd already beaten him there. He was busy inspecting the guest register, having removed it with almost surgical delicacy from under the arm of the slumbering Miles.

"Hill, howdy," he nodded. "Didn't know you were the night owl. Say I'm sorry about pickin' you up like that, givin' your ol' lady a scare. Stupid of me. But, hey, I like that purse..."

"Hush," Buddy cut him off and snatched the book from his hands. "We got problems."

Buddy began studying the entries. Forgoing glasses, he strained his eyes at the page.

"It's Perlmutter you're lookin' for, isn't it? I was wonderin' myself. His name's in there but it ain't L. Perlmutter, it's this R."

"He's dead."

"R?"

"R's here. L's dead," Buddy informed him and read on. "R is Label's son. R's a middle-aged hippie." Suddenly he punched the page. "Damn! Damn it to hell!"

Miles rocketed awake. "Yes...? Yes! What can I do for you sirs?"

They seemed not to hear him. Hunched, the two old soldiers were fixed on a certain signature. The script was elegant, florid yet bold—an artist's autograph or an explorer's. Just the kind of person they'd be proud to have at their reunion. But the name itself was a problem. Worse. The name was a waking nightmare.

EIGHT

Sitting on the corner of his bed, naked except for his boxer shorts and eyeglasses, his St. Christopher's medal, Francis Spagnola enjoyed a smoke. Celebrated with it, triumphantly puffing, for the night had been just swell. No one had blamed him for being a fuck-up, for not taking over that machine gun on the ridge and getting them all captured. The name Eisenhower wasn't so much as mentioned. It was like being back in his POW support group—better, in fact, because he hadn't had Carruthers to lean on.

He smoked and confronted himself in the full-length mirror on the wall. Rolls of fat, gelatinous layers of it cascading from his shoulders to his lap, varicose veins and liver spots, hair in scraggly patches on his head. The body of a man who had every reason to be miserable and yet he wasn't. He was giddy and still rather drunk and jubilant like some little kid. He could barely wait for tomorrow and for the tomorrow after that one. Six full days of it, imagine. Who would have guessed that being back in Saint-Vith would be so liberating—that a reunion, of all things, might free him.

☆ ☆ ☆

In her mirror, Alma Wheatty removed her makeup. Cotton balls dipped in cold cream whipped in swift surgical passes across her cheeks. Not her favorite time of the day, to be sure, and not today especially after traveling for nearly 24 hours, drinking too much and then being "on" through an endless dinner. Yet she felt recharged, rejuvenated. Her plans had proceeded splendidly, from her first request for an invitation to tonight, when she fit right in with the men. With one man in particular, though they hadn't really talked yet, had hardly met. She had feelings about such things, Alma.

She brushed her teeth and took her calcium pills, her vitamins E and B1; placed the rollers around her hair and camouflaged them under a net. More creams, these rubbed in and not off, and several drops for her eyes. Capped, white-faced and teary, over seventy and well past midnight she wasn't a pretty sight, she knew, not just plain but ugly. And yet, that same knowledge assured her that tomorrow she'd look much different. Tomorrow she'd be coifed and painted, pushed up and put together. Presentable, available. Not at all a bad bargain, Alma thought, for a man of senior tastes.

☆ ☆ ☆

If before he was drained, aching, desperate for bed, now he was all of those things and anxious to boot. First Richard Perlmutter in the bar, a nice enough man, but still there was something about him—he couldn't quite pin it. Smarmy. And then the name in the register. The name that could blow this reunion wide open and defeat the mission the Major had given him—*nothing unbecoming*. Buddy Hill climbed the stairs, one at a tormenting time, then dragged himself down a feebly lit hallway to his room.

Leaning into it with all his weight, as though it were made of steel instead of plywood, he pushed through the door. Kaye had left it open for him, probably expecting him to walk in any minute and not spend another half-hour downstairs. But he had and she, rather than fretting as Buddy had expected, had gotten undressed, into her nightgown and under the covers in bed. He didn't know if he should be relieved or not—or insulted. As if his wife were already preparing for the future as Buddy had decided it, practicing life without him.

He looked at her as he quietly laid her purse on the night table next to her and started to loosen his tie. She lay on her back, a corpse's pose, and like a corpse her mouth was ajar, dentureless, her hair blanched and stringy. Her skin had a silvery sheen. Still, he couldn't help seeing her as he remembered her just after the war, no longer the little girl down the street.

Chrysalis: the only word for it. Two and a half years he's gone and in the interim she buds, she blossoms. His first sight of her literally takes his breath away—that upturned nose, the pert, pursed lips, hair the color of cornsilk. Her eyes, though merely brown, have a fire to them, and her body…even clothed, the thought of it makes him quiver. Yet of all these exquisite parts, none arouses him more than her hands. With their pale, spindly fingers, the palms like porcelain cups, her hands bespeak all of her delicacy, her unthinkable possibilities in bed.

But they waited. Not like folks today, screwing first and only then getting intimate, back then they abstained, interminably it seemed, through the wedding ceremony and then the reception. Finally, all at once, they were alone, facing one another in the honeymoon suite at the old Hollyhock Hotel in Des Moines. Undressing one another. Naked.

To think that he hadn't been killed on the ridge, crossing the Rhine or in dozens of smaller engagements, that he had lived to experience that night! The memory of it would recur to him over the years and often at the strangest of times. At work, he'd suddenly be seized by the image of those hands on his chest, around his erection, her entire body free to be touched and tasted. "Mr. Hill. Mr. Hill, are you all right?" the secretary would inquire, and he'd go on smiling dreamily for a moment before snapping back to dictation.

They experimented, explored new couplings, secret obscenities, convinced that they were the first couple in history ever to go down on each other, to fuck four times in a single night. Then, very gradually, the fire began to sputter. A child came, Buddy's career beckoned. Routine, struggle, then that child's agonizing death, which had the strange effect of rekindling their passion for a while, their desperation. The flame lasted long enough to bring Allison into the world before it, too, subsided.

Their lovemaking regressed from weekly to monthly then ceased all together just short of their seventies. The subject was never discussed, never regretted, but simply understood.

Buddy watched his wife purring open-mouthed in bed, her arthritic hands clawing the covers. Gently, he lifted each of those hands and laid them evenly at her sides; drew the covers to her chin and puffed up the ends of her pillow. With the back of his finger, he traced the crease in her brow.

So the years had changed them, replacing the once-vital tissue of their love, cell by cell, with firmer elements—calcified. And if the remnant was alive, less sensual, it was also more durable and pure.

He finished unfastening his tie and went to work on his cardigan and shirt, his loafers and corduroy slacks. He took off his underwear and put on the pajamas that Kaye had unpacked and laid out for him at the foot of the bed. Then, after brushing his teeth and taking his pills, he shimmied under the blanket next to her and reached to turn out the lamp. Only then he remembered the purse.

He clicked it open and emptied its contents on the blanket over his chest. For all he knew it was all there—the compact, the tissues, the deerskin wallet he'd bought her some birthdays ago and inside it the credit card she rarely used and the fifty-dollar bill she always kept, just in case. And the photographs, a miniature album of them, each in its laminated leaf.

There was the two of them on their thirtieth anniversary, contently middle-aged, Kaye with her golf course fitness posing arm in arm with the manager of Rutherford Savings and Loan, a man at the height of his administrative prowess. Buddy warmed to this image of himself and his wife twenty years before, and warmed, too, to the next leaf with its portrait of Allison, circa 1969, in braces and long straight hair parted down the middle.

But the third picture was hard—too hard, even now that he could at least bring himself to look at it. Robert at four years old, just before his sickness. Freckled and flaxen-haired, a scattering of milkdrop teeth. Buddy had so few memories of him—a fine sand, they seemed to have filtered through his fist—so that only filaments remained: his christening ceremony, that Halloween he dressed as a cat. An autumn day in the park where they watched some bigger boys launching water rockets. "Up! Up!" his son had laughed as the bright blue missile arced high into the bluer sky. "Go, Daddy, let's go!" the boy exclaimed, tugging on his father's arm. He could still hear that laugh, and feel the tugging, lying on his bed in Saint-Vith.

He turned the page, quickly, and found himself face-to-mischievous-grin with Melissa. He raised the album to his eyes. A recent photo; Melissa as he'd seen her at the airport, in calico and pigtails, fixing to blow a bubble into his face. Calling him Granapple. Emotions collided within him—adoration, for one, but also regret, sudden and piercing. He would not be seeing her this Christmas nor most likely any other, he recalled. Period.

Buddy returned the photographs to the purse and the purse to the night table, then stretched to switch off the lamp. He would go to sleep with that image of Melissa etched in his mind, he told himself as he turned his body toward his wife's and spooned her. He would try to sleep, thinking of nothing, not the past and certainly not the future, distant or otherwise. Not about tomorrow or that ghastly name in the register. Nothing to do with the reunion.

☆ ☆ ☆

On the bed, smoking a miniature cigar, Richard Perlmutter lay fidgety with thoughts. What a thrill it had been at last seeing the men—the Major, Spagnola—beholding them in the flesh. And what a pleasure meeting Buddy Hill, who turned out to be much as Richard imagined him, a regular joe. Strange, though, the way Buddy had reacted to the invitation list, and strange his rushing out of the bar—Richard could not understand it. Again, he experienced the sense that he'd overlooked something, that fleet, almost dizzying tweak. Richard tried to clear his brain and concentrate—a task he found difficult in normal circumstances and impossible now, with a woman lying naked next to him.

She was coiled with her back to him, exposing the 'S' of her spine, her full ruddy ass, and the parabola of her thighs. Her body rose and fell laboriously, laden with post-coital slumber.

Yvonne, she'd called herself at the bar. Sturdy peasant girl, none too bright or too beautiful, of the type who'd been servicing foreigners in these parts for years, centuries perhaps, hoping for a ticket out of here or merely a generous tip. A piece, literally, of history.

Part of Richard reproached himself for drinking too much, succumbing to the barmaid's temptation. But another part was busy imagining his father in bed with a woman like this, a local, some lonely night during the war. Unlikely, Richard concluded. His father's loves were all of a type: delicate-looking ingénues with refined but ultimately deferring intellects—hardly this Yvonne. But perhaps his father was different back then, before he became the illustrious scholar. Perhaps, once, a roll in the hay with a half-illiterate wench would not have been beneath Leonard Perlmutter, would in fact have made his day.

Richard pulled pensively on his cigar. He tried to think about tomorrow when Buddy would introduce him to the men—whether or not they'd accept him, Label's son. His thoughts ran through his theory about the battle—the perfidy, the conspiracies—and then back to his father, the possibility that somewhere around Saint-Vith lived a sibling whom he, Richard, had never met. A sister. Yvonne!

His breath seemed to snag on the smoke. Hacking, Richard assured himself that had she been born during the war, Yvonne would be ten years older than he was, instead of the other way around. He stubbed out the cigar, removed and folded his glasses. *Stop thinking,* he ordered himself. *Stop thinking you can still drink half the night and fuck the other. You're not exactly twenty anymore.*

He shut out the light finally and lay listening to Yvonne's breathing. Still, he couldn't sleep. Instead he reflected on history, what a funny business it was, fungible and open to all sorts of interpretations. And yet there remained certain irreducible facts. There *had* been a war, for example—the Second World War—and a battle fought in these parts. It was a fact that the 133rd had lost that battle, with most of its men captured or wounded or killed. Yet, after the war, the commander of that unit had returned to Saint-Vith in a futile search for bodies. The commander had remained here for six months, Richard remembered from the file, until November 1945, about the time of his father's discharge.

☆ ☆ ☆

Pieter stood and stared. For the longest time he didn't move but remained framed in the doorway and peering into steam. Entire minutes he stood without knowing why, only that the scene he saw was a key to something: a memory just beyond conjuring, a horror.

Pity, Pieter thought, since the evening had been so pleasant. More than pleasant—a treat, what with the way Hollister and Pringle adopted him almost, made him feel right at home. One of the boys, as if nothing unusual had happened to him during the battle. Nothing untoward. He couldn't remember, in fact, when he last spent so much time in the company of others just talking and eating and enjoying himself.

After it was over, Pieter eased up the stairs to his room. His valise was waiting for him there, all of his tools in order. The bed was turned down, the linen inviting. After such an arduous journey, the stress, he had no other thought than to slip between those covers and conk out. Only first he would draw a bath.

Wrapped only in a towel, he pattered across the cold linoleum floor. But he only got as far as the door and there he saw it. Mounted on porcelain paws, with copper spigots, swan-shaped. The only original piece in the room if not in the entire hotel, in the entire village probably.

Pieter studied the tub. He wrestled with his memories, straining to pin them down. Some connection with the battle. He saw himself, half-blinded by smoke, climbing the stairway toward a door that suddenly burst open, unleashing a torrent of steam. Someone pushed by—Pieter closed his eyes and tried to picture him, his dripping-wet uniform, the red hair. All at once it occurred to him: *Featherstone*! Of course! But why hadn't Pieter recognized him immediately? The shelling, the shock of battle, Pieter reasoned. Only now, more than a half a century later, did the truth seem obvious to him. It was Dean Featherstone running past him on those stairs, out of the hotel and into the jaws of battle.

Pieter opened his eyes and again saw the tub. The same tub, perhaps, that Featherstone had been bathing in. Poor bastard, the old mason thought, blown to bits before he ever reached the forest, probably. Which was why his body had never been found.

But what did Featherstone's fate have to do with his, Pieter wondered. Wrapped in his towel, in the doorway, he fought to make sense of it—his flight through the forest, the footprints he saw, the farmhouse... He remained there for an hour or more, standing and staring, half-frozen.

☆ ☆ ☆

He ran his fingertips across the water, gently, so that the surface was barely disturbed, so that the water felt almost like skin. Young skin: smooth and unblemished, with that certain suppleness and give. Such textures had been his weakness in life—one of several, actually, fine food and cleanliness being others—and the need for them had driven him to extremes. They'd brought him low and broken his heart and yet, even at this frightfully advanced age, he craved them. Some addictions you can never be weaned of, he had concluded. Some desires just never died.

Disrobed, perched on the rim of the bathtub, he stroked the water and mused. How had they ever thought to make him a soldier—an officer, no less? As a child he'd never played sports, never gone in for that he-man stuff. Had never wanted to kill anything, surely. And yet he came from a certain class, a certain schooling, that ruled out any place in the ranks. One look at his record was enough to merit him lieutenant's bars; another made him a captain. Promotions came regularly—swiftly as his commanders got killed—and soon he was a full-bird colonel, barely a kid himself and already leading a battalion. But apart from signing orders, he'd never truly led anybody. There were other, *real* officers for that.

They gave him a rank, a unit, and then they gave him a war. None of that Hollywood kitsch but a real war of brains and intestines oozing, of shit in your foxhole and piss running down your pants, of fear as cold and massive, as impassable as the polar icecap. Not the kind of place for a man with desires such as his, with weaknesses.

Ironic, then, that it was there, in war, that he'd found his ultimate desire. Dean. Hair the red of glowing embers, that diamond-glint blue of the eyes. A mere private of nineteen and yet dominating and wise beyond his years. Aware of the contradictions in the world, even of his own name—Featherstone—all at once gossamer and hard.

Love is an unpredictable thing. It breaks out when it wants to, mindless of schedules and plans—like battles. And just as one might fall in battle, so, too, in war can a man fall in love. So he found himself in wartime, against all expectations, utterly smitten, suffering through each morning's inspection, reviewing rows of scabrous, ill-smelling men before at last reaching Dean, his jewel.

The nights they'd spent together, furtively in his tent, with the sentries posted at a distance. The joy he felt stroking the flat of his stomach, the curve of his alabaster cheek. He would have given him anything, the silver eagles from his shirt. But in the end Dean only spurned him, teased and mocked him. Was it any wonder he wanted revenge?

A minor vengeance, modest by wartime standards: he'd sent Dean on a little errand, down to Saint-Vith. A hostile town, true, but with the war only weeks from ending, there seemed no danger in it. The peasants would only be happy to help.

So off Dean went and on the Germans came. The battle. Those six days and nights, by far the worst of his life, on that ridge where that jackass of a Major insisted on digging in and making a stand, hopeless though it was. Shells exploding, dirt and pine boughs raining into the foxhole where he had hidden unscathed, but where the screams of the wounded reached him anyway. He felt nothing for them, only worry for Dean. Worry to the point of madness, for Dean had never returned.

Then it was time to surrender. Slowly he rose from his hole, resurrected but with part of him still dead, and descended with his hands raised from the ridge. In the meadow—or what used to be a meadow, a killing field now—the men gathered at gunpoint. German infantry, themselves looking half-starved and crazed, beat the Americans into line. They beat him as well, an officer, until Joachim arrived and saved him.

Sage, discerning Joachim. With his riding crop and that "Von" prefixed to his name, he had no need to establish his pedigree, and intuitively recognized it in others. Even in a man who'd spent a week in a hole, exposed to the elements, muck-covered. Without hesitation, Joachim approached him, clicked his heels, saluted with his crop. And he had saluted back, feeling all at once an affinity for this man with eagles on his coat much like those on his own. Kindred birds.

"Follow me," Joachim told him in English, an invitation, not an order, and led him away to his command car. He could still remember the faces of the men as he drove off, that mongrel look of bitterness and yearning, of pain. Not unlike the expression he saw now, so many years later, staring into the water's reflection.

Discerning and prescient Joachim, knowing even in that moment of minuscule victory that Germany's war was lost. That there'd be a hefty bill to pay for that shindy the Nazis had thrown in Europe. Already plotting his and his comrades' escape, making the right connections within certain American circles. All he needed was a nexus, a point man who knew the ropes, who had the proper rank and credentials. Someone impeccable. Of course he would be paid for his services, handsomely even, for if nothing else Joachim was a man of honor. Diamonds, cut and uncut, for each GI body obtained, for each identity whose owner no longer needed it.

A perfect plan, really, returning to Saint-Vith with Graves Registration, searching for MIAs. Half the job had been done for him already. A local urchin, the orphaned butcher's son, had combed the forest for stiffs, had stuffed them into his sack and stored them in his cold house. Even the paperwork was handled—Perlmutter, the company clerk, he'd returned as well. Perlmutter, with his eye for detail and his fluent German and French, was willing to do anything to serve his country, and to support that wench he'd knocked up.

The last of the great romantics, Perlmutter, but then again who was he to judge? Yes, he wanted to help Joachim and yes, he welcomed the reward, but the truth had never eluded him. Neither for friendship nor for wealth had he returned to Saint-Vith. He'd come back searching for Dean.

Why, specifically, had he sent Dean away, he wondered as he dipped the first of his toes in the tub. Vaguely he remembered a night in his tent, his table set with bread and cheese, the preserves he'd been saving since Paris, a bottle of Rhenish wine. He recalled the glow of the hurricane lamp and its reflection in Dean's laughing eyes. Maliciously, he laughed when his commander reached out to touch him, called him "priss" and "cream puff." And that's when the anger began.

Anger uncorked and left to breathe all night, its bouquet was ripe by morning. By the time reveille sounded, he'd already tasted revenge. To this day the scene recurred in his dreams: Dean sauntering out of camp, into the forest with his rifle slung over his shoulder, pausing to snap a twig from a tree and slip it into his mouth. Dean turning back with lazy defiance and shooting him the biggest go-fuck-yourself grin.

The water temperature was perfect now, precisely the way he liked it. He read somewhere that Churchill, too, had a fondness for bathing, for surfaces silken against his skin. Even great men have their weaknesses, he reasoned, and not just the might-have-been great.

One foot inside, then two, then bending forward onto his knees like a Mohammedan bent in prayer. Next, easing back onto his rump, he slid smoothly down until his head came to rest beneath the sprockets, each one as sharp as a knife.

His body—white, blubbery—buoyed slightly before settling, garnished with ringlets of steam. He regretted for a moment not having called for room service—if this wreck of a hotel actually *had* room service—and having that fetching young bellhop, Miles he called himself, bring him a carafe, some pâté de foie gras with biscuits. He might have had it served him in the tub.

Tomorrow perhaps, he promised himself; tonight there was serious work. He had to plan his next moves. How to avoid that redneck Major, that dimwit Hill and the whole antediluvian mob, at least until he retrieved the diamonds. There was chance, however slim, that they were still in the cold house, still in the butcher's possession. According to Miles, he lived in the same old cottage, an aging idiot now, bearing his meats in a sack. But still dangerous, he reckoned as he fingered the scar on his shoulder, recalling how that idiot had stabbed him.

The diamonds, left behind when he was forced to flee Saint-Vith in a hurry, they were his only hope now with the Harper's scandal still bleeding him, and creditors hot on his trail. He'd nearly given up when suddenly the invitation arrived. The perfect disguise for journeying back inconspicuously—the reunion, his ideal alibi.

He needed money desperately, and yet his weaknesses persisted. As did his guilt. He brought up his arms and hugged himself and shook remembering Dean, the person he'd loved so completely, the boy he had sent to his death.

Book Two

THE SECRET OF SANDPIT RIDGE

ONE

He had a way of smiling, Buddy, that totally altered his face. His mouth stretched and his nose extended—a bow and its arrow—his eyes reduced to slits. Twinkles and dimples previously hidden suddenly broke out and glowed. Smiling like that, Kaye could hardly recognize him, much less tell what that smile was for. "Is that happiness or hurt I'm seeing?" she would ask him, knowing how eager Buddy was to please her always, knowing how pride prevented him from revealing pain. She wanted to ask him again as he waited on the staircase several steps below her. Was that smile really meant for her, the old woman cautiously descending one foot at a time, balancing on her cane, or was it for himself—for the ache in his bones and the regrets of a hasty decision?

But "You go on" was all Kaye Hill managed to say to him. "I'll catch up with you later."

"Hup-to, Kitty. You're doing fine." Buddy smiled at her again, crinkling up his face even tighter. It was the most he could do, a man unaccustomed to expressing such feelings, to tell her how grateful he was for her company, for her willingness to put aside her anger.

From below them in the lobby rose a farrago of noise: coughing, shouting, the whoosh of polyester on rayon, the whine of a hearing aid or two. Old people's sounds accompanied by an old people's smell, overripe and medicinal.

"What time did you get in last night? I don't remember you coming to bed."

"Not too long after you," Buddy replied as he reached out for her forearm and cupped it. He seemed incapable of telling her truths anymore, much less how much he loved her. "You were out like a light."

What good would the truth have done her, Buddy pondered. The night had been one of his worst ever, wracked with cold sweats and dreams of ice-choked rivers. He fretted endlessly about the reunion, which could easily become a fiasco. How could he tell her all that without incurring one of her infamous *I told you so*'s, without her demanding that they pack up and fly off at once?

It was too late. He was committed to staying in Saint-Vith, and couldn't leave the Major, the men. Not now especially, with this new kind of danger approaching. Having failed once to return to the ridge—in the war—he wasn't going to do it again. As long his endurance enabled him, this time he was digging in.

The noise and smells intensified as Buddy neared the bottom of the stairs. He half expected the crisis to have broken out already, bedlam. But hazarding into the lobby with his wife on his arm, holding on to her as much as she to him, he encountered a different scene.

The guests gathered around the Major, who was pressed up close to a young woman, tall and dark-haired. An expensive camera hung around her neck, and her hands held a notebook and a pencil. The Texan was talking expansively as usual, arms sweeping across entire swaths of countryside, of battlefields and time. The woman scribbled fast to keep up.

Buddy didn't enter the circle, but dallied off to the side. He tried to catch the Major's attention, but all he received was a roll of the eyes and that same vainglorious grin, as if to ask, *can I help it, Hill, if she likes me?*

The young woman indeed seemed intrigued by him—by all of them, eager to hear their stories. Only Alma's expression was dour. Having gone to such lengths putting herself together that morning—hair curled, makeup meticulously applied, having chosen her pink cashmere skirt and matching vest, her décolleté blouse and boots—all with the Major in mind, she suddenly found herself upstaged.

Within the cluster of listeners, a hand rose and waved to Buddy—

Spagnola's, giving him the thumbs-up. Other men motioned at Buddy as well, but he just smiled his ambiguous smile. With the Major so preoccupied, he thought it best to keep vigilant, guarding against unwelcome intruders.

Buddy scanned the lobby, peered up the staircases, and double-checked the exits. Miles, or Waldemar, still sat behind the desk, while Kuhlmann, the driver, stood in front of it. But then another man made his entrance. A full head taller than Kuhlmann and twice as wide at least, sixty-something and balding, with a belly reminiscent of a bass drum. A well-dressed man—tailored suit, Italian shoes—exuding an air of affluence.

The man returned Buddy's stare and after exchanging a whisper with Kuhlmann, the two of them approached.

"Mr. Hill," Kuhlmann bowed, "Mrs. Hill. I wish you to meet Herr Hermansdorfer. He is the owner of this hotel."

"A pleasure, Mr. Hermans…," Kaye began, then turned to her husband for help.

"Hermansdorfer," Buddy obliged. "You have a very comfortable place here, sir." Lying, he realized, was slowly becoming his forte.

Kuhlmann translated and the portly man smiled. Fat nose, thick lips—his features were as rounded and soft as the driver's were angular. Hair very black and pomaded. He spoke, finally, delivering what Buddy sensed was an often-recited speech in German.

"Mr. Hermansdorfer wishes you to know that he was only a boy during the war but that he knows all about the battle you and your comrades fought here." Kuhlmann paused, as if reluctant to go any further. A sharp look from his boss, though—he *understood* English at least—prodded him. "A great battle that we owe our freedom to. In the name of the people of Saint-Vith who have elected him, Herr Hermansdorfer wishes to say thank you."

"Elected him?" Buddy asked. "You *elect* your hotel owners?" He asided to Kaye, "Democracy at work."

Hermansdorfer laughed, jiggling a succession of chins. But Kuhlmann remained straight-faced. "Herr Hermansdorfer," he stated, "is also the mayor of this town."

"Jah, I am zee mayor," Hermansdorfer affirmed, with a measurable expanse of girth. "Burgemeister."

"Well, Mr. Mayor, you got my vote," Buddy said. He thrust out his hand for a moist and beefy shake. "And who's that?"

Buddy motioned at the young woman who was still commanding the Major's attention—his and the rest of the group's; who was still scribbling fiercely, as though his every word were writ.

"Journalist," Kuhlmann scowled. "*Paris Match*. She has family near here, she says, in Houffalize. She wants to write about the battle. About you."

"Well, I can think of one man who'll be happy to talk," Buddy remarked, and Kuhlmann agreed, "At least one."

Hermansdorfer didn't hear them, though. He was too busy beaming at the journalist, bubbling with his hands planted proudly on his paunch. "*Paris Match*," he chortled, "Wunderbar."

☆ ☆ ☆

"Burgemeister was he," Kaye sneered as they wandered toward breakfast. "Had a few burgers too many, if you ask me. And you might have said something about the bed, Edwin. *And* the heating."

Buddy touched her forearm. "Yup, I might have," he said, all the while still looking over his shoulder, making sure that no one unwelcome was following. The lobby was empty, though, with the sole exception of Pieter.

Buddy glimpsed the mason slipping off in his dun-colored parka, in heavy work gloves and a stevedore's cap, as he lugged his valise toward the exit. If Pieter saw Buddy he did not acknowledge him, didn't look anywhere but ahead. His jaw was set and his eyes fastened on some distant and minuscule point. He barged through the door and out into a brilliant morning, and never once looked back.

Inside Bayonet Hall, Buddy and Kaye took their place at the breakfast table, alongside Maurice Pringle, again in his yachting jacket, his cravat and indignant veneer. Friends called him Ham, the couple from Iowa heard, a short-wave enthusiast who, when he wasn't chatting with captains at sea, sold nautical antiques out of his house in Jeckell Island, Georgia. "Ever want a good grapnel, a bilge pump—we're talking original stuff here—you just give me a call." His pudgy fingers were always in motion thumping the table or raking his beard. "Just call and ask for Ham. I'm always home, and there's nobody else there but me."

Billings was seated as well, also examining his food. Grumbling over the lumps in his oatmeal and the lamentable absence of honey. "You fight a war for these people, this is what you get." A widower from Brookfield, Missouri, Billings had been an insurance appraiser—"cynicism an asset," he said—before retiring to long afternoons playing cards at the VFW, to a succession of medical specialists. "Hobbies?" he frowned when Kaye asked him. "How 'bout staying alive."

Phil Conforti joined them, having first misplaced then located his wife alone in the Bastogne Bar. He guided Mary back to the table, held out her chair and unfolded a napkin in her lap, all the while looking up and smiling at Kaye and Buddy, telling them, "Can you believe it, a girl like this going for a *schlub* like me?"

They ate, partaking of fare once again overabundant—sausage, bacon, steaming mounds of eggs. "Next course, angioplasty," Phil said. "Bypasses for dessert."

The conversation settled on the mundane issues, on pensions and health care plans, grandchildren for those who had them, the weather. Things they'd talk about with anyone of their age, their preoccupations, encountered outside the Wal-Mart back home. Nobody mentioned the reunion per se or why they'd decided to attend. Nobody spoke of the battle except, ironically, Spagnola.

The retired wrecker found himself sitting next to the young reporter from Paris who, with her camera and notebook, her look of indefatigable interest, did not have to prompt him to speak.

"I wasn't what you'd call a natural soldier," he told her. "Not like the Major over there or any of these guys. Fact was, I was scared shitless." He paused to shovel some eggs into his mouth, then, chewing, spoke on.

"Too scared to be of much good to anybody." He looked down the length of the table, at Stan Morgan and Jimmy Rob, as if to seek confirmation, hoping they wouldn't supply it.

"We were all scared," the Vicar, positioned on Spagnola's right, cut in. "Anybody who says he wasn't, Miss, either has a bad memory or trouble telling the truth."

The woman regarded him with eyes set deep in her face, hazel eyes sheltered by dark untended brows. "And you, were you wounded, Father?"

The Vicar laughed. "Reverend will do. You know…Miss?"

"Mirelle. My first name is Claire." Her English was fluent but with the merest trace of an accent—heavy 'th's, a faintly rolled 'r'.

"You know, Miss Mirelle, I was wounded on the first day of the battle, the very first barrage. A piece of metal no bigger than this"—he held up his pinky—"pierced me right here," and pointed it at his brow. "Cut the optic nerve."

"My God," breathed the reporter, a stark-featured woman in a collarless white shirt and plush violet blazer. Nut and raven played in her French-braided hair, olive and cream in her skin. The pencil she wrote with was chewed.

"Precisely my thought at the time. My God!" Tommy exclaimed. "But there *was* a bright side. Because of my wound I got evacuated. I wasn't killed. I was never even taken prisoner."

"You see, that's where the courage comes in: seeing the good in every situation, even if that situation looks dark." This was Genie's contribution, Tommy's wife. She laid both her hands on the back of her husband's and massaged them. "Faith is the key, Miss. *And* love."

"Love and faith," Claire repeated, writing fast. Her entire face seemed to be taken up in the effort—her wide, full-lipped mouth grimly puckered, a twist in her plug of a nose. "And some of you were captured, no?"

She was addressing the entire table now, and in response, Rob and Hollister nodded. Morgan seemed not to hear. Only Spagnola actually answered her, at length again and while reaching for a second link of sausage.

"Being captured was even worse than being in the battle, if you can imagine it," he said. "The cold, the humiliation, I never got over it. In fact I still go to this POW support group, every damn week, and I'm the oldest guy there, all the rest from Vietnam and Korea and stuff. I'm the oldest and Captain Carruthers—got that, Car-ru-thers—the Captain's the group leader and he thinks I'm just now making progress..."

He couldn't help himself, blabbing. It felt so good talking to this girl and through her to the rest of the guests around him. "Once you've been a POW, there's a part of you that never gets out," Spagnola admitted, and with a chomp on her pencil, nose scrunching, Claire quoted him verbatim.

The meal proceeded pleasantly enough, so far according to plan. Coffee and pastries were served by Miles, assisted by the barmaid from the night before. She looked worse for wear, the morning revealing dark circles around her eyes, a face pleated with lines. The two of them bustled, for there were no other waiters—a skeleton staff—no cooks or concierges. Hermansdorfer watched them from the far end of the hall, gloating it seemed, with that same sated smile and his belly extended imperiously.

Of Saint-Vith's mayor, the Major was an older, thinner reflection. He, too, wore his self-contented grin and was trying it out on Alma now, the former nurse having maneuvered herself into a place next to his at the table, moving in swiftly when the reporter's attention was diverted. The Major never missed a beat, though. He rambled on—no longer about the war but all about his ranch outside of San Marco, Texas, five hundred acres, about a rare strain of Arabians he'd been breeding. What he talked about never mattered, Alma realized, as long as the subject was himself and the listener, preferably, a woman. She couldn't say she minded it; on the contrary, she found his rambling entertaining, his attention flattering. *This man isn't wounded*, she reminded herself, *he isn't about to die*.

Halfway into a one-sided discussion of cattle branding, the Major interrupted himself—"excuse me, darlin'"—and rapped a spoon against his juice glass. He stood, not a tall man but straight in the back, with thumbs hitched behind a fist-sized belt buckle in the shape of a coiling snake.

"Your attention, men. Please. Ladies. Thank you. I want to welcome you all again to the beautiful Hotel Ardennes in historic Saint-Vith, Belgium."

Laughter rippled across the hall, followed by scattered applause. Hermansdorfer, oblivious to the joke, was laughing and clapping too.

The Major's glass again sounded. "Now, men, here are your orders and I expect you to follow them exactly. First, there'll be no cavorting in Houffalize, at least not with the ladies..." He paused for another swell of laugher. "And as for the ridge, ain't nobody goin' up there on his own, not before the end of the week and our big closing ceremony. Our own Sweet Martinson's up there right now cuttin' us a right fine memorial and I don't want nobody seein' it 'til it's done, y'hear?"

"Yes-sah!" somebody called out, and there were more laughs, more clapping. The Major peered down the lengthy crook of his nose, surveyed the modest assemblage of old men and women hunching, and was happy. He didn't grin but actually smiled, revealing teeth that were white and even and mostly his own. "And another thing," he continued. "There'll be no fraternizing with the locals. No drinking black market booze and no..."

The Major halted. He squinted hard and screwed up the face that a moment before had been beaming. Noticing the change, Buddy Hill swerved in his chair to see a dark, long-haired man standing at the entrance to the hall. Dungarees, motorcycle jacket—a bum off the street, or so he seemed, except for the gold-rimmed spectacles.

Buddy waved at him, urging him to enter. "Pardon me, Major," he said. "Folks. Here's someone I think you should meet."

Kaye, confused, tugged on his cardigan. "What's going on? Who *is* that?"

"It's all right, Kitty," he assured her quietly, then stood to announce: "This young man—come in, Richard, don't be shy—this young man's name is Richard Perlmutter. That's right, Perlmutter. And I believe he has something to say to you."

He held an inviting hand open to Richard and at the same time shot the dumbfounded Major a wink.

"'Morning everyone," Richard said, shuffling forward.

"Speak up!" growled Stan Morgan with a hand to his ear. "Can't hear you if you mumble."

Richard tried again, louder: "Good morning, I said. It's a great pleasure for me to meet you all." He stood next to the Major, took his hand and shook it. "This man, for example, I've heard so much about him from my father. About all of you. You, Mr. Gimpel, and Mr. McCloski, you. You're kind of like legends to me."

The old men gaped at him, at one another, clueless.

"Who'd you say you were?" asked Jimmy Rob.

Hollister answered him, "Perlmutter," and leveled one of his surviving fingers at Richard. "Why, you must be Label's boy."

"Yes, Label's boy," Richard smiled briefly. "But I'm afraid Label, as you called him, can't be with you today."

"Yeah, well, what do you expect from that goldbricking do-nothing clerk?"

This crack—from Pringle—sparked new bursts of laughter, so blaring that Richard's next words were lost. Only Morgan seemed to catch them, his hearing aids having winnowed the noise.

"Hold on! Quiet everybody!" Morgan pounded his table. "Shut up! Then, with silence restored, he looked at Richard. "What did you say?"

"I said that my father, Professor Leonard Perlmutter, is dead."

A collective groan swept over the tables. Whispers of "Label...*dead?*"

Richard rushed to console them. "He would've loved to have been with you here today, I know. And I like to think he'd have wanted me to come in his place."

"Richard's a historian, just like his dad," Buddy explained. He walked over to the younger man and put an arm around him. "He's even done a study of our battle, you know, got some ideas he wants to share."

The Major at last slapped his thigh. "Well goddamn!" He, too, looped an arm around Richard. "Welcome, son, welcome. Consider yourself an honorary member of the 133rd!"

A full-blown ovation followed, partially standing. And that was that. The diners went back into their food, back to their small talk as if nothing of significance had happened—reacting to Label's passing as they might have during the war, when death was common and life potentially short.

The transition astonished Richard as he accepted a seat from the Major and Alma filled up his plate. He didn't eat, though, and hardly noticed when Yvonne, the barmaid-turned-waitress, hastened to pour his coffee. He was too preoccupied watching the men, amazed at the gusto with which they ate, as if this breakfast might be their last, as though they were once again digging in.

☆ ☆ ☆

An hour had been allotted between the end of breakfast and the first of the reunion's tours. Back in the war, they'd be ready to move out in a moment's notice, now it took forever to get the men up and down those stairs and in and out of the bathroom; to bundle them up in several layers of winter clothing, to find their gloves and hats. There were medicines to take and braces to secure. Items such as purses and wallets, glasses and rings, had a peculiar way of wandering off and had to be searched for frantically.

"You hardly touched your food this morning," Kaye remarked from the far side of their bed as Buddy stooped carefully looking under it.

"You haven't seen my other sports shoe, have you? I thought they'd be warmer than the loafers."

"Barely touched it last night, too."

He rifled the outer pockets of his suitcase. "I was sure you packed them both."

"You have to eat, Edwin. At least that."

He tossed the single sneaker into the closet, rolled his shoulders and sighed. "It's the pills. They kill the pain, sure, and everything else with 'em."

"It's not just the pain." Kaye glared at him. She leaned over her cane with a scowl and one eye closed in the reproving pose he feared most. "You're nervous about something. About this silly reunion."

"It's not silly..."

"Silly to worry about, then. You see it's going fine. All the old fogies are here—Roger with his bimbo wife, that Major who can't shut his trap for a second, and Spagnola... What could possibly go wrong?"

He looked down at the floor and then up at her, their gazes meeting midway over the bed. "Nothing, Kitty. Nothing can go wrong," he said as he pushed his arms through his overcoat. "Did you see my scarf around anywhere?"

☆ ☆ ☆

Behind the wheel of his minibus, Kuhlmann looked impatient. He had waited for half an hour, engine idling, while his passengers mounted the three small serrated stairs and took their seats behind him. They climbed and groaned and griped, as if aging were the world's worst tragedy for these Americans, as if life had owed them more. *Fools*, Kuhlmann's sneer seemed to say, even as he greeted them in turn.

"Hell of a morning," Spagnola shivered, with a clutch of his jacket's collar. "Good to see you so bright."

"Yes," said Kuhlmann.

Spagnola found a seat behind Buddy and Kaye Hill and leaning forward whispered, "How old you think that guy is?"

"Beats me," Buddy whispered back, "anywhere between fifty and seventy-five. Ageless, kind of."

Spagnola snorted. "Ageless maybe, but I wonder what he did during the war."

The bus was loaded finally, the veterans all present and accounted for. Richard Perlmutter was invited to join, and the reporter from Paris, Claire. The Mercedes engine whirred, the heater hummed full blast, fogging up the windows. The bus pulled out from Saint-Vith.

Down the neatly aligned streets, past the modern buildings, red-brick and drab, it passed, until finally it broke free of the town. The bus sailed through a countryside that, in the eyes of the men at least, had scarcely changed. The same undulating hills, the forest still choking the road as though hell-bent on reclaiming it.

Rubbing the window with his sleeve, Spagnola looked out and tried to imagine the Germans advancing, churning up the macadam with their Tiger tanks, the biggest in their arsenal. So they had come that first day of the battle, with their grinding treads, their cannon and machine guns blazing.

He remembered meeting a man in the stalag, couldn't remember his name, only the story he told. He'd been driving a jeep, minding his own business, when suddenly there was this big gray tank in the way. The man leaned on his horn, honked like a madman, hollering, "hey, asshole, out of the way! Out of the way!" until the tank's turret started swiveling slowly, slowly, cannon leveled. And slowly the man's eyes widened and his hands rose up, for sure enough there on the turret was painted a big black Bavarian cross. Spagnola remembered envying that story—*If you got to fall prisoner, fall funny*, he thought—and wishing it had been his own.

Elsewhere in the bus, other windows were being rubbed.

"Everything looks familiar, and nothing," Billings caviled, but nobody responded to him; they were all too busy looking.

"Incredible," Alma said, "like we'd left it yesterday."

She had planted herself next to the Major, a ballsy move considering that he was seated far in the back of the bus, with plenty of empty places up front. But there was no time for shyness, not at this stage in life. Now she was leaning against him as the two of them peered out of his window. She could feel his body beneath his coat, still taut, still vital.

The Major gazed through the glass. "I can see those sons-of-bitches coming through those trees over there, in their snow suits, coming steady and firing. I tried to stop 'em at first, me and a coupla the boys. Took us a .50 cal and a bazooka and laid up the sweetest lil' ol' ambush. You shoulda seen it, Helen."

"Alma."

"Everybody else is running. I grabbed one of them, a full colonel.

'Hold on there, colonel,' I told 'im. 'Ain't nothin' out there but Krauts.' And he just looks at me with eyes like Roman candles and starts hollerin' 'Run for it, Major, we'll all be killed!'"

The Major came up for air. "You don't mind me running on like this?"

"Not at all," said Alma. She smiled, and even pinched his arm. "It's what I'm here for. Run."

"Well, run is what we *didn't* do. We just waited till the Jerry column came, couple of Tiger tanks and those sons-of-bitches in the woods, let 'em get real close, two hundred yards maybe, and then—*pow*. I gave everybody a turn on that .50 cal, loved shootin' that gun, and then me and Rhys took out the lead tank with the bazooka. Wasn't more'n twenty feet away, practically on top of us. Good man, Rhys, loaded that bazooka twice before he got the wires right—his hands were that cold, shakin'—and all that time that tank's just getting closer and closer. 'Take your time, Bobby,' I tell him. 'Take your time.' Kid got killed later, though, bullet straight here, in the neck. Up on the ridge."

"I had to take 'em there," the Major said to the window. "Couldn't have escaped by that time even if we wanted to. A fine defensive position, that ridge, clear fields of fire, dirt you could dig in, even in winter. Mighta held out a day or two longer, maybe, if relief had come. But, you know, with Hill gone and Pappy, my best machine gunner missing, Sweet with the B.A.R.... Shit, but didn't we put up a helluva fight anyhow? You should have been there."

"I *was* there," Alma reminded him.

The Major looked confused for a moment, closing an eye at Alma. But then his grin returned. "Sure you were, honey," he comforted her, and cupped her hand in his.

Richard ignored the scenery. He was busy contemplating his own reflection in the glass plate separating his seat from the driver's—that and peeking sidelong at Claire, the journalist, seated next to him, trying to decide whether she was pretty or not, fretting over whether she'd ask him questions like: *what do you do for a living?*

But she didn't ask, she said, "Too bad about your father," while regarding his dreamy reflection. She had already written his name in her notebook—Perlmutter—and next to it, *l'innocent*.

"What?"

"Your father. I was sorry to hear that he died. Was it sudden?"

"Hardly. ALS."

Solemnly she nodded. "Lou Gehrig's disease. Horrible."

She was pretty all right, Richard acknowledged. Pretty but strange-looking with her bas relief cheekbones, a prominent brow. A millimeter wider and her mouth would have been comic, not sensuous, he thought. Her lips almost looked swollen.

"You're a writer…"

"A *struggling* writer," she corrected him. "I believe the precise word is freelancer."

"And your English is very good."

"It should be. I studied in the States, at Berkeley, and I lived in New York for a while. Actually, my grandfather was American, you know. A soldier."

She couldn't be more than twenty-five, Richard guessed, yet in the fleshiness beneath her jaw he could already envisage the future double chin, to betray an inner softness.

Claire continued, "He was killed in this battle everyone here talks about, when my grandmother was still pregnant. My father never knew him."

"You're a *local* writer then."

"If you call Paris local. That is where I live, though I try to visit my grandmother as often as I can. Her house is not far from here, in a village called Houffalize. Funny name, Houffalize, no?"

Richard smiled at her—the name was quirky indeed— but his smile went unreciprocated. Inwardly soft, perhaps, but outside this Claire was hard-baked, he realized. Layers upon layers protected her.

"That is how I heard about the reunion," Claire told him. "From my grandmother. She is quite old now and not well, but she still reads the papers. And since I had grown up hearing her stories about those brave and handsome GIs—*and* since I needed a byline, bad, I thought: why not suggest it to my editor?"

"And he went for it."

"Liked it, you mean? Oh yes, he liked it very much," she exclaimed, nearly—but not quite—excitedly. At that instant, her eyes and lips seemed to narrow, and her tone precipitously dropped. "And you, Richard, why did you come here? Was it because of your father? Did you have a sense of duty, of"—she pronounced it in French—"camaraderie?"

"Camaraderie may be taking it a bit far. Curiosity. I always wanted to meet these guys. Maybe through them get to know my father a little better. He was a distant kind of man."

To his consternation he saw that she was writing down his every word. Accustomed to quoting other sources, it didn't please him being cited himself.

"Distant, yes," Claire recorded. "Yet these men seemed very close to him. What was it they called him—Lanny? Able? *Label.* Was that his real name?"

"Nickname," Richard informed her. "Though I never knew why. His real name was Leonard."

"He was some kind of teacher, yes? A historian…"

"A historian, yes. Leonard Perlmutter, professor emeritus, author of twenty books. You mean you've never heard of him?"

He was baiting her and the frown she gave him seemed to take it. But her next comment caught him off-guard: "You sound envious of him."

"Envious?" Richard repeated, nonplussed. No one had ever asked him that question; he never asked himself. "I guess I was," he admitted. "I envied his success—his life. He not only wrote history, you see, he'd lived it."

"And you, Richard, you are a historian as well, am I right?"

He took his time answering her, studying his reflection in the glass. For a moment he considered telling her about his theories, about the research he'd done on the battle and the book he planned to write. But in the end he decided against it. "Me?" Richard replied finally, with a shrug and a trace of a sigh. "I am my father's son."

An hour's drive outside the town, the bus came to a halt beside an open field. Pine-bound, bleached and matted by frost, the field was like a dozen others they had passed with the exception of the markers bordering it. Memorials with the insignias of various regiments, allied governments, royal families, the Veterans of Foreign Wars. An iron plaque informed visitors that the field belonged to the nearby village of Malmedy and that here, on December 17, 1944, some 86 American GIs, POWs, were shot by the Waffen SS.

The doors hissed open, frigid air rushed in, and yet the veterans rose to meet it. Wordlessly, without complaint this time, they filed through the aisle and down the stairs to stand, shivering, alongside that field.

"I remember it so well," somebody said finally. Hollister. The wind beat steadily—a thumping, rug-dusting sound—whisking off his words. "They marched us past here the day we were captured. I remember seeing the bodies half-buried in the snow. I tried not to look. I tried not to count them all."

"There was a tank right here," Roger Gimpel contributed. Willa, conspicuously miserable, clung to his arm, but for once he seemed unaware of her. "A King Tiger. There, where Alma's standing."

He pointed at her, perched over one of the memorials several yards distant from the group. Chin in her fur-lined collar, wind worrying her hair.

Saddened, Alma also felt guilty. She heard about this place during the battle, rumors she at first refused to believe. The Germans were soldiers, too, she told herself, with honor. They wouldn't shoot prisoners in cold blood. She'd dismissed the rumors and now felt guilty about it, confronting the barren field.

"Yeah, it was a Tiger all right. I saw it, plain as day." This was Jimmy Rob. Small, wiry, a wick of a man, Rob had aged well, retaining his hair, his slimness, but also a penchant for sharp, sudden head movements, as if snipers were still lurking about. "And Jerries all around it, just standing there smoking our Lucky Strikes."

"Laughing."

"Laughing and taking pot shots at them bodies."

"Coulda been us, men," the Major said. In his cowboy hat, his sheepskin coat and gloves, he had the look of a senior Marlboro Man, but his manner was conspicuously dour. "Damned straight, it coulda been us."

There were no more remarks, no more recollections. Some moments passed and then, without prompting, Tommy Vorhees stepped forward and recited the Lord's Prayer. Tall and chalky in his shale-gray coat, he fit well with the rest of the memorials—unseeing but meant to be seen.

"Amen," the visitors murmured.

They stood for a second longer, gazing at the field and the heavy gray clouds maneuvering in the sky above it. Then, after stooping to gather mementos—a pebble, slivers of brittle grass—they stood while Claire snapped their picture, and bundled back to the bus.

Ten minutes later, Malmedy was well behind them, but the gloom in the bus persisted. Faces long and pale even on pleasant occasions appeared to hang lower, waner.

Kaye groaned to herself: *this is what I have to look forward to, six whole days of it.* She squeezed Buddy's arm, nevertheless. He appeared genuinely distraught, grimacing in a way that could not be mistaken for a smile. "You've taken your medication, yeah?"

"Yeah," said Buddy Hill.

"That was hard for you, wasn't it?"

"Yeah."

"Those poor boys..."

"Yeah, poor..."

Great heart, caring soul—that's what her husband was, able to mourn for men he had never known and well over fifty years later. And yet unable to feel for her, the woman he'd lived with nearly as long. She stroked his arm and wondered again just what she was supposed to feel—anger, sadness, gratitude for the pain he was sparing her? Sighing, she joined Buddy in staring through the window, at the trees, stiff in funereal review.

"Could I maybe have your attention for a moment?"

A dozen faces shot up, eyes widened. The silence on the bus had become almost sacrosanct, and someone had dared to break it. And not just someone but, the veterans saw, that son of Label Perlmutter. He stood at the head of the aisle, leaning against the glass partition to steady himself, facing them. A nice enough young man but also somewhat strange in his dungaree clothes and ponytail, the motorcycle jacket with all those belts and zippers. Trying to look *too* young.

"Might I, please? Thank you."

He waited until he was sure they were all looking at him, reminded himself to speak loudly and slowly, enunciating. He was conscious of Claire scrutinizing him.

"I know this is kind of irregular," Richard began, "but I thought seeing that my father is no longer with us, and seeing that I'm something of a historian too, well, I thought that I might…that *you* might let me share with you some of my insights into the battle."

He paused to let his meaning sink in. Sure enough, there was "You tell us, boy, just like your ol' man!" The Major started applauding, hooting from the back of the bus. "Tell us 'bout the battle!"

It was difficult to know whether the old rancher was being serious or merely teasing him. Richard couldn't dwell on it, though. When would he get another opportunity like this, all the men together and focused exclusively on him, a golden chance to try out his theory?

"Any event in history can been interpreted in an infinite number of ways, seen from an endless selection of angles. Depending on the prejudices of the person regarding it, on his or her *perceptions*."

The faces gawked at him, vacant. They hadn't understood a word he said, Richard realized. He would have to start slower, throw out an example or two.

"Take the Malmedy massacre. A horrific incident by any account, and yet…and yet, try to see it from *another point of view*."

"What kind of point you had in mind?" Hollister wondered. "The corpses'?"

His remark spawned some giggles in the bus, less like real laughter than nervous twitter.

"No, not the corpses," Richard chuckled along, then suddenly went deadpan. "The Germans."

"Careful, boy," the Major grunted.

Buddy whispered to Kaye, "He's got to be kidding."

Their reaction did not surprise Richard; he was prepared for it. He held his hands up, as if to halt a stampede.

"Just think about it for a second. Put yourself in their place. It's you, the Wehrmacht, who's surrounded, confronting an enemy who outnumbers you ten to one, who has a hundred times as many planes, tanks, artillery pieces. Who's about to invade your homeland. Put all the other considerations aside—Nazism, the Holocaust—I'm not saying they're unimportant, but try to see the situation as the simple soldier did. As *you* might have in *their* boots."

"Okay, I'm in their boots," Pringle snarled. "So what?"

"So you got yourselves a lot of prisoners. More prisoners than you can handle. You're low on ammunition, got armies closing in on you from either side. You're tired, cold, hungry. You *know* the feeling."

He paused to let this sink in. So far not bad: no riotous protests, no one ordering him to shut the fuck up. A head or two was even nodding, he swore. They were ready for that next, more radical, step.

"Now say some of those prisoners make a move—prisoners who just a few hours ago killed your best pal. Say one of them goes for a concealed weapon, a .45."

A groan bowled down the aisle.

"Witnesses, both German and GI, later testified that one officer did make such a move."

"Like hell they did!" Phil Conforti hollered. "I read the interviews—it was all in *Stars and Stripes*. There was nothing about any gun!" He was already halfway out of his seat, with Mary struggling to restrain him. "Where'd you get that crap?"

"From the archives," Richard replied. "In files the government wouldn't have wanted you to see during the war, with all due respect to *Stars and Stripes*."

"They shot those boys again and again—I saw 'em!" McCloski, rising, roared. Too tall for the minibus, he hunched his shoulders and strained his neck, coughed violently before roaring again, "Shot 'em when they were dead already, buried in the snow!"

"No snow," said Richard.

"What do mean 'no snow'?"

Richard removed his glasses and wiped them slowly on his sleeve. "No *deep* snow, anyway." He hooped the stems around his ears. "A light powdering, perhaps, on the first day of the battle, but not enough to bury anyone."

Pringle growled: "How do you *know* that?"

"Daily reports, U.S. Army Department of Meteorology. The snow you 'remember'"—he wiggled two fingers on each hand—"was from photos taken after the battle, when the bodies were tagged. Snow didn't fall here heavily until December 25th, Christmas Day, when you were already well into Germany."

"And the Tiger tank?" Roger leapt in, his face a four-alarm red. "I suppose I didn't see that there either, did I?"

"No *Tiga*," Richard said, smiling, trying to make light of Roger's accent. "According to military intelligence, there were no Tigers in this sector at all. The tank you saw was probably a Panther Ausf A, a much smaller vehicle."

They were all on their feet now, up in arms, even Billings, tottering on his walker. Kuhlmann, looking more amused than anxious, nevertheless asked them to please take their seats, but the veterans ignored him. They were too busy ranting at Richard.

"There were Tigers, you bet there were Tigers!"

"Tigers and heaps of snow!"

Through the commotion, between the heads bobbing like whitecaps around him, Buddy caught sight of the Major. He stood ramrod straight and purplish, impervious as Alma tried to calm him. His eyes caught Buddy's and practically etched in the word: *unbecoming*.

But what was Buddy to do? Positioned closest to Richard, clearly he was supposed to step in and end the discussion, period, get the men quieted again. But he could barely find the energy to get to his feet, much less intervene forcibly. Exhaustion like a shroud enveloped him.

"There you go, white as a sheet again," Kaye warned. She hooked a finger into his pants pocket, in case he, too, tried to rise. He didn't. Buddy merely sighed, "Dependable, my ass," but his words were lost in the shouting.

They all were shouting—Rob denouncing anyone who said they knew more about the battle than the men who fought it, meaning—Pringle added—the Perlmutters, father *and* son.

"There are many truths in the world, Richard," the Vicar declared, "but some are truer than others."

They shouted and then yelped as the bus took a hairpin curve—Kuhlmann hardly slowed for it—and bodies careened in the aisle. Then, as they righted themselves, a single hand rose and waved excitedly.

"S'cuse me! Pardon me, teach!"

He'd been sitting quietly thinking about Malmedy, about the men who hadn't had a chance in hell, thinking about Private Eisenhower. Spagnola was thinking about what a flimsy thing the truth really is—what is known and is not known and by whom—so arbitrary. Then Richard started his talk.

"Over here!" Spagnola bellowed, "I have a question!"

Finally, thought Richard, *somebody with a rational response*. "Yes? What is it?"

Clinging to the coat racks, a paunchy cruciform, Spagnola slid forward. "My question is...how do *you* know *you* know what you saw?"

Richard winced at him, hunched his shoulders in an effort to understand. "Come again?"

"I said, 'how do *you* know what *you* know is the truth?' I mean, you read them weather reports, right? No snow until the 25th. Or so you remember. But somebody else might remember it different—'heavy snow on the 17th,' it coulda said. Or maybe the guy that wrote that report got it wrong. Maybe he meant to write 'flurries on the 25th and on the 17th a goddamn blizzard,' only he never got the chance. Maybe just then, he had to run out to use the latrine. Ever eat a can of GI beans? It can do that to you, you know. Now *that's* the truth."

Winded, Spagnola paused for breath. He was going to continue, address that tricky question of tanks, but then the cheering started. It began in the back of the bus, with Alma and then, after Alma elbowed him, the Major, and from there it rolled up the aisle, through Hollister and Croker and Stan Morgan. Buddy, enlivened suddenly, started yodeling, "Spa-a-a-a-a-gnola!"

Spagnola turned, reversing his hands on the coat racks, and bowed as gracefully as he could. And by bowing, he revealed Richard retreating to his seat.

"What was *that* about?" Claire asked him.

"Nothing," Richard grunted. He felt humiliated, frustrated. Criticism he could take, even obloquy, but not being made fun of in public. And not by a bunch of amateurs, and aged amateurs at that. For a second he could almost understand how his father might have felt, each time they called him Label.

TWO

The edge of the forest had receded over the years, away from the burgeoning town, like a sea pushed back by silt. Sea-like, its shoreline was shallow at first with clumps of trees and a public park to be waded through before plunging into evergreen depths.

Pieter strode unerringly, by instinct almost. He held the map drawn for him by Miles at the hotel, but he barely consulted it. He didn't need to. It was as though Saint-Vith hadn't changed at all, was a hamlet still and he was young and sturdy, a soldier and a farm boy with a future.

But why then, Pieter asked himself, did he lose his way the first night of the battle? Of course, there'd been the shelling, his tumble down the hotel stairs, Tully's death. Yet he'd been in barrages before and saw men die, lots of men. His back was always a problem. No, something set him off course that night. Something diverted him.

Pieter lumbered through the park, past a playground. The children stopped to gawp at him, an old, gaunt Goliath in a parka and cap, lugging a leather valise. Their laughter followed him as he wound around the public lavatories, behind a wooden bench, to where the path began.

Twenty paces within, the forest enveloped him, the trees lined trunk to trunk, their branches intertwined. The village sounds—swishing traffic, the children's laughs—were replaced by the forest's own noises: animals twittering, the spontaneous crackle of twigs.

He walked intently, eyes ahead, workboots crunching the dried needle bed of the path. Just being back in the forest, even in daylight, set his heart racing, his mind again wondering what might have happened if he hadn't gotten lost that night. His entire life would have changed. He would have married Meg, as planned, built a house, raised a family. The children in the park who'd laughed at him would be about the age of his and Meg's own grandkids by now, and he'd take them to the park to play. So many ifs, Pieter reproached himself, so much flame and air. He dispelled them and picked up his pace, thinking of nothing but stone.

It was there, waiting for him, right where Label wrote. The stone. A hundred yards or so down the path, in the clearing where the meadow used to be, close by the base of the ridge. A boulder larger than Pieter pictured it, almost as tall as he and several times wider, covered by a canvas tarp. Its shape evoked the image of an old man brooding, The rock would be gloomy, he imagined—basalt or obsidian, the usual funerary fare, but when he pulled the tarp away, Pieter gasped.

The stone was beautiful. A Belgian granite, dove-gray and richly crystaled. Quartz that caught the meager light then released it, iridescent. He pulled off his gloves and let his callused fingertips roam over the folds and the creases, the spurs and ripples, sensing densities and depths.

The quarryman had already done half the work. Three days, four maximum, was all Pieter needed to finish the job, if the weather and his back held up.

Pieter knelt carefully, reverently, and fumbled inside his valise. He found what he wanted—the number 4 mallet and his air-hardened chisel—and selected a place on the rock.

Alone in the forest, in his woolen cap and wind-whipped parka, the man known as Sweet started cutting.

☆ ☆ ☆

"Aw, I don't know. Ask me something else—about my career at the bank. Anything."

Buddy's face had darkened, a shade above his usual ruddiness, when Claire posed the question. He was squirming, fidgeting with his silverware, and Kaye clearly enjoyed it.

"Go on, Edwin. Tell her. The scariest thing that ever happened to you in the war. Tell her it was coming home and meeting me."

Kaye and Claire shared a laugh, an alliance, while Buddy tittered nervously. He was prepared to talk about many things—banking, football—but not about the war. Not with a total stranger at least, recording every word.

They sat at a roadside café, nibbling sandwiches, sipping cappuccinos. What talk there was seemed subdued now, the victim of a ruthless day of touring, of the biting cold and of sites that drained them emotionally. After Malmedy, there was the sloping hillside outside of Schönberg—quite scenic, actually—but it was there that thousands of men from the 106th Division found themselves cut off and surrounded and surrendered en masse to the Germans. Later still the group came to the crossroads near Baugnez, the scene of yet another massacre, this one of Battery B of the 285th Battalion. The precious villages of Stavelot, Trois Ponts, Amblève—all housed memorials to the Americans' resistance, their gallant, hopeless resistance.

Too much loss, so many lives unlived—the veterans sat benumbed by it, while Claire saw her chance. With their defenses down, anguish exposed, the men were easy marks for interviews. Carefully she chose her prey, a quiet yet authoritative man, an outwardly smiling type who, she sensed, was hauling some secret burden.

"You really want to know? The *scariest?*"

Claire nodded avidly, and Buddy could see that she was serious, that she wouldn't make light of his answer. "It had nothing to do with the battle," he said. His words were sullen, suddenly, almost whispered. "Not that the battle wasn't scary. It's just that I wasn't around at the end of it, you might have heard. Left the ridge on the third day to help one of my noncoms—that's a sergeant—Papino his name was. He had frostbite. Well, after that, I couldn't, you know, get back. Lots of Germans around. The shelling was heavy…very heavy."

Buddy sipped, once, twice. He seemed to have trouble continuing.

"Edwin…" Kaye interjected after a moment, as though regretting that she'd egged him on, but Buddy, after a nod, resumed: "No, the scariest thing happened three months later, at the crossing of the Rhine. I'd been assigned to another outfit—Label had seen to that—and there we were about to cross the river in these big, flat-bottomed, wooden boats, me and twelve other guys I'd never even met before. Replacements, all of them. Kids."

"But 'don't worry,' the officers told me. 'You're going to get smoke cover out there, we promise. We're going to blast the other shore to kingdom come.' And, hell, I believed 'em, though I should of known better by that point, two years in the Army. Turns out, it was *them* who shelled *our* shore, the Germans, and we had to drag those boats under fire. Weighed a ton. We got out and wouldn't you know it—no smoke. Not a whiff. What we got instead was flares, enemy flares."

Buddy had turned to Claire finally, dared to make contact with those eyes. "Ever see a flare go off?" he asked her.

Claire shook her head.

"Actually, you don't see it at first. You hear it. 'Pock!'"—ten fingers flicked out from his fists—"An experienced soldier will know what that sound means and that second he'll be hitting the dirt. Only there was no dirt to hit out there, only wood and the water, and nobody else understood it but me. I tried to get those kids to get low but they didn't listen. They were sitting straight when the sky lit up, and then the machine guns started firing."

"We were sitting ducks. I know it's a cliché and all, but there's no other word for it. Bullets smacking the water all around, hitting some of my men, too, though I didn't know it. Then, right next to us, another boat gets it. One second it's there and then—splinters. Nothing. I was sure we were next. Ever have that feeling? That any moment you just weren't going to *be* anymore?"

"All the time," Claire laughed, but neither of the Hills laughed with her. Quickly, she took up her camera. "Just act natural," she advised, as if either of them could act otherwise.

"But I went on being, I guess," Buddy said as he posed. "I made it to the other shore and got those kids out of there. Most of 'em were killed later anyway, I heard, up in the hills. Me, I hung around the boat a while.

Some private had been shot through and through. I waited 'til he died."

"A terrible experience. Awful." Claire kept scribbling while she spoke. "No wonder it was your scariest."

"But it wasn't. I haven't even *got* to the scary part."

"Shame on you!" Buddy's wife scolded him; she even slapped his wrist. "The girl's trying to write a serious story and you're teasing her."

"Not at all. This *is* the scary part."

"No sooner did I leave the boat when a machine gun bullet came and creased my helmet—one inch lower and I wouldn't be sitting here, no sir. Last thing I remember was some Jerry in the hills begging for mercy—*Nein! Nein!* like that—and then screaming when some Thompson gun cut him down. After that, I was out cold, who knows, an hour or more."

"But when I come to, the first thing I see is this house. One of those old German houses, you know, gingerbread-like. I picked myself out of the mud and started heading for it. I had to be crazy, of course—a *German* house—but I was so damned tired, more tired than I'd ever been in my life up 'til then, that I just had to find a place to lay my head a little."

"I go up and find the door's open, yet nobody seems to be home. Inside, flare-light shines through the windows and what I can see is amazing: rugs and chairs and sofas—good stuff, fine stuff. This tidy little kitchen and a dining room with china plates all stacked behind glass. Outside the world's on fire and in there, in this house, everything's perfect. Peace."

"I climb up the stairs. There's a hall at the top and at the end of the hall, a bedroom. A bedroom with a bed like nothing I've ever seen before—I grew up poor, you know. A gigantic goosefeather bed with satin pillows and a bedspread of pure silk. A big white canopy like you see in the movies. I see that bed and all I want to do is to lie down on it. Someone comes in and shoots me, I don't care. All I want is rest."

"I don't like where this is headed," Kaye fretted. "How come you never told me this before?"

"Hold on, Kitty. Let me finish." Now it was his turn to slap her hand, playfully.

"So I lie down. Dirty boots, bloody uniform, everything. I stretch out on my back with my head on those pillows and my arms at my sides, and it's like I'm floating. Like sailing. Suddenly, I don't care about anything—about the war, about getting through it, nothing. I feel my rifle slipping to the floor and I don't even reach over to stop it. I'm just sinking—or rising, I don't know. So this is what death is like, I think, and all this time I've been fighting it."

"I slept. Minutes maybe, hours. No dreams, not even that awareness that you're sleeping. But then I feel something tugging—all of sudden. Somebody is tugging on my sleeve. 'No,' I think, 'no, leave me alone. I don't want to go.' I never wanted to get up again. I wanted to go on sleeping forever."

"But the tugging gets harder and harder. Like pulling me up from this deep warm well. I open my eyes —it's dawn outside and I see this. . .*figure*. I think: this is it, now I *am* going to die. But the figure doesn't move, just stands there, and then slowly I begin to understand. This is a child. Boy or girl, I can't tell. 'Hi,' I started to say, but with that the kid just turns around and runs out of the room. Just like that."

Buddy stopped, out of breath, sweating. Kaye was gaping at him. For as long as she'd known him, even when he had a few, she never heard him talk so much, and surely never about the war. Never about his feelings. Must be the medication.

Claire would have gaped as well but she was just too busy writing. A fabulous story; her editor was going to love it. "So that was it," she said, "the scariest thing, being wakened by that child."

Buddy shook his head. "No. The scariest thing was getting up, getting off that bed and lifting my rifle off the floor. The scariest thing was going back to my life, Miss, to the war, and knowing it was a long way from over."

Some time after her talk with Buddy, Claire began another, this one with Tommy Vorhees. The ideal pair, he and Genie: five kids, fourteen grandchildren, all of them members of his church. A man who'd always known his calling, even before the war, which was why they'd nicknamed him Vicar. No crises in his life, at least none he cared to speak of, except for that matter of sightlessness, and even that he turned into grace.

"The Lord sought fit to test me," Vorhees told her. "A test of faith."

And his wife confirmed it: "Passed it, too. Flying colors."

The Vorhees: so loving and inspiring and *boring*, entirely too cloying for her readers. She needed something meatier, more visceral—another Buddy Hill.

Claire retreated to the café entrance where she flipped to a fresh page in her notebook, found a pencil not yet chewed. She adjusted her camera for light.

"Aliens."

She practically jumped. Against the wall next to her—had he been there all along?—leaned Richard Perlmutter.

"I didn't see you…"

"Those huge ears of theirs," he said, raising his chin at the veterans. "Kind of makes them look like aliens, don't you think? Extraterrestrials."

Crouched over their tables, blanched by afternoon light, the men *could* seem otherworldly, Claire agreed.

"People's ears get bigger as they age," she explained. "My grandmother told me."

"Bigger and deafer, it seems. The longer they live, the less they're willing to listen to anything that doesn't…"

"To listen for God," the journalist interrupted.

"Huh?"

"What my grandmother told me. Why old people's ears grow—to listen for God."

"And you believe this?"

"I believe," Clair said coldly, "that you should try listening to them for once. The way *they* saw things. The way *they* remember. Try listening to Buddy Hill."

Richard shot back: "You mean just write down everything they say, uncritically, like you do, hoping for some sentimental scoop?" He was trying to sound tough and hold his ground, but he couldn't help noticing how tall she was, statuesque, and the roundness of her lapels.

Claire's mouth hung open—a voluptuous mouth, Richard noticed that, too—before clamping into a scowl. He could have killed himself for being so impetuous, so certifiably and downright dumb. He would have told her that, too, if just then Claire hadn't turned and huffed away. If just then Kuhlmann hadn't marched into the café and announced that the coffee break was over.

"You heard 'im, gentlemen, ladies," the Major barked, "move out!" And no one gave him guff.

☆ ☆ ☆

Dusk and the bus returned to Saint-Vith. Inside it was silent again, though not because of sadness. Everyone was fast asleep. The Hills, Kaye's purrs and Buddy's cantankerous snores, harmonized more or less, with their heads teepeed together. Spagnola curled up in his bowling jacket with his arms stiffly folded, a position he'd often slept in ever since the war. Billings, Morgan, the Confortis and the Gimpels—all slumbering, adding to the sibilant hum that nearly droned out the engine's.

Only Alma was wide awake, more alert than she'd felt in days. Tucked in the crook of her elbow was a man's arm; his hand lay on her lap and his head on her shoulder. The Major slept and Alma daydreamed, tried to reconstruct the hodgepodge of events that would lead her life from her hometown of Joshua Tree, California, through a dozen southern Army posts, to Europe, Korea, and Vietnam, then back to California again. And what next? Texas? She saw herself on a sprawling ranch, like Jean Arthur in *Shane*, in an apron and gingham dress, sounding the bell at mealtimes. A girlish fantasy, she knew—at her age, it'd be more like Mammy Yokum—but then why not indulge it? After all she'd been through and seen, didn't she deserve her whimsy?

Alma looked down at the balding head propped under her jaw. She strained to examine the skin with its embroidery of broken veins (he'd done some imbibing, this one) and obligatory liver spots, the great beaked nose and eyelids as thin and crinkled as wafers. She wondered what secrets that head contained, what tales of pain and desolation that was the lode of anyone who'd lived as long as they had—a cynical view, admittedly, but she'd had all her experience to prove it. Lying in bed talking with an older man was like debriefing a soldier after a battle. Once the bluster was through, that toughness and bravado, then the crying came, the howling. She wondered how long it would take him to reach that point, how long it'd take her, digging, to touch it.

Finally, after putting off the notion for as many minutes as she dared, she pondered the million-dollar question: could he still or couldn't he? As a man of, say, seventy-eight, he looked healthy enough; no conspicuous disabilities. No pallor in the lips that might bespeak a kidney problem and no impairments of speech or motor coordination. He didn't even wear glasses. Yet, experience again told her, you can't tell an engine by its hood. Crucial parts, from prostate up to medulla oblongata, had to be in reasonable working order to get to that place where age wouldn't matter anymore, where Alma still needed to go.

No problem, she concluded, *either way*. He could be DOA and still she'd bring him round again—she'd done it innumerable times. With CPR or, if need be, a hammer blow punch to his chest. She wasn't a nurse for nothing, thought Alma Wheatty, adept at resuscitation.

The bus reached the outskirts of the town and burrowed through its darkening streets. In preparation for arriving at the hotel, Kuhlmann flicked on the aisle lights and brusquely aroused his passengers. There were moans and curses, a chorus of hacking and one sharp, anonymous fart.

"I swear that guy was in the Wehrmacht," Croker grumbled.

Hollister yawned, "too young."

"Maybe. Or maybe it's the winters here," Croker said, rising, "Preserved him."

The others rose as well, slowly, plaintively, but the Major remained inert. Alma tried shrugging the shoulder he slept on, jiggling her elbow and pinching his hand. Nothing. Then, by shifting down in her seat, she lowered her mouth to his ear. "Darlin'," she whispered, unable to call him the Major, but realizing that she didn't know his real name. She cooed,

"Time to wake up, sugar," and briefly, tenderly enough to leave him wondering just what had woken him, kissed his leathery cheek.

☆ ☆ ☆

I'm too old for this, he inwardly whined as he swatted the branches away. The ground was cold and the air even colder, like he was breathing shards of glass. Though he'd always enjoyed remarkable health, uncanny vigor in spite of his indulgences, he was never the outdoorsy type. Give him a city any day, he thought, unsnagging his scarf from a pinecone. Give him sidewalks and nouvelle cuisine, elevators and central heating. A man of civilization, he was, of basic human amenities.

He hated the forest and yet he plied on, stumbling. "There is a path there, very straight, marked—you can't miss it," that sweet boy, Miles, had assured him. Yet he *had* missed it, somehow, and now he staggered as saplings lashed out at him and needles jabbed at his face.

Quite a sight he made. In his long, black dress coat, his pearly cashmere scarf, he imagined he looked like some Harvard Club dandy detrained at the very wrong stop. If only they could see him at Harper's Academy now, see what lengths they'd driven him to and for what—a slight indiscretion, a momentary indulgence of weakness?

At least none of the veterans had seen him, not yet. Surely they'd discovered his presence already, had noted his name on the register—they weren't *that* stupid. Yet they hadn't come looking for him, either, preferring to wait until he made his appearance at the reunion, at which point they'd deal with it, somehow. Still, he was taking no chances, breakfasting in his room and tarrying there until well after the bus had departed. Only then did he steal out of the kitchen entrance, into an alleyway that led out behind the town square, to a park where he could slip undetected into the forest.

He had just sidestepped some brambles, ducked under a bough, when his shoe—his wingtipped, city shoe—caught on a root and twisted. He fell in a long, slow-motion roll, tumbled and landed with a thud. Five minutes later, he was still sitting cross-legged on the leaf bed, cradling and massaging his ankle. Trying to remember how this forest—this hell—had once held the promise of bliss.

Of big bucks, a bundle to be made playing on that quirkiest of human organs: the heart. Banking on people's need to bury their precious departed, to plant them in the ground and secure them with a tombstone; to put *themselves* to rest. People needed their gravesites, especially for soldiers, their deaths so distant and cruel. Did it matter, ultimately, *which* soldier they actually interred?

He had exploited these quirks, he and Joachim and his friends, and he'd nearly cashed in on them, too. But the venture had failed, like so many others in his life, and now he sat, a weak, penniless, mirthless old man, alone and blundering in the forest.

With the aid of a mercifully placed tree stump, he managed to jack himself up. He brushed off his sleeves, pulled on his scarf and his gloves. His shoes had been scuffed, he regretted, and his ankle was starting to throb. But the cold was worsening—crystallizing—and there really was no other choice. Either freeze where he was or somehow falter on.

He suspected that he was slogging in circles. Behind him, he could still hear the sounds of Saint-Vith—engines puttering, children laughing in some playground. Then, from somewhere ahead, came another noise, different. A sharp, insistent rataplan, like somebody banging on stone. He lumbered toward it, wondering if the noise was actually in his head, a preliminary sign of frostbite. Only when he reached the edge of a clearing did he see the hunk of granite and the tall man smacking it with a hammer.

A tall, odd-looking man in a woolen cap and brown, bulky parka. It took him a while, peering from behind the trees, to realize that this was Pieter Martinson, the hayseed lug they used to call Sweet. There had been some mention of him in the invitation, something about carving a memorial. Sweet had paid no attention to it at the time, too stunned by the fact of the invitation itself. All those years without so much as a postcard from the veterans, and suddenly this. Suddenly a reunion in Belgium.

What was he to make of it, he wondered. That the men had finally forgiven his conduct during the battle and, later, his hasty departure with Joachim? That nobody remembered Dean? Unlikely, he reasoned. Chances were they hated him still, might even kill him if the chance arose, provided they still had the strength.

No, the invitation was a blunder, an error by that egghead Perlmutter's son—what was his name? Richard. The son who had been so gracious, almost filial, on the phone, confirming his rsvp.

The men hated him, but it didn't matter: he had his alibi. He could return to Saint-Vith without arousing suspicion, could stay at the Hotel Ardennes and yet manage to avoid the veterans. Slipping unnoticed out of town, past the police or any old villager who might remember him, he could sneak into the forest as well.

He detoured wide around the clearing, keeping low, grateful for the racket the mason made that camouflaged his own crepitation. He struggled forward until he spied some figures in front of him. Gray figures, dense and triangular, frozen in time and place.

Dragon's teeth. Crisply arrayed, symmetrical—if not for the lichen coating them, they might have been molded yesterday. They knew how to work, those Germans. Something he always respected about them, about Joachim. It was Joachim's idea to exchange the identities, to take them from those who no longer needed them and affix them to people who did. And to pay for it all: diamonds—that, too, was Joachim's brainstorm. Sequestered from niggardly Jews, no doubt, hidden from the advancing Russians, the diamonds were totally untraceable. So ingenious a plan, so neat and foolproof only a fool could have ruined it.

He threaded through the dragon's teeth and tottered some twenty yards beyond, until another clearing appeared and within it, a cottage of sorts, rebuilt from the one that was destroyed in the war. One thing remained unchanged, however, unmistakable. Half-hidden in a hollow, tenebrous and crude: the cold house.

He approached it cautiously, as quietly as his wingtips could crunch. He stepped up to the tree line. There was no one in sight, no yelping farm dogs either. Slowly he entered the yard, sidled down to the hollow. Still, nobody.

It all appeared too easy. The lock on the door looked to be a century old at least. How hard would it be to bust it open with a rock, to slip inside and scratch around a bit? Minutes, maybe, but that was all he would need. Once he found what he wanted, he'd be out of there quick, away from this forest, far from Saint-Vith and the fucking reunion. He'd catch the next plane back to the States—better yet, Bermuda—and to an entire world of weaknesses, indulging them until the day he died.

Such fantasies would have to wait, though. Nothing would happen today. First he would scout out his position—that much he'd learned as an officer—reconnoiter his enemy, never underestimating his strength. For the enemy *was* strong, still, according to Miles, capable of wielding huge weights—sides of beef, whole pigs—and hauling them through the forest. Such a man might not take kindly to some nattily dressed foreigner snooping about his yard. Such a man, however half-witted, might have a decent memory.

He hurried away from the hollow, back the way he came—between the dragon's teeth, around the clearing, this time finding the path. He hitched to the rhythm of Martinson's hammering—steadier now, less adamant—driven by the thought of his hotel room, of the bath he would take to soak his ankle, to soothe his ravaged skin. He thought of the dinner he'd order from room service, the brazed orange mallard, garden vegetables, a Chardonnay. Perhaps Miles could serve it to him in the tub...

He stepped briskly now, no longer breathless anymore or even footsore. The sun had broken through the clouds overhead, slicing through the branches, and for a moment the forest itself looked gilded. It was then, transfixed, that he stopped and remembered Dean.

The boy with the sun in his hair, multiple suns in his eyes. Dean the first time he saw him, on inspection, dogtags resplendent on his chest. Dean in combat, a prodigy on his machine gun, playing it for the enemy's dance. And in the forest, at night in his tent by lamplight, Dean's fingers alighting on his epaulettes, stroking his eagles' wings. Whispering coyly, "fraternizing with the men, now, are we?"

So he remembered him, in those and a hundred other scenes. Cocky, gallant, not quite real—ethereal. He'd be an old man by now, of course, as wasted as any of those veterans, half-dotty and deaf. Or more probably, a scattering of moldy bones. How he longed to embrace them—the bones—to gather them and plant them in the ground. He found himself searching for them, in spite of himself. Checking behind bushes, under copses, his eyes raking the bed. An old man alone, scavenging in the forest. He and his quirky heart.

☆ ☆ ☆

In the lobby, by the front desk with the register in his hand, the Major gave Buddy yet another of his interrogating looks. He'd been darting them all day, dishing them out at every opportunity—on the bus, at Malmedy and in the café—whenever Buddy's gaze chanced in his direction. It was a look that asked, *Where is he already?* Asked, *Are we just going to sit here and wait?*

"What say you and me go up there right now and knock on his door?" the Major finally proposed.

"Maybe he's not in. Maybe he's down with the ladies in Houffalize. Maybe he's brought one back."

Buddy's maybes earned him nothing but frowns. No, Houffalize was out of the question, as were any ladies. "Still, I don't think it's wise to go up. We don't want to make a scene."

"A scene!" the Major shouted. "A *scene?*" his voice booming about the lobby. "What happens if he just shows up here, in the middle of a meal or something. At the ceremony!"

Buddy was desperately tired, drained by the day and by the effort of hauling himself through it. All he wanted was to get up to his room and into his bed, napping with Kaye before dinner. The Major hardly looked better, flushed and glassy-eyed.

"No use getting worked up about this, least not yet," Buddy advised him. "For all we know he's going home tomorrow."

"He has reservations through the week," the boy behind the desk, Miles, cut in. The two guests merely growled at him.

"No matter," Buddy continued. "We'll deal with it if and when he shows up. Just, let's not jump the gun."

"Jump the gun—you're one to talk," the Major snapped at him, and next nearly barked at Miles. "You say he went up an hour ago, that he ain't been down here since?"

"Yes, sir."

"I want to know when he leaves. You just call me, night or day, anytime, you got that, son?" The Major extracted several bills from his wallet and pushed them across the desk.

"Yes, sir!"

"That's it, then." The Major clapped his hands. He slapped Buddy hard on the back. "And you get some rest, Hill," he counseled. "You look like a pile of shit."

The two men separated and faded toward their respective staircases. The Major, bow-legged and bent slightly, and Buddy stiff, his spine a monorail of pain. Miles watched them ascend. He carefully folded the American dollars and inserted them in his vest pocket, next to the similar sum he'd received only an hour before, and for much the same information—the comings and goings of the veterans.

☆ ☆ ☆

One last tap, a delicate one to remove a spur of granite, and Pieter lowered his tools. He stepped back, fists propped in his flanks, and surveyed his first day's progress. Not bad for an old man, he admitted. The face of the memorial, where the legend would be borne, was already delineated, and the stone's inner secrets—scintillating crystals, filigreed swirls—revealed. Soon he'd be ready for sanding, for polishing and inscribing—all according to schedule. Years had passed since he carved outdoors like this, standing, and he was proud of himself, Pieter Martinson. The men would take pride as well.

How swiftly the time had sped. Here it was dusk already and he felt as if he just arrived, was not in the least bit tired. Though his hands were numb and the tip of his nose, Pieter was mindless of the plummeting temperature. The forest, as dark and solitary as his basement, cloistered him. But there had been moments during the day, between mallet blows, when he thought he heard sounds—creaks, rattles, like those made by his staircase back home—and sensed he was no longer alone. Then the forest grew silent again. His suspicions passed and his mind went back to the carving.

He blew on his hands and retrieved his gloves, bent carefully, returning his tools to the valise. Over the stone Pieter dragged the tarp, and anchored its edges with dirt. He noticed again how the marble, once draped, had a melancholy cast, hunched and reflective. It reminded him of the Medici tombs—those wistful Sybils—or a senior version of The Thinker.

Pieter turned to the path, doddering, his torso ballast for the valise. Twigs and leaves cracked sharply beneath his boots, so loudly that he never heard the footsteps following his closely through the forest.

THREE

The trick, he learned, was to force himself awake an hour ahead of time, bundle up and tiptoe down the stairway undetected. Risky business, he realized, what with the erratic way old people slept. Any one of them could be up at that hour, wandering the halls with apnea or a tricky bladder, and liable to discover him descending.

But so far his luck had held out. For the second morning straight he managed to make it through the lobby even before Miles got to work; to slip into the so-called Bayonet Hall and then through the double doors to the kitchen. Past the walk-in refrigerator, the long metal table on which the hotel prepared its "delicacies," and then to the service entrance. A bit of chicanery was required here, folding a small piece of cardboard he'd torn from one of the fruit boxes and inserting it in the latch in such a way that the door wouldn't lock behind him.

Simple, really. Five minutes after leaving the minimal comforts of his room, he was out in the breath-snatching cold, in an alleyway richly appointed with trash. But he was outside just the same, and once he ignored his swollen ankle, the calluses raised by his wingtips, he'd be on his way out of the village and back through the trees, heading once again for the cold house.

☆ ☆ ☆

The Bayonet Hall was set for breakfast, the sugared rolls heaped, eggs and sausage steaming. Steam also rose from the pots of freshly brewed coffee held by Miles and Yvonne, positioned in opposite corners. Even Hermansdorfer stopped by, belly-barreling through the door to see that all was in order. It was, immaculately so, yet still the hotelier frowned. The hall was virtually empty. The veterans had yet to arrive.

Morgan and Hollister alone had managed to get up in time, taking up the end of one table where Hollister dug in and Morgan poured himself a glass of juice and promptly dozed off again. Presently, they were joined by Claire, in jeans and a bulky fisherman's sweater this morning, more eager than elegant and a shade too chipper for waspish old men at that hour. But Hollister didn't seem to mind.

"Two 'l's, that's right," he told her, leaning over her notebook and spraying it slightly as he spoke. He tended to do that—spray—ever since suffering a stroke several years ago, and to apologize whenever he did.

The stroke had brought about his early retirement as a high school phys. ed. teacher, had left him with a crick in his neck and a twist in his mouth, giving an immutable expression of sweetness. It was all okay by him, though, for now he had more time to spend with his grandchildren—eight at last count—and to get in some serious fly-fishing. His wife, Carol, had meanwhile become devoted to a certain TV evangelist, and was often away on the mission circuit, volunteering. A pretty quiet life, maybe boring at times, but Greg Hollister could not complain.

Claire made a show of writing this down without pausing to ask him what phys. ed. meant, or fly-fishing. She looked up at his face—an owl's flat face with a pinched nose, an owl's thorny eyebrows. From there, her eyes fell to his right hand as it reached for a croissant, at the stubs between its index and forefinger.

"You're not really interested in grandchildren..."

Claire endeavored a smile. She liked this Hollister already and would have liked him even more if he told her a marketable story.

"Funny about that," Hollister said, indicating the hand still perched on the roll.

"Funny?"

"Funny 'cause I never got a scratch before it. Funny 'cause in war you can hold your head this way"—he tilted to one side—"or that, and it's the difference between a close call and kingdom come."

"Kingdom come..."

"Death, dear. But I held my head all sorts of ways and nothing so much as touched me, not even up on the ridge."

"But then we got captured, yeah, and the Germans start marching us across Germany. The cold was just awful, and we were without gloves, without scarves, nothing. Until finally...." He held up the hand to show her, framed her in the gap above the stubs. "Black as coal. Frostbite."

"I'd seen enough of it," Hollister went on. "I knew what had to be done. There was this medic—didn't know his name, never got a chance to thank him. He did a hell of a job, though, don't you think, considering he used his razor."

Claire's pencil fell on the table. "I think I may be sick."

Hollister shrugged. "No big deal, really. It didn't hurt much, and with some sulfa and the snow, it never even got infected. It was just kind of funny, that's all."

"Again funny? Why funny?"

"'Cause before the war I was a pitcher, you know, baseball. A good one, too, had a curve ball you couldn't touch. Senior year I got scouted by the pros, got offered a place on the Cards—the Cardinals, a major league team. But then my number came up and I was off overseas. Rolling, crawling, I was always guarding this hand, kept it close to my body, like this. I wouldn't have cared if they blew my ears off, just as long as that hand was protected."

Claire had stopped writing. She was gnawing on the pencil, disfiguring it. "You call this funny..."

"Sure do. If I'd played in the majors I wouldn't have met my wife, Carol, or had four beautiful sons. Would never have taught phys. ed. at Thomas Jefferson High in Burnsville, North Carolina."

"Carolina?" Stan Morgan, awakening suddenly, sputtered. He took a sip of his juice. "I was in Carolina once."

Hollister leaned over Claire's notebook again. His hand again reached for her wrist, touching it this time. "That's Burnsville with *two* 'l's," he said.

In another corner of the hall, at a table that had been set but was unlikely to be occupied, Richard sipped his coffee. Claire's interview was already in progress when he'd entered, and he sat watching it from afar—watched Hollister's gesturing with his pollarded hand and Morgan intermittently dozing. He observed the way the woman listened—*really* listened—with her shoulders hunkered forward, a whole body affair. He wished he hadn't been so abrupt with her in the café, wished he had an opportunity to apologize and explain. Richard studied her, such an unusual looking girl, today in the fisherman's sweater that made her look less like a journalist than a student wearing her boyfriend's clothes. He wondered if she had a boyfriend, wondered how her hair would fall, unbraided.

"You do not sleep much this night?"

Snatched from his revery, scowling, Richard looked up. Yvonne with a coffeepot stood over him.

"No thanks to you," he mumbled.

He felt guilty seeing her this morning, having slept with her again that night. Their sex had been competent—better than competent, adroit—and when it was over he watched as she rose uncomplainingly, dressed and made her herself up for yet another twelve-hour shift. Richard felt guilt but also revulsion—at her but also with himself for succumbing—and annoyance, because he needed to be alone.

He needed to go over his theory and the way he'd present it to the men, had been sorting through his father's files again, mentally, when Yvonne came knocking on his door.

Leaning to fill his cup, Yvonne brushed his cheek with her breast. "They miss you," she said.

"And I miss them," Richard assured her. He looked up at her face that was neither beautiful nor ugly but just tired, its shadows permanent.

Yvonne giggled again and then, to Richard's relief, she left him. Several of the veterans had just straggled in, and Herr Hermansdorfer was signaling to serve them.

"Oh, Lord, *yes*," Alma responded when the waitress offered her coffee.

The former nurse looked worn, in spite of her efforts to disguise it. No coat of cosmetics could hide half the night she'd waited for a certain knock on her door. For the sight of that bald, beak-nosed bastard in a robe and slippers, two glasses and a bottle of champagne, greeting her, "Evenin', sugar."

But he never came. The door stayed unknocked and her bed half-empty, and it must have been near dawn when she drifted off finally, curled around her pillow. Still, it took more than a no-show to throw Alma Wheatty, and she wasn't disheartened yet. The day's schedule was a long one—more battlefields, more bus rides—and another night lay ahead.

"This, too, please," Alma requested, holding up another coffee cup for the waitress to fill. "My friend is coming down in a minute," she added, thinking that at worst she could drink it herself.

Spagnola was tired too, but deliciously so. He, too, had spent much of the night sleepless, mind racing. The previous day had left him exhilarated, pleased as punch over the way he fit in so effortlessly with the men, the way he'd entertained them laying into that Perlmutter creep, and made them laugh, just as he had in the war.

Between flipovers of his pillow, he'd composed a letter to Captain Carruthers and other members of his group. He'd reminded them of his earlier fears and how they all proved baseless, of how time had erased all differences—soldiers and goofballs, heroes and sneaks—and left them so humbly, vulnerably human. That was where freedom was, he'd tell them, in the realization of that oneness, a communion of sorts. He'd never actually *write* the letter, of course, was too embarrassed about his penmanship and spelling, but he thought it nevertheless and set it to memory. Someday he'd recite it back home.

He limped buoyantly into the hall, red-faced and huffing, and plopped down next to Alma. "Morning!" he exclaimed as he reached for the bun basket and then for the deviled eggs. "In' this something!"

Then the rest of them sidled in: the Gimpels in matching green ski outfits that accentuated Roger's paunch and Willa's cleavage; the even odder couple of Harry Croker and Maurice Pringle, the first thin and unforgivingly angular and the second soft and rotund. As if onto a bandstand, the Confortis strode in. Phil intoned, "Welcome to World War II, the sequel," while Mary smiled and smiled. McCloski lumbered and Rob seemed to bounce; Billings grumbled on his walker. Genie Vorhees ushered her husband, and lastly, trailing the procession, came the Hills.

"Morning. Morning, folks," Buddy chimed.

His mood was upbeat, the result of a good night's rest, a respite from harassing dreams. There were good days and bad days being sick, yet he'd known right from waking that this one was exceptionally good. There'd be no more sparring with Kaye, no dragging himself breathless through the motions. As though he'd never seen that name inscribed in the register, as though the entire reunion wasn't in doubt. He patted Billings' pate. "Nice cut you got there, Sam," he said. He winked at Hollister and Claire. "Easy Greg, she's a minor."

A full five minutes passed before the Major ambled in. Alma saw him first and was about to beckon him to the empty seat next to hers, but instead she changed her mind. Better to let out the reel a bit, she reasoned, let him come to her. From the looks of him, though—hunched, sunk-eyed, unshaven, as if he'd been binging all night— she wasn't sure he could make it. She was just about to write him off, forget about him and switch her sights elsewhere, when the Major sauntered over and seized that empty seat. "Private," he nodded at Spagnola, and squeezed her knee under the table. "Nurse."

They ate heartily, purposefully, but without passion.

"Everything tastes the same to me these days," Pringle lamented. He was swabbing his toast with jam and butter. Crumbs, like castaways, clung to his beard. "Reminds me of C-rations."

"Are you kidding?" Phil Conforti replied, his mouth half-full. "C-rations were great. The best. That bully beef stuff—like a cow fresh out of the blender."

"Who remembers any of that anyway? You think anybody remembers us?" This was Rob's complaint, issued while inspecting a wedge of quiche, sniffing it with rabbit-like twitches. "Ask some kid what he knows of Double-U Double-U Two and he thinks you're talking about a Website."

Groans of agreement around the table.

"E-mail," someone sighed.

"Mobile phones."

"Genetic engineering."

"The 21st century," said Hollister, shaking his head. "Each morning I look in the mirror and there's this ancient geezer looking back at me. I can't figure it."

The others shook their heads as well, bewildered.

"Fact is, we've come to the front of the line."

This was McCloski. A big man with a St. Bernard's mug, jowled and droopy. Features like balls of wet clay hastily slapped on his face. He spoke into his coffee cup, coughed at it.

Pringle raised his eyebrows and asked, "Excuse me?"

"You know, like when you're waiting at the bank or something, at the bakery. You wait while other folks are getting served. And the line gets shorter and shorter up ahead of you and longer in the back. Then all of sudden there you are, right at the front, and all that's left is that one single word."

"*Word*, Ralph?" Hollister pressed him. "What word are you talking about?"

McCloski swigged his coffee, coughed again, and scowled. "Next."

☆ ☆ ☆

One lousy padlock, that's all there was. Old and rust-encrusted, easily broken by a crowbar or, lacking that, a rock. There were plenty of those around the yard; he selected one, a stone little bigger than his fist. It wouldn't make too loud a sound, he figured, like a branch cracking. One lock: amazing when one thought of the treasures potentially waiting inside. He struck it once, twice, and the iron gave way. The door, by itself, swung open.

A coldness breathed into his face, chillier than the air outside, if that was possible, metallic. He stooped down—the lintel was low, barely high enough for a child—and entered. The darkness seemed total, but he could sense the forms hovering around his head. Adjusting, his eyes began to pick out the glistening ribs, the frozen flesh and cartilage. A dozen carcasses—cows, hogs—hung on hooks from the ceiling.

He smiled, resisted the urge to giggle. The cold house was exactly as he remembered it; more meat, perhaps, and no cadavers, but otherwise nothing had changed. There was every reason to believe that the diamonds were there too, still buried, unredeemed. But where? Under the floor, most likely, embedded in ice. He'd need a flashlight to work with, and tools.

Why had he chosen this of all places, he wondered. The idea seemed clever enough at the time, even ironic: ice inside ice. Practical, too, for the cold house was where the bodies were stored. Fortunately, the boy didn't give a fig about jewels, didn't understand their worth, the imbecile, just as long as he got his cash. Twenty U.S. dollars for every lucky corpse that would soon attain new life, a new beginning, with one of Joachim's friends.

He knelt down, knees crackling, and brushed his fingers across the floor. The surface was coarse with striated ice and the drippings of freshly killed meat. Yes, tools were needed, sharp tools. A hammer and chisel like those Pieter Martinson was using, chipping away at his stone. Perhaps he could borrow them one day, just for a while, when the old geek wasn't looking.

He anchored a hand on each thigh and rose slowly, and as he did, caught sight of a strange sort of shining in front of him. Bluish, shimmering, a nimbus around the meat. He started toward it, pushing through the dangling slabs and haunches, gliding as if toward a beacon.

The source of that light was only a few feet away—tough to gauge it in the darkness—behind one last carcass. He stretched out his hand to push it aside, but then halted. He heard something. Between the scratch of his own footsteps and the squeal of the hooks and chains, he detected a faint crunching noise in the yard outside, like boots crushing the frost.

Panicking, he backed away, knocking as he did into ribcages and haunches, until finally he reached the door. He stuck his head out and looked around and thought he saw a hulking figure, in a dull-colored greatcoat and floppy hat, disappearing behind the cottage. Any second that figure could return and make straight for the cold house. Bumping his head as he ducked under the lintel, he glanced one last time around the yard before tottering, on gelid legs, back into the forest.

The plaque was almost complete. A full three feet by four and a half, with beveled, feather-edged borders sliced deep in the rock. So he had envisioned the memorial, the plaque dug in as the unit had been on the ridge, the epitaph firmly entrenched. The rock itself suggestive of an elderly yet still muscular figure lost in ambivalent thoughts.

Pieter Martinson laid down his mallet. He screwed the ball of his fists hard into his flanks and craned his neck as far as he dared. The work was taking its toll. The strenuous walk each day back and forth from the hotel, the weight of his tools, and then the eight or ten hours straight he put in, without so much as a coffee break, hammering. It was enough to exhaust even a thirty-year-old, to strain even the strongest of backs.

The sky was an industrial gray, Pieter noticed, practically touching the treetops. He recalled a similar sky the morning of the battle, recalled thinking *some weather's coming*, and how he'd hoped to reach the bivouac before snowfall. It was his big fear now—snow. Imagine having to wade out here, to clear a swath around the rock and then keep brushing off its surface. Snow did strange things to stone. Hairline flaws, otherwise observable, vanished in the wetness and cold. One wrong tap, one secret fissure, and the entire facade could crumble.

Pieter retrieved the mallet and positioned a number 8 chisel on the stone. He was about to begin tapping when, out of the corner of his eye, he spied a man at the far end of the clearing. A man, dressed most incongruously—in a dark dinner coat, a cream-colored scarf. Pieter only caught a glimpse of him, but in that glimpse he could tell that the man was not young. He moved with difficulty, puffing, as if he were running away.

Pieter thought about calling out to the man, asking if he needed help. Before he could, though, the man veered through the trees and vanished.

Pieter remembered the previous day, the strange sounds he heard while returning to the village, the sense that someone was following him. Strange indeed, for moments later another person appeared at the end of the clearing–much larger than the other man, lumbering, in a weather-beaten hat and greatcoat. He, too, disappeared into the forest.

Something strange is going on, Pieter thought to himself, but resisted the urge to find out. Whatever it was was none of his business, and he musn't get involved. His business was carving, with less than three days left to finish the job and a blizzard possibly brewing. He tried to forget what he had seen, to concentrate on the task in front of him. Pieter raised the mallet and struck once, twice, on the chisel's flattened head. He worked uninterruptedly, thinking of nothing, as the memorial emerged from the stone.

☆ ☆ ☆

There might have been a battle in the Bayonet Hall, from the look of the tables. Splotches of spilled coffee, rivulets of juice, eggs and bread crumbs stippling the table. Breakfast was technically over, but no one moved. The hotel, though grossly overheated, was far-and-away preferable to the Arctic outside. The boy from the front desk and the floozy from the bar were still filling cups, even when they weren't entirely empty, and Hermansdorfer smiled from a corner. They could have sat there all day, Kaye thought as she helped herself to another bun that she had no real intention of eating, dropped one on Buddy's plate as well. Just as long as that ghoul Kuhlmann didn't come and drag them out to the bus. Sweating, stuffed, she was content to stay just where she was.

And Claire was content to have her there—to have all of the guests gathered around their tables where she could work them systematically, approaching them with her pencil in her teeth and her notebook open, ready to record their stories.

With Hollister behind her, she started on Stan Morgan, with a short, shouted Q & A that devolved into a tour of the various pins on his lapels: the Community Church, the Lion's Club. He told her about his years in the service—the Postal Service—first on the route in Evanston, and then in the district office; about his late wife, Martha, a school caféteria cook, and the decade he spent as a widower; about his stamp collection and his miniature car collection, but about his experience in the Army—nothing. "I was a soldier," shrugged Morgan.

"Yes, but what about the war?"

"Come again?"

"The *battle*!"

"Oh, *that*." Recoiling, he seemed to shrink inside his suit. He pushed the glasses up his nose with fingers thick and stiff, like rolls of Lincoln pennies. "I survived it. I was captured, and I survived that, too."

"No incident you'd want to tell me about? No acts of heroism?"

Morgan gazed at the floor, nodding. "Reported a cat burglary once. Broad daylight, right on my route."

She considered taking his picture, but then thought again. A generic old man—round-faced, balding—who had probably been generic in middle age as well and before that, your average, nondescript kid. For ten minutes Claire listened to him but never wrote a word.

"One last question, Mr. Morgan, if you do not mind. Why the reunion?"

He tilted his head and tapped his hearing aid. "The reunion you say?"

"Yes, the reunion."

"Well, you know how it is. Me and Martha, we never had any children...and it's Christmas time." He tugged on his lapels and, with the back of his fingers, brushed some lint from his pins. "It's good to spend it with people."

Claire left Stan Morgan and drifted across the hall, to the table occupied by the Gimpels and Jimmy Rob. Willa was expanding on a vacation they had taken in Spain, just the two of them, in Marbella on the Costa del Sol—"*Real* Europe, nothing like this"—while Roger fumbled with a book-sized box of pills.

"And the food..." Willa kissed her fingers as she peered inside the box. "Don't forget the brown ones, dear. Beta-carotin, good for the liver."

Roger made a face as he swallowed. Sheathed in green nylon, with his red fleshy face, his look was vaguely vegetable.

"The service, too, hand and foot." Willa was back in Marbella. She was shaking her coffee cup, bell-like, and her bracelets jangled. "None of this insufferable waiting..."

While Willa waited for her refill, Claire leaned closer to Rob.

"How did *you* survive the battle?"

"Oh, Jesus," he groaned. "Je-sus." His hands—delicate hands, trembling—fluttered across the table.

"Did you think you were going to die? Were you very lucky?"

Rob stared anxiously into a plate littered with half-nibbled carrot sticks. "Questions like that...I'm not very good at 'em."

"What was it like being captured, then? Did the Germans treat you terribly?"

"One could say that..."

Claire frowned—she couldn't hide her disappointment. Under the name Stan Moran, she wrote in her notebook *Jimmy Rob*, and next to it the same word: *Rien*.

"My brother," Rob said suddenly.

"Excuse me?"

"I survived because of Bertie, my brother."

She went for her camera. "Just a background shot," she assured him. With his gray curly hair, white teeth, and guileless, almost childlike expression, Rob was sure to arouse readers' sympathies, Claire was certain. "Please now," she said when she'd finished snapping, "tell me about Bertie."

"Big guy, Bertie. His real name's Bertrand, but no one called him that. Big guy, not like me. Played hockey. And when the war came, they put him in the Rangers."

"How, then, did he..."

"Save me? Well, you don't know Bertie. You didn't know our mother, only person he was ever afraid of. She told him before he went off that he'd better take care of me or else. Our Ma."

"So he saved you?"

"Like I said. As soon as the Germans break through he steals this jeep and heads off to where he thinks I'm posted, around Saint-Vith. He finds some division headquarters and walks up to this officer—a general, Bertie tells it—and asks where's Private James Rob of the 133rd. Well, this officer guy, he's half shell-shocked himself and he says, 'How the hell I'm supposed to know. He's probably out there dead with the rest of 'em.' So Bertie takes this guy by the collar and lifts him off the floor and says, 'Tell me where he is or I'll twist your fuckin' head off.' Excuse my French."

Rob paused and rubbed his slender jaw. His hands kept moving, kept straightening—his shirtcuffs, his fork—as his story steadily unwound.

"He found me all right, dug in on that ridge on the second day of the battle. I was scared to death and so cold...and then, out of the fog, I hear my name being called—Jimmy! Private Jimmy Rob! And I cry back: 'Over here!' And just like that he drops into my hole and gives me a pair of gloves—you believe it, we didn't have gloves—and a scarf and an extra Army blanket. Socks me in the arm and he says, 'You get hurt, Ma's gonna whup me, so don't even *think* about it.'"

"Did you?"

"Did I what?"

"Think about it?"

"Try not to, a hundred Germans coming at you. But those gloves, boy, and that scarf—it doesn't take much when you've got nothing. Later, after we were liberated, he found me again, this time in a field hospital in Leipzig. He came every day bringing me extra rations, fresh meat and greens, get my strength up. And every day he'd sock me in the arm and say, 'See what you did, I'm in deep shit with Ma.'"

Claire wrote fast, wishing she had mastered shorthand. Here at last was a truly great story, a surefire bylined feature. All it wanted was an ending, something with meaning, with pathos. "That's quite a brother you had. Is he still…?"

"Bertie. Oh yeah. Though I haven't seen him in, oh God, five, six years at least. Our wives didn't like each other much, you know how it is, and then me being in Albany and him all the way out in Sacramento. I was thinking, though, we really should hook up again someday. Maybe after the reunion."

Claire's pencil went still, suddenly, and she fought to suppress a sigh. So much for pathos. If only they had stayed best friends through life, or if Bertie had died prematurely—*anything* but bickering wives. Already she was looking around the hall in search of another story.

"The people, too, you should see them," Willa was saying now that her coffee had come, now that Roger had taken his pills. "So cultured and refined. Nothing like the Spanish we have in America."

Rob asked Claire, "Would you like to hear about my realty business?" He was fully warmed up now, flattered and wired. "I did pretty good with it, you know."

But Claire only nodded. She had fixed her sights on the Major's table, realizing, finally, what any seasoned reporter would have picked up instantly. *He* was her scoop. Images of ranches, of cowboys on the range and then—flash forward—of war and suffering, his hopeless battle on the ridge. The Major: a character straight out of an airport novel, bigger than life even as he neared the end of it. Rob was talking real estate and Claire pretended to write, but she kept one eye on that other table and waited for her moment to move.

Richard watched her watching. He could see where her eyes were staring and who her next subject would be, and for a second, he almost envied the Major. He envied all of them, even Stan Morgan, even Billings, for having a story to tell. He, too, wanted a story, and a story that someone might hear. Like his father's. He sipped his fourth cup of coffee and felt his stomach jittering. His brain was working fast. All the men were gathered at their tables, compliant and subdued. Now was his chance, perhaps his very last.

The ringing of glass and silver wrought silence in the hall. The Major stood, spoon in hand like a miniature scepter. He'd been regaling Alma with the tale of a three-day poker game just after the war, five-card stud with characters with names like Louie Two-Foot and Miloxi Bob, in which he bet everything he owned—the drilling rights, the ranch—on a pair of lousy eights. A breath-stopping tale, everyone, even Spagnola, had stopped eating to hear it.

But just as the Major had seen his opponents and raised them, Kuhlmann entered the hall. In his hat and trench coat, his skullface and scar, he might have been a spy coming in from the cold instead of a driver whose mere presence meant that the bus was running outside.

"Sorry, folks, looks like the ending's got to wait," the Major said, and the entire table groaned. He winked at Alma, "Tonight," before peering down the table at Buddy.

"Lieutenant Hill!"

Buddy looked around him as if there were another Lieutenant Hill on the site.

"Lieutenant, the men are ready to move out?" The Major's hand made little uplifting movements, egging Buddy on.

"Right," Buddy muttered. He cleared his throat and mustered some pep. "Ready for action, sir!"

"Thank you, Lieutenant. Now listen up, these are our orders for today: first, we're goin' to this place called Liege, to the American military cemetery there. Pay our respects to the boys who died for us."

"Can you really be so sure?"

The Major, squinting, glanced around the hall. "Pardon me?"

"I asked, how can you be sure?"

From his chair, Richard Perlmutter stood.

"Hold on there, son," the Major checked him. "We're happy to have you here, for your father's sake and all, but you can't be causin' a fracas."

"I know, I know. I was hasty yesterday, I admit it, and arrogant. But I've studied the battle inside and out, and I just have this one last question. Let me ask it, please, and then I'll sit down and shut up. Promise."

Richard waited for a response—there was none—and so he repeated, "*How can you be so sure?*"

"So sure about *what?*" Pringle demanded.

"About what the Major said, that all of those men died for you?"

The Major hissed from behind him, "What are you getting at, son?"

"Think," Richard told them. "Half a million Allied soldiers crammed into one front, and opposing them, a hundred thousand Germans, low on ammunition, low on food, exhausted. How, then, did those Germans know just where to strike where the American line was the weakest, in Saint-Vith?"

Desperate looks darted from the Major to Buddy Hill. *Stop him*, they urged.

"He wants me to say something," Buddy whispered to Kaye, and had just started to move when her hand clasped hard on his shoulder.

"Stay," she commanded him. "Major wants it stopped, let *him* stop it."

Richard's eyes, meanwhile, had widened with excitement. His face was flushed and his hands flew gesturing. The single question had multiplied: "Why didn't U.S. intelligence, which had broken all the German codes, have any knowledge of this? How was it that the Germans came out with weapons *you* knew nothing about—the Tiger tank, the jet fighter—and had no answer for? You, the world's biggest, richest army?"

McCloski, with his sledgehammer hand, pounded on the table. Others also pounded—Croker, Rob, Phil Conforti. But only Spagnola spoke, removing his Caterpillar cap and scratching his pate. "I don't know, Richie, I ain't been to college or nothing, and I don't know squat about history, but hey, some guy's trying to blow your balls off, it's education enough for me."

The men laughed uneasily and this time Richard laughed, too. "Please understand that I'm not trying to say you men were in any way less intelligent or less brave—on the contrary, you fought one very tough battle. I'm only suggesting that, from inside your foxholes, it might have been hard for you to see the whole picture."

The laughter had ceased, the protests, too. The hall fell silent. Richard's eyes swept across the veterans, meeting as many of their eyes as he could, before falling again on Claire. She was writing in her notebook now, writing furiously, her lip between her teeth. He called to the man by the door, "Ten minutes, Mr. Kuhlmann, no more."

The driver nodded.

Richard reclaimed his chair and straddled it in reverse. Leaning over the backrest, his tone lowering and expression turning severe, he started:

"Though technically enemies, Germany and America had one crucial thing in common..."

☆ ☆ ☆

It was just before the clearing or thereabouts, just as Martinson and his rock came into view, that he realized he was being followed. At first he thought the footsteps were his own, echoing. But then, as the cadences parted, as the crackle of twigs and swishing branches grew louder in the forest behind him—louder and closer—he knew that he was not alone.

Rushing had never been his forte, not even in his youth. He was never the hurrying type, always preferring to be late for a meeting rather than run to arrive on time. But now, pursued, he worked himself up to a pace he hadn't equaled in many years—since the war, perhaps, dashing for cover.

He rushed and cut across the end of the clearing where there was a good chance that Martinson could see him. He no longer cared, and for a moment actually considered going up and saying good day to the gaffer, but only for a moment. Avoiding Martinson, he hurried across the end of the clearing and ducked headlong back into the woods.

He blundered, he ran, yet he couldn't seem to put distance between them—between himself and the man closing in. Nor could he find the trail, had no idea what direction he was heading or where the town might be. He imagined himself being overtaken finally, tackled, dispatched, and his body left where nobody would ever find it. His ultimate nightmare: dying alone, unidentified. Unburied.

He ran and tears stung his eyes and cheeks. They dribbled over his lips as he uttered the name he hadn't heard in well over fifty years.

"Dean," he rasped, and it sounded so strange to him, pitched in his own voice. "Dean!" he shouted, and then nearly burst out crying when someone up ahead responded.

"Deandeandean!" the children laughed as they scurried around the playground in the park.

Somehow, unknowingly, he'd reached the edge of the town.

He strolled into Saint-Vith as though nothing had happened, re-knotted his scarf and plucked the burrs from his sleeves. He felt wonderful, suddenly, relieved and exhilarated. A feeling he'd experienced coming down from the ridge after the battle and surrendering himself to Joachim.

He did not return to the hotel directly. He detoured instead around the square, peering into the windows of the souvenir shops, at the kitschy porcelain miniatures, toy tanks, lighters in the shape of grenades. At a newsstand, he browsed through some magazines. The square was all but empty; nobody was on his tail.

He angled, now, toward the hotel, driven by the thought of breakfast—eggs benedict, café au lait—served to his room by Miles. To the bathtub, where he'd be basting his body for hours. His pace picked up again, effortlessly now, and then all at once he stopped. In front of the hotel, he saw, the minibus was idling.

The old bastards hadn't left yet. They were still inside the hotel—in their rooms, probably, refusing to face the cold, or gossiping down in the lobby. It meant that he could not risk a regular entry; the front door was no longer safe. No, he'd have to return the way he left: down the alley behind the hotel, through the service entrance and into the kitchen and around the bar before slipping up into his room.

He retraced his steps to the farthest end of the square, turned, and made his approach. Stealthily past the front of the hotel, the bus, and then to the rear, between the overflowing bins of garbage. He veered around them, into the alley, and nearly smacked right into him.

A giant. A colossus, two heads taller than any normal man, he seemed, and as wide as the alley itself. He had come from the other direction—from the forest, apparently—and had entered the alley at exactly the same moment. In a filthy greatcoat, an even filthier hat, he hunched and snorted and gazed with eyes as small and dark as bullet holes. His smell was worse than the bins'.

They stood and confronted one another, the elderly gentleman and the ogre. They said nothing, hardly moved, until finally the older man nodded. "Comment ça va, mon garçon?"

And then he dashed. As fast as he could in his wingtips, scarf and coat flapping, actually sprinted for the door at the other end of the alley. He lunged for the door he'd had the foresight to leave open, its bolt jammed with cardboard, and twisted the handle. The footsteps behind him grew louder, closer, were nearly on top of him. The door opened and, squeezing inside, he threw his entire weight against it, locking it. The handle began rattling madly.

He backed into the kitchen and then, whirling, found himself face-to-perky-face with Miles.

"Oh, it's you, sir. Good morning, sir!" he chirped, sleeves rolled up and his arms sunk elbow-deep in suds. "You surprised me."

"Apologies. I saw the bus outside and those people I asked you about, I'd rather not run into them yet."

A distinct clicking noise from the door; the bolt shifting to open. *The monster has a key. He's coming into the kitchen!*

He pushed past the desk boy, propelled himself along the metal table, knocked over a stack of dishes. Ahead of him was a double door that just then parted to admit the seedy barmaid with a tray and an empty coffeepot. He nearly toppled her as well.

"Merde!" she spat.

Miles called after him, "But, sir, they're not outside, those people…"

But he couldn't hear him. Could only hear the rear entrance clacking shut and the thud of boots on linoleum. He barreled through the double doors and out into the raw fluorescence.

☆ ☆ ☆

Most of the men were already on their feet and the others rising hollering, "Bullshit!" and "you're crazy!" at Richard who, virtually alone, remained seated.

He had just finished telling them his theory, how the German offensive of December 1944 had been secretly coordinated with right-wing American generals who wanted a negotiated peace on the Western Front in order to confront the Eastern. Together, America and Germany could prevent the Soviets from entering Berlin and then push them back to Russia. Needed only was a modest breakthrough in the Ardennes, a neat little stalemate on which to base the armistice. The Bulge, the desperate battle for the ridge, it was all a plot, claimed Richard.

"You're out of your fucking gourd," howled Billings, rattling his walker while Gimpel and McCloski stomped toward Richard in a huff. Alma was close behind them—Alma who, until now, had kept aloof from the hubbub, a men's affair, but who'd finally lost her cool, barking, "You can blow it out your ass, buster."

Buddy Hill watched the scene with horror. He needed no more cues from the Major, no more prompting. The situation was unbecoming in the extreme. He freed himself of Kaye's grasp and moved to impose himself between Richard and his detractors, when the double doors swung open.

Stan Morgan noticed him first. Stan, who could hardly hear what Richard was saying and was unclear on what all the ruckus was about, now shouted at the top of his lungs. "Gosh!"

Hollister was the next to notice. "Holy shit!" he cried, and then McCloski: "Can't be..."

The Major turned pale and faltered, so that Alma had to catch him by the arm, and Buddy staggered backwards to Kaye.

"What's happening? Who's this?" Tommy Vorhees asked Genie, but when Genie turned to Rob all he said was, "You don't want to know..."

Expressions of horror, of disgust, and yet nobody moved; nobody was capable.

Spagnola, alone, stepped forward, and formed a cogent question: "You? Here?"

He received no answer. Instead, he watched as the intruder strode through the tables, nodding at the guests as though they were lined in review. He reached the front of the hall, next to the Major, turned and rocked back and forth on his heels. "As you were, men," said Adrian Rifesnider, "As you were."

FOUR

Harry Croker caught the eye of Maurice Pringle and a memory passed between them.

They had just emerged from their foxholes, risen like the newly dead. Bones cracking, uniforms stiff, faces white where they weren't blackened. They hadn't slept more than an hour or two for any night of the six, couldn't have, what with the shelling and the cold, could not remember their last hot meal. With jagged pain, they lifted their arms and on wobbly knees began trundling down the face of the ridge.

Others had already gathered on the meadow, huddled like so many sheep. Germans, many of them no more than kids, butted them with their guns, relieved them of rings and watches. Only one of them stood apart, an officer to tell from his insignia—long-faced and handsome in a frosty manner, blond at the temples, his eyes a ceramic blue. And on his cap, the skull-and-crossbones of the Waffen SS. He looked on disinterestedly, smoking, and then motioned for one of the prisoners to be brought to him. He wanted their commanding officer.

All eyes were on them as the SS man offered the colonel a cigarette (a Lucky Strike, it was later said) and engaged him in conversation that grew quickly, visibly, cordial. Soon they were laughing together, laughing with a third of the battalion dead or missing and the survivors at gunpoint, freezing. And when the time came to march those remnants off—the first of a hundred miles' marching—that laughter hounded them through the woods.

That was the point when Pfc. Croker turned to Corporal Pringle, a man who had shared his foxhole often but who was scarcely recognizable to him now, and drew a finger across his neck. Pringle followed suit: a quick, clean slice through the jugular. So, without so much as a word passing between them, the pact was made. If they ever got out of this alive, they promised, they would kill that slimy bastard. They'd slit his fucking throat.

In the Bayonet Hall of the Hotel Ardennes, in Saint-Vith fifty-five years later, Croker repeated the gesture. The finger was crooked now, the neck lined, but the meaning remained unmistakable, the memory shared. Pringle nodded in acknowledgment. He and Croker then returned their eyes to where all the others' were pinned.

"Isn't this a surprise?" the Major clapped. He was laboring to show that nothing was abnormal, slaving to extemporize. "Y'all remember the Colonel, don't you?"

"Adrian, please."

A silent moment followed, icy silence. The men were standing in a cluster now, glowering, while the women—Willa, Mary, Genie, even Alma—hung back. Only Claire ventured to come forward, and to peek between the cantilevered shoulders.

What she saw was an old man, probably not much older than the Major, and yet something about him—the pabulum of his chins, the bloated nose and cheeks—spoke of some deeper decay. Thin, gingery hair, professionally coiffed, hand-tailored clothes. A man of class, portly and proud of it.

"What's going on?" she asked the person closest to her—Richard. "Who is he?"

He had recognized the face immediately—older perhaps, sallower—remembered it from the clippings in his father's files. And the voice was the voice that had RSVP'd shortly after his father's death. "You heard him. Colonel Rifesnider, commander of the 133rd. Seems he's joined the reunion."

The Major stammered on: "We thought, you see, this being our last big gathering and all..."

"Yes, we thought...," Buddy rushed to add, but then stopped short, stumped.

Phil Conforti had plenty of words, though, and furious. "Who invited him? Who in his right mind would do that?"

The former colonel looked around the room. He shrugged slightly, shuffled, but stayed mum.

"I did."

Heads turned this way and that, confused, before alighting one after another on Richard.

"*You?*" Billings scowled, as if Richard's theory hadn't been hurtful enough, that he had struck them with this as well.

"I invited everyone from the 133rd," Richard said. "Everyone my father listed."

Suddenly they turned on Richard, as though Rifesnider were not even there.

"Your father wouldn't have dared," Pringle spat.

"Never in a million years," cried McCloski.

The Major hurried between the men, trying to calm them. Buddy tried, too, though sluggishly. He felt dizzy and nauseous suddenly; the walls began to spin. Kaye, taking notice, started toward her husband, but paused at the sound of someone loudly clearing his throat—Kuhlmann.

The scarecrow-like driver stood in his trench coat, one sleeve raised toward the door. "My apologies, *mein damen und herren*," he said hollowly, "The bus can no longer wait."

☆ ☆ ☆

Nobody spoke, not even whispered, throughout the entire trip. Not because of the cold or the sight of an old battlefield, not because someone had died. A silence not of pain but of supreme resentment. The veterans rode wordlessly and seethed.

Rifesnider had joined them on the bus. Without being asked, without asking, certainly, he had simply climbed aboard and taken the only seat open to him, next to Richard Perlmutter.

They sat and said nothing to one another, the two pariahs, exchanging sidelong glances.

Rifesnider was astounded by what he saw. Take off twenty years, cut off that ridiculous ponytail, and Richard was the image of his father. The resemblance did little to calm him, though; on the contrary, the sight of Label's face only deepened the headmaster's anxiety. Narrowly he'd escaped his pursuer—escaped a ferocious beating or worse—only to find himself stuck on a bus with these bumpkins. Once they'd seen him, he had no choice but to tag along, whether they wanted him or not. The reunion had been his alibi, but now that he was part of it, how could he slip away? How could he get back to the cold house?

Richard's glimpse betrayed a smile, momentary and contrived. He felt sorry for having screwed up again, for convincing no one with the theory of his battle, for inviting this man whom nobody wanted around. Sorry but also curious. What was it about this Rifesnider that everybody so desperately despised? Once again he sensed he was missing something, much as he felt perusing his father's files. He remembered the fastidiousness of Rifesnider's affidavits—the remains of each German soldier so exactingly described, the handwriting so neat. The handwriting looked familiar, somehow, and yet he still couldn't place it. He could not place anything, glancing and smiling again at Rifesnider, dumbly this time.

Elsewhere in the bus there were other glances exchanged, other smiles, all rueful. Vengeful. Claire didn't get it. She saw how Rifesnider's appearance had stunned and rankled the veterans, but she hadn't an inkling why. Nor was anyone particularly eager to explain. The men seemed too troubled to notice her, much less to fill her in.

"They hate him."

She craned her neck. Stan Morgan was leaning over the back of her seat, chin propped on his arms.

"So I see," said Claire. "And perhaps you could tell me why?"

"Many reasons."

"Give me one."

Behind their glasses, Morgan's eyes brightened briefly, as if from some sudden jolt. "He didn't fight. Not on the ridge, not before it, either. And then when we surrendered, he went off with the Krauts."

"Krauts?"

"The Germans. This officer they had, this SS bastard. He went off with him."

Claire had already opened her notebook, was already transcribing his words. "And then?"

"And then nothing. We never saw him after that. We'd always pegged him for a good-for-nothing, but there he became a traitor, too. Some boys swore that if they ever caught him again they'd turn him in or simply shoot him themselves."

"And now?"

"What say?"

Claire half-turned to him, raised her voice as high as she could without exceeding a whisper. "Now? Would they shoot him now, after all this time?"

The reporter was thinking headlines, anticipating her editor's delight at this stirring chronicle of closure. But then Stan Morgan smirked at her, cheeks inflating, glasses pinched up his nose.

"Depends," he said.

"Depends on what?"

"Depends if we get a gun."

Seated behind Morgan, laboring not to but inescapably listening in, Kaye heard his talk of killing someone, of hatred and guns, and dejectedly shook her head. She was holding her husband's hand, kneading it. All of his joints felt knit.

"Just let it go," she advised him, "ignore it." But Buddy's tension only stiffened; ignoring it, Kaye knew, was not possible, not for the man who had spent his life tending to other people's problems. And as a problem, Rifesnider was not about to go away. She could see that now in the veterans' expressions—frigid, fixed—and the severe straightness of their backs. On the bus, riding across Belgium, they looked like they were hurling toward battle.

☆ ☆ ☆

Liege was a relief, at first. The clipped hedges and disciplined lawns, the paths strictly lined with poplars. So neat, so symmetrically soothing to the eye. And the flag, America's flag, flapping in this foreign wind, waving to them: a candy-striped patch of home.

Buddy saluted it as he exited the bus, then immediately set to shivering. As wintry as it was in Saint-Vith, the temperature in Liege was lower, solidly lodged below zero. The sky was low, churning gray and menacing. The sun was a pewtered presence.

The veterans descended the bus and immediately huddled for heat. Room was found for Claire in the crowd, even for Richard—if nothing else, a hale, warm-blooded body. All except for Rifesnider. He stood in the lee of the bus with hands thrust into his dinner coat, with his collars raised and his painstaking haircut disheveled. His knees had begun to knock.

"I'm going to ask him over," Willa Gimpel told Roger and had started to wave, when her husband jammed her hand down.

"Don't you dare," he hissed. "Don't even think about it."

Genie Vorhees thought she should try as well. "Tommy, please…" But all she received was a shake of his head, as if even the *appearance* of seeing Rifesnider was odious.

No one said another word about it, and so they waited, the men together and their former colonel apart, until the last of the passengers—the Major and Alma—joined them.

"Perfect day for a cemetery, eh, Major?" Hollister stuttered. But his erstwhile commander said nothing. Only Alma answered, grunting through lips as pale and knurly as scars.

"Think *we're* cold," she said as her eyes swept across the field. "Imagine how *they* feel?"

The headstones lay before them, as far as anyone could see. Row after row of them, evenly spaced and uniform, like sprockets on an infinite reel. An eerie sight, silent except for a tractor purling somewhere, and the wind whistling faintly through the stones.

Who'd have thought there'd be so many? That was the question the veterans asked themselves silently—that and, *why them and not me?* It was one thing to talk about numbers—ten, twenty thousand dead—and quite another to see them. To walk through the crosses and the occasional star, reading the names, the ages, until the mind no longer absorbed; feeling guilty about it at first, and then moving on, wondering at what point homage might be said to have been paid already, duty done.

They regrouped near a central memorial, an obelisk engraved with the names of battles. There the visitors stood once more with their teeth chattering, knocking the heels of their shoes, and waited for someone to speak. They all looked—he could *feel* them looking—at Tommy.

"A life is a lot to give for a country," he began as Genie helped him forward toward the obelisk. "One life, I don't care what anybody says, it's an awful lot. Think about it: all the good meals you've eaten, playing with your kids, making love—*making love*—and the countless sweet breaths you draw every day. All that and in one instant, gone, just like that, snatched from you. Stolen. So gone that you can't even question the injustice of it all. Those questions are left for us, now, aren't they? The living."

Tommy Vorhees, the Vicar, paused. With a finger, he wiped a tear from behind his dark glasses, and swayed. For a moment he looked as though the emotions were too powerful, even for him. He swallowed hard, though, and continued:

"We have all the questions, but none of the answers. We want to be grateful for surviving, yet we know that we're here today because somebody else isn't. We want to say that there was some reason why we lived—some goodness on our part, some special purpose—and yet there are thousands of good men lying here, men with purposes far better than fertilizing this lawn. Good men died as well and bad men went home."

With this, all eyes, even Vorhees' it seemed, shifted to Rifesnider. He had hung back from the memorial, out of earshot, and wanly smiled at the stares.

"We want to say," the Vicar went on, "that these men died for us, for our freedom and way of life. And yet who among the beautiful young boys buried here wouldn't trade places with us, old and useless and decrepit as we are, right now? This very frostbitten minute."

And that was it. No consoling note to end on, no prayer. Tommy Vorhees stepped back from the obelisk, reaching behind him for Genie's hand. Another interlude of quiet followed, uneasy now, as thoughts invariably gravitated to the bus, to the heating system and the seats. They waited to hear the Major say "dismissed," but instead heard Kuhlmann's voice, gruff and discordant, rebounding off the stones. "Here we are! Wait! One second!"

The driver was zigzagging through the rows, trampling over graves as he shortcutted toward the obelisk. One hand held his hat to his head and the other a bouquet of roses.

"Sorry. They were not so easy to find," he huffed to the Major when he trotted up to the memorial.

But the Major merely nodded to him, and slipped him some cash for the flowers. Then, taking the bouquet, presenting it as he would a firearm, he laid it before the obelisk.

"I ain't got much to say for a change," he croaked, turning back and removing his Stetson. "Only the sadness I feel that our boys could not have been buried here. Must've been months 'fore anybody came looking for 'em, I reckon, and by that time…But that don't mean we can't remember them here, and do 'em honor. So for you, for Tully and Rhys and Captain Toth. For Barkin…"

"And Featherstone," Rob called out. "For Dean Featherstone." And all eyes, narrowing, again aimed at Rifesnider.

"For Dean Featherstone," the Major repeated. "For all of you brave and wonderful boys, we salute you." And he did—they all did, crisply.

Alone among the men, no veteran, Richard did not salute. He had barely registered the Vicar's words, scarcely noticed the cold. He was far too immersed in his own jumbled thoughts, and striving desperately to sort them.

"Toth. Rhys. Tully…"

He was staring at the headstones, mumbling to himself, and seemed not to notice when Claire addressed him.

"Good work this morning," she said. "First that speech—where do you get such ideas?—and then this man you invited." She snapped a picture of the men around the obelisk and then, swerving the lens, another of Rifesnider standing alone. "Can you believe the way they hate him?"

"Dean Featherstone…"

The camera lowered and the face behind it was hard. "You have not heard a word that I said. That anybody says. These men, their courage—*that* is important, not your silly theories."

Her cheeks, he noticed, darkened as she scolded him, a sudden blaze of beauty. But not even that could hold him. "Something I missed…"

"I know," Claire sneered as she turned and left him. "Life."

The Major saluted again and signaled the ceremony's end. The veterans filed past him toward the bus, all except for Alma. He circled the obelisk and gazed out at the cemetery, eyes raking the rows. He saw her, finally, or what he assumed was her, a thin dark figure hunched over one of the stones.

The Major went to her, found her with her hair wind-slapped and her makeup running rivulets down her face. It took him a second to realize that this was a woman crying.

"He wanted me to be his girl…"

The Major looked down at the cross. *Lionel Fowles, Capt. 27 Inf. Btn*, it said.

She sniveled into the fur of her collar. "We were in the church, in Saint-Vith, completely surrounded as far as we knew, expecting any second the Germans to come bursting in. I didn't know what they'd do to me, a woman. And there were so many wounded, some so bad—I thought they'd shoot them."

"But in comes Lionel. He'd taken some metal in his chest already—it didn't look good—but he was so strong and broad-shouldered—somebody later said he'd played hockey for Cornell. So full of self-confidence, we just did what he said."

"There was a Sherman tank parked not far away, he said, pretty shot up but still running. He told us to round up all the stretchers we could, anybody who could walk. He got us all moving—me, two doctors, a couple of orderlies and the wounded—and he led us out there, into that hell. Shells exploding, people screaming. But Lionel led us. I trusted him."

She fished through her handbag for a tissue, swabbed her nose and tapped the ducts of her eyes.

"The tank was there, sure enough, shot up like he said, but damn, it ran. It sped, like this big old jalopy with all of us hanging on for life, trying to keep the wounded from rolling off. Bombs, bullets everywhere, but when I look up there's Lionel up on the front of that tank, standing there with his Thompson firing."

"Somehow he got us out. We got behind our lines. I wanted to thank him—hell, I wanted to marry the guy! But he'd never got off that tank. He was still lying there, this rock of a man all shivering pale and curling. Gut-shot, bad, hardly any external bleeding, and he'd lost so much blood already...

"I stayed with him. He wanted me to be his girl and I said, 'Don't you know it, sweetheart.' I think her name was Sue."

Alma started crying again; the tissue was useless. The Major felt useless as well, examining the tips of his boots. "Wait here," he said finally. "Don't move."

He bandied all the way back to the obelisk, and returned wheezing and red-faced, sweating beneath his hat. "Here," he gasped, and pressed a long-stemmed rose into her hand.

Alma knelt and laid the rose on the ground. "What will happen now?" she sobbed. "Who will visit them when we're gone?"

The Major, for once, was mute. He had no words, only his grin, more pained now than glib, and an arm that he put around Alma's shoulders, that both held her and led her from the grave.

☆ ☆ ☆

The afternoon stretched and crept at a glacial pace. Another long bus ride, an indifferent lunch, and then onto the bus again—all in chilling silence. Not until Kuhlmann turned into a tree-lined country lane, with veterans looking around in puzzlement, did the Major at last speak up. "Got a little surprise for you all here. The man at the hotel, Hermans…whatever, he set it up. Said you'd like it. Let's hope so."

"I say we'd had enough surprises for one day," Croker groused.

McCloski agreed, "For a lifetime."

"Why can't we just go back to the hotel?" whined Willa Gimpel, and Roger, prompted by an elbow to his flank, went along. "Willa's right. Enough already."

But the bus plied on, following the lane until it eventually spilled into a yard. A schoolyard, fittingly equipped with swings and a jungle gym, a soccer field with goals. The school itself was a converted country manor, retired behind a copse.

The minibus came to a halt and was almost immediately surrounded, assaulted by shouts and shrieks of laughter. Children, several dozen of them, had already poured out of the house and more were following, dashing toward the bus to gape through its windows at the alien beings inside.

"What do they want from us?" asked Rob with a sudden jerk of his head.

"They want to meet you," the Major explained. "They've heard all about you from their granddaddies, about how you beat the bad ol' Nazis. You, Rob—every one of you—you're heroes."

Heroes. Spagnola heard this but couldn't get the description to stick. Heroism was the last thing he'd see in himself, in his or in anybody's eyes. And yet here were two tow-headed kids craning to peek through his window, mouths open, eyes ablaze. He flitted his fingers at them and they flitted tiny fingers back. He felt himself surrendering to their smiles.

Getting off the bus proved a hazardous affair, as the veterans were nearly tackled by their hosts. Kaye clung to Buddy, who in turn latched on to Hollister and Hollister to the door. Billings was in particular trouble, with a threesome of eight-year-olds dangling from his walker. Injury was averted, though, when the teacher finally caught up with his kids. A demure man in his late twenties—thin, bland, prematurely balding—he pried them away, told them in both French and German to go gently with the Americans, that while they had been soldiers once, young and muscular, they were much much older now and breakable.

"They are very…how do you say…?"

"Excited," offered Kuhlmann as he descended, bored-looking, from the bus.

"Excited, *jah*!" cheered the teacher, and waved a feminine hand round his kids. "You fight to make zem free."

That same hand now motioned toward the schoolhouse and they moved, the old and the unfathomably young, together through the trees.

The camera clicked and—"Oui!"—Claire congratulated herself. It was one of those photos she could visualize exactly even before it was developed: of Spagnola walking with his head in the air, striding in spite of his limp, and his hands in the hands of two little blond kids, a boy and a girl.

She was going to take another shot of them, just in case, when she realized she had run out of film. Her "oui" turned to "merde" as she rifled her camera case for another roll. It was then, reloading, that she heard the voice murmuring somewhere behind her. Under a brace of pine trees, hunched with his hands deep in his jacket pockets, stood Richard. He was talking to himself again, upbraiding himself.

"You got to get the connection. December, November…"

She called to him, "You are not joining them? I think this is a good place to see what your father really did here."

"Barkin…Featherstone. *Damn* it."

She muttered another "merde," cursing her curiosity. She went over and stood next to him, just to see what he was grumbling at.

Three old headstones, dark gray and deeply eroded, askew. But the inscriptions were still legible—in German, and the dates: December 1944.

"Werhmacht?"

Richard shook his head. He pointed to the unit designation beneath the names. "SS."

"Amazing that they would keep them here, next to the school."

"They were here before the school, before that teacher was born. Anyway, the kids wouldn't know…"

"Perhaps it is better that they don't." She gathered the collars of her pea coat and framed her face. "It's freezing out here," she said. "We should go inside."

Richard sought a respite in that face, gazing at it, but it only deepened his bewilderment. "I'm missing something…"

"You are missing something now," she said, with a swing of her chin toward the school.

"Barkin…Toth. Their bodies were never found. All those graves we saw at the cemetery…Doesn't that strike you as strange?"

Claire shook her head. "War strikes me as strange. *You* strike me as strange."

"And yet they were all listed in my father's files as living still. He even had their addresses."

"I don't understand."

"Neither do I," Richard muttered. "Not yet. But there's someone here who might…"

He lifted his eyes toward the schoolhouse. The children and their guests were all within now and singing spiritedly. Only one man remained outside.

"It's kind of cold out here, don't you think?" Richard asked as he and Claire approached. "I am sure it is warmer in there."

Adrian Rifesnider smiled at them brightly. "I rather doubt that," he said.

"You came back, didn't you? To Saint-Vith, after the war. Graves Registration."

The smile quickly wilted. "If you say so."

"The corpses you found, they were all Germans. SS men."

Rifesnider took a breath. A frown of impatience drifted across his lips, as if the two of them, Richard and Claire, were pupils at his old academy, pests.

"You've never been in war, have you?" he asked them. "Either of you? Quite an arbitrary thing, really. A shell falls into a foxhole and two men are killed. One of them appears to be untouched, just sitting there, thinking, though his brain's been turned into mush. As for the other…well, there is no other. He's gone. No blood. No bones. Not so much as a dogtag."

Richard felt the heat rise to his face; he could see his glasses fog.

"But there must have been something… They weren't all killed by shellfire."

"Animals. The forest has animals. And villagers, not all of them sympathetic, you might say, to the Allied cause."

Richard glared at him, at the glib expression, his prim, pouty mouth.

"You're lying."

"How dare you," Claire started at Richard, but he didn't let her finish.

"You found those bodies all right but you didn't report them. You did something else with them. Something…"

Rifesnider's smile returned, brighter than before, and steely.

"Perhaps that's a question you could have asked your father," he said, then turned back to Claire. "I think, mademoiselle, your friend was right. It might be warmer inside."

With that he left them, veering toward the trill of children singing, to the thrum of old people clapping along.

FIVE

It was as if the entire morning had never happened, not the visit to the cemetery, not Rifesnider. The children had seen to that. Their music, their vivaciousness and warmth, had made everything else seem petty by comparison, made everything for once seem worth it.

The afterglow of the schoolhouse remained with them throughout the ride back to Saint-Vith, at dinner where spontaneously songs were sung—"Skylark" and "Where or When?" and "Moon River"—and many spirits drunk. Spagnola tried harmonizing with Phil and Mary, coaxed McCloski into a discordant duet. Even the Major was seen to be crooning. Buddy, who ignored Kaye's warnings and drank too much, later needed her help mounting the stairs to their room.

Spread-eagled on the bed, he felt his shoes and trousers lifting off of him, sensed a blanket drifting softly onto his chest. A light went out, the room fell silent. In the darkness, in the peace, Buddy began his dream.

The bed he lies on is not the hotel bed—not polyester-stiff but satiny and pliant, mellifluous. He sinks even as he sleeps, plunging through strata of unconsciousness. Aware, somehow, that he again has his clothes on—not his corduroys, no cardigan, but a uniform soiled with mud. With blood. He has not been wounded, though, not even scratched, just tired. Terribly, immeasurably tired.

Deeper he falls, lulled by the chatter of machine guns. This is the sleep of the complacently dead and he vows never to wake from it.

But then the tugging comes. He'd been expecting it, of course; he has dreamt this dream before. The gentle pulling on his fingers, inching up to his wrist, his sleeve. The pull becoming a yank, hauling him up from the depths.

Surrendering finally, he awakens and sits up in bed. Just in time to see the child dashing, as usual, from the room. Only this time he swears he sees her—a girl. A flail of long black braid, a flash of patent leather. He finds himself crying, "Don't. Come back. Wait!"

He opened his eyes to nothing—darkness, the ceiling. His chest was heaving, breath short. He wondered if he were having a seizure, tried to remember if heart attacks were on Sorgenson's list of symptoms, things to expect in the final months. Buddy glanced over at Kaye, purring imperturbably as ever, and was pleased that he hadn't wakened her. Gingerly as possible, he swung out of the bed and found and donned his clothes. Tiptoeing, he slipped out of the room, into the grainy corridor light, and made his way downstairs.

He hardly knew what he was doing, only that he had to, desperately. His watch said 1 o'clock, and given the time difference, there was still a chance that he could catch her. The lobby was deserted—no Miles snoozing, no Hermansdorfer dawdling about. Only the Christmas tree and the fireplace alternately blinking.

And the phone on the reception desk unlocked.

He picked it up and dialed, charging the call to his card. Then he waited while bings and beeps resounded in the receiver—volleying, he imagined, with the fireplace and the tree. Until someone on the other end picked up.

"Allison? Is that you?"

"Who is this…Dad?"

He could hear Paul grunting in the background, asking if the call was for him.

"Hey, greetings from Belgium!"

"Dad, oh Dad, gosh…" He liked her best in moments like this, off-guard and again the little girl, could almost see her skipping rope alone again in their den. "It must be the middle of the night where you are? Are you okay? Mom?"

"Fine. Fine. Everyone. And, hey, good news: we won the war!"

She didn't laugh, didn't react except to snap at Paul who was probably tapping her shoulder. "It's for me, for chrissakes, it's Dad..."

And then he heard it. Behind Allison, behind Paul, a sound like a bubbling brook. "Lemmespeak! Lemmespeak!"

"Isn't she supposed to be in bed?" Allison asked, and though the question was not intended for him, Buddy answered it.

"It's all right. Put her on. Two minutes. Please."

A short silence, then heavy breathing. She was there, with him; he could feel it.

"Melissa?"

"Missy," she said sharply.

"Sorry. Silly me...Missy?"

"Hi, Granapple! Hi!"

"Hi to you, too, Miss!"

"Are you still there, far away? Are you still fighting..." She turned her mouth from the phone. "Who's he fighting again?"

"Nobody! Nobody's fighting. We're just having fun!"

"Granapple...I did some new horses for you. Blue horses. I even drew the hooves."

"Blue horses. *With* hooves. I am one lucky guy..."

"But you have to come here and get them. On your way back from there—that place. For Christmas."

"Well, now, Missy, Grandma says..."

"I don't care what Grandma says, I want you to come."

A strange noise leaked through his receiver, soft but unnerving. He knew what it was, of course, only he did not want to admit it.

"Missy, darling, don't cry..."

"I want you to come. You have to come. It's not fair."

He started blubbering, "Okay, okay. Listen, listen, I'll tell you what..." without any real idea what he was going to say, what promises he'd make without the slightest chance of keeping them. But Allison spared him the trouble.

"You see, I told you it was past her bedtime," he heard her gripe as she snatched the phone from her daughter.

"Sorry, Dad…Gosh, now we'll never get her down."

"*I'm* sorry."

"She was right about one thing though—you really should be coming here."

"Yeah, well, you know how it is with your Ma. Order's an order."

"Still…I didn't like the way you looked at Kennedy. I've never seen you like that." She hesitated here, held her breath for a question he sensed she had been formulating ever since. "Is there something you and Mom aren't telling me? If there is…I'm a grown woman now, a scientist."

Buddy affected his best belly-laugh; it barreled around the lobby.

"No, no, no secrets. No mysteries. Just your parents getting old. And as for Kennedy…you know me and airports. Travel is trouble, that's what I always say."

He lied through his teeth and it worked. A few more pleasantries were said, warm wishes conveyed—Buddy's for Paul and from Allison to her mother. Then Allison said that the call must be costing him a fortune, and he knew that there was nothing left to say. It was time for him to hang up.

"Kiss her for me, will you? Twice. And tell her I love her and can't wait to see those horses."

"Sure thing, Dad," his daughter, now with an edge in her voice, promised him.

"Right then."

"Right."

"Good-bye."

The pings and the buzzes returned, louder now but emptier. In the fireplace, on the tree, the lights blinked gaudily, forlornly.

☆ ☆ ☆

In the sink of his hotel room, Pieter Martinson cleaned his tools. The mallet, breaded with granite dust, the chisels rust-darkened. First rule of the master craftsman: take good care of your tools. Wipe them down and oil them every evening, return each one to its place. The fact that he was in Belgium, thousands of miles from his workbench, would not change that. He scrubbed and dried them, scoured them with a sharp wire brush—all exhaustively, lovingly almost, struggling against the tremors in his hand.

The shaking had begun that evening at dinner time, the minute he entered the hall. It had been a good day's work for him; the bulk of the sculpture was finished, and all that remained was the close incising, the sanding, the buffing. But the long hours outdoors, bending over, had taken their toll on his back. Returning to the hotel, walking crookedly, Pieter was not in the mood for some weepy old men gabbing about the machine-made memorials they'd seen at the cemetery, and the countless boys who fell—fell but never broke—in battle.

Then he heard the singing. It echoed through the lobby and for an instant Pieter wondered if some other veterans' group was just beginning its tour. But the young man behind the reception desk, though half asleep and hooked up to his Discman, managed to point a finger at Bayonet Hall, wriggling in such a way as to indicate that, yes, those were Pieter's buddies caroling.

Plodding through the double doors, Pieter was treated to the sight of a dozen hoisted glasses, of the Major swaying like a metronome between Alma and Buddy Hill. Everyone was there—McCloski, Rob, the Gimpels and the Confortis, celebrating. Billings tapped along with his walker.

There was another person present, too, Pieter noticed, somebody new, seated at a table alone. Pieter was sure he knew him—it wasn't so much his looks as his attitude—yet he could not quite place him. The man acknowledged the gawky parka-clad figure at the door, raised his glass to him and smiled.

"Easy, Sweet," Hollister told Pieter, taking hold of his arm, when he saw the mason's jawbones go slack. "Just pretend like he isn't here."

Pieter muttered. "Him…Here…He *came*." His muscles knotted, the color—what little he had of it—drained from his face, but otherwise said nothing. He sat, rather, and ate, and even joined in a song or two, struggling not to stare.

Only later when he had returned to his room, while scouring his chisel, did Pieter admit to himself just who, exactly, the new man was. He was the man who, one December day fifty-five years ago, sent Dean Featherstone down to Saint-Vith on an errand—an errand from which he never returned. Because of that man, Pieter's life was changed forever; he still divided it between before that day and after. That man—Colonel Rifesnider—now had the gall to greet him and even toast him. And he was staying in this hotel, under the same roof, this very minute.

Pieter regarded himself in the mirror. So haggard-looking, pale. A face that had, over the years of hard work, acquired the hue of headstones but none of the peace that those headstones counseled. An old haggard man blanched with anger, that's what he was, tremulously clutching a chisel.

☆ ☆ ☆

For the fifth time Richard turned and fluffed his pillow. He glanced at his luminous watch and listened as doors opened and shut in the hallway outside and feet shuffled unevenly on the floor. The older you get, the more trouble you have sleeping, his father once told him, and Richard thought, *that's it, I'm aging*. Pretty soon he would be just like the codgers at the reunion, drippy-eyed and retelling the same stories endlessly.

But there were other factors conspiring to keep Richard awake. There was the memory of Rifesnider sneering at him. If only he'd been a kid again, Richard fantasized, he might have knocked that sneer clean off the bastard, tackled and throttled him until he revealed the real reason he returned to Saint-Vith after the war. Not out of any sense of duty—no way, Richard was convinced. No, Rifesnider came for the bodies. German or American, Richard wasn't sure, but it had something to do with the bodies…

And somehow his father was involved. But why, Richard wondered, would Leonard Perlmutter have associated himself with such a man, and under what circumstances? Again, mentally, Richard searched through his father's files, through the photo of the stone farmhouse and the receipts from some Belgian bank, through Rifesnider's meticulous affidavits. Again he came up with nothing.

More footsteps outside. Old or young? Sometimes it was hard to tell. He was fully expecting Yvonne to show up, thumping on his door and inquiring why she hadn't seen him in the bar. His sudden coldness toward her was cruel, perhaps, but then again she certainly was no novice at such things. She knew the ropes, he assuaged himself; he'd be sure to tip her generously when he left.

But still he found himself waiting impatiently for that knock. *Don't do this again, asshole*, Richard finally and inwardly moaned. *Not now*. He punched his pillow and punched himself in the forehead. He was lying awake for Claire.

There, he admitted it, and he allowed himself to remember her: Claire on the bus, in the roadside café and the schoolyard. The ferrous eyes. Her broad, almost homely features fused in that uncanny beauty.

I've got to be nuts. A woman half his age and not even his student. Who couldn't seem to stand him much, much less be attracted to him.

Richard turned again fitfully, wrestling with the angels of his thoughts. Trying to pin them to earthlier subjects—graves, for instance, and names, to Tully and Barkin and Toth. But his mind kept creeping back to pictures of a pencil rutted with teethmarks. There were her braids again suddenly, her breasts…

A knock on the door. A woman's knock, Richard could tell, soft-knuckled, demure. His heartbeat quickened, his breath cut short in gasps. He didn't dare to move.

"Ri-shard…," entreated the voice through the door. A sad voice, husky with whiskey and smoke. "Rishard!" she hissed, knocked once more, then retreated down the hall.

Curled, a pillow wrapped around his head, he waited for the footsteps to fade. He lay there sleepless and feeling old, feeling relieved and lovesick at once. Yvonne had left him, but Claire would never arrive.

☆ ☆ ☆

Down another length of corridor, different footsteps, softer, shoeless. Another knock on another door, but no hesitation now; a crisp knock, once and to the point. And this time somebody answered.

"I thought you could use this," Alma said, and raised a bottle of champagne. "Helluva day."

She was wearing only a bathrobe, with her hair combed out and dangling. The hallway lights were hardly kind to her, especially now with much of her makeup removed. But the warmth of her face was undepleted, and her cleavage, strategically revealed, looked deep.

"Yeah, well, I reckon you're right 'bout that," the Major, scratching his bristles, agreed. Minus his cowboy boots, barefoot also, he looked shorter, barely Alma's height, and surprisingly boyish in his pajamas. Boy-like, he blushed at the sight of her, even while he grinned.

It took a second, but he finally held out his hand to her—an open palm on which she could lay her fingers and let herself be drawn.

"And good thing you brought that bottle with you," he said as she entered. "Reckon I'll be needin' that, too."

☆ ☆ ☆

In a different room, Spagnola lay thrashing. His dreams were like a roiling stew. Belt-straps echoing in the pantry, jungles where the parakeets were killed. A prisoner on his knees and begging, praying like a martyr for mercy…

Startling up in his bed, Spagnola threw off the covers that were twisted and sodden with sweat. He fumbled on the nightstand and knocked over the lamp before finding his glasses and his cigarette pack, lit a match and struggled to steady it. He smoked but the smoke was just another image unfurling, and madly he fanned it away.

Rifesnider. It was all Rifesnider's fault, Spagnola concluded. Everything had been going so right before he came, damned near perfect, and then—*pow*—the memories, the horrors. Like he was back in the support group again but without the slightest support. The mere sight of him had done that—that smug, self-righteous smirk from a man who was twice the coward Spagnola was yet never seemed to have paid for it, who left them stranded on that ridge when they might have escaped behind American lines. Men had died because of Rifesnider, he told himself, men had fallen captive.

Spagnola dragged deeply on his cigarette, fought to clear his head. In all truth he couldn't remember why, exactly, they dug in on the ridge, whether it was Rifesnider's lack of decision or the Major's eagerness to fight. In the end it didn't matter, really. He still felt the hate gathering inside him, consolidating like a ball of all the poisons his body had stored. He considered calling Captain Carruthers—he knew his home number by heart—but then saw what time it was, just before dawn, and realized that he couldn't, that it was too late at night back in Jersey.

Instead, he tugged on his socks and his trousers, his sweatshirt and bowling jacket. Flipping on his Caterpillar hat, Spagnola tiptoed out of his room and crept, gimpy and wheezing, as quietly as he could down the stairs.

Not until he crossed the lobby and reached the front door did Spagnola hesitate, wondering whether he might not be risking his health, or what remained of it. The cold: what if it was too much for his heart? He remembered those toughs in the black leather jackets, the punks who'd sniggered at the bus, and he worried about getting mugged.

"Aw, shit," Spagnola said out loud and heaved his bulk through the door and out into the predawn darkness. Into air like frozen oil. Spagnola reeled under it, a massive weight on his chest; he hacked violently and spat. But the paroxysm soon passed. He zipped up his jacket and yanked down his cap and hobbled off in a direction that he somehow instinctively knew.

He just did. Like a ball-and-chain, wrecking, knows which way to swing. He turned right off the town square, followed an alley to a broader road and hung left. Streetlights flared above the pavement. His footsteps reported like shots.

And there it was. He recognized it instantly, though the facade was cloaked in shadows, its portals sealed with night. The steps were time-hollowed and slippery, and he climbed them with care, reaching out to the archway which, he noticed, was no longer pockmarked with bullet holes. "Wha'dya know," Spagnola said as his hand slid from the marble to the worm-eaten woodwork of the door. Brushing off the front of his jacket, removing his cap, Spagnola entered the church.

The darkness inside was different—multilayered, mysterious—broken only by the candles flickering in the apse. He made his way between the pews, approached the altar and knelt. Only then, after genuflecting, did Spagnola dare to look up. He did and swept off his glasses, wiped the lenses on his jacket hem and, blinking, looked again.

A miracle. The stained glass window was completely restored to the way it looked before the battle. The peasant Jesus again hung on his cross, still crude and unshaven, clad in his tattered cloth. And still radiant, the first glow of dawn lambent behind his head, his arms outstretched to encompass the world, its horrors and its beauty, the present and all of the past.

What had he ever done to hurt anybody, Spagnola asked himself. Had he ever been so selfish or cruel to deserve the anguish he suffered as a child, the trauma of the war, his sterile marriage and unloving kids? His life might have taken different courses: a nice cushy Army job, true love, devoted family. But had he ever once complained? Why, then, when he finally admitted a grudge, some anger, why did it torture him so? Why was he spiked with guilt?

Spagnola prayed. Long and fervidly, on his knees and clutching his St. Christopher's medal, he prayed for the dead—his parents, his wife—and for his sons, wherever they were. For the boys who never came home he prayed, and for one in particular—for Eisenhower, groveling for his life in the snow. In twirling puffs his words ascended. Tears scalded his cheeks.

He prayed and another miracle happened. Dawn. All at once the window turned effulgent. The blue of the loincloth, the ocherous flesh, the scarlet—all rained down on him suddenly, anointing him.

He's a lot like me, isn't he? Spagnola realized as he raised his face to the colors. And if that were true, he wondered, if this Christ, poor and simple, could forgive the fatcats who betrayed him, might not he, Francis Spagnola, do likewise?

Latching on to a pew, he managed to get to his feet again. His knees hurt him, his phlebitis; his breath was coming in gasps. And yet he felt unburdened, strangely, and relieved. Spagnola almost felt free.

He crossed himself and quickly left the altar. He was eager to get back to the hotel, to get back into bed for an hour of shut-eye before breakfast. Out on the street, though, Spagnola chanced to glance up and saw, looking down at him, that same buck-toothed snicker, those slyly jeering eyes. Perched once again on the roof, the gargoyle bared its talons at him and laughed.

SIX

Spagnola returned from the church, teary-eyed, and heard crying coming from the hotel.

Real crying, tortured and shrill, it resounded out of the lobby and into the street where Spagnola, approaching, heard it plain. But he was hard-pressed to locate its source, even after stomping inside. There was Kuhlmann standing sentry by the desk, impassive as usual, and Hermansdorfer with his paunch and expression both drooping. In a far corner, beyond the ersatz hearth, the veterans had gathered in a tight circle around someone—adult or child, Spagnola couldn't tell—bawling.

Shouldering his way between Rob and McCloski, Spagnola caught his first glimpse of her. A dowdy, dough-faced woman with jumbo mother-of-pearl glasses and a frizz of red hair, no real neck to speak of. Late sixties, perhaps, though she dressed much younger—plaid skirt and tartan sweater— girlish. She sobbed and the guests gawked at her with their shoulders rounded, heads sunk. Alma plied her with tissues.

"What's her problem?"

"Featherstone," whispered Rob.

Spagnola took a moment to register. "Dean?"

"You heard him," McCloski said. "Dean Featherstone."

Spagnola was incredulous. Apart from her hair color, there was nothing about the woman in any way evocative of the young man who had been, by anybody's estimates, even Spagnola's, dashing. "What is she...what?...His cousin?"

"Kid sister," Hollister, leaning over, explained. "Last saw him just before he shipped out."

As if taking her cue, the woman wailed, "I remember him in that uniform. So handsome. A man already. Magnificent."

She managed to get the last word out before bursting into torso-wrenching sobs. She accepted another two tissues from Alma and Genie and dealt each of them a clarion blow.

"I was only eight at the time," she hastened to add to the two older women. "But *oh* do I remember."

Alma peered across the circle at the Major. Between them they had not had a minute's sleep that night, spending it on the bed, drinking, talking, retracing the courses of their lives. She had told him about Vance, her poor late husband, and about her bittersweet love of the job, nursing the wounded—those she could save—to the point where they no longer needed her. She confessed to her attempts to hold on to that feeling for as long as she could, traveling great distances, keeping up the front. She told him about the reunions.

The Major told her things as well—about captivity, the months in the stalag, the marches... They talked and at dawn they had parted. Tonight, though, there might be more, Alma appeased herself as she plucked another tissue from her purse. That is, if the Major's health held up.

Blanched, the veins in his cheeks seemed illuminated, and perspiration cobbled his brow. Sleeplessness, booze, had exacted a price from him, Alma knew, but none as high as the reunion itself, Rifesnider's appearance yesterday and now this, this Muriel Radowicz, née Featherstone, a widow of Dayton, Ohio.

She, too, had received an invitation, thanks to that bumbler, Richard Perlmutter. An invitation made out to her brother, that had bounced from address to address before finally reaching hers. Then, after weeks of deliberation, a day ago, Muriel decided to accept.

"You don't know how I suffered, just thinking about it," she whimpered. "I mean, who am I to barge in on you like this—you don't know me from Adam, right? But when I thought about him. *Dean...*"

"Oh, Jesus...it's okay, lady, really," stammered Pringle.

"No trouble at all," Morgan said, and offered his own well-worn hankie.

"You're perfectly welcome here," the Vicar added. "One of us."

"One of us," echoed Genie.

But the warmth of these words only thawed her quicker. Muriel melted; she flowed.

The Major glanced around despairingly for support. He was no damned good with women's blubbering, especially this woman's, like an oil rig gushing. It was one of the things he liked about Alma, the fact that she could deal with entire wards of wounded, and never once lose her cool. Yet when he looked to her now, imploringly, all he received was a shrug.

Which was a far sight more than he got from Buddy Hill. The one-time lieutenant was busy comforting Kaye who, in a kind of female herd mentality, was sniffling along with Muriel. So were Mary Conforti and Genie and even Willa Gimpel. Especially Willa Gimpel, biting on a knuckle as mascara bled from her eyes.

The Major looked again—to Phil and Roger and Harry Croker, to Billings. All were as helpless as he was. And the one person who should have been doing something, who was personally responsible for this mess, Richard, was hiding behind Claire, the journalist, as she scratched away in her notebook.

"Excuse me, please. Beg your pardon..."

Somebody was threading through the crowd, pressing inward—just who the Major couldn't catch just at first, and neither could Buddy, pre-occupied with Kaye.

"If I could just..."

The Major visibly gasped. The very man who had quarreled with Featherstone, who'd sent him on that errand to Saint-Vith, was now approaching his sister.

"Good morning, ma'am," he introduced himself, and took the woman's hand. "I was your brother's commanding officer."

In a tone as soft as talc, tenderly, Rifesnider hushed her. He swept a silken handkerchief from his blazer's pocket and dabbed it around and underneath her glasses. Then, in the one move no one thought to make, that was so out of character for folks of their class and generation, Adrian Rifesnider embraced her.

He hugged her fully, patted her hair and kissed the top of her head, all the while speaking in a voice just loud enough for the others to hear.

"Yes, yes. We all loved Dean. He was a very special boy. Terribly special, as you and I know. Yet there were many Deans in the 133rd, other special boys who didn't come home. Which is part of the reason we've gathered here, to honor their memory."

He paused, still holding her, but turning to the men as he said, "Honoring them with dignity, with reserve, and of course we'd like you to take part in that honoring. Do you think you can manage that?"

Muriel looked up at him through misted lenses, snuffled loudly, and nodded. She smiled at Rifesnider and Rifesnider simpered back before announcing, "Men, ladies, the former Miss Muriel Featherstone."

No one applauded. No one said anything. Only Willa Gimpel who clapped and cried all at once. "Isn't this *beautiful*!"

☆ ☆ ☆

After breakfast, the plan called for a walking tour around modern Saint-Vith—a pharmaceutical plant, a rehabilitation program for wayward teenagers, the factory where they made those quaint porcelain miniatures, and as a special treat, a tour through the brewery, an exact replica of the one destroyed during the war. Wheelchairs would be provided for those unable to walk that distance, and comforters against the cold. And a four-course lunch, courtesy of the Burgemeister's office, would be served—so declared Hermansdorfer, who was also leading the tour.

"Don't...," Richard began as Claire gathered her notebook and camera. "Don't go...yet."

He'd taken the liberty of seating himself next to her while she conducted her interviews, listening intently as if they were vital to his work as well. The waiting was torture. Richard desperately needed to talk to her, but he didn't dare interrupt, nor would he even look at her, for fear of staring.

But now the proprietor had made his pronouncement and the veterans were struggling to their feet.

"What I mean is...Come with me."

Claire's only response was a short, sharp glance that seemed to question Richard's sanity. Ignoring him, she set her eyes on Muriel Featherstone, across the hall at a table alone with Rifesnider. Claire watched as the former headmaster helped her on with her coat.

"Now there's a story," the journalist said under her breath.

"*I'm* your story!" Richard blurted out and then, when she glared at him, he leapt to correct himself. "I've got a *better* story. Much better. Sensational."

"You look tired," was all Claire said.

"Yeah, well, I haven't been sleeping much."

Just then Yvonne sauntered by, prim in her waitress's smock, hair neatly bunned. But her face, caught by the light, looked devastated. For the third time she held up her coffeepot to Richard, and for the third time he shook his head and declined.

Claire frowned, "I can imagine."

"No...it's not that..." His tongue felt the size of a lollipop, cleaving to his palate. "What I'm trying to tell you is, I have the story you're looking for. The one you *need*."

"Tombstones, bodies," she smirked, stretching into her hooded pea coat. "I know your stories."

"Body snatching, that's my hunch. Body switching."

"A hunch, you say?"

"I'm being serious, listen. It's something to do with Rifesnider. He was here after the war, in Saint-Vith—you heard him, he admitted it. It's all in my father's papers. The Army sent him to find the remains of missing American men, only he didn't find any—at least that's what he claimed—only Germans. But the missing Americans, they're still listed as alive!"

Richard had been whispering—hissing really, but loudly enough for some of the veterans to hear. They looked at him now querulously as they exited pass his table.

"Keep your voice down, you'll upset them," Claire hissed back. She regarded him peevishly. "What is it exactly that you are trying to say?"

"I don't know. Or I do know, I just haven't put my finger on it."

"Please," Claire groaned, and stood on her tiptoes to relocate Muriel in the crowd.

She'd lost sight of her but could hear her crying again; could see the veterans flocking around her once more, handkerchiefs fluttering.

Claire moved toward where the throng was thickest, but Richard grabbed her by the sleeve. The gesture shocked him and Claire no less. She glared at the hand restraining her.

"I need you," Richard muttered, letting go suddenly then fumbling for reasons why. "You speak French, German. Mine are rusty, both of them."

Claire hesitated. She looked at him hard, caught his eyes finally and held them. "Body snatching, you say…Rifesnider."

"Scoop of the century."

"And where do we find this scoop?"

Shrugging like a child, beaming, "Where I always find it," Richard said. "In the archives."

☆ ☆ ☆

The man behind the counter barely looked up when they entered, his face burrowed inside a newspaper. It took nearly half a minute of standing there, clearing throats, tapping on the countertop, before he finally acknowledged them, raising his screwed-up snout and squinting at them.

"Jah?"

Claire grunted "the nerve…," but Richard shushed her. He was used to this type of archivist, his ego inflated inversely to the puny size of his library. Saint-Vith's library, though modern and well-lit, appeared to be deserted.

Richard instructed her, "Ask him for the files for 1945. Births, deaths, marriage. Everything from all the villages around here. Oh, and police records—arrests, complaints, that sort of thing."

"Why deaths? Why marriages?"

"I don't know. Just ask him."

Claire translated and the archivist screwed up his nose even tighter, winced again revealing rows of pointy teeth. He closed his paper and tugged on the knot of his tie. Rising slowly, a young man but with all the vim of a seventy-year-old, he browsed through the stacks behind him, and here and there pulled a file from the shelf.

It took over an hour, but in the end several dozen dossiers found their way to one of the reading tables.

"What now?" asked Claire. She looked exasperated already, daunted by the piles of yellowing documents.

"We read."

"Read what? *For* what?"

"All of this."

He tried to sound businesslike, to corral the excitement he invariably felt in the presence of primary sources.

"Look for something unusual, something that catches your eye, even if you can't say why. A name, a date. It's difficult to explain... Just go with your instincts."

Claire simply leered at him. Her eyes narrowed as if to mimic the archivist. "Instincts...," she said, "*right*."

They read. Richard flipped through the documents, surfed them in the way he trained himself for years. He rationed his glances at Claire. In one, he picked out the swirls in her knuckles; in another, the mole on the line of her jaw. Her earlobes were on the large side, he noticed, and her nape, exposed while she toyed with her hair, looked ruddy. He could have studied her all afternoon, indulging, yet each time they wandered, he wrenched his eyes back to the page, back to his methodical search.

What *was* he looking for? Death certificates, perhaps, of males aged nineteen to twenty-five, reports of unidentified bodies found sometime around 1945. Looking for a name that might ring a bell—a Toth or a Barkin—or some indication of place of burial. But even if he found any of this, what would it mean? He still didn't know, only that somewhere along the way the pieces would start to fall together. That he'd understand suddenly, finally, what was missing from his father's files.

The morning passed, and the early afternoon, but without the slightest revelation. Richard had rummaged through hundreds of documents, through hundreds of lives—their deeds and marriage certificates, mortgages and wills. But none of them showed any tie to Rifesnider, to bodies found in and around the town. No city ordinances, no declarations by the occupying force, Allied or German. Just people living out their existences quietly, unobtrusively, in Saint-Vith or one of the surrounding villages, gliding over that one glitch—World War II—as smoothly as snakes over logs.

"Zippo," he slapped another file onto the stack of those already read. "You?"

"Same."

"Hungry?"

"Bored. I think you should buy me coffee."

They left the archive and hurried to a small corner café. Three round tables, all empty, and a stunted old woman seated behind a counter, half-hidden by the espresso machine.

"A storm is coming," Claire shivered. "Just think, you will finally get your snow."

Richard frowned. He blew onto his balled hands, wanted to blow onto hers as well, and signaled for two cappuccinos.

"You're not letting me forget that bus business, are you? Or what I said at breakfast. I was impetuous, okay? I was obnoxious."

"Impetuous. Obnoxious," she confirmed.

"I admit it. Now can we just...move on?"

"Move on? I would not think that is like you..."

He shook his head, befuddled.

"Your father, you don't move on from him. You have this thing about him, no? This obsession. It is why you came to Saint-Vith."

He laughed, he shrugged. "I didn't really know him very well. We didn't, you know, talk. Except about history."

"He never told you stories about when he was young? The war—he never spoke of his experiences?"

The cappuccinos arrived, delivered by the woman, dwarfish and plump. He crushed a sugar cube into his cup and ponderously stirred. "Once. One story. About something that happened to him before he went to Europe, when he was waiting to ship out in New York."

She went for her notebook and pencil—an instinct—and just as unthinkingly Richard reached out and touched her hand.

"I'll tell you," he said, "but you've got to promise me not to write."

Claire glowered at him, closed an incredulous eye, but in the end consented. "Promise," she said, and so let Richard begin:

"The unit had a twenty-four-hour leave in New York, a final fling before shipping out to England. He awoke that morning, my father told me, with this feeling. Something told him that he had to go to Grand Central Station. The strangest thing, he couldn't shake it. So, while the rest of the guys went off to get drunk and laid, my father, the boy who always did what he was told, found himself headed for midtown.

"It's a big place, Grand Central, cavernous. Thousands of people, soldiers, commuters, bustling. And my father doesn't even know why he's there. He wanders around a bit, totally lost, cursing himself for missing his last big day, and that's when he sees her."

"Your future mother, yes?"

"No—*his* mother! She's just sitting there on one of the marble benches. I never knew her really—she died when I was, like, three—but I can see her there anyway. Fat wool coat, calf stockings and clunky shoes, with a bag full of goodies she made for him—kugle, chopped liver: Jewish food. 'Ma!' he calls out, 'Ma!' And then she sees him and calls out too, 'Label!' She had that same feeling too, without knowing why, to go to New York and Grand Central!"

"That is where he got his name," Claire commented, lowering her cup.

Richard blinked at her. There was foam on her upper lip.

"Label. *She* gave it to him, your grandmother, not the men."

A pause while the logic sank in. "My God...you're right. Of *course*. I always thought that it had to do with him being the company clerk—you know, paper clips, labels. But no...Label. His Yiddish name."

Claire smiled; for the very first time she smiled at him. "I liked it when you told that story," she said. "You looked like this little boy."

He dropped another cube into his coffee and stirred. Anything to hide his blush.

"A lucky boy," Claire murmured. "I never knew my father. He left my mother when she was pregnant with me. Just picked up and left us in Paris. That is how I grew up. *La petite batarde Belge*, children called me."

Richard said nothing. He wanted to ask her if she had ever heard from her father again, if she'd ever tried to locate him, but before he could, she pressed on:

"They say he is in Germany somewhere, or Austria, working at jobs here and there. I do not know. He has never tried to contact me. He does not even call his own mother in Houffalize."

The dogged ambition, her toughness and her pencil-chewing—suddenly they made sense to Richard. "Hence your interest in older people—father images."

He half-expected her to laugh at him, to tell him to mind his own business. But to his astonishment, Claire actually sighed. "Sometimes it feels like I was *born* old."

"Older men..."

Now she did laugh—a short, bitter chuckle—before gazing straight into his eyes. "Now and then, yes. Older men."

The little woman came out from behind her counter, took their cups and smiled at them, prattling to them in German.

"She thinks we are a charming couple," Claire interpreted. "It's nice to see happy couples these days, she said."

He laughed, too loudly, and overpaid the bill. Like some junior on prom night, he scrambled to hold her chair.

"Such a gentleman," she said as she tersely pulled on her coat. "But you must not get the wrong idea, Dr. Perlmutter. It would never work."

He felt himself pouting, kid-like again. "Why not?"

"Like you said before, a hunch." Claire buttoned her coat and retrieved her notebook. She retrieved her pencil as well, and inserted it between her teeth.

☆ ☆ ☆

Maybe it was that second glass of local beer, the knockwurst or the cheese, but Buddy was feeling awful. All the junk he had eaten was waiting, he imagined, like a muzzle-loaded bomb to come shooting out the way it entered. His spine felt embedded in pain. He was popping his pills constantly now, ignoring the two-hour intervals, secreting them so Kaye wouldn't see—all with diminishing effect. The disease that he had seen all too clearly on Dr. Sorgenson's X-rays, that was giving him less than a year to live, was boring into him. Digging in as doggedly as the men once did on the ridge, so that only massive surgery could dislodge it—maybe, if Buddy weren't so dead-set opposed.

Or was he? Struggling to keep his attention on the young factory worker, a blonde girl with skin as glossy as the porcelain miniatures she held, her eyes the same watery blue, Buddy began to wonder.

It wasn't that he was afraid of death or of any sort of divine retribution. For all his churchgoing, his basic belief in a God, he never concerned himself with heaven or hell, preferring to cross those rivers when he met them. As for the pain, he simply dealt with it, period. Rather, the fear was of becoming a burden to himself and to others, Kaye especially. Those fears still hounded him, but then so, too, did the fear he felt listening to Melissa's voice on the phone that morning, her anger and her hurt. He dreaded causing her anguish.

"First we take the paste, here, and we combine it with the chopped-up glass," Kuhlmann was saying, translating with measurably less enthusiasm than the ebullient German girl explaining the art of porcelain-making. "Next, we pour it in the mold and then it is time for the oven..."

Kaye whispered, "I think you should go back to the hotel. I want you to rest."

"What do you think, Kitty," he replied, ignoring her. "Wouldn't these look good in our den?"

He motioned at a row of bonneted Bo-peeps, each of them hugging a lamb.

"I do," she said. "Something to remember you by."

At the tour's end, Hermansdorfer handed out free samples—tiny glass skiffs of the same design, Buddy noted, as the boat he rowed across the Rhine.

"How charming," Willa Gimpel exclaimed, and "how *generous*," before anyone realized that the gifts were only bait, tempting them into the shop.

Rows of pink-tongued poodles, of swans and Teutonic maids were revealed to them as Kuhlmann opened a door. Blandly, he announced: "A ten percent discount for all our special guests. Courtesy of the Hotel Ardennes."

The veterans, together with Muriel and Rifesnider, set to perusing the wares. She pretended to admire the statuettes, all the while plumbing him for information. "You said you knew Dean well. It may sound silly, an old widow like me crying for someone she hasn't seen since she was a little girl…maybe I am a little silly, but I need to know about him, too. *Anything*."

Rifesnider allowed himself a frown. He had stuck by the woman all morning, alternatively consoling and cajoling her, keeping the other veterans away. The last thing he wanted was for one of them to get a word in with her about the nature of his relationship with Dean—those special attentions, the nights alone in his tent. The errand. But even he had his limits. With her stringy red hair and formless body, those preposterous glasses, Muriel was just too repulsive, too effusive in her mourning for a person she scarcely recalled, much less loved in the way he, Adrian Rifesnider, still loved him.

"As I said, a very special young man. Sensitive, charming, and a great soldier as well. A boon to the entire outfit."

"I know all that already. I heard. But..."

"But what? What else can I tell you?"

A pudgy hand covered Muriel's mouth, hiding the lips that again began to tremble. "How he died..."

Rifesnider breathed deeply. He straightened himself, looking somber, all the while glancing about to ensure that no one was within earshot.

"I assume you read the report. Killed in a crossfire, I believe, on the first day of the battle."

"Yes," she breathed. "But is that all? Nothing more. It all seems so...sketchy."

He placed one hand on her shoulder while the other reached for his handkerchief. There was going to be another scene, right here in the gift shop, and he didn't think he could stand it. Leave now, he told himself, before it's too late. *Do what you came to do.*

"You must understand, dear, this was war. Awful confusion, every man struggling to save himself. That there was any report at all on Dean's death was a miracle. Fortunately I survived to write it myself, after my release from captivity."

"Oh, Dean, poor boy. Sweet Deany..." Muriel broke down again, a salvo of thunderous sobs that threatened to unsettle the statues.

"Will you look at this!" He picked up the largest of them, of a milkmaid with twin buckets balanced across her back. "Isn't it precious?"

Muriel ceased crying for a second, long enough to spy the price tag. "God, that's outrageous!"

"Don't be silly. My treat," Rifesnider said. "I insist. You wait here, browse a bit. I'll have the young lady wrap it up for you."

He snatched the statue and left her protesting, strode toward the register and doled out the last of his cash. A hefty price, but none too exorbitant to be free of her finally. Free of all of them—that stick-in-the-mud Major and that meathead Spagnola, and Buddy Hill, the nobody. In just a few hours' time he'd be far away from here, along with the diamonds he'd earned with his own hard work and ingenuity, that were due to him these fifty-five years.

The veterans, he saw, were absorbed in their pedestrian shopping. He buttoned his coat and hitched up its collars and slipped deftly out of the door. Undetected, unmissed, Rifesnider rushed to the forest.

☆ ☆ ☆

His work was as good as done. The weather had held up and so had his back, and after three days of solid carving, the memorial had definitively emerged.

Not a bad job, Pieter allowed himself to admit, stepping away from it. Just the effect he wanted, the textures, the subtle shadowing. Even the most delicate parts—the snake-and-sword emblem—looked precise. All that remained was the sanding and the buffing, and for that he had a special tool, unique in his valise, battery powered.

The electric sander wobbled in his hands, whining sonorously and reaming through his back. Still, it was vastly easier than doing the job manually, and quicker. For the first time since his chisel bit stone, his mind could afford to drift.

It settled, first, on the reunion, on what a fine idea it was in the end attending it, and on the men, how much he sincerely liked them. But then he remembered Rifesnider and the wobbling of the sander intensified, so violently that Pieter had to shut it off for a moment and steady himself. Then, again sanding, he resolved to think about something else. He found himself thinking about Meg.

There was the memory of the last time he saw her, down in the basement of his parents' home. He was already practicing his new craft of stone carving, because farming was too hard on his back. Down there, interred, he received her, and Meg did all the talking.

"I know what you went through over there—I mean I don't *know*, I *understand*, just as I understand the difficulties you've had coming home, the way people have acted toward you. So cruel. As if any of them had actually ever *been* in a battle…"

This was the new Meg Housen—the rebel, the speech-maker, hardly the exquisitely shy girl he'd known before the war. And beautiful: full-breasted, tumid in her jeans, a citrusy smell about her. Or was it pine? She frightened him terribly, as if the slightest contact with her—a touch—could shatter him.

"But it's not just them, is it, Pieter? It's you." She paused and swallowed the dank basement air. "*Mostly* you, actually. You're just not the same person. The war changed you—you *let* it change you. That special something you had inside, that goodness—maybe it's still in there, I don't know, but it just seems that it's gone somewhere." She held up two fists and opened them suddenly. "Gone."

Speechless, he simply stared at her. Her face had reddened so, her freckles had almost vanished. Her eyes behind her glasses looked blurry. Pieter couldn't tell if she were merely angry or angry but also sad, or maybe anxious to get the whole thing over with.

"I'm leaving in two days, you're aware, and I just wanted to say that I'm willing to give it a try again—a try, I'm saying, nothing more than that. If you want to. You can come and we can live together for a while. See how it goes. Don't look so shocked, Pieter. You know how my thinking's changed."

From her cheek and forehead she brushed away imaginary hairs, and scratched the bridge of her nose. The old code existed still, it seemed, only the messages had changed. This one said: *I did what I had to do—my duty—and now I have to move on.*

And she had, he later learned. Armed with a Ph.D., she took on Washington, fighting first for civil rights, and later still in favor of abortion and the environment. Marriage, divorce, a financial scandal in the '70s, nothing had stopped her. Last reports had her heading a senior citizens' lobbying group, an aged but spunky advocate.

But they never talked again. Word would arrive sometime, through neighbors, but then folks moved away or passed on. The country lane that once linked their houses was paved and sealed with strip malls. Yet Pieter always carried the memory of their last encounter. In the forest so many years later, sanding, he could still hear her footsteps ascending his basement stairs, a lamentable sound, followed by lapidary silence.

He turned the sander up to full power, grounding down his thoughts, honing them to the single task at hand. In the dust and the buzz, he saw and heard nothing else. Nor did he notice while, behind him, his valise was quietly opened and parts of its contents removed.

☆ ☆ ☆

Still nothing. Not even so much as a hint.

He heaved another file on the stacks that now towered above their table. They were working in the library again, Richard and Claire. The chairs were closer together now, their shoetips almost touching. They read, but superficially, flipping through the files, distracted.

From behind the front desk, the archivist cleared his throat. He tapped his watch and screwed up his snout: closing time, it meant. Richard's fingers splayed in the air, begging five more minutes, but the archivist shook his ferret-face, no.

"Damn," Richard muttered, and was just about to shut a file of police reports when suddenly his chin jerked backward. "Whoa! Will you look at this!"

He pushed the file at her, but Claire hardly glanced. She seemed absorbed in other papers, a file marked *Nees/Gedurt*. Births.

"What is it?"

"You tell me?"

With a sigh and an effort, she left her document for his. "It's a complaint of some kind," she told him. "Break-in and entry…assault. Of a minor, it says. Armand Bougilet. Orphaned, illiterate—there, he's made his mark."

"Yes. *Yes…*" Richard was leaning against her, unconsciously clasping her arm. "And who is the man accused?"

"An American soldier. An officer." Her breath cut short. She paused, gazing, then read: "Adrian Rifesnider."

"And the date?"

"November 15, 1945."

"Bingo!" Richard shot out of his chair and snatched the file from her hands. "I gotta make a copy of this."

Another spat followed with the archivist who, it turned out, spoke English perfectly well and vehemently.

"No photos now!" he growled at Richard, all the while slapping his watch. "The library is closed five minutes!"

Richard tried humoring him, complimented the filing system, the archivist's paisley tie. He paid double for the photocopy and rushed it back to Claire.

The stack on the table almost completely obscured her, but not so completely that Richard missed seeing her tear something—a piece of paper—from one of the files. He watched her quickly fold it and stuff it inside her coat pocket.

Richard saw but said nothing, too enthralled by his own discovery. Triumphantly, he waved the report.

"November 15, 1945, the day that Rifesnider left Saint-Vith. The day he resigned his commission! Don't you get it?"

Claire stared at him blankly while Richard rattled on:

"This is it, the lead we needed. Tomorrow we can buttonhole Rifesnider, confront him with the facts. He'll have to tell us everything." He planted his fists on the table and leaned over them. "Let's celebrate," he exclaimed. "Bottle of wine? Champagne!"

Schmuck, he reproved himself the minute he suggested it. He remembered what she told him at the café—*it will never work*—and here he was coming on to her again, flirting like a total ass.

But, "Yes, wine. A whole bottle," Claire replied, albeit without enthusiasm, with a surrendering sigh.

☆ ☆ ☆

They staggered in, feet dragging, heads slung. They returned, Spagnola limping, and the waddling Morgan and Croker. Billings on his walker and Kaye Hill with her cane, a stunned Mary Conforti led by a sorely weathered Phil. Three-fingered Hollister, the blind Vicar, and Roger Gimpel, his face a five-alarm red. Walking wounded, Alma thought watching them; they looked like they'd just fought a battle. It looked as though they had lost.

None seemed more defeated than the Major, wan and trembling. Alma positioned herself next to him, and not only out of affection, but from a genuine fear that he'd fall.

She whispered an order in his ear, "Right after dinner, buster, it's straight up to bed."

But the Major merely winked at her. "My thought exactly, sugar."

Spagnola also longed for his bed and would have skipped dinner just to crawl into it, but now he was saddled with Muriel. Abandoned by Rifesnider at the factory, the relentlessly crying woman had latched on to Spagnola, who alone could make her laugh.

"Knock. Knock."

"Who's there?" sobbed Muriel as she accepted Spagnola's handkerchief.

Spagnola sighed and gritted his teeth. This was all Rifesnider's fault—everything was, he concluded. He wanted to tell Muriel to can it already, to leave him alone and let him go up to his bed. But all that he said to her was, blandly, "Banana."

Dinner was a brief, mostly joyless affair. Appetites were low, suppressed by the five different tastings they'd been treated to, the beer, the cheese, the knockwurst. Though Hermansdorfer had his heart set on it, not a single hand was raised when asked for takers on a night of traditional Walloonian music. The veterans ate, they drank and griped, going through the motions, and hardly noticed Pieter when he entered.

He stood in the doorway with his gangly arms akimbo, his face uncommonly flushed. He peered around the tables and then, wincing as he bent, peered underneath them as well. Willa Gimpel waved at him and the Confortis pulled out a chair, but instead of joining them he merely mumbled—in Swedish, thought Rob, seated closest—before turning and exiting again.

"What's the problem, soldier?" Alma asked as he lumbered past her in the lobby. The Major perked, "How's the cuttin', boy?"

The two had left the dinner early, were already ambling toward the stairs. But now they paused and watched as Pieter plodded over to Miles. There, on top of the desk, was the mason's valise. He yanked down its zipper and opened it wide.

"Will you look at that!"

They looked, Alma and the Major, at the valise and then at one another. They looked at Miles, who shrugged.

"My tools," Pieter groaned. "Somebody stole them."

The Major rolled forward onto his toes, raised himself and glimpsed. "Seems all in order to me."

"Well, they're not. They're *not*! The flashlight's gone. My chisel..."

His face darkened, his eyes unnaturally bulged. Alma suddenly found herself less preoccupied with the Major's health and seriously concerned about Pieter's.

The mason jerked the zipper shut again and, with a surprising burst of strength, whisked the valise from the desk. Trailing dust and parka flaps, he stomped up the stairs, leaving the three of them speechless in the lobby.

"Reckon it's the excitement," the Major said finally. "Finishin' his memorial and all."

Alma told him, "Speaking of excitement, I think you've had more than enough for one night." She twisted his string tie around her fist and pulled it gently away from the desk, back in the direction of the stairs.

"Beggin' your pardon, Ma'am, but the day's just beginning."

"We'll see," she said, and patted him gently on the cheek. "We'll see."

She began leading him up the stairs, but after only a few steps he hesitated, and called down to the lobby below.

"And you there, Waldemar!!"

"He prefers Miles," Alma whispered.

"Waldemar, Miles, whatthefuck. If Colonel Rifesnider ever gets his prissy ass back here, tell him..."

Alma patted him again, harder this time, and added an elbow to his ribs.

"Tell him the dinner's on me."

SEVEN

"Damnedest thing. There I was an officer, a man who'd seen his share of the world, enough for sixteen lifetimes. But I'd never been a kid, really. I'd never really *lived.*"

Alma stroked the strands of wiry hair on the head she cradled in her lap. She took a sip from the whiskey bottle, then held it to the Major's lips, tipping it gently. With her finger, she herded a trickle of liquid back into the corner of his mouth.

The Major had been talking for an hour straight, hardly pausing for breath. No more about his memories of the stalag, the stories that had horrified her the night before, but now about other parts of his past, the personal ones.

About his childhood, how his mother's early death had left him with a father—"combination rattlesnake and cowpie"—who put him to work on the ranch cleaning stalls, shoveling shit, driving stakes for fences. No weekends, no holidays, just work before he went off to school every morning and again when he came home afternoons. "Drinkin' was the best thing he ever taught me. A ten-year-old with a taste for bourbon."

He opened his mouth for another slug, and Alma supplied it.

"Taught me how to fight, too. Or more like how to duck a punch. Could pack a haymaker, that old sonofabitch, specially when he was soused."

Then the war broke out and he rushed to enlist for it early.

"Snuck off in the middle of the night, never told nobody. Sent one postcard from basic, that's all, another from OTS, but I never got nothin' in return. Not even overseas. Didn't even learn the old bastard had croaked before I got home. And that's when it started."

"It," for the Major, was fun. Nights, weeks, lost on drunken binges, fast cars, faster women. An unlimited budget from the ranch he inherited as the only next-of-kin. He hardly had a memory of it, so wild was the time. He barely remembered Josie.

"A sportin' gal, is what they used to call 'em, knew what she was doin' between the sheets. Only with me she got herself knocked up but good, and took off for somewhere. I never did see her again."

He wouldn't have mentioned her, either, lying on the bed with Alma, she in a nightgown and he in pajamas—not the most romantic topic, another woman. But Alma had insisted that he tell her everything, unexpunged, and so he spoke.

"Year later, there's a ring on my door but I'm passed out on a sofa somewhere with a bottle in my hand, and by the time I answer it, there's nobody there. Just this basket with a baby in it—just like you see in the movies—and a note sayin' 'see the kid inside, he's yours.'"

A son. Wendell, he called him, Wendell Jr., which in time got shortened to Wendy.

"Hell of a kid. Gorgeous to look at—blue eyes, sandy hair. Right then I swore he'd have everything I never did. He was gonna enjoy his growin' up. Both of us were."

They were pals. They were drinking buddies from the moment Wendy turned fifteen, and not too long after that, whoring buddies as well. "He always got the pretty ones, damn 'im." Thursday nights, they'd pack into the Major's Dodge and tear down to the border, raise holy hell in some honky-tonk Mexican town, then crawl back on Sunday to sleep it off and nurse their hangovers and see the local doctor about the clap.

"Me and Wendy, best friend I ever had. Maybe my only friend."

Why, then, had the kid left him, the Major wondered. Just up and bolted the day after his eighteenth birthday.

"To feel his independence, of course," Alma reminded him. "Like his old man."

"And like his old man, Wendy enlisted in the service. The Marines, for chrissakes. And there's this friggin' war on."

On home leave, his last before shipping out, Wendy joined his father for one last bash—the best, the wildest, the Major described it.

"Matamoros was never the same again, trust me."

Then he was gone. Six months later the letter arrived. "We regret to inform you..."

"Of all the times I could have bought it—should have—and never got so much as a scratch. And he goes and steps on a mine in some God-fuckin' hamlet I never heard of and nobody'll ever remember. A land-mine. Wendy. My son..."

She felt his body tremble, the entire length of it, and when she tried to ply him with more whiskey, it simply ran off his chin. They had reached a point in the conversation she knew too well, the stage where her medical training left off and the woman still in her took over. Slowly arching, she leaned over and kissed him on the lips. Kept kissing him, unbuttoning his pajamas while the other reached for the lamp. Lovemaking in the light could be, at their age, disappointing.

"I could be Josie for you, if you like."

"No, just you tonight, darlin'. Just Alma."

Just Alma. A strange order to fill. Some time had passed since she had been with a man, and longer still since she'd been with a man as herself. How might it feel to be loved for who and what she was and not as someone else imagined her? It was going to take getting used to, she figured.

She felt her gown rising, the night air bracing her skin. She lay back on the bed and closed her eyes and thought of her name, sheepishly at first and then intensely with the first of his intimate touches. Alma, *her* name: she could've shouted it out.

☆ ☆ ☆

They not only shared a bottle of wine but, en route to the hotel, they stopped off and bought another. Now Richard was quiet in the way he became whenever he drank too much—quiet but whimsical as Claire held forth with her views of the world, of life and human relationships.

"Power. Money. Fame. It is all about sex. Everything is just about sex."

"Except for sex," Richard giggled. "Which is about everything—power, money, fame—*but* sex."

If she agreed she didn't acknowledge it, but merely sipped the bottle and rambled on, tripped and knocked into his shoulder. For Richard, the blow was simply sublime.

They stumbled into the lobby and almost physically into Mr. Hermansdorfer ambling out from the bar. He, too, had been drinking—port, Richard imagined—alone with his Walloonian music, was red-faced and low but smiled broadly the minute he recognized the journalist, and even managed a bow.

"Connaissez-vouz cet homme?" Richard asked him. He held out the copy of the police report, pointed to a name on the page. "Cet homme—ici."

He held the document at arm's length, grimacing. His eyes then suddenly bulged.

"C'est Armand!" Hermansdorfer declared, "C'est mon boucher!" He hunched his shoulders and marched in place, zombie-like, then squiggled a stubby finger around his temple.

"It seems your man is a rather large butcher," Claire interpreted. "Large and stupid."

"Yeah, but clever enough to go and complain to the police." Richard turned back to Hermansdorfer, asking him, "Alors, il est en vie…Est-ce que je peux le trouver?"

The hotelier threw up his hands. "Bien sur!"

He took Richard to the front desk, solicited pen and paper from Miles, and proceeded to draw out a map of the forest—the path through the woods and across the clearing, to the cottage of Armand the butcher.

"I thought you said your French was rusty," Claire frowned at Richard when he returned.

"Trusty, I said, trusty."

He folded and pocketed the map, said merci to Hermansdorfer and the boy, then reached out and took Claire's hand. Just took it suddenly, without calculating, but then he couldn't let go. The hot pulp of her palm, her elegant fingers entwining…

She let him hold it as they moved toward the stairs. Until, pausing, she said, "Not a good idea, Perlmutter." She drank from the bottle and wiped her lips with her wrist. "Not good at all. I have luggage."

"Baggage."

"That, too."

Richard ignored her. He felt light-headed and dizzy yet preternaturally focused. The unthinkable of just a few hours ago was actually happening: Claire ascending to his room. What might occur there he couldn't imagine, didn't dare to, his dreams were already exceeded. He simply kept climbing, as oblivious to her warning as he was to Hermansdorfer in the lobby winking at Miles, gloating at the promise of publicity.

☆ ☆ ☆

In short, finely calibrated motions, Buddy removed his shoes. The slightest jar launched shock waves of pain through his body, not only in the small of his back now, but in his thighs and pelvis, his neck and shoulder blades. He took off his socks, peeling them ever so delicately, and then, inhaling, held his breath for the colossal task of standing and unzipping his pants.

Kaye in the bathroom spit out her mouthwash and called, "Look at you. You can barely undress yourself."

"Been a long day," Buddy sighed. He unhitched his belt, lowered his fly, struggled to keep his movements fluid. "Kaye…"

In the doorway, framed in fluorescence, she looked spectral, her hair white, her gown milky.

"You should be home in your bed, resting. If you're going to die, for Lord's sake, you might as well do it in comfort."

"Kitty…"

"Don't Kitty me, please. It's not that easy, Edwin."

She had moved into the bedroom, clutching at the doorknob, the walls, the night table with her crooked hands, because she had left her cane by the bed. But she shook her head violently when he stepped forward to help her. In his skivvies now, hardly the image of chivalry, he stood aside as Kaye passed.

"I thought we made a deal. We weren't going to have this conversation any more."

"What conversation? Since when do we, the high and mighty Hills, ever have"—she raised her nose, her brows, in imitation snobbery—"*conversations?*"

"You know what I mean..."

"You mean you told me your decision and that was it. Period. Like I was one of your customers at the bank." She lowered her voice, imitating his "'Fraid, ma'am, your request for credit's been denied."

"I thought I was being..."

"Dependable. Don't I know it? Dependable Buddy Hill. Pillar of the community, man of steel. Just like you were at Bobby's funeral."

She did not have to elaborate. The memory was Buddy's most vivid: the open grave, the sun shining—irreverently, it seemed, for it really should have been raining. He stood through the service rigidly, looking tough. Inside, though he was fractured, a heap of shattered glass. The slightest jolt, he thought, would scatter him.

Kaye inquired, "Did you ever stop and ask yourself what *I* felt about it?" more softly now, tempered by her mention of their son.

Buddy lay down on the bed, pulled the covers over him. His wife was talking to him but his mind was still by the graveside. He saw the pastor close his book, the tiny casket lowering...

"Did you ever ask whether I was mad at you or heartbroken? Did you ever ask if I was, you know..."

She slid into bed next to him but immediately turned away and switched off the light.

"What?" he asked after an interval, in the darkness. "You were what?"

"Scared, Edwin. I'm scared."

He thought about rolling over and curling around her, two spoons like in the old days. He thought of hugging her, though he wasn't at all sure she would let him or that he could manage it, so enervated he felt by the pain. He sighed and settled for an utterance:

"Me too," said Buddy, "Me, too."

☆ ☆ ☆

The plash of water on porcelain was a salve to his ravaged soul. The sound filled his ears where his heartbeat still thundered, filled his brain still reeling with fears. His fingers were shaking as well, so radically that he could barely adjust the taps. The bath might be too hot or too cold this evening, but Rifesnider did not care. Just as long as it was wet and deep and cleansing. As long as it would help him forget.

But of course he couldn't forget, nor would he, for the rest of his living days. The night's indelible marks. The beam from Martinson's flashlight playing on the trees, probing for the path. The crunch of his shoes on the mulch. The cold, the unspeakable almost unbreathable cold on his face, and the sweat flowing clammy beneath his coat. Yet he floated through the forest as if in some undulating dream, gliding until he came upon the shadow, huddled and dark, in the hollow behind the farm.

There was no light in the farm, no sound in the night except for the squeal of the wooden door opening. He ducked under the lintel and entered a cold more thorough than the night's—thicker somehow, bleak. Kneeling, he shone the flashlight on the floor, its strata of crystals and blood. Somewhere, he believed, were the outlines of a hole, a foot deep, half that wide, that he himself had dug—he with that moron looking on—then covered with a plug of ice.

But he found nothing. Filaments of gristle, bone chips, a rusted iron nail. The hole was gone and with it, the diamonds. The imbecile had taken them after all, and Adrian Rifesnider was an imbecile for imagining otherwise. As much a fool today as he was fifty-five years ago, that day when he entered the cold house.

He had asked the boy to meet him there, their usual rendezvous. Only this was no usual meeting, no wordless exchange of human remains for dollars. He was furious, fed up with the butcher's son who he suspected was holding out on him, hoarding bodies for other, perhaps higher bidders, and utterly exasperated by the search. Six months he had been in Saint-Vith, six months since V-E Day, and while the world danced and began life anew, he'd lingered in this sinkhole, ferreting out the rotten and the dead.

Of course he made a fortune from it—Joachim and his friends were generous to a fault. Stashed away stones priceless enough to keep him in high style forever, to pay off Perlmutter and return to America a king. And yet he felt miserable. Empty, anxious, vexed. Of all the corpses he had found and identified, renamed and buried, one still eluded him. The only one that mattered.

What would he have done had he found his body, Rifesnider wondered, embraced it? That is, if there was enough of it left to embrace. Bury it? Absolutely, a sumptuous tomb—none of that anonymous military shit. A mausoleum cut from the finest marble with flowers endowed for years and room inside for two. One thing was certain, no former SS thug was going to get his identity, no matter how many diamonds he paid. No Hans or Rolph or Karl, no killer, would bear the name, the records, the life, of Dean Featherstone.

Frustrations. Finding nothing. Feeling nothing—Rifesnider remembered that now, trailing his still-frozen fingers through the tub. He remembered the numbness of that day in November, with the temperature outside already nearing zero, and far below that in the cold house.

"You've got something you're hiding, don't you?" he accosted the boy. "Cachez-tu quelque chose, n'est pas?"

But the boy just stood there, face, eyes, vacant of any thought, any significant intelligence. But he understood, somewhere in that simpleton's brain of his, he comprehended.

"Ou est-il? Ou!"

Rifesnider shook him, clasping his knotty little shoulders. He touched the boy, and suddenly he realized how long it had been, how desperately he had missed it. Suddenly, in the cold, in the darkness, he was touching him everywhere—on his cheeks, his chest—but the boy just stood there as still and dumb as the slabs of meat dangling from the rafters above him.

He might have gone on touching him, indulging his weakness, if not for that unexpected sparkle. From somewhere in the back of the cold house, beyond the carcasses—a refraction of the daylight seeping through the door. Very bright, blue-tinged.

Bedazzled, he left the boy and began moving toward it, pushing through the quarters and the ribs. The light grew brighter, it seemed, brilliant and then all at once blinding—or was it the pain that blinded him? The stunning pain that bored through his shoulder, so searingly that for a moment he thought that he might have been shot.

He stumbled out of the cold house with the pincers still stuck in him. In his back, through the scapula and in front, just above the chest—a little deeper and it would have pierced a lung, or wider, his heart. He groaned, spewing blood, as he pulled the barbs from his flesh.

How he got back to Saint-Vith—that was a blank. Rifesnider recalled being stitched by a doctor whom he paid double not to record it; recalled, just as his wounds were being dressed, Perlmutter bursting in to say that the boy had gone to the police—the boy who knew everything, enough to get the both of them hanged.

They had to act quickly. Certain individuals had to be notified, American and German, and papers had to be burnt. There could be no going back for the diamonds, unfortunately, not with the police prowling about. Though Perlmutter wanted to stay—he and his whore—there was nothing to be done about it. He, too, had to vanish at once.

Rifesnider twisted the star-shaped sprockets. The tub was filled almost to the brink, would surely spill over once his corpulence lowered inside. That didn't matter to him, either, as long as he could submerge himself, purge himself of the miraculous horror he witnessed.

The light—he had seen it again in the cold house, seemingly self-emanating, glimmering. He glided toward it, slipping on his wingtips. No boy to stop him now, no pincers…

Whether he gasped or screamed, he no longer remembered, only that he dropped the flashlight then groped for it madly on the floor. He tried to look once more at the light, couldn't, and instead ran headlong out of the cold house and back into the forest. He forced himself to think about nothing, only the tub, his ablution.

He was naked now. His clothes, rent and burr-studded, lay in a heap on the floor; he had not had the strength to arrange them. Listlessly, Rifesnider waited for Miles to enter—the door was unlocked—bearing him his supper. Pâté de foie gras and the house's best Chablis, the feast to be served in his bath. He would ask the boy to do that for him, and perhaps throw in a back rub as well. A gentle massage of his breast and shoulder, kneading the soft scarred skin. The least he could do for an old tired veteran, who had fought for his freedom in the war.

One foot dipped, then two. The water just right, as it happened. From there onto his knees and then leaning backward, slowly, easing himself down in reverse. Always the same routine: a ritual. Lengthening, simmering, he would lie and wait for his meal to be delivered—for deliverance, through pleasure, from the scintillating image of Dean.

☆ ☆ ☆

It was a new experience for Pieter, insomnia, a solid sleeper at home. Not exactly wakefulness but not quite dozing either. Something in between, rather—a no-man's-land. His dreams not dreams really, but fantasies. But the blood looked exceptionally real.

He was carving. Bent over his work in his usual back-straining hunch, shoulders revolving, head pitched, as his mallet pounded the chisel. Pieter sculpted apace, making good progress on the likeness supine before him.

Only the likeness was already formed. The stone was not stone but flesh and viscera which the chisel cut through unchecked. Scarlet blood flowed down its blade, coating the mallet, his fist. Skin unwound and bone dissevered, more pliant than the softest marble. Zealously he carved, not creating but destroying for once, and the likeness he defaced was Rifesnider's.

☆ ☆ ☆

"Steh auf, los! Aufstehen! Steh sofort auf!"

The guard was screaming at the top of his voice. That hawking, barking way Germans yelled, though the voice was barely adolescent. A kid maybe fifteen, sixteen tops, with a greasy uniform and an Afrika Korps cap, entirely the wrong color for Europe. For Bavaria or wherever the hell they were, laboring in a quarry. Twelve hours a day with no rest, next to no food, yet anybody who sat down was to be executed. Shot on the spot—those were the orders, and if there was anything this boy, this brute, understood it was orders.

"Steh auf oder ich erschießdich!" he yelled with the Mauser pressed to his cheek, the muzzle leveled point-blank at Eisenhower.

Spagnola tried to play casual, clowning as always, "C'mon kid, no time to lie down on the job. We won't get overtime that way."

But Eisenhower didn't get up. He could scarcely raise his head, yet when he did it was only to show these sad-dog eyes, the face not much older than the guard's but infant-like somehow, innocent.

"Eins…zwei!"

"Listen to me, you numskull," Spagnola, no longer joking, spat. "This bastard's serious."

He could have jumped the guard, of course. Though weak, a sack of bones himself, he was larger than the German. At least he might have deflected the rifle.

"Zum letzten mal, steh auf, sag ich! Steh endlich auf!"

But Spagnola did nothing. He didn't intercede, didn't reach out to the GI slumped in snow for fear of what the guard might do to him. The guard maybe sixteen and a killer already with a killer's pitted face, teeth black and eyes hollow, his mind blinkered by orders.

"Damnit! Eisenhower!"

He could have called for help, Spagnola. He could have begged. A man who spent so much of his life genuflecting, he might have fallen to his knees and pleaded.

"Drei!"

The shot sounded too sharp—more a *dack* than a *boom*—to have blasted the boy's throat away, yet it did. Blood and tissue sprayed onto the snow, across Spagnola's coat. Yet not a sound from the boy—no scream, not even a grunt. The only noise was of the killer's boots, several sizes too big, sloshing away, and of Spagnola weeping, "Why didn't you get up when I told you..."

Not between sleep and fantasy Spagnola lay but between different poles entirely: guilt and remembrance. He stared at a ceiling the color of dirty snow. He remembered returning to the stable where the other POWs were billeted and told them in a rather off-the-cuff way how that dumbass kid Eisenhower had been transferred to another detail. If the story seemed implausible, nobody took him to task, not even about the blood stains on his coat. No one had the strength.

But Spagnola had questioned himself, that night and most others since. Silent, monstrous questions, so secret not even his support group could hear about it, not even Carruthers. The crime for which there was no expiation, no release. Until now perhaps, in Saint-Vith. Here was a chance to do what should have been done over fifty years ago. But would he have the courage, Spagnola wondered, did he have the rage?

☆ ☆ ☆

Claire sat cross-legged on his bed, clasping her stocking feet. Claire. She swigged the wine intermittently, raising the bottle high to her lips so that he could watch her throat contracting. Her hair, unbraided, flowed in obsidian whorls. Beneath her camisole—the room was hot and she'd removed her sweater—her breasts were shifting subtly.

"And your second wife?" she frowned.

"Same story. Student. Unending insane sex at first, and later, equally insane boredom."

"You have a pattern, Richard."

"Yeah, like you don't." He took the bottle and plugged. "Your Berkeley dean, or whoever he was. We all have patterns. *Life* is one big pattern."

"I will drink to that," she said, and snatched the bottle back from him.

The bobbing throat, the lips lustrous with wine—Richard watched her intently, yet what he felt wasn't sexual. Rather, it was a sensation he experienced only once or twice in his life before, the feeling of falling helplessly.

She licked the corners of her mouth. "You sound like my father. The little my mother told me about him. Oh, the romance at first, the cheap dinners in Montparnasse, couscous by candlelight, homemade wine. Making love all day in his loft. Yes, she told me that, my mother, do you believe it?"

"And then he left her."

She laughed; again her bitter laugh. "One morning and she wakes up alone in their bed. No note, no address or phone number. Only me—comment est-ce qu'on dit?—a going-away present."

If so, what a gift! he could have told her. But what he said was worse: "I'm not your father..."

She appeared not to hear him, though. "I would like to be in love like my grandmother was. With a handsome soldier who came to defend me. They *were* in love, you know. She always told me. And they would have stayed that way, too, if it was not for this *fucking* battle."

Her sudden vehemence unsettled him. He wondered how he should react to it, to confront it or indulge it. He changed the subject instead. "Did you ever try looking into his family in the States—your grandfather's, I mean. Brothers? Cousins?"

Claire shook her head. "They were not married, you see. They never had time. Quite a scandal for the family—we are very traditional out here. They would not even mention his name. And then I came along.

First my father and then me, both of us bastards."

She gazed for a moment at her coat slung over a chair in the corner, and then back at Richard whose face had inched closer to hers. His nose almost touching her nose their eyes were linked and dancing.

Their lips moved closer to the point where magnetism took over and then, quite suddenly, they met. Careening around her mouth and neck, her cheeks and forehead, his kisses were beyond his control. Hers were furious, too, though less with passion, he felt, than something else—anger, perhaps.

They kissed, and Claire reclined to receive his body, arched her back to let him unbutton her jeans. He kissed each of her ribs and her clavicle, kissed her armpits before daring to proceed to her breasts. *This is really happening*, he had to remind himself as his tongue traced a line to her navel, as his fingers slipped under her panties and for the first time he heard her moan.

☆ ☆ ☆

There was no movement in the bed, not even the spontaneous fidgetings of sleep. No sounds, either, after the sudden, catch-breath grunt that had wakened her, followed by the long and diminishing breath. The hand on her thigh that contracted violently, furling like a leaf aflame—that trembled, then froze, and fell listless.

Alma lay there now, eyes wide and her body very still, afraid to move or to so much as call out his name. Because she knew that she wouldn't be answered. Because she was a nurse with over a half-century and three major wars' experience, and knew when a patient was gone.

She would go through the motions, of course. CPR, direct chest massage, reaching down his throat for his tongue. She'd grab his hair, slap and punch his face, spitting, *you fucking lousy asshole prick, you pull this shit on me…*

Then she would cry. Forehead rested in the crook of his neck, Alma would weep as she'd wept in the cemetery, for all the soldiers, young and aged, defeated finally by time. And for herself, perhaps more than anyone, she'd cry. Dying alone, with no children or grandchildren to comfort her, and no other identity to assume. Taken by death as she was so rarely in life, by love, as nobody but Alma Wheatty.

☆ ☆ ☆

A shuffle in the hallway.

"What's that?" she asked, and her body went rigid.

"Relax," Richard whispered. He had just removed her panties, had inhaled her full-woman aroma and was inches away from tasting her. "It's nothing," he said, and resumed the trawl of his tongue.

She clenched a handful of his hair. "No, it's not nothing. Something's happened. Go and see."

"Please, Claire..."

"You have to. I can't do this until you do."

With a groan, Richard got up from the bed, fumbled for his pants and shirt. He was still buttoning them when he peeked out into the hall, when he caught sight of the barmaid rushing toward him.

"No...shit...Yvonne. You can't come in here!"

But she wasn't coming for Richard. She didn't even look at him, but scurried straight past his door to another one three rooms away and pounded on it.

"Mr. Hill! Is that you in there. Mr. Hill! Wake up now please! You must come quick!"

Other doors opened, groggy faces in the cracks. In seconds, the hall was crowded with old men in baggy pajamas, baffled and murmuring and gazing around disoriented. Buddy was the last to appear.

"What's the matter? What's happened?"

"You must come! You must..."

They followed her as fast as they could, slippers flapping, tying up their bathrobes haphazardly. Up the stairs to the floor above where most of the men had already gathered.

"What's the big idea?" Rob asked around. "Where's the fire?"

"In McCloski's room," Pringle offered.

But McCloski was there as well, Golem-like in his skivvies and T-shirt. "It's Conforti, then."

"Not us, we're fine," said Phil as he shepherded his wife, Mary, down the hall. The Vicar was guided, too, by Genie, and Roger Gimpel by Willa as she whined, "I knew something would go wrong here, I told you…."

"Calm down everybody, just stay calm," Buddy urged them, though his face, pale and sleep-creased, was the least serene of all.

Hollister at last threw up his hands. "Then why are we standing here?"

"This way! This way!" Yvonne urged him. If Buddy's was pale, her complexion was chalky, her hair stood literally on end. "In here!"

Light poured from an open room which they entered, single file. Inside, on the still-made bed, sat a young man with his head in his hands and weeping.

Stan Morgan bent over him. "It's the kid from the desk," he announced, and everyone could see it was Miles.

Buddy held him by the shoulders. "What happened, son?"

Trembling, the boy just managed to point.

"Zere! He means here!" Yvonne was pointing as well, at the bathroom.

Buddy went in first, striding but then stopping short before his bare feet stomped on the glass. Shards of a broken bottle, of a snifter and some plate, glittered on the floor, in a montage of pâté and wine.

"Jesus…"

So riveted was Buddy by the mess, and so relieved that he hadn't stepped in it, that he took another moment or two to finally notice the tub. "Jesus Christ…"

Stiff, white as tile, he emerged and faced the veterans.

"What is it, Hill?"

"Whose room is this?"

Buddy offered no answers, not even to Kaye who just then trundled through the door. He merely returned to the boy.

"Tell me *exactly* what happened."

Between his fingers, sniffling, Miles told him of the order he had received for room service—Room 26—very late at night but his orders were to do everything possible for the Americans. He brought it up and the door was open; there was no need to knock. But the room was empty. He called out—no answer. "Then I saw the light in the bathroom. Then I saw…" the boy broke off in sobs.

Meanwhile, in the bathroom, gasp followed choking gasp—"My God! I'll be damned…"—as the veterans took turns peering in.

The guests were all crowded around the bed now, everybody talking at once. They parted when Mr. Hermansdorfer entered. Summoned from his home, in a heavy woolen coat over a powder-blue training outfit, he too, went to the bathroom. He grunted in disgust at the floor and then gagged at the sight of the tub, empty except for the water. The water was tinted scarlet with blood.

"Who is zis?" he came out asking, dispensing with any translation. "Who does zis room belong?" he repeated, but all he received was shrugs.

Only Buddy, glancing at the clothes on the floor, at the burr-spangled coat, the gloves, the scarf, spoke finally. He muttered as if to himself, "Rifesnider."

Pieter was the next to arrive. He walked sullenly through the men as he might through a conflux of mourners, to the bed where he knelt and retrieved several items from the floor—a mallet and chisel and a flashlight. "My tools," was all he explained.

Then Spagnola, shambling in, smoking. "A party, huh," he said. "Wasn't I invited?"

Commotion, confusion, too many people in too small a room, all of them jabbering. In the midst of it all, with Rob and Hollister, Buddy tried to confer.

"What could have happened to him?" Rob wondered.

Hollister speculated, "Could've slipped, I guess. Happens all the time to folks our age. And those sprockets are pretty sharp."

Hermansdorfer, joining the group, nodded zealously, "Sharp, yes, very sharp," desperately afraid of a scandal.

"Cut his head—you know how head wounds bleed—and went out to find a doctor," Hollister continued imagining. "You'll see, any minute now, the bastard'll be back with a bandage."

But Rob asked, "Why go out to find a doctor? In that cold outside...Why not just pick up the phone?"

Buddy kept to himself, however, only halfway paying attention. Instead, he scoured the room, examining the faces, exchanging puzzled glances with Kaye. He suspected that all the men were asking themselves the same questions: what in God's name they were doing here, at 2 A.M., in the boondocks of Belgium, with a serious crisis on their hands? And where the hell was the Major?

"I knew it. I told Roger that this whole reunion idea was loony," Willa droned on to anyone willing to listen.

Phil Conforti worried, "Do you think we ought to call the police?"

"The police," echoed Mary, clapping.

"Don't want no police." Billings raised and dropped his walker, as if to punctuate his point. "No...goddamn...police."

"We're on vacation," recalled Pringle. "We didn't come here for trouble."

Croker snorted, "As if we should give two shits what happened to that no-good sonofabitch."

The Vicar, pulling away from Genie, homed in on Croker's voice. "Let's try to get a handle on this, can we?"

"Police? Did someone say something about police?" fretted Morgan.

The ruckus mounted. A dozen old people bickering, a sniveling boy on the bed. The hotelier babbling reassurances, the barmaid with a bottle, suddenly, and shots for anyone who asked. Utterly distracted, no one noticed that Alma had entered the room.

She dragged herself, rather, and leaned briefly against the doorway. In a wrinkled nightgown, her hair a tangled morass, she looked like a ragamuffin. Her face, without makeup, was fallow.

Kaye spied her first and thought, *what hurricane hit her?* But then her logic dawned: Army nurse, combat experience, what better person for a wounded man to seek? She asked, "He was with you, wasn't he?"

Up and down, Alma nodded.

"Is there anything we can do to help?"

Another nod, this time side-to-side.

All at once the hubbub ceased. Silence, broken only by Miles' whimpering, clutched the room. Buddy joined his wife facing Alma.

"The wound was too deep?" he plied her. "The bleeding?"

Alma stared blankly now; she blinked into the bathroom light.

"After he fell in the tub and cut his head...that's what happened, we think."

Not a sound from Alma Wheatty, a half-shrug.

"Rifesnider, Alma. We're talking about Colonel Rifesnider."

She looked at Buddy, finally, and indulged an ironic grin.

"Not Rifesnider," Alma corrected him. "Not the Colonel," she said. "The Major."

Book Three

THE LADIES OF HOUFFALIZE

ONE

Countless canopies descending in the night, infiltrating the trees to stealthily gather—an invasion. Snowfall in the Ardennes, in December. Not the onslaught that had been threatening for days now, but merely a healthy sprinkling. Snow as there may or may not have been during the battle here many years ago. A soldier's snow: pure and munificent, silently enshrouding.

Through the night, the forest, the old man tramped. Hat and shoulders powdered, his coattails sequined with ice. He trudged, unhampered by either cold or darkness, the direction etched in his soul. He plowed through the branches to the clearing where the moonlight rose bluish from the snow. Past the shadow of the stone—hunched, foreboding—that one of the Americans had carved. Between the dragon's teeth, their blades now delicately sheathed.

The farm was not far, just beyond the trees. Grunting, he pulled on the iron pincers and heaved the oilskin sack on his back. The weight tremendous but no greater than many of the carcasses he had carried. Blood, as usual, dripped from his coattails, only to be absorbed by the snow.

He quickened his pace, chugging steam, huffing. Already he could see himself barefoot before his fire, with a cigarette and his bottle—rewards for his hard day's work. For his cleverness in protecting what had always been his, that nobody could ever steal.

All these years he had kept it, ever since the battle. A treasure more valuable than any he collected in the forest, rare and beautiful and perfect. The one treasure that he had not found but had rather found *him*, had waited for him motionless in the cold house. Imagine chancing upon it, just when he had given up hope. In the dark with the cannons still booming and his father dead, he was a scared and hungry boy, completely alone. A boy who had never known peace, only beatings, who'd always been treated like a animal. Then, suddenly, this: remarkable, powerful, immortal.

So he hid it from the Americans, from the officer who would have paid plenty for it, no doubt. Who would have stolen it that day he came to the cold house—looking for the diamonds, the officer said, but what he really wanted was clear. His hands were groping, lunging for a throat, but all they found were the pincers. He ran, bleeding, back to Saint-Vith, packed his bags and fled. And to make sure the officer would never come back, a complaint was filed against him with the police.

But that was a long time ago, the old man realized, though just how long he could not reckon. And now the officer had returned, together with other Americans, the fat and the lame. The officer had come back, and the old man knew why—not for the stones, but once again for the secret. Aged, enfeebled, the officer wanted the power. He longed for the magic of youth. And so he had to be stopped.

Through the last weave of branches the old man saw it, a shadow inscribed on shadows, a presence intimated by snow. The cold house he had always preserved, stocking it faithfully with ice, and that had, in turn, preserved him, kept him strong and solitary while others grew weak and dependent. That fed him while so many starved, and shielded him from the hands of intruders.

They were one, the old man and the cold house. The two of them inside one another, frozen. He gave the pincers a final tug, hitched up the sack and its contents. He was almost there, nearly safe, where forms dangled reverently in darkness. Where slabs of meat like silent priests tended to a glimmering altar.

TWO

Stan Morgan picked up a marbled cinnamon roll and examined it. Turned it this way and that, then placed it back in the basket. He did the same with a folded slice of salami, and then the potato salad, surreptitiously dipping his fork and tasting it straight from the bowl. It was like chow line in the Army, no place for etiquette or highfalutin manners. Take what you want and scarf it. Fact was, he didn't give a damn anymore, after all those years acting properly with the Postal Service, deferring to customers, to supervisors and union chiefs. Kowtowing to his late wife as well, whose people—housing contractors, big deal—had always looked down on him.

He didn't care. He was seventy-eight years old, functionally deaf and showing signs of degenerative blindness. It was 7 A.M. after a sleepless, shock-filled night, with snow outside and death upstairs, and nobody but him in the hall. And if he took a bite of bacon—he did—then dropped it back on the plate, who would be the wiser? Who the hell would tell him, an old soldier, what he could and he could not do?

Not Croker and Pringle, certainly. They came in a few minutes after Morgan, made a beeline for the buffet but then just stood there, gabbing.

"You call that an investigation?"

"Well, they tried," Pringle said. "You saw what condition that floor was in, all that pâté crap all over it. Then half of us bumbling in." He lifted a fork from the table and held it, sneering, to the light. "Go find a fingerprint in that."

"Still," Croker observed. "I get the feeling our host here—what's-his-name, Hermansberg—wanted the police in and out as quick as possible. Not too many questions asked. Bad for business."

He smiled and the lines in his face seem to deepen. Thin, symmetrical lines, like the kind he once sketched at his table. A draftsman, Harry Croker had been, an industrial engineer with a passion for exactitude. That same precision was still evident in his appearance, in the steely pentangle of his crewcut, the streaks that were his eyes and lips.

"Not that it's going to help him much," Croker continued.

"Not one iota," Pringle agreed. "Right after breakfast, I'm packing."

"Farewell Colonel Rifesnider. Farewell Saint-Vith."

They exchanged a look, fleeting but sharp.

"Too bad about the Major, though," Pringle added.

"Too bad."

That said, together they inspected the food. Croker lifted the lid from one of the heated tureens. Prunes were stewing inside, and Pringle bent over to sniff them.

"If you don't mind!" Morgan, unnoticed by the two of them, bellowed out from the corner, "You know how many germs that spreads?"

The others dribbled in. Hollister, Rob, McCloski. Some after only a few hours' sleep, most with none, long-faced and foot-dragging. Billings advancing crab-like. They hauled themselves to the buffet table as parched men would to water, faces stooped to the food. The couples—the Vorhees, Confortis and Gimpels, and the Hills, Buddy and Kaye—arrived, all shuffling. There was not much talk, only the clank and scrape of silverware—a strangely war-like noise—and the usual clacking of dentures. Spagnola showed up and Pieter Martinson, valise in hand, and a devastated Richard Perlmutter.

Only Claire seemed awake, ebullient even, buoyed by the stupendous story that had just plopped into her lap: the sudden death of one veteran, apparently in the throes of passion, the violent disappearance of another. Banner headline stuff, a career-maker. She would not wait for the diners to sit down, but accosted them at the buffet with her camera and notebook, her half-gnawed pencil pointing. "Tell me, Mr. McCloski, did you hate the Colonel, too?"

"Mike."

"Adrian, no?" She turned to Richard to confirm. "His first name *was* Adrian…"

"No, ma'am, *I'm* Mike. It's my name."

"Sorry. Silly… So, Mike, did you?"

McCloski piled his plate with scrambled eggs, stared at the mountain he constructed, then plowed it off again. "Don't you want to hear my life story?" he asked her. He reached out to spear some pancakes, but then allowed them to slide off his fork.

"Well, no, no actually. What I really want to know is how you felt about Rifesnider?"

"I was a miner, you know. Pennsylvania coal. My father, too. You don't want to hear how it was in the mines before the war? How it was after?"

Claire leaned over the table, tried to interpose herself between McCloski and the juice pitcher he was contemplating. "Rifesnider?"

"It was dark," Mike McCloski said and paused to cough up a wad of phlegm, hawking it into one of the napkins. "Then it got darker." With that he walked away.

Claire tried with Phil Conforti as well. He was helping Mary select her food, returning to the table most of the rolls and sausages she'd stacked on her plate, restoring them surreptitiously.

"Rifesnider?" he scowled. "Bah! You want an interesting story, let me tell you about the wet dream I had on the ridge. No kidding, a wet dream, right there in my foxhole, under fire. Now *that's* a story."

Claire couldn't tell if he was joking or not, merely putting her off.

"Or about Private Boot—good ol' Cal—our unit's first KIA. In the fields above Normandy, the kid sees some horses, big horses, you know, the kind they have on the beer commercials. Clydesdales. And Cal being a country boy, he says, 'hell, I can ride that!' But the horse throws him and steps on his chest." He squeezed a toasted roll, crunching it. "Calvin Boot, Killed in Action by a horse."

Conforti might have gone on, tale after irrelevant tale, but Mary at last interrupted him. "Answer the young woman, Philip," she commanded. "Tell her how you hated that man all your life and how you wished you could get your hands on him—those were your words, weren't they?"

She plucked a powdered cruller from a basket and dropped it on her plate, and just as nimbly, her husband shunted it back. And in the same motion he asked, "Sure you don't want to hear about that dream? It was starring Gene Tierney."

Roger Gimbel ignored her entirely. Willa, alone, volunteered, describing the former colonel as a nice man, "a gentleman," much like a certain McGeorge she'd known—"his *first* name was McGeorge"—who had also hit his head in the bathtub. "Would've drowned, too, if I hadn't arrived there in time."

Stymied, perturbed, Claire bit so hard into her pencil it finally snapped in half.

Richard tried to assuage her: "Why don't you just take some breakfast? We should eat and get out of here."

She gave him a wintry look, as if he, and not half the men there, were doddery.

"The forest, remember? The butcher? Armand?"

"You are still thinking about that? After all that has happened last night?"

He didn't respond immediately, not until Yvonne had finished laying a platter of waffles in front of him, averting her eyes before slinking back into the kitchen. Only then he insisted, "But the project…"

"My project is *this*," Claire stressed with a drum on the table. "This. Now. Not something that happened a hundred years ago."

Richard pouted. He felt ashamed doing it, but he couldn't help himself, his jaw and mouth drooping. But to his surprise the pathos worked. Head tilted, eyebrows arched, Claire pouted back.

"Okay. Okay. We'll take that walk later, yes. Just let me get my interviews," she said and brushed her fingertips across his face. That touch was more than enough for him. Snatching a croissant, he followed her.

They came and they ate and, in time, the men talked as well, in half-completed mumbles.

"Touching, I think," Hollister was saying, "the way he went."

Rob nodded solemnly. "Fitting. Very fitting."

"We should all be so lucky," Billings concluded, and the three of them shared a smile.

But Genie Vorhees wasn't smiling. She pursed her mouth and stiffened stolidly in her chair. "I hardly agree," she said. "I hardly think it's touching that an unwed couple engages in inappropriate relations, and certainly not fitting that one of them dies in the act."

"You've got to be kidding!" Kaye, silent until now, acidly cut in. "We're talking about consenting adults, Genie. Consenting *senior citizens*." She looked to Buddy for support, but saw his mind was elsewhere, and so turned back to the Vicar. "I've been a church-going Methodist all my life, but I say we've got to be a little flexible in these matters."

The Vicar's hands were wrestling. "I think," he began, swallowed, and started again. "I think it's a matter of conscience," he said, and the two women moaned in unison—"Come *on*"—and continued to argue between them.

Muriel Featherstone, meanwhile, made her entry. She, alone, had not been in Rifesnider's room that night, had taken a sleeping pill and snored straight through the bedlam. Someone—Miles perhaps—must have told her, though, for she was weeping with unprecedented intensity. "First Dean, and now this…" Blowsy, shoulder-shaking sobs.

But nobody ran to her. Nobody paid her much attention, not even Spagnola, who merely passed her a napkin. He, too, was preoccupied, staring at Pieter, studying him. For the first time since arriving in Saint-Vith, the mason had joined the veterans for breakfast, and yet he ate nothing. Spagnola watched him, herding his eggs from one side of his plate to another.

"What?" Pieter finally asked.

"Nothing," Spagnola shrugged. He sipped his coffee and scowled, "You'd think these people could brew…" And then, interrupting himself:

"You get your tools okay?"

Pieter leered at him. "Fine. Fine."

"Good. Good. I was just wondering..."

"Wondering what?"

"Like...what were your tools doing in his room anyway?"

"How am I supposed to know? You think I know?" Pieter drew a wrist across his mouth, swiped some nonexistent crumbs. "He stole them."

The face Spagnola made was incredulous. "*Stole* them?"

"My God," Pieter groaned. "As if those detectives weren't enough..."

In a huff he stood and snatched the parka from the back of his chair, turned and bustled out of the hall, across the lobby where he nearly collided with Hermansdorfer.

Though sunken, the proprietor's eyes beamed with cordiality; his chins were consecutive smiles. "Guten Tag!" he greeted Pieter but received no reply. Then, strutting into the hall, equipping himself with a coffee pot to personally replenish their cups, he greeted each of the veterans. Their reaction was no warmer than Pieter's. No depth of his fawning could appease them, not after that night full of terrors, not after he had them interrogated.

Assigned the task were a pair of cheaply clad, beer-reeking, plainclothesmen whose English may or may not have sufficed to understand the answers they solicited; who didn't seem that curious anyway, only in getting back to whatever bed or bar Hermansdorfer had dragged them from. Two frumpy, middle-aged cops who never took their coats off, scratching at their little notepads as they asked the same exact question, "Did you know zis Colonel Rifemeister?"

The responses were no less the identical: "That's Rifesnider. Rifesnider. And yeah I knew him."

"Did you not like him?"

"Yes, I did not like him."

"Did he have many—how do you say—enemies?"

"Didn't have no friends."

"Any person who would want to hurt him? One of ze guests perhaps?"

"Sure, but we're just a bunch of old-timers, remember? We can barely hurt ourselves."

The imposition—that was what annoyed them, and the implication. Bad enough dealing with the shock of it all, but then having to go on the defense. "They're only doing their job," Kaye had said in an effort to calm Buddy, to avoid yet another tragedy. "The police and Hermansdorfer."

"They could've at least waited 'til morning, the bastards."

"They want it over with now. Tonight," she explained as their turn to be questioned arrived. "We all do."

So the police had done their work and gone, and here was Hermansdorfer, smiling his false fat smile and pouring coffee as if it were punch, as if nothing unusual had happened, another festive breakfast. He smiled and poured and then he met Jimmy Rob.

"So, Mr. Hotel Owner. Mr. Mayor, what's next?" The much smaller, slighter man snarled at him. "What do you do with the body?"

The proprietor merely blinked; he tried to shake his head.

"Yeah, I know, you don't speak English. Still...what are you going to do with the Major's body? Have you called the embassy yet? Looked into next-of-kin?"

"Next of...vat zis you say?" He looked around for help.

"Brothers, sisters," Hollister offered. "Family members."

"Kids, you blockhead. Children!" With a stomp of his walker, Billings was on his feet, shouting not only at Hermansdorfer, suddenly, but at everybody. "Is this whole situation crazy or am I the only one? One stiff upstairs, another outside somewhere—I got enough problems, thank you. I don't need this shit."

Scattered "yeah"s were heard around the hall. "None of us need it," said Croker.

"I think..." Mary Conforti stood, suddenly, twisting her hand from Phil's. She declared, "I think we should all go home," and sat down again.

Buddy listened to these words with horror. Old men, death was again what it had been for them in the war—bad luck—a thing to be shunned, kept a distance from. Bad luck even mentioning it. He listened and could hear the Major's warning—*nothing unbecoming*—but felt helpless to do anything about it. Weary and sick, he wanted only to sleep.

"I say we pack up our things," Roger, at Willa's urging, proposed. "We can pack up the Major, too."

"Good idea."

"Pack up."

"We don't need no memorial service, thank you," McCloski said. "And no night with no ladies of Houffalize."

His words had the timbre of finality; no one felt a further need to speak. But then someone did, a frailer voice, cracking. Not quite audible at first, and only as heads turned, as eyes winced then widened at the woman in the doorway, did her meaning reach them.

"No next-of-kin."

Toddling at first, then steadying herself, Alma stepped between the tables. No longer disheveled as she had been during the night, but again put together, fastidiously—tightly fitted knit skirt, heels and heavy makeup. She walked with her face held high to the fluorescence in a faintly decadent cast. "No kids. No brothers or sisters. Nobody," said Alma. "Except us."

"I said we could take him," Roger reminded the men. "I ship things all the time."

Box him and ship him back to Texas, Rob suggested. "He'd like that, I'm sure."

But Alma disagreed. "That's not what he wanted. I think I know what he wanted and it's not that."

"What then?"

She blew and pushed the hair from her face, shifted her weight onto one heel. "You'll see," she said, "but it'll have to wait until tomorrow."

Protests bellowed. "Not tomorrow. Today!"

"I'm leaving."

"Me, too."

"Now."

Buddy didn't know where to look first—at Hollister or McCloski, Billings or Morgan—their faces contorted suddenly, masks of their former masks. Such anger, such disappointment. Only Kuhlmann, the driver, entering quietly and taking up his position near the door, seemed to enjoy himself, a smirk on his scar-crossed face.

Croker made to leave. "I'm going up to my room," he said. "Say we all meet in the lobby again, one hour."

"Hour's fine," said Pringle.

They were all on their feet now, all marching past him, while Buddy just stood and stared. His head swam in the din and the hall appeared to be spinning. Any moment, he feared, he might faint.

"Edwin?" Kaye pressed him.

But he didn't faint. Instead, "Wait!" he shouted suddenly, with an upward stab of his arms. "Wait," he repeated, softer but no less obstinate as he stepped in front of the departing veterans, bodily blocking their path. "Can we just hold on here a minute?"

Rob practically barked at him. "Let us by, Hill. Enough's enough."

"War's over, Buddy," Phil told him.

Still, Buddy would not move. His body seemed to go rigid. "I need…I need more time."

"Time?" wondered Croker. "How *much* time?"

"A little. A little more than a little. 'Til tonight."

Hollister objected, "No way," and Willa hissed, "*Do* something, Roger."

Detaching himself from Genie, the Vicar approached Buddy, stood almost face-to-face with him. He whispered, "'Fraid you're asking a bit much here, Buddy. These men are tired—we all are, even you. I think we should give it a rest."

"I made a promise."

"Promise?"

"A vow if you like. You believe in vows, don't you, Vicar?"

The blind man thought a moment, inclined his head, and nodded.

"I need 'til tonight," Buddy whispered in return, and then repeated it loudly to the others: "'Til tonight. If everybody will just wait here. Relax. I'm sure the hotel will make you comfortable." He glanced at Hermansdorfer who, the gist sinking in, bowed back at him.

"And where are you going to be?" Morgan wanted to know.

"I have to leave for a while… I can't tell you where just yet. But trust me, I'll be back."

"Yeah," Pringle scoffed, "Where have we heard that before!" And cackles rattled the hall.

Buddy ignored them. He quickly conferred with Hermansdorfer, and consulted Kuhlmann as well. Only then, after some agreement was reached, did he again address the men. "By eight o'clock tonight. You have my word on it. Now who will stay?"

The men looked at him, they looked at each other.

"I will. I'll stay," said Alma.

"I will stay!" piped Claire—too eagerly, she realized, and slapped a hand across her mouth. But Richard showed no reservations. He nearly came to attention as he cawed, "I'm staying, too!"

Alma, Claire and Richard—hardly the choicest lineup, not one of them from the 133rd. Without at least some of the men concurring, the unit would disband, Buddy knew, would surrender and march off, once again, defeated.

"You can count me in."

The immediate circle of Rob and McCloski, Pringle and the Vicar parted slightly, then broke to allow for Spagnola's shambling entry. "In the airport," he told the veterans, "this man saved my butt." He wobbled next to his former officer, and aligned his shoulders with his. "I probably should get my head examined, but I'm with you, Lieutenant."

Shoes scrapped the linoleum, groans rent the air. Someone lamented, "Oh, Jesus," and someone else: "What can you do?"

"We stay," Croker yielded. "But only until eight. Any later and this hotel's got total vacancy, y'understand?"

He did and more clearly than he had anything in the last few days, in months perhaps. Buddy turned and signaled to Kuhlmann, and the two of them headed for the door. But that's where Kaye was waiting, pinioned on her cane, implacably announcing, "I am *not* staying."

"Aw, Kitty, not now," Buddy began, not wanting to beg her in front of all these people. "Later I'll explain…"

"Don't have to, Edwin." She held up one hand, resilient if bony, while the other pressed down on her cane. She looked almost ferocious for a second, formidable, and yet he detected a gleam in her eye, that shift of her mouth he remembered from the mornings when she would straighten his tie before work, or evenings, as she slipped beside him into bed. An expression so familiar that Buddy was hardly surprised when she taunted him, "I'm not staying, you old fool," and informed him. "I'm going with you."

THREE

A flurry, that's what it was in the battle, Buddy mused. Doilies on the branches, lacy coverlet on the ground. Somehow his memory had deepened it, imagined huge snowdrifts and banks. Memory can do that, twist an event until you're not even sure that it happened. *That's what reunions are really about,* he concluded as the car wound its way through the forest. *That's why we gather.* To confirm. To verify. To know, just before we sleep, that our dreams just might have been real.

Buddy Hill stared out of his window, at the trees lightly sugared with snow. His hand was in Kaye's, though the two of them had hardly spoken, no more than the few words he told her en route to the car—where they were going and why. Strangely, she hadn't protested, hadn't scolded him right then and there and ordered him back into the hotel. Somehow, she had sensed his purpose anyway. Inclining her head as if to say, "yes, that makes sense," she continued walking, a half-step ahead of him at least.

"How much longer we got?" Buddy asked, reminding himself of Allison many years ago as a little girl, on long car rides, nagging.

But Kuhlmann didn't seem to mind. He glanced at the clock on his dashboard, then up at his rearview mirror, at the old American couple hand-holding in the back seat of his car. "Thirty minutes to the station. I believe we shall be on time."

He said this matter-of-factly, tonelessly, without any attempt to reassure them. Bare-headed, coatless in the car, he seemed even ghastlier.

The scar appeared to slash across his forehead, to graze a brow and slice through his nose before plowing into the flesh of his cheek. Glimpsing it in the rearview mirror, Kaye felt herself stiffen. Her hand contracted in Buddy's.

"Car accident?" he asked, leaning over the front seat and motioning at the scar—not on Kuhlmann's face directly, but in the mirror.

The driver looked up and saw where Buddy was pointing. "No. Not exactly."

"Hunting, then?"

"You might say..."

"How *might* I say?" Insistence now girded his voice, one of the handier inflections Buddy had perfected, dealing with debtors at the bank.

Kuhlmann understood this—there was no escape—and begrudged his passenger a sigh. "In the war. It is from the war."

"World War Two?"

"There has not been another. Not here."

"But you must have been a kid back then. A civilian."

"A kid, yes," the scarred man said as his hands made fists on the wheel. "But a ci-vi-lian?"—he pronounced it carefully—"No."

The war was ending. Everybody knew that, though the Americans had yet to cross into Germany. It was over. *Kaput*, Kuhlmann said. But then the soldiers came, SS, and told them that everyone must fight. For the Fuhrer. For the Fatherland. Anyone who could carry a gun. "They did not have to force me. I wanted to go."

"But Germany," Buddy pressed him. "*Nazi* Germany."

"I hated the French. We all hated the French—my father, *his* father. And I liked Germany. I won't lie. Many people do, but not me. I liked Hitler. But what did I know?" The driver almost laughed. "I was only fifteen!"

Only fifteen but they stuck a uniform on him—pieces of uniform—and gave him a gun, teaching him how to shoot it, to use the bayonet and toss a dummy grenade. Two weeks of training before the battle. Then there they were, crouching in the darkness, in the forest as the shells growled and shrieked overhead. A sergeant, grizzled veteran of the Russian front, went bandying between them, making sure their rifles were unlocked, helmets buckled, imparting last words of advice.

"He pinched my cheek. '*Kind*,' he said, 'You stay right behind me. Keep your head low and stop for nobody. Nobody, you hear.'"

A whistle blew. The command—*vorwärts*! Suddenly, everyone was on their feet—teenagers, pensioners, the scattering of real soldiers among them—moving fast through the trees, between the tank traps. Marching on an objective they did not know, could not see. Tough going at first, what with the branches, the too-big boots and the trousers that kept creeping up his backside. He tried to remember to keep his rifle hip-height, muzzle down, to walk head up but hunched, all the while struggling to stay behind that sergeant whose name he no longer remembered.

All at once, they were out of the forest and crossing a clearing. Beautiful, fog-swept and shimmering, silent except for the faint jangle of gear and buckles, of boots padding and labored breath. He would have liked to have paused for a moment, dropping to one knee to admire the stars peeking through the clouds and inhale the tart piney air. But the line was moving still, moving faster, and it took all his energy just to stay close to the sergeant, the nimbus of his figure in the mist.

Bright flickering sparks broke in the darkness in front of them. Sparks that turned to fire and leaped out at them, tore through them. He heard screams, saw people in the point line collapse. "*Vorwärts*! *Vorwärts*!!" some officer was howling, but he could barely hear him, for all the machine guns chattering, the grenade blasts.

"The sergeant, the sergeant, I was telling myself, over and over. Stay with him."

And he did, advancing toward some elevated position where the enemy was dug in and firing. Until the sergeant suddenly crumbled and fell.

"I ran to him but could not help him. He did not have any…" He paused, took note of Kaye, open-mouthed, in the mirror. "He was dead."

He remained by the sergeant's body, crying, as the unit stumbled a few sorry meters more, into the wall of fire. Some of the soldiers had begun to fall back, though, against orders. First two or three, then all of them, scurrying for their lives, dying even in retreat.

He felt someone tugging on his coat. Someone urging him to run for it. It took him a moment to snap to, to realize that he had to leave the sergeant now and save his own life. He pulled himself to his feet, started to turn and then…"

"And then?" Buddy pressed.

"How is it called, a bullet that hits something hard—a rock—and flies up?"

"Ricochet."

"Ah, like the French. Ricochet, yes. You see what it did," Kuhlmann said and raised his face to the mirror.

They had left him for dead, face-down and motionless in the blood-sodden snow. Not until the next attack, the next wave charging and repulsed, did someone—he never learned who—notice that he was breathing still and haul him back through the woods.

They sutured him, stitched him, gave him a pill of some sort to kill the pain, totally useless. They told him to report to his unit, that he could walk, fire a rifle, fight. But he'd had his fill of battle. Escaping in the confusion, he made it to Saint-Vith—what was left of it—found his family and hid with them in a coal cellar for ten straight days, while the war rumbled over their heads.

"Let me get this straight," said Buddy Hill. "That's who we were fighting, a bunch of old guys and kids?"

"Edwin, please," Kaye reproached him. She pinched his wrist, a clear sign that she wanted the subject changed.

He hissed back, "Hold it, Kitty," and returned to Kuhlmann. "Kids and old guys, that's who my outfit surrendered to?"

The driver smiled—for the first time. "Many of us, yes."

Buddy mulled this over, massaging his chin. "Don't say," he muttered and ended his pondering with a shrug. "Sorry about that wound of yours, then. Nothing personal."

"No, nothing personal, of course," Kuhlmann repeated. "I would have done the same to you."

An icy moment ensued, stares gelling in the mirror. Kaye pinched his wrist again, harder now, but Buddy would not react. An entire second passed before the former banker emitted a sound that Kaye was not quite sure she recognized. A raspy, clipped, coughing noise, as if some object were clogging his throat. Another second until Kaye realized that he wasn't choking but laughing—dry, bitter laughter—and that Kuhlmann was laughing too.

They drove like that, through the snow-dusted pines, the macadam slick now with meltage, the remainder of the distance to the train station. Kaye, relaxing finally, sunk her head on her husband's shoulder. The engine whirred and the old men prattled, improbably lulling her to sleep.

☆ ☆ ☆

Richard glowered at her. For over an hour now, while his third cup of coffee went cold, Claire had been interviewing yet another veteran. Or not so much interviewing as listening inertly as he ignored her questions about Rifesnider and repeated the same sclerotic stories of how life had screwed Harold Billings.

There was the marriage that hadn't amounted to much ("Not what you'd call love at first sight, or last"), the son and the daughter who never appreciated the good things they had or learned the meaning of hard work; the failed businesses—a hardware store, wholesaling carpets, the car rental franchise—that were always the fault of stingy creditors and tardy suppliers, bad timing and the economy. Rapacious lawyers were a particular object of hate, rapacious doctors too once the illnesses set in.

"They tell you life is a game, but I say to hell with that. Games you sometimes win."

And then the most harrowing loss of all, his hair, what had been, for Billings, a talisman, a source of consolation. Thick and wavy once, it had withered and shed, exposing moles and warts that he never imagined hiding there. Hairlessness: more than the strokes, worse than the walker, this was his ultimate defeat.

"You know what?" He pushed his face close to Claire's.

"No, Mr. Billings, what?"

"Everybody tells you how rough it was on that ridge. No heat, no sleep, Jerries attacking us day and night, a living hell. Well, I got a secret for you, lady..."

He peered conspiratorially around the hall. Except for Alma and Pringle, seated far from each other, each in a separate world, the place was empty. The others had gone back to their rooms to sleep the day away, waiting for Buddy to return.

"Yes?"

"I'd go back there in a second," Billings confided. "Just to be young and strong on that ridge again, full head of hair 'neath my helmet."

He took hold of his walker and, with the sum of his bitterness, hoisted himself up. "One second, that's all I want, and trash everything since."

"Edifying," Richard remarked as Billings teetered off. "Is that enough for your story yet? Can we get to the *real* story now?"

But Claire scarcely acknowledged him. She was already staring at Alma, already formulating her questions. She would have to move quickly, she realized; the old nurse had finished her coffee and was about to get up from her table. Claire rose first and hustled toward her, a predatory gait that was not quite a run but no saunter either, a trajectory that would place her between Alma and the door.

"Mrs. Wheatty. Madam..."

Alma turned sharply. A look of annoyance plied across her face, towing a saccharin smile. "Wasting your time with me, Miss."

"You knew him." She was already reaching for her notebook. "You knew the Major well."

Alma looked off; her smile was distant too. "No, not very well."

She shook her head, shrugging slightly, as if to banish a thought. "But why are we talking about death? Things past? Here..." She snatched the pencil from Claire's grip, snatched her notebook as well and flipped it shut before handing them both to Richard. "Go outside, you two, take a walk. Live."

"You heard the lady," Richard remarked. "Nurse's orders."

Claire appeared to have heard nothing—not Alma, not him—and showed every sign of staying for one more interview at least. Richard studied her, her beauty accentuated, he thought, by her lack of sleep and her dishevelment. Was her mood more than just a product of her frustration, her confusion over her relationship with yet another, much older, man? He remembered the document. Torn from its file and stuffed in her pocket—perhaps that was the source of her funk.

He thought about confronting her outright, demanding to read what she had taken, but the opportunity passed. Already she was heading across the hall, pen and notebook poised—and already he was following her—toward Pringle.

☆ ☆ ☆

Not forests and hamlets anymore, but a gray industrial blur sped outside his window, broken only intermittently by the burst of a passing freight. *People don't ride on trains they way they used to*, Buddy silently observed. Once he had crossed the continental United States in one, a troop train, three straight days and nights, and his teeth felt loose when it halted. Once trains were in their lives, in their music: *can't you hear the whistle, blowin' down the trestle, oowee*—in the rhythm, eight-to-the-bar—*a clickety-clack echoing back the blues*. Perhaps, he considered, he had lived too long after all, belonged to a different world that few folks nowadays could relate to, with their e-mail and satellite dishes, their instant communication that left them no time whatsoever to talk. His was a lost world, simple with its goods and bads, its comforting finality. Buddy watched the blight flash past and found that his foot was tapping, a melody jingling in his head. *Breakfast in the diner, notheing could be finer than to have your ham-n'-eggs in Carolina*.

The melody, the motion, kept him from fixating on his pain. A solid rod of it now radiated from his hips to his shoulders. Nauseated, dizzy, he almost missed the little man with the hydraulic drill he once imagined boring into his spine, missed the Major's face grinning at him. He said face grinning at him. He said none of this to Kaye, though, never complained even as the carriage jerked and rumbled. Rather, he looked at her and smiled and held that smile until she glanced up from her magazine and returned it. There was peace in this moment, the two of them embarked on a journey of substance, however uncertain its goal, and he did not want to spoil it. As long as they kept going, he thought, they'd never have to stop.

He closed his eyes but tried not to sleep, knowing that he would only be yanked awake again by some phantom hand and forced to fight on in the world. All was white behind his lids, and he imagined a countryside brightly mantled with snow. He heard the tracks' rattle, like the distant crackle of gunfire…

"A volunteer! We need a volunteer!" Buddy heard someone shout. The Major. And he heard himself answering. "What's wrong?"

"Papino. Goddamnit. His feet…"

Lt. Hill peered above his foxhole. Tentatively, painfully, like an infant emerging at birth, he blinked into the raw winter light. An hour had passed since the last assault, three hours since the one before that. Sniper fire still pinged through the trees. Around him the ridge looked hellish, littered with shit and shell casings, smoking craters and body parts. A nightmare, it seemed a miracle that any of them were still alive, himself included.

"How bad?"

"Bad. Frozen solid. We've gotta get him out of here."

Buddy was half ice himself, and the other half aching bones and muscle. Still, he managed to run doubled over, skidding, to Pappy's position. He found the sergeant crouched in his hole, propped up on his gun. Snot icicles dangled from his moustache, and an unlit cigar from his teeth. His face had gone ghostly white.

"What's the problem, sergeant?" Buddy asked as he rolled into the foxhole beside him.

Pappy motioned to his boots and Buddy could see the leather, the laces, grotesquely stretched.

"No way, lieutenant, I ain't leaving."

Buddy felt his stomach turn. While the men might have liked him some and vaguely admired the Major, Pappy they respected. Pappy they revered. Without him, the outfit was sunk.

"Stay and you're *not* leaving," Buddy told him. "Ever."

"I ain't going," the noncom repeated. He squirmed to the lip of the foxhole, twisted his torso and aimed his gun at the meadow.

"Don't be stupid," Buddy said quietly as he pulled him back into the hole. "Ho, Major," he hollered, "I'm with Pappy! I'm taking him!"

The answer echoed, "Just get your ass back here on the double, Hill. We need you."

"Roger."

With God-knows-what power, Buddy dragged Pappy to his feet and draped one of the sergeant's arms over his shoulder. To the men on the ridge, Buddy shouted, "Cover me!"

The ridge erupted with M-1 and machine gun fire. The meadow geysered with dirt. "Say hi to the ladies for me, Pappy!" one soldier cheered from his foxhole, and then another, "Hey, Pappy, don't forget to write!" And even from the far end of the meadow, some Germans chanted, "Pah-py! Pah-py!"

Together, limping, Buddy and Pappy began their descent down the ridge. Before them was the forest, a few hundred yards of it, and beyond that the ruins of Saint-Vith. Whether any of it was still in GI hands, he had no way of knowing, only that he had to deliver Pappy to a field station and then hustle back, all without getting himself shot.

"This is suicide. You know that, Lieutenant."

"Just shut your face and help me here. Shit, you weigh a ton."

They lumbered, a three-legged man, through the trees as shrapnel whizzed through the branches. A hundred yards on, the forest thinned out to a field. Through the snow-laced gusts, Buddy could see the village in front of him, a gray and smoking form. He grasped Pappy tight around the shoulder, lowered his head, and pressed on. Suddenly the sergeant yanked him to the ground. He pushed Buddy into a drainage ditch flowing with semi-solid muck.

Buddy glared at him, "What the f..." only to have Pappy's hand clamp over his mouth. The sergeant's finger pointed upward before lightly touching his lips. The lips formed the word: *Krauts*.

Buddy did not understand at first, not until he heard the crunch of hobnail boots. They passed right above them, inconceivably missing them, blinded, perhaps, by the wind. A patrol of five in white winter camouflage, bunched together, incautious. Buddy reached for his webbelt and unhitched a grenade. He started to pull the pin.

Once again, Pappy's hand stopped him. It snatched the grenade away. "No!" Pappy nodded, and for a moment Buddy was furious. Damn if he were going to die and not take a few of those bastards with him.

"I coulda got 'em," Buddy hissed when the patrol had passed. "One grenade, the Thompson."

"Yeah, and if the grenade missed? Thompson jammed?" Pappy chided him, treated him to a green-toothed grin. If lower in rank, he was older than Buddy by a year or two, had survived Sicily and North Africa and before that, growing up in the Bronx. "You said we had a chance, remember? I kind of like to have it."

Drenched, mud-covered and shivering, they emerged from the ditch and continued toward the village. Pappy could barely walk now, totally numb below the ankles, and Buddy had to carry him. Between the smoldering houses, down the cratered, churned-up streets, they slipped from alley to alley, pausing behind the rubble to check if the way was clear. Until Buddy spied some wounded men—Americans—on stretchers being borne into a church.

Hit repeatedly by 88s, its ceiling collapsed and stained glass windows shattered, the church was hardly more than a ruin itself. The crypt, though, still provided shelter, and there Buddy found the station. Dozens of men sprawled out on the bare flagstones, some writhing but others motionless, most of them steeped in blood. Doctors labored by candlelight. A chaplain administered last rites. An Army nurse hurried past Buddy, and without thinking, he reached out and grabbed her by the arm. "Hold it."

The nurse merely smiled at him. "Howdy to you, too, lieutenant."

"My sergeant, here. He's got frostbite, real bad."

"I see. Well, we're kind of short-handed here, but you lay him down, make him comfortable, and we'll get around to him soon enough."

A plain but kind-faced woman, with gore-mottled hands, cheeks sallow with exhaustion. "Don't I know you from somewhere?" Pappy asked her as Buddy eased him to the floor.

"Sure, soldier, sure you do..."

He stayed with him for a while, rustling up a cup of coffee, a blanket that some other poor bastard no longer needed. He lit two cigarettes and tucked one in Pappy's mouth. Bombs, meanwhile, thudded overhead, and wounded filled the crypt—men without limbs, burnt men, all of them ceaselessly moaning.

"I got to be getting back." Buddy glanced at his watch, warily, as if he were already late for an appointment.

"You're not going anywhere," Pappy muttered. He had had his morphine, was liltingly drifting to sleep. "Not back, anyways."

"I promised..."

"You promised shit. Go back and you're dead. Simple. Try to get out of here, get behind our lines, you got a chance. Maybe." Pappy said this matter-of-factly, not grinning anymore, his face as gray as a deathmask's. He reached up and clutched his lieutenant's collars. "No going back, lieutenant," he managed to grunt before slipping down to the blanket. "That's an order."

Screeching brakes, like the shriek of an incoming shell, and a violent jolt to his back. Buddy's eyes opened. The train was pulling in to the station. He watched Kaye, waited until she closed her magazine before saying, "I didn't sleep."

"I know."

"You can feel it."

"Even if I were in the next car," said Kaye.

She, too, had stayed awake, reading but not really reading, feeling oddly excited. Perhaps it was the thought of Paris—no, not the Paris of her dreams but a grubby suburb, yet far enough from the Hotel Ardennes.

Away from death, both long ago and recent. Or maybe it had to do with her husband? The sense of sharing a future with him for a change and not just a past, a purpose. She'd admired the way he stood up to the men, made his decision—quirky as it was—and stuck to it. A spark of the old Edwin Hill she married.

Pity he wasn't that spunky about his illness, Mrs. Hill found herself wishing; pity they both weren't. If only she could rib him about it, point at his lap and laugh, "you're not using them anyway," as if referring to an old set of golf clubs. "What do you say we just chuck 'em?"

But she wouldn't. She didn't laugh that way anymore, certainly not about that. Instead, Kaye would sit and pretend to read, imagine that they were really vacationing in Paris. And when Buddy rose, slouching and stiff, she'd get up as well, and follow him down the aisle.

☆ ☆ ☆

Spagnola paced his room. Twenty feet by twelve, he already had it measured and measured again. From the bedposts to the radiator, from the window to the shelves, he stepped in evenly gauged hobbles, counting off to himself. A smothering space, yet there was something reassuring about it. He was a man who had always lived alone, even in the company of others—soldiers, a wife, his sons—and lived in fear as well. A suspect in crimes he never committed, a fugitive from the few that he had.

He smoked his fourth cigarette of the hour, coughed and limped, and confessed to Captain Carruthers silently. Spagnola imagined him, the Captain, with his divine corona of hair, and the group, a heavenly host. They looked at him and nodded and listened. "It's okay, Francis," they said, and never once judged him. They never asked about the blood on his hands but accepted him simply, and there was forgiveness, there was freedom, in that.

He paced and smoked, counted and coughed, and decided he'd had enough of the reunion. A bad idea from start to finish; stupid of him to have hoped it would be otherwise. No closure, no peace, just the reopening of many old wounds, and the ripping apart of some new ones. No escape, but surrender again and confinement.

But he did not have to take it anymore, wouldn't. He would wait until eight o'clock—keep his word—until Buddy returned, but not one minute longer. Then he was out of here back to Brussels and the first plane to Newark, to Tuesday night bowling and Thursday's Knights of Columbus, and Wednesdays with the POWs, his favorite. Back to his house in Kearny, New Jersey, and to pacing its empty rooms.

☆ ☆ ☆

Alma laid the clothes on the bed, alongside the body. Such small clothes, the shirt no bigger than a boy's, it seemed, the pants narrow-waisted and short. Wearing them, though, he appeared much broader, a man of prodigious dimensions. A larger-than-life type, folks no doubt called him, and it only made sense that the Major would shrink accordingly, now that the he was dead.

He lay on his back, hollow-cheeked, his hook-nose thrust in the air, reminding her of an ancient Egyptian mummy she once saw displayed in a museum. And like a king of old, the Major, too, was deserving of dignity. Which was why, after his death, she had taken the trouble of returning him to his pajamas. Which was why she was dressing him now. Alma rose from the bed, walked over and opened the window. The cold would help preserve him, she knew, at least until the funeral. Winter gushed in, swirled under her skirt and whipped around the corners of the room. It ruffled the pajamas, and for a moment made the Major seem to stir.

He was just another corpse, she told herself, one of the great many she had seen in her career. But of course this corpse was different. Only hours before it had been alive and making love to her, vibrant and adoring her for herself.

No, not another corpse, not by a long shot, Alma admitted, as the tears cooled stinging on her cheeks. The carpenters would arrive soon—Hermansdorfer had assured her. The box they would build would be simple but strong, of the finest Ardennes pine. The Major would have liked that, she believed, the ruggedness of it, the total absence of airs. Just as he would like the resting place she had planned for him, a place that in a way was his home.

Delicately, she opened his pajama front and withdrew his arms from the sleeves. Then she turned to the shirt, checkered red with stiff flared collars and rhinestone snaps galore. A boy's first rodeo shirt, so it seemed to her. *How on earth did he ever fit in that thing?* Alma wondered before sighing and drawing a wrist under each of her eyes. Before lifting his body—quite light, in fact—to dress it.

☆ ☆ ☆

Within his valise there was any number of whatchucallits, tools that had no proper name, no predetermined function, at least not in the stone-cutting trade. Usually they were intended for different purposes entirely—a section of autojack, a fingernail brush, miniature bellows, a baster from some customer's kitchen—acquiring a function that only he could appreciate and could rarely do without.

Of these, one was especially priceless, adored even, for it was always the last tool Pieter touched. It had its own name—not a whatchucallit, but the thingamajig—though the dentist who once scraped plaque with it probably had a more technical term. For Pieter it served to grind filaments from the inscription, correcting imperfections that nobody would ever see but that he, the master, couldn't countenance. He liked the heft of it in his hand, the top-heavy weight, the textured grip, and in spite of the cold, removed his glove to wield it.

Through the letters, deep in the grooves, Pieter worked. Picking, blowing, peering inside with one eye closed, and then picking again, painstakingly. The job was almost finished. One of the largest stones he ever cut, among the most personal, and yet there was none of the satisfaction he usually felt completing even the commonest memorials. None of the pride. He felt only a deep-seated exhaustion, an emptiness, and the spasms in his back threatening to buckle.

His original hope, that the reunion would somehow reveal to him just what, exactly, happened to him in the battle, had faded. There had been clues, perhaps—the hotel, the bathtub, his daily walks through the woods—but they all led him nowhere. Ahead of him stood a wall, thick as ice but opaque.

Also groundless was the hope that the men might accept him again fully, but he had spent much of the reunion alone, as secluded in the forest as he was in his basement back home, exploited for his craftsmanship. Even Rifesnider's disappearance, welcomed though it was, brought him no solace. Some of the men, he believed, even suspected him. *That strange man, Martinson, that loner,* he imagined them thinking, *who knows what he's capable of?*

Pieter wanted only to be done with it now. Whether there was a ceremony as planned, whether it was ever unveiled, he would finish the memorial as he'd pledged to do, fulfilling his duty and honor. He would return then to his workbench and the letters of gratitude above it, to the yellowed photo of the girl in jeans, the hairbun and the tortoiseshell glasses. Get down, finally, to the jobs he'd always set out for himself to do but had never quite found the time. A stone for Herbert Shanks, his classmate killed in the Pacific, he'd carve, and a stone for a man they called Sweet.

With his thingamajig, Pieter Martinson dredged the depths of the lettering. Scouring hard, one hand braced on his back. So focused that he scarcely heard the crunching snow, the crackle of twigs and leaves, behind him. And when he did—by the time he realized that he was not alone, not in his basement but in a forest where any stranger could creep up on him, it was too late.

"Mr. Martinson. Hello."

Pieter whirled—too fast, he felt it in his back—and brandished his tool, ready to defend his stone.

"Easy, Pieter. It's only us. Remember?"

He squinted at the two figures behind him, a man and a younger woman, trying to place them. Then, lowering the thingamajig and his eyes, he muttered, "Sorry, I didn't recognize you."

"We did not mean to scare you," Claire said. "We were just out for a walk, you see. Exploring."

Richard hazarded a step. "Can we see what you've done?"

The mason stood in front of his carving, threw back his shoulders to hide it. "Not until it's finished."

"But…"

"It's the way I work. Please."

"We understand, Mr. Martinson," Claire apologized as she caught the hem of Richard's motorcycle jacket and pulled him back. "We won't disturb you." She replaced her camera's lens cover and closed her notebook. "Still, I would like to interview you at some point. About your life, that is."

Pieter looked away for a second, seemingly lost in a thought. "I cut stones. Headstones. It's what I do and what I've always done. There's nothing more to write."

"Yes. And I hear you're quite an artist at it. The best. I also wanted to know your feelings about the reunion. You know, now with the Major dead. About Mr. Rifesnider."

He turned back to the memorial, bent and returned to dredging. "I have nothing to say."

"Did you hate him, too? Were you one of those who wanted him to disappear?"

Now it was Richard tugging her coat, drawing her away. "You have a good day, Mr. Martinson," he called out to him, and shot her an urgent look.

☆ ☆ ☆

"All I wanted was a question or two," Claire complained when they were again within the woods.

"One question or two too many."

The day had proceeded poorly. First Billings then Alma and finally Pringle, a total bust. The portly man in the yachting jacket had indeed talked about boats—schooners, skiffs, and catamarans—only it turned out he had never actually owned one, lived in Brookfield, Missouri, nowhere near any body of water, a supervisor for the Board of Ed. Boats were merely a hobby, he explained, like the ham radios he liked constructing. One day, though, he hoped to go on a cruise.

He talked at length until Claire asked him about Rifesnider, and then the man went mum. He folded his arms over his crossed-oars patch and sunk his beard into his cravat. "Not going there, no sir," Pringle grunted, and there the interview died.

Pringle left and the hall was empty. Claire, bereft of excuses, had no choice but to follow Richard out to the forest and to go searching for this butcher person, this Armand.

Not a happy excursion, to be sure. Through the searing cold air and over the slick forest floor, Claire shuffled along inconsolably. So she let him know that her real story was back at the hotel, with the men, and not out here, chasing a crime from the ancient past that would scarcely interest an archivist anymore, much less the readers of *Paris Match*.

"Slow down, will you," she puffed when Richard had gotten well ahead of her. She fell back onto one of the concrete cones interspersed between the trees, blew into her hands and swiped the hair from her face.

"Dragon's teeth," noted Richard.

"What?"

"The thing you're sitting on. The Germans built them to stop American tanks, as if the Americans had tanks around here to stop. But you know those Germans—think of everything. Dragon's teeth."

"Right." She frowned and rolled her eyes, pretended to inspect her camera.

Richard backtracked and rested against the cone next to hers. He looked at her, marveling at the ruddiness the cold aroused in her cheeks, the ebony luster of her hair. He longed to lean over and kiss her, even on the forehead, but feared that she would only turn away. Something had happened to her since the previous night, through the morning and its serial disappointments. He felt, instinctively, he was losing her.

"Must you?" she snapped when he lit up a miniature cigar.

He snuffed it out on the concrete. "What's up, Mirelle? Too cold for you?"

She would not answer him, didn't nod. Her gaze was deep in the snow.

"Or is it that piece of paper? The one you stuffed in your pocket at the library. I saw you."

Her face went rigid.

"Here, let me take a look at it. It's probably nothing."

"It is not *nothing*," Claire said finally, shrinking into her coat.

"Well, I can't know unless I see it." He held out his hand. "Give it to me."

She reached into her pocket and passed it to him, all the while looking away. Richard removed his glasses, cleaned them on his jacket, restored them and read.

A birth certificate. He saw that right away. A baby boy, Jean-Claude Mirelle, born in the district of Saint-Vith-Houffalize on November 14, 1945. There was the mark of the midwife, the magistrate's seal, and then spaces for the parents' names. Sabine Mirelle, the mother, was blocked in one of these, and next to it, the father. That was the name that Richard's eyes fixed on, blinked at, tried to keep in focus. Two fingers pinched the bridge of his nose, then slid under his glasses to massage the rims of his eyes. Yet, when he removed those fingers and his glasses dropped back into place, the signature was still there, neat and curiously familiar. And so was the name: Dean Featherstone.

"I did not say anything to Muriel. I mean, what *could* I say. 'Hello, you never met me or even knew I existed but, you know, we are related?'"

Claire kept babbling but Richard barely heard her. He was concentrating on the dates, calculating.

"Maybe she would take me home with her, to Michigan or Wyoming or whatever. Meet my whole new family."

"It's falsified."

"And maybe there is some money put away, insurance, inheritance. Think, Richard, I could be rich."

"He *can't* be the father…"

"And what a headline it will make! I will win the fucking Pulitzer."

He hollered at her, "It wasn't Featherstone!"

Claire fell silent. She glared at him; her eyes were glazed with tears. "No?"

"Couldn't be. Not if your grandfather died in the battle—that *is* what your grandmother said?—in December of '45. Not if Featherstone did. This kid was conceived *aft*er that, the earliest January."

"Oh..."

"We can always ask her, of course. Tonight, if there's time, or tomorrow after the ceremony."

"Yes. Whatever..."

"Let's not worry about it now," Richard said. He creased the paper along its folds and stuck it in his own jacket's pocket. "It's getting late."

He offered his hand again and she took it now, let herself be led from the teeth. He walked briskly, following Hermansdorfer's hand-drawn map. Only a short distance remained to the farm. But then Claire stopped suddenly, with a violent jerk to his shoulder. Richard swung around, for the first time furious at her, only to hear her whimper, "What if he didn't die?"

"Who?"

"Nobody *saw* him get killed, right? No *body* was ever found." A tear streamed down her face. "What if he's still..."

Richard yanked her hand and thundered forward. "Later," he snapped. "We'll ask your grandmother."

☆ ☆ ☆

Buddy handed the address to the cab driver, who mumbled something in French and stepped on the gas. Winding through the Paris traffic, Buddy squeezed Kaye's hand and gave her a look that said *so far so good.*

From the Gare du Nord they crossed the Pont de Neuilly, into the outlying districts of the city. Not the Paris that Buddy helped liberate in the war—twelve times liberating it, the unit moving back and forth—

with the picturesque cafés, banner-festooned boulevards, beautiful women. This, rather, was the dark side of Paris, the one never seen on postcards. Filthy streets, half-crumbling buildings—all seemed to be melting in a slur of snow flurries and drizzle, in consecutive shades of gray.

"Lord," gasped Kaye, and her husband echoed her, "Lord is right."

But neither of them was prepared for the place where the cab finally stopped. Again, he showed the address to the driver, and again the man nodded and mumbled. Though there was no sign on the street or building number, Buddy knew they had arrived.

"I think you should wait here. I think I should do this alone."

"Are you sure, Edwin?"

He bent through the cab window and kissed her forehead. "I'll be back," he said, slipping his hand from her grip. "Promise."

The staircase was worse than the street outside—darker, dirtier, a gallery of obscene graffiti reeking of urine and spoiled fruit. Buddy climbed, at first reluctant to lean against the walls, but by the second flight resting heavily on them. He paused on the landing, struggling to catch his breath, not at all sure he could continue but then, with a gulp of air, plugging on. Through wailing echoes of North African music, the shrieks of some family squabble. Another flight, another landing, until at last he came to the door. Again, there was no name or number, but Buddy nevertheless knocked.

No answer. He counted to three, slowly, and began to knock again when the door swung open. An Asian woman, middle-aged, very short and bland-faced, confronted him, and Buddy backed off muttering apologies. Clearly he had made a mistake.

"Who's there?" A weak, raspy voice wavered from somewhere inside the apartment. "Who's at the door?"

"Il y a un vieil homme a la porte," the woman called out, but never took her eyes off Buddy. "Un Américain."

"Let him in, for chrissakes. Let him in."

The woman lowered her gaze and stepped aside. "Entrez, si'l vous plait."

Buddy entered a salon of sorts, furnished only with a fluff-bleeding sofa and a television set on which the *Ed Sullivan Show* might have been watched. Dust thickened the air, along with a dirty sock smell and a whiff of stale tobacco.

"Venez par ici," the woman motioned to him, moving into another room, a kitchen. Buddy could see pans and utensils nailed to the wall, a stack of filthy dishes in the sink, and at a small, slightly tilted table, the back of a man in a bathrobe.

"Thank you. That'll be all for today, Madam Lee."

"D'accord," the woman said. "Au revoir, Monsieur," and retreated, leaving Buddy alone.

"You believe it? More'n fifty years in this friggin' city, and I can't even speak the lingo." The man twisted in his chair. "Howya doin', Buddy?"

Buddy restrained a gasp. "You're...not surprised to see me..."

"I had a feelin' somebody'd show up. The invitation and all. Figures it'd be you."

Buddy would not have recognized him—not at first glance, anyway, nor at second. Jowls and bags scalloped his face, cataracts clouded his eyes. There were scabs on his lips and on his scalp, a chain of pinkish growths. Yet there was that quality about him—the undauntedness, the tobacco-cured growl of his voice—that remained unaltered, unmistakable.

"I need you," Buddy said finally, fresh out of small talk.

His laugh was the same, too, gruff and irreverent. "You got to be kidding."

"I wish I were. A lot of things've happened—at the reunion, I mean. Bad things. I can tell you about them on the way, but right now I *need* you to come with me."

The old man in the bathrobe looked around his kitchen, at the unwashed dishes, the grease-encrusted stove. "I was a big fish in the war, wunt I? No general, maybe, but I got respect. But back home, what was I—a nothing, a big fat zero, that's what. A public school janitor. You'da stayed here too."

His eyes swung now to the wall, to the curls of mustardy paper and a calendar with cars no longer made. "It wunt so bad in the early days. A guy could do just fine on an Army pension and a coupla words of Fransay. Pack of cigarettes. The ol' *voulez-vous coucher*. You remember. Even had a wife for a while—*me*. Good woman, actually, took care of me and all. But, you know how it is, bad feet, bad breaks, and before you know it, *pow*, no more broads, no booze, and you're down to your last cigar." He smiled and revealed his blackened teeth. "I'm dying, Buddy," he said.

Now it was Buddy who laughed. "Yeah, and who isn't?"

He shrugged and tweaked his moustache. He still had the moustache, a slender mantel, and mounted over it, that same battered trophy of a nose. "Suppose I owe you, don't I?"

"Suppose you do."

"How long, then?"

"Two days. Extra pair of socks, underwear. Toothbrush, if you ever use one."

He snickered and Buddy snickered with him. "Double time, then. There's a taxi waiting outside."

Descending the stairs proved even harder than climbing them. The two men leaned on one another, grunting, swearing, recalling a similar journey fifty-five years ago, slogging together through the snow.

"At least there're no Jerry patrols," Buddy panted.

They made the entrance, finally, and staggered out to the street. The passenger window of the cab opened, and Kaye glared at them with a mixture of shock and concern. Yet when they approached, as Buddy began, "Here she is, the girl of my dreams—Kitty, I'd like you to meet…," her face softened and her hand reached out.

"No need for introductions," she said. "So good you could join us."

He took her hand in both of his and wouldn't let go, not until Buddy reminded him that they had a train to catch, that certain men were waiting for him still, in Saint-Vith.

☆ ☆ ☆

Claire would not let go of his hand, but only held it tighter. At first he thought it was out of gratitude, for telling her that the document was fake, but now, as the farm came into view, Richard was no longer sure. Not that he was so sure about the document, either. Was it really impossible that Featherstone was the father? Weirder things happened in war. And the dates—the battle in December '44, the birth the following November—was there really no way of reconciling them? He rifled his mind for answers, rummaged it. Again, he had that feeling that he'd missed something, of not seeing trees—aptly, in the Ardennes—for the forest.

Clutching, Claire crunched his knuckles.

"What now?" he carped.

"I don't know. This place."

She was referring to the yard they had just entered. A scruffy patch of ice, mud and snow—and specks of something else, ruddier. Opposite them was an old-fashioned cottage, a throwback to the 1800s with an outhouse and a well, no visible hookup to electricity. Another structure—lower, darker—was half-hidden in a depression in the woods, and it was there that Richard guided her.

She gasped, "Where are you taking me?"

"Quiet. You'll see."

"I do not like it here. I want to go."

"I thought I saw someone moving…," Richard said.

He had, briefly, a shadow scurrying from the yard into the forest. It could be the butcher, Richard speculated; perhaps he was shy of strangers.

"Richard, please." She started to dig in her heels.

"Claire…" He reproached her, with a sharp single wrench of her hand. "Enough."

He towed her toward the squat stone house behind the cottage. Footprints, big footprints, seemed to lead inside, through the stunted door, and Richard made to follow them, but Claire again demurred.

"Look…"

She pointed at a track of soiled snow near the cottage, at a large oilskin sack abandoned there. The sack, positioned upright, was very full.

Twisting out of Claire's grip, Richard approached.

Holes, he saw, had been punctured in the sack's upper flanks—for the rope, Richard reasoned, for hauling it—and from those holes oozed some liquid, brownish like those specks on the ground. "Who knows, maybe Rifesnider's inside?" he laughed as he seized the sack and pulled downward.

A headless neck. Bloody veins, cartilage, bone appeared, and Richard heard a scream. He, too, was shocked, recoiling from the sack, and required a second to regain his composure. But by then it was too late; Claire had already fled.

"It's only a pig!" he called after her, "Hey, the man's a butcher, remember?"

Richard glanced at the sack, at the carcass, and then at the dark stone structure in the hollow. He wanted to enter it, take a look-see inside, but in the end he merely cursed. He ran, fast for a man his age, with his jacket and ponytail flailing, into the forest after Claire.

☆ ☆ ☆

Pieter oiled the stone. A special oil he used only for such occasions, a combination linseed, rosin, and lemon. It brought out the glitter in the quartz, emboldened the relief of the plaque. He stepped away, one hand on his back and the other with the oily rag still raised, as though in an act of surrender. Then, pocketing the rag, reaching down very slowly, he retrieved the canvas tarpaulin and lifted it over the top of the stone.

That's that, he thought, wiping his hands together. Whether or not they held the ceremony tomorrow, whether he ever saw any of the veterans again, the unit had its memorial. He sighed deeply, mightily, as he sometimes did in his basement, completing a hefty job. Here, though, the sound was absorbed by the forest and snatched away by the wind. No matter, Pieter shrugged, the entire experience would soon be behind him, buried where it always belonged.

Retrieving his valise, he dropped the rag inside, zipped it closed, and lifted its leather handles. He lifted carefully, allowing the weight to displace evenly throughout the body—while he gazed across the meadow. Stitching across unblemished stretch of snow, he saw, were footprints—Richard and Claire's, most likely. They crossed the clearing before disappearing into the trees.

For an entire minute Pieter stood there, oblivious to the valise's weight, to the widening shadows of twilight. He stared and cringed, squinted and groped. Footprints in the snow, at dusk, leading into the forest. Footprints…

☆ ☆ ☆

The Bayonet Hall was empty. No more smorgasbord, no beer or wine or coffee. The tables uncovered—naked Formica—and the walls bare, the floor sheening ice-like in the neon. There was no clock, either, but at precisely eight, the door opened and the first of the veterans entered.

Croker, flat-topped head angled forward, his skinny frame bent, as if some vacuum were sucking him in. Then came Rob, no less lean but nervous, hesitant, and behind him Pringle, sauntering. McCloski lumbered and Willa minced, egging Roger along. The Vorhees, the Confortis, a waddling, sleepy-eyed Stan Morgan. Hollister and Billings, inching. They gathered in the hall and mulled, muttering, brooding over the time. Only when Spagnola walked in, escorted by Alma, did the assembly grow quiet and remained quiet a full minute longer until Croker finally spoke up:

"Well?"

"As well as can be expected," Alma replied. "Thank you."

"It's after eight."

"So it is," said Spagnola with a glance at his watchless wrist. He limped toward them.

"So, we had a deal," McCloski said. "No Buddy, end of reunion."

Spagnola chewed on his nail. A part of him was also eager to leave, but another part—the larger one—stayed loyal to Buddy. "What's the matter with you guys," he asked them finally. "Ain't you never heard of a grace period?"

"Grace schmace," Willa snarled. "We want to go home already."

"Home, yes. Home would be nice," chimed Mary.

Phil interpreted: "What she means is, Buddy didn't show up like he said, therefore we don't have to wait for him anymore."

"Fifty-five years is enough, I'd say," huffed Pringle.

"And I say, screw it," Billings spat. "Get the driver, call a cab. We're quitting."

Then everyone, all at once, was shouting. Clamoring, complaining. And Spagnola, summoning his limited breath, strove to holler above them: "What if his car got stuck? What if he had a flat? How can you just *leave* him like that?"

Until Rob yelled back at him—"What do you mean 'How can we leave him?'"—and the hall went silent again. "You, of all people," he continued. "Where the hell were you when we needed you on the ridge? Hiding, that's where."

"That's not fair…"

"And that kid," Phil interrupted. "The kid who went out with you on that work detail and didn't come back. What's his name…?"

"Eisenhower!" Hollister barked. His perennially kind face had gone brittle suddenly, tight-lipped and cross. "Tell us, what really happened to Eisenhower?"

Alma put her arm around the man's shoulder, hugged and protected him. "All of you leave him alone, Who gave you the Medal of Honor?"

Croker practically lunged at her. "And who are *you*, lady? You weren't even up there. You're not even one of us."

"A man-chaser, that's what she is, and she caught him all right," Roger sniggered. "Cold."

"Which I'd take any day over the brain-dead bimbo you got," Alma fumed.

The shouting intensified—a furor—yet more people entered the hall: Muriel Featherstone, composed for a change but then losing that composure as soon as she heard the argument. "Oh, this is terrible, just terrible," she bawled. "If my brother had only seen this..."

Fresh back from their run through the woods, breathless, Richard and Claire arrived, clueless as to what was happening.

"Can I ask what this disagreement is about?" the journalist began. Already, she had produced her notebook.

"No!" Rob pounced. "No, you can't. And put that thing away. Interview's over."

Richard rushed forward, "You don't have to be so rude. Any of you," and then reared back, retreating before a chorus of "Shut *up*!'s."

The Vicar, alone, urged calm. "I think we can discuss this in a civil fashion, don't you think? We owe that to each other..."

"Easy for you to say, Vicar," McCloski sneered. "You weren't in the stalag with the rest of us. You were never a POW."

"My ass I wasn't. Will you look at these," he strained, pointing at his darkened glasses. Genie tried to intervene, pulled on her husband's arm—"Tommy, please"—but he curtly shrugged her off. "You all got out eventually, but I've stayed a prisoner ever since. Every stinking day!"

The door opened and closed again. Pieter stood there, in his woolen cap and soiled parka, vagabond-like, toting his valise.

"I heard the noise..."

Stan Morgan, closest to him, explained, "The men are going 'cause Buddy didn't show. They were just saying good-bye."

"You mean there won't be a ceremony after all? Nobody'll see the stone?"

"Ah, so that's it? The stone," Hollister accosted him, pointing an accusing stump. "That's the reason you came."

"I didn't...no."

"I'd have thought he'd be ashamed to show his face," Pringle asided to Croker, brash enough for everyone to hear.

"What do you mean?" Pieter asked. Confused, beleaguered, he released his grip on the valise. It crashed, contents clanging, on the floor.

Roger suggested, "Could be he came for Rifesnider. Maybe it's him he came to *cahve*."

"His tools *were* in the room," recalled Rob, "And to think we called him Sweet."

"I'd like to see the stone!" Mary said with a clap, at which Billings snarled, "Clam her up, will you, Phil."

"Clam yourself," Phil shot back. "Nobody talks down to my wife, you…cripple."

"Or maybe it was the fat man," Croker said, meaning Spagnola. "Or both of them. The company clown and the company coward, taking revenge."

Sniggers seared through the hall. Croker laughed outright.

"Enough! All of you, enough!" Alma roared. "*You're* the ones who should be ashamed. A bunch of impotent bullies."

They started coming toward her. First McCloski, then Hollister and Rob, then Pringle. Their faces lurid, sweating, hands shaking. Roger and Billings, Croker and Phil Conforti. Spagnola and Pieter were moving as well, imposing themselves between Alma and the men. Muriel wailed and Claire scrawled while Richard looked away in disgust. No one heard the Vicar pleading and no one noticed as the door to the hall opened slowly, and Stan, after squinting, after shaking his head half-dazed, suddenly came to attention.

"What's *his* problem?" Croker asked Billings, but Billings had straightened before his walker. Hollister gave a two-fingered salute.

Then they were all doing it: McCloski, Pringle, Rob. All of them stopped short and went rigid. Croker jabbed his chin out and Roger's paunch recoiled. A clicking of heels from Phil. Spagnola watched them, flabbergasted. Pieter had frozen as well. "Jesus, Mary…"

"You're a disgrace to that uniform, kid," he heard a groggy voice say, and Spagnola was about to snort, "*what* uniform?" when he, too, turned stiff.

"Always knew you'd make a lousy soldier."

"Yes, sir," Spagnola said.

"Don't 'sir' me, private. It's 'yes, sergeant.'"

"Yes, sir! Sergeant, sir!"

Braced between Buddy and Kaye, an arm on each of theirs, he shuffled. He passed in front of his men.

"Great to see you, Sarge," Phil Conforti said.

Rob lowered his eyes—"Evening"—and Pringle did, too, the man in the yacht jacket adding, "You're looking good."

"Like fuck I am. And quit grinning."

Each of them greeted him. Each of them deferred.

"Sarge."

"Pappy."

"Sergeant Papino."

Genie, responding to her husband's inquiries, whispered into his ear. "I'll be damned," he said. And Claire, informed by Richard, gazed at the ceiling, "thank you, God," and flipped to a new page in her notebook. Muriel cried—out of sadness or joy—and Willa still whined about going home, but nobody heard her.

Between the rows of reverent veterans, he doddered. Alma approached and offered to take Kaye's place assisting him, asking him, "How're those feet doin', soldier?"

"Not bad. Can still do a Lindy, you'll see."

"Wager I will."

He reached the back of the hall. Then, turning, he released himself from his helpers' grasp, faltered a bit but managed to keep his balance.

"Situation?" he demanded of Buddy.

"Like I said, one dead, one missing."

Pappy nodded, took this in. "Supplies?"

"Best chow in town."

Finally he addressed the men: "Orders are we're supposed to hold out here one more day. Have a ceremony of some kind, dedicate a stone. Party later in Houffalize, with the ladies. S'no chickenshit assignment, I admit, but if there's anybody here who thinks he can't hack it, that it's time to give ourselves up, well, I'm listenin'..."

Not a word. Apart from some coughing, a hearing aid's hum, there wasn't a sound.

"Then it's settled. We stay." Through glassy, heavily hooded eyes, he looked around at the men. His hands started shaking slightly, then his body, but when Alma and Buddy moved toward him, he churlishly waved them away. "What the hell you gawking at?" he asked. "Dismissed."

They rushed at him, broke ranks and embraced him. "Easy, boys, easy, this ain't the same Pappy," he panted and choked, but he couldn't convince them otherwise.

FOUR

The Bastogne Bar was hopping, relatively, as it hadn't since the reunion's first night. Though no toasts were raised, the drinks went down fast—as fast as Yvonne could pour—and laughter rang through the glasses. Teetering on their stools, several of the men recalled the time when McCloski, sick while riding in convoy, shat out of the back of their truck. A fierce wind was blowing, and it carried the crap straight into the following vehicle's windshield ("You shoulda seen that driver's face!" howled Rob). Or when Hollister went to divisional HQ to have a tooth pulled and ended up stealing the general's mascot, a duck. A reward was posted for the bird, word of it reaching them at B Company when they were still busy sucking the bones.

"Rifesnider heard about it and wanted to court-martial you," Pringle remembered.

"He was only sore 'cause he didn't have a duck himself."

"He would have *had* it all right, knowing Rifesnider," Billings winked. "Then he would've eaten it."

They whinnied and guffawed and held out their glasses for refills. Wiping his mouth, Croker wondered, "What *really* happened to that bastard?"

Billings snorted, "Do we really care?" and the heads around him nodded.

Except for McCloski's. "Ask me, it was all a trick," he said, and paused while the others looked at him blankly. "One bathtub, lots of red dye or pig's blood—doesn't take much—and the whole reunion's screwed." The miner chugged his shot. "Rifesnider's revenge."

"He's right," Hollister agreed. "I don't see our hotel owner sweating over it. Maybe Rifesnider paid him off. *And* the police."

"Sounds likely to me," said Rob.

"Or, he actually *was* killed."

They turned, open-mouthed, to Stan Morgan, having almost forgotten he was there. "I mean, any one of us could've done it," Stan said. "Would've. Right? Even Sweet over there." He motioned at Pieter, drinking alone in one corner. "Even Spagnola."

They glanced at Spagnola, drunk and hunched over his table, and then at one another. "Okay," Stan conceded. "Maybe not Spagnola," and the men started laughing again, uproariously.

Though vaguely aware of that laughter, and that he was its target, Spagnola didn't care. He scarcely missed a beat, telling the story of his life and pouring another Cutty for his listener.

"A wrecker, worked with the big balls. And my wife, Harriet, she had the biggest ones of all." He cupped his hands under his chest and jiggled them. "Yeah, but then she croaked and the boys moved away. Wasn't much left to do so I joined the Knights of Columbus, Tuesday night bowling. And then there's the group."

"The group?"

"My POW support group. Every Wednesday for two hours. Guys from Korea, Vietnam—I'm the only one left from the Big One. We tell our stories over and over so we can get used to them, kind of, you know, get over the trauma."

"Oh yeah, the trauma. I nearly forgot."

"Captain Carruthers—he's the group leader, a Navy pilot, a POW himself—he says that I'm making real good progress—I'm here, ain't I, at the reunion? Wouldn't of thought about it before. Couldn't be sitting here, drinking and talking with you."

He refilled both glasses and lit two cigarettes at once, puffing on one and proffering the other.

"I was too hard on you," Pappy said and his lips trembled. He pulled on his drink and dragged on his butt, yet the trembling continued. "Too goddamn hard..."

"No, you got it all wrong." Spagnola laid a hand on his former sergeant's wrist. "I had no business being in the infantry, but you knew that if you didn't bust my ass I'd never make it. Fact is, Sarge, you saved my life."

Pappy's wrist quivered under Spagnola's hand, but Spagnola kept it there while, with the other hand, he reached again for the bottle. "Say, ever been to New Jersey, Pap, to Kearny? Nice place, quiet. And I got this big old empty house..."

At another table, at the other end of the bar, Alma Wheatty was also hearing of houses. Houses of the Lord, of worship, the various pulpits Tommy had held, each one higher than the previous, culminating in The First Episcopal of Johnson City, New York: the pinnacle. Not Park Avenue, not St. John the Divine's, but a solid, hard-working community, hard-praying. "What I always wanted," the Vicar confessed. He rubbed his shoulder against Genie's. "What *we* always wanted."

"I never knew what I wanted," Alma replied with a stir of her gin and tonic. "It might have been the Major. We could have had a few years...."

Genie started in, "No offense, Mrs. Wheatty, " but her husband interrupted.

"You should be thankful," he reminded Alma. "The way the two of you came together, if only for a moment, after all these years. A miracle."

Alma shrugged and chewed on her lower lip. How strange to be told such things by a man in a collar, whose glasses refracted the particolored lights of the bar. A man she met over fifty years ago, briefly. She looked up at Genie. "I've met Tommy before," Alma said flatly. "Before the reunion, I mean. In the war."

The Vicar appeared to gape at her, while Genie seemed confused. "I don't follow..."

"They brought him in during the battle. There were so many

wounded, I couldn't spend much time with just one. But there he was on a stretcher on the floor in the church, head all bandaged, and his eyes…"

She turned now to Tommy. "I asked you, 'Hey, private, how you feelin'?' And you said, 'Not bad, Ma'am, but I can't see a lick.'

"I thought about lying to you," Alma continued. "Telling you that it was only bullet flash, but you had this expression…Then you spoke to me."

"I remember this, vaguely " Tommy muttered. "A nurse…"

"You told me about your fiancée. About Genie."

"Because I knew already."

"Knew what?" Genie pressed.

"Knew that I would never see you again." He turned to Alma. "And that's when I asked you."

"Yes."

Genie cried, "Asked him what?"

"He asked to touch my face," Alma told her, though she was still addressing the Vicar. "Only my face. Because…"

"Because I wanted to preserve it," Tommy explained to his wife. "It's hard to explain. By making her face yours, touching it, somehow I thought I could keep it inside me forever."

Genie looked confused, afraid and flustered. "And did you?"

With his long, pale fingers he traced her cheek, her forehead, and gently pinched her chin. "It's the same face I see now. Your eighteen-year-old face, it's never changed. Alma did that."

Alma shrugged again, this time blushing. "Best role I ever played," she said, though neither of the Vorhees understood her. "You were right, Reverend, about the miracles, the moments. Most of them we spend alone."

She was speaking to the both of them now, but looking at neither. Her eyes had crossed the bar to where Pieter Martinson sat on a stool apart from the others, stooped and sullen and staring into his glass. The glass, as far as she could tell, was empty, except for several cubes of ice. Pieter was staring into ice.

Buddy also noticed him staring, was worried about Pieter and nearly said something to Kaye. They were seated at an impromptu "couples" table, along with the Confortis and the Gimpels. Willa, on her third or fourth Black Russian, was boring them with stories of "me and my Roger" on various vacations—Alaska, the Seychelles Islands, London, Mozambique—while Roger chortled along, his face insalubriously reddening.

Mary, alone, dared interrupt them, commenting on the chairs—"Do you think they're colonial? They look colonial, don't they, Phil?"—and recalling a wedding they once performed at, the son of a Westchester congressman, where the guests simply would not let them quit.

"'Encore!' they kept shouting. 'Bravo! Encore!'"

"Great night, Mary, one of our best," Phil said and clasped her applauding hands. He smiled at the others, "Sorry."

But Willa hadn't paused. "The natives were buff naked. *All* of them, men *and* women. And tattooed. Yoohoo!" She brandished her empty glass at the barmaid. "You think my Roger's blushing now, you should have seem him then, surrounded by all these big black boobs."

Roger, nearly vermilion, twittered, and Phil twittered, too, and Mary. Only Kaye remained staid, her jaw archly set, and Buddy, who'd been keeping his eyes on Pieter when his eyes somehow closed. His chin drifted to his chest and his breathing lengthened.

"Edwin. Edwin, not here."

He heard voices from far away, noises, but it was the tug on his sleeve that finally salvaged him. "Yes? What?" He rose from his sleep like a man from deep water, gasping and shaking his head. "Was I snoring?"

"Everything but. And no wonder, what with what you've been through today," said Kaye. Rising, she apologized to the other couples, "Time for this old soldier to hit the sack."

Buddy mumbled apologies as well. He availed himself of his wife's cane, struggled to his feet. The room was revolving; his head was a leaden plug. The pain had become permanent now, a possessing, harrowing, demon.

"Thanks again, Lieutenant," Phil said. "You truly deserve that rest."

Roger toasted him, "We always knew you'd come back."

They left the bar, Buddy and Kaye, and entered the lobby. At the front desk, slumped, Miles sleeping as usual, Discman affixed to his ears. And in front of the fake fireplace, confronting the tree, sat Muriel Firestone. The coppery light of the electric flames, the tree's iridescence, made her face look long-dead, decomposing. But her fingers were very much alive and methodically tearing a tissue. Buddy started toward her, but Kaye held him back. She shook her head "no," and kept him on course to the staircase.

They had only one flight to climb, but it felt like a long one, a steep one, with Kaye for once taking the lead and Buddy angled against her. They climbed slowly, one step at a time, and were soon passed by another, sprightlier, couple.

"Mr. and Mrs. Hill, goodnight."

"Again, helluva job today, Buddy."

Richard and Claire. They seemed to zoom by, pausing only for Claire to wave and Richard to slap Buddy's shoulder. Then again they soared, trailing behind them a heady scent of wine and perfume, leather and sweat. They appeared to be holding hands.

Buddy croaked, "You remember that?"

"Let's get you to bed," was Kaye's reply, said with a frown and a dip of her brow, meaning she did but preferred not to dwell on it.

☆ ☆ ☆

"We could visit your grandmother tonight, if you want. It's still early. Or take a rest. Whatever."

She smiled at him, a vaguely lascivious smile. They had gone out to another pub in town, to be alone for a while and to celebrate and now, three wine glasses later, Claire was tripping up the stairs. "Whatever," she laughed.

Her mood had changed precipitously since Pappy's arrival. Frustrated at first, frightened after their trip through the forest, she turned chipper suddenly, punchy from lack of sleep. She had her story—*Sergeant Saves*

Old Outfit—and nothing else mattered. Not the Rifesnider mystery, not even her own. Not another word was said about her father's birth certificate and who it claimed his father was.

Richard did not begrudge her. All the time in the bar, and now on the steps, he remained astonished by her, enthralled by her verdigris eyes, the bounteous sweep of her mouth. He liked the fact that she could change like that, from glum to jaunty and probably back again. Her unpredictable, protean quality.

At the door, he fumbled with his keys a bit, nervous. The scene was all too familiar to him from his college days. The nights returning to his dorm with some social psych major he'd hit on at a dance, the shared understanding of what was going to happen inside: the groping, the imploring, hooks and hesitations undone. *A quarter of a century ago, holy shit*, he thought, turning the key and standing aside to let Claire, not much beyond college age herself, enter first.

She dropped across the bed, exclaiming, "Oh. Heaven," and he watched her—the elliptical thighs, the flat of her stomach and the sudden rise of her breasts. Already he was plotting the removal of her sweater, the peeling off of her jeans. He blushed to feel himself tremble.

"Excuse me a second," Richard stammered. "I'll be right back," and ducked into the bathroom. He wanted to empty his bladder before anything serious got started, to wash his face and brush his teeth, but mostly to clear his mind of clutter.

Unlike Claire, Richard could not forget the certificate. Even when he gazed at her, he saw it still with its date and signatures, a palimpsest. He thought of it as he peed, as quietly as he could, and was thinking of it again at the sink where, in the mirror, he caught sight of the middle-aged man wincing back at him. A whitening at the temples, that looseness around the jaw—all were revealed under brutal fluorescence. Crow's feet, eye-sacks, the teeth permanently stained. When he opened his shirt to wash his armpits, the flesh seemed to sag from his collarbone. The image occurred to him of overripe fruit, of butter left out on the counter all night. Yet here he was with a ponytail, with John Lennon glasses and a girl on the bed outside young enough to be his daughter.

Richard imagined how he would look to her naked, with his handlebar fat and graying chest hairs; pictured his past-its-prime body next to hers, lissome and flowering. A repulsive thought, he admitted. What, then, did she see in him? *Oh, yes, the father thing*, Richard remembered. Poor girl. She didn't know how lucky she'd been growing up without one. How different his life might have been if he weren't the son of Prof. Leonard G. Perlmutter—G for Gershon, a tenebrous family secret—if he wasn't the son of Label.

Still fixating on his father, Richard buttoned up his shirt, replaced his glasses, and started out of the bathroom. His father…the date: November 1945. The realization struck him, though he failed to make sense of it at first. The police report about Rifesnider, Claire's father's birth—both occurred about the same time as *his* father's discharge. They were all linked, somehow—the coincidence was too great. *Holy shit*, Richard muttered again, this time out loud.

He rushed, exclaiming "Claire, you're not going to believe this!" more anxious to tell her than to make love to her. But no answer came from the bedroom, no sound except that of soft, measured breathing.

Sprawled on the bed with her notebook clutched to her throat, Claire lay sleeping. Deeply, contentedly she slept, and not even Richard with all his startling revelations, his desires, could rouse her.

☆ ☆ ☆

Nothing would wake him now, he was set on it. Not the bombs, not the shouts, no pint-sized intruder tugging on his sleeve. He was sinking into a sleep as dark and enshrouding as the river outside, turning in undulating currents.

Buddy was dreaming again; his recurring dream about the house and the bed by the Rhine. He knew it, yet the dream had textures and dimensions. He could actually *feel* the wetness in his boots, smell the mud on his uniform. The machine guns in the hillsides were rattling. But at the same time his senses seemed to be departing him, sloughing off. He would lie here forever, eternally at peace. All else could rage on—the war, the world—without him.

This was his decision and he'd stick to it. The vow repeated in his head, a mantra, even as he slept, even as the footsteps approached. As always, they were a child's footsteps, but this time he was prepared for them. Melissa or no Melissa, she would just have to leave him be, to understand that his time had come, he was tired, and wanted only to sleep.

It began, again, the tugging. He tried to ignore it; he still wasn't getting up. The kid could tug all night.

"Hey you..."

The voice was high but not feminine: a boy's voice. Familiar but distant.

"Hey you, get up."

The tugging intensified. "No. Please..."

"But you can't give up now, not yet. It's not time. You have to live." The boy insisted, "Look at me."

He didn't want to look. He knew what he'd see if he did.

But the boy began to cry. "Daddy. *Dad*-dy!"

"Don't, shhhh," Buddy begged him. "You don't have to..." And he opened his eyes, just a crack, peering from one dream into this one, wondrous and bright.

"Don't cry," he said to the boy by his bedside. The boy who had left him so many years before, stolen from his life by polio. "Don't cry, Robert," Buddy told him. "See, I'm up. I'm getting up."

"Promise?"

"Promise," he said and reached out for the cheek with its galaxy of freckles, to the star-lit gold of his hair. "Oh, Bobby...," he wept and the child seemed to smile at him. A pitying and affectionate smile, it was the last thing Buddy saw as his son dissolved into daylight.

"Edwin?" asked the lump under the covers next to him. "Are you all right? The pain—can't you sleep?"

He smoothed the grizzled tassels of her hair. "Nothing's wrong, Kitty, I'm fine. Very fine." Buddy assured her. "It's morning."

FIVE

They gathered in the lobby, dressed in their Sunday clothes: ties on the men, the women in skirts or pantsuits, somberly colored. They muttered their good mornings but mostly just nodded at one another. There wasn't much more to say. This was the moment they'd returned for, whatever their individual motivations and however differently things turned out. Now came the encounter, the closure. Time to reunite with the ridge.

Hermansdorfer was on hand, funereal in his long, black coat and matching homburg, flanked by Yvonne in dark glasses, her head wrapped in a shawl. Miles in R&B mode—reflector shades, ash-gray turtleneck—cradling a trumpet. Kuhlmann arrived in his usual attire, trenchcoat and hat, but with the grin for once lost from his face. Others from the town had shown up as well—the young woman from the porcelain shop, the teacher from the schoolhouse, even the frumpy policemen who were supposedly in search of Rifesnider. All had come to lend hands to those who needed them, their backs to the box that was presently wheeled out on a gurney.

They parted to let it through. A simple pinewood box, draped with the flag that the hotel flew whenever Americans were expected. Behind walked Alma in black, or near-black clothes, head lowered, silently escorted by the Vicar. The murmuring, what little there had been, subsided. The lobby grew perfectly still.

"Well, I suppose that's it," said Buddy Hill. "Pappy?"

Hanging on Spagnola's arm, the former sergeant saluted. "All present and accounted for, sir."

"Good. Let's do what we came for, then." Cupping Kaye's elbow, Buddy turned to the door. "Let's move out."

Raggedly they filed behind the gurney, out into the spanking cold. A small tractor waited there with a trailer onto which Hermansdorfer, and the policemen, the teacher and Kuhlmann, lifting gently, transferred the coffin. The others then joined them—Hollister, Rob, the Gimpels and the Vorhees—shivering, rocking from foot to foot, huddled around the trailer as if somehow it could give off heat. The last to exit was McCloski, the tallest of the bunch, able to reach up above the door to the dining hall. He emerged now with what he'd taken down—the M-1 rifle with its bayonet fixed and a GI helmet, still fitted with its camouflage netting.

The old miner nodded at Buddy, who in turn motioned to Miles behind the tractor's wheel. The engine turned, the trailer buckled then rolled. The veterans followed, doddering many of them, struggling, but remaining in step more or less in a slow procession across the square, through the park and into the forest.

On the trail, still partially snow-covered, the progress was slower. The line repeatedly halted as someone stopped to regain his or her breath or improve a grip on a walking aid. A clangorous noise accompanied them—twigs snapping, wheezes and coughs—that was hardly reverential. Then, a hundred yards in, the passage grew too narrow for the tractor. The coffin was again lifted onto as many shoulders as could bear it, not just Miles's and the policemen's, but also Hollister's and Rob's, Croker's and Phil Conforti's. Alma took a corner as well. Buddy, too, moved to help, only to find his lapels caught in Kaye's fist. "Don't even think about it," she said.

Straggling, just about spent, at last they reached the clearing. Pieter Martinson was already there waiting for them, in his parka and under it, a dark and outdated suit, a midnight serge tie, that was his standard attire for funerals, for witnessing his handiwork unveiled.

"Everything's ready?" Buddy asked him.

"Ready, Lieutenant."

Buddy stepped up to the base of the ridge, where the scrub of what had been the meadow met the stony soil and scree. There, the snow had been hardened by Pieter's boots, packed into a slippery sheet that Buddy inched across in order to grab hold of the tarp. He looked up at the covered stone and felt a sickening twist in his stomach. It seemed to him gnome-shaped, hunchbacked, gnarled. Precisely the kind of memorial that one would expect from the gloomy Martinson, but not one that the men might want to be remembered by. But it was too late to dwell on that. They were already running behind schedule, on borrowed strength and warmth. The ceremony would have to start.

In a semicircle they gathered around the stone. Buddy spoke first, reluctantly. Apart from the occasional retirement address, a pep talk to his staff at the bank, he had always avoided speeches. But there was no choice here—the men depended on him—and no time to sort out his thoughts. He spoke simply, off the cuff, with his hands at his sides and his face leveled, as if to address his troops:

"Men of Company B, citizens of Saint-Vith, friends. We've come today to pay tribute to the battle we fought here. A battle we didn't win, true, but not for want of trying. Not for lack of guts."

His eyes shifted downward, at his snow-dappled shoes, and his tone seem to lower as well. "Some of our best buddies died here, in the cold, far away from their homes and loved ones. Horrible deaths. Others, like the Vicar here, like Hollister, were hurt in ways that changed their whole lives, and I guess all of us bear the scars in one way or another. We didn't win, but we did what we had to do. Our conduct was not in any way—as a friend of mine used to say..." He smiled briefly at the coffin. "Unbecoming."

"What does it mean today?" he continued. "What can it mean to anybody in this cockamamie world of ours, with its video games and space shuttles, a world spinning faster than any of us can keep up with? What does it matter what one group of men did on one nameless ridge over a half century ago, in a battle nobody remembers? Not much, I reckon, but it matters to us. By God, it matters to us."

"Think," said Buddy Hill, "think back to how we were then, so strong and bursting with life, with passion. Think of all we came through from Normandy and France to here, to these woods. Remember how we'd sit around, telling stories, or go down to Houffalize, to the ladies. Those ladies—they were there to dance, *only* to dance, but did we ever dance with 'em. For hours and hours, never once needing rest, dancing until the sun came up and it was time to go back to the camp. We were young and that was the glory of it. Young and powerful and brave..."

He choked suddenly, cleaved by a poleax of pain. Kaye moved toward him, but he raised his hand to stop her. Swallowing, Buddy strove on. "That's what we gave here, our youth. That's what we put on this line. And that's what we've come back for, those of us who're left, to remember. To celebrate. Yes, celebrate. We fought one hell of a battle, gentlemen, and nothing, not sore bones or weak eyes or high blood pressure, can ever take that away from us."

Buddy stepped back and allowed Genie to come forward, assisting the Vicar. Ramrod straight, his long, pale face angled upward toward the treetops, he spoke solemnly, quoting from the Bible, "When thou goest forth into battle against thine enemies and seest horses and chariots and soldiers greater than thou, be not afraid. Let not your hearts be faint and do not tremble, for the Lord, thy God, is with thee."

Next came Hermansdorfer, now adorned with a great gold-plated chain around his neck, the symbol of his municipal office. Consulting a clipboard, he delivered a speech, long-winded and in German that no one but the locals could understand. Yet he spoke in a somber tone, gesturing toward the ridge, the stone, and none of the veterans interrupted him.

Lastly, and by her own request, rose Muriel Featherstone. Muriel, half-buried in a bushy fur coat, with a matching muff and hat, produced a piece of paper that appeared to be tear-stained and, sniffling, she recited the Binyon poem: "They shall not grow old as we who are left grow old. Age will not weary them, nor the years condemn. At the going down of the sun and in the morning, we will remember them."

Then there was silence, awkward and reverent at once. "I guess there's nothing left to it," Buddy shrugged. "Sweet?"

A second passed before Pieter realized that he was being summoned. He hurried to stand, front and center, beside Buddy. "Any words, Sweet? Anything you'd like to say?"

The mason looked at him quizzically, the faintest blush on his cheeks. "No…nothing…no," he stuttered, and reached for the hem of the tarp. But short of seizing it, he froze. "Yes," he said, and rising, turned and faced the crowd. "Thank you. I want to thank you all."

Together, Buddy and Pieter pulled the tarp away. All at once a sound went up from the veterans, a rhapsody of sighing and gasps. Buddy was breathless. The sculpture was nothing like he had pictured it, no mournful, mud-colored slab, no breast-beating tribute to failure. Instead there was the stone—smooth, pearly, ablaze with shimmers and glints. There was the form, not stunted and furled, but stalwart, a prow-like block slanted toward the forest, dug in and hell-bent on resistance. And on its face, boldly bordered and stamped with the sword and the snake, the inscription:

> On this ridge, in December 1944, we, the men of B Company of the 133rd Infantry Battalion of the United States Army, fought for six days and nights against superior enemy forces.We did our duty. We gave it our best. Remember Us.

Buddy started to read it out loud—Pieter was too shy—but he had barely pronounced the second word when the veterans started rushing. Lunging, they converged on the stone, touching it, almost hugging it. They hugged Pieter too—younger men would have hoisted him—and slapped his back hard, though he scarcely minded it. Instamatics came out and Hermansdorfer was drafted into service snapping pictures of the entire group posed around the memorial. There was laughter, suddenly, a sense of communal relief. As though the weight of that stone had been lifted from each of them and laid to rest here, by the ridge.

Arriving late, unnoticed in the commotion, were Claire and Richard. They came panting up the path, holding hands but releasing them just as they entered the clearing. Claire with her face windburnt and her hair wild, and Richard looking worse for the trek and winded, closer in shape to the veterans than to her.

"What'd we miss?" Richard choked, drawing up to Kuhlmann.

The driver's eyes stayed trained on the memorial, on the revelry of old people around it. "Speeches, prayers, the usual," he said.

Richard remained with Kuhlmann, an odd pair—motorcycle jacket and trenchcoat, ponytail and pate—watching from afar, while Claire waded into the fray. Soon she was taking everyone's photo, individually—portrait quality, she said, fit for framing. She had gone through an entire roll, and was working on a second, when Buddy at last interceded. "It's time," he said, stepping between the photographer and the stone. He motioned toward the path, to the coffin nestled on the snow and to Alma standing sentry-like over it. "Somebody's waiting."

Again, the box was lifted and behind it the veterans thronged. Slowly, uncertainly, they started up the ridge. Beneath the shallow snow, the soil was rocky and shifting. Gaining purchase, even with good shoes and strong knees, was difficult. Miles, the teacher, the policemen—all those carrying the coffin kept slipping backward, and soon Hermansdorfer himself pitched in, even Kuhlmann. The others were too busy bearing themselves and others less capable of climbing.

"It was easier coming down, I recall," puffed Croker.

Pringle hawked, "'Specially that last time."

"I'm ready to surrender again," Stan Morgan choked. "Just show me where."

Spagnola was helping Pappy, his arm hooped around his waist, shoving him.

"Come on, Sergeant, you can do it."

"You just keep that hand where it is. Any lower and I'll bust it."

But Spagnola also had to be pushed, by Rob and McCloski, while Hollister assisted the Vicar and Roger hauled his wife, stumbling, grousing about her heels.

The ridge that they once scooted up, mounted and descended a dozen times daily before the battle, that they defended without complaint, was now taking them forever to scale, cursing at every step. Buddy was starting to fret. Hostile-looking clouds were advancing from the east, creeping up and overrunning the sun. Soon, it could be snowing again. The veterans could be trapped in the forest.

"Next time you pick a fight, make it someplace flat," Kaye grumbled as she offered to share her cane with Buddy.

"Next time," Buddy conceded, "it'll be Iowa."

Stan Morgan moaned and Billings swore. A commotion rose from the ridge, shrill as an enemy charge. What little solemnity remained had dissipated; the ceremony was becoming a rout. Buddy was inclined to call the whole thing off, to tell them that climbing was just too hazardous in this weather. "Hold on, everybody," he began, barely gathering his breath. "Let's all stop just where we are."

But before anybody could heed him, or even register what he'd said, another voice came rumbling down the hill. "Goddamn it—it's mine!"

"Mine, too!"

A third voice resounded, no less amazed. "And mine! Jesus..."

Buddy grunted, he sucked in his pain and summoned up the strength to propel him the final few yards to the top. He arrived, rasping, only to have his breath cut short.

Hollister, Pringle, Croker, Rob: each was standing knee-deep in a depression, mesmerized, gazing at the meadow below.

"Home sweet home," said McCloski as he sunk into a hollow half-filled with pine needles.

Pappy instructed Spagnola, "Slow, slowly," as he helped him into his foxhole. "Right, that's good," the old sergeant sighed, as though he were being eased into a bath.

"And this one here was mine," Spagnola announced. He climbed down carefully, good leg first. "Recognize it anywhere."

"Don't know how," cracked Pringle. "You never saw the top of it."

Spagnola looked at him. He gawked at the others, uncertain how to react. But then they decided for him. Clutching their bellies, swaying in their holes, the men exploded with laughter. Peals of it reported through the forest, and Spagnola laughed, too.

Buddy alone remained silent, thinking *See, I did come back*, as he located his old position. He looked around at the other men, each standing in his hole as if they were trying out their own graves—that or rising up from them. His eyes turned to another hole, empty and freshly dug by Hermansdorfer's staff—the one position that would not be surrendered, ever.

It took a few minutes more, but eventually the team carrying the coffin reached the crest of the ridge. The men clambered out from their foxholes and assembled again, shoulder to shoulder, on the ridge. There they watched as the Major's coffin was lowered. They blew on their mitts and took turns passing a shovel, each contributing a spadeful of dirt that thudded like distant shellfire. Alma came last in line, but when offered, she refused the shovel, preferring instead her hands. She scooped two fistfuls of soil and allowed it to filter through her fingers. Buddy asked her if she would like to speak, but this, too, she declined. "Rest yourself, darlin'," was all she said, and slapped her hands clean.

There were no more words, no speeches or prayers. Never a formal man, or religious, the Major would have wanted it that way, they knew. There was only taps, played by Miles, clear and dolorous and with only a hint of syncopation, while the men stood at attention and saluted. McCloski planted the rifle, bayonet down, at the head of the grave, and crowned its stock with a helmet.

☆ ☆ ☆

"Do you think she'll be angry?"

"Why angry?"

"You told her you'd come back yesterday. You told her you'd call. Now all of sudden you show up with some strange older man." He clicked his tongue. "I know I'd be ticked."

"Ah, but you are not my grandmother. She has not been angry in years."

They had been crossing the village of Houffalize, only a mile or so down the road from Saint-Vith but half a century removed. The cottages with their mullioned windows and gabled roofs, the winding cobblestone alleys—all of it unchanged since the war. They passed the church, the butchershop and a patisserie, the pub where, the veterans claimed, the ladies liked to dance.

He tried to imagine being a soldier on leave from the front, fresh out of the horror, pressing his bristly cheek to the temple of a woman who looked like Claire. No wonder they remembered it so fondly, the veterans, the sweetest memory of their lives.

He knew how they felt. That very morning he had awakened with Claire's head on his shoulder, her hair draped over his neck.

Returning from the bathroom to find her asleep on his bed, he had not disturbed her, but had carefully laid down beside her, staring at her for an hour or more until he, too, finally drifted off. They had slept together—literally—clutching one another while entirely clothed. Only in the early morning had he dared to kiss her—first her nape and then the niches behind her ears. Claire responded, groggily at first, then frantically, a clash of teeth and tongues. His hand cupped her breast while the other unbuttoned her pants, her zipper. Ravenous, he licked the length of her throat.

Then, suddenly, her finger was on his lips, halting him. Claire pulled away and rasped: "Let's not. Not now." There were interviews she had to complete that morning—"Why rush this?" she asked. Her grandmother was waiting in Houffalize.

They hadn't made love, but he still had the taste of her mouth in his and the promise of real lovemaking later. That, alone, could sustain him, but since then Claire had been acting differently—distantly, her morning's adoration replaced by a mild form of reproof. Her smile was like that of a loving mother upbraiding her scrape-kneed son.

"You will enjoy meeting her, Grand-mère," Claire continued. "She has a great sense of humor—ironic, like yours." Again that reproachful smile. "You two have a lot in common."

Richard hated that smile. Quickly, he changed the subject. "She has to know more than she's told you—about your grandfather, I mean."

"For instance?"

"For instance what he looked like. Was he a redhead? Was he handsome, cool? What was his rank and where was he buried? I suppose you've been to the grave..."

"Well...no," Claire confessed.

"Great. We'll just have to ask your grandmother, then. If he really died in the battle, like she said, she's sure to know where he's buried."

"Yes. She'll know. Of course..."

Her demeanor had changed suddenly, though he had done nothing to change it. He knew that her father's birth was somehow linked to the date of Rifesnider's flight and that of his own father's discharge—the coincidence was too great—and that all three were tied to Dean Featherstone. Yet he hadn't shared that knowledge with Claire, loath to disturb her sleep, and now because it was all he had to lord over her, his sole grounds for pitying *her*.

They reached the outskirts of the village and began climbing a small hill. At the top stood a stone farmhouse that Richard could've sworn he'd seen somewhere before, but couldn't quite place. Again that stymied feeling, that there was something important he'd missed.

The sensation intensified as they entered a yard with its stacks of firewood and compost heaps, all snow-topped. A freshly roasted smell consorted with the piquancy of pines. At the door, Claire knocked once, twice, then let them both inside.

They wiped their shoes and pegged their coats before entering an old-fashioned salon, with antique furniture and throw rugs. Christmas tree and crackling hearth, a mantel lined with knickknacks. And slumped in a settee with knitting on her lap, an old and desiccated lady.

Claire whispered, "Grand-mère," reaching out to touch her but recoiling before she could. "Grand-mère..."

"She's sleeping, Claire. Let her sleep." Richard was looking around the room, at the mantel with its tiny bells and picture frames, those ubiquitous porcelain miniatures.

"Are you sure? Is she breathing?"

"She's snoring, can't you hear?"

"Check her, Richard." She clasped his leather sleeve. "Please."

He put down the frame he was holding—a picture of Claire as a little girl—and relented. "Oh, Jesus…"

Her skin had that cellophane texture, the weightlessness, of fine Mediterranean pastry. He lifted her hand to feel for a pulse but the old woman suddenly flinched. Her eyes, liquid-blue behind spectacles, flicked open.

"Qu'est-ce qu'il y a?"

Claire hurried to explain, apologizing for not calling, recounting the latest events, introducing her friend—all in a single breath. The grandmother blinked, nodded, appeared to take this in, but her eyes never wandered from Richard. She glared at him, as though not quite sure he was real.

"Enchantè, Madame," he began. He found himself staring at her in return, but without quite knowing why. "Je m'appelle Richard."

But before he could say another word, the old woman cut him off with the most horrendous of sounds—wheezing, gagging—as if she were having an attack. He turned to Claire, helpless, "What do we do?"

"Nothing," Claire assured him. "She's laughing."

"Laughing?"

Dextrous suddenly, the old woman sprung from her chair. In clunky black shoes and a long woolen skirt—in spite of them—she shimmied across the room and into a broom closet, emerging with a yellowed shoebox. Back in her chair, cackling, she shifted through an assortment of junk until she extracted a picture frame not unlike the one Richard had been holding. She gave it to Claire, who glanced at it once, then examined it closely before she, too, broke out laughing.

"What is going on here?" Richard demanded. "What's so funny?"

Biting her lips, Claire strove to compose herself. "She does not know where my grandfather is buried," she said, then handed him the frame. "But you do."

Peering out of the frame was a face much like his own. The same wire-rimmed glasses perched between the prominent forehead and nose. The same retiring mouth, the hair prone to waviness. It could have been Richard except for the fact that the photo was old, black and white and yellowing, and its subject was a corporal in uniform.

"C'est lui! C'est lui!" the old woman whinnied.

"Oui, Grand-mère, c'est lui," Claire agreed and could no longer contain her laughter. "It *is* him, Richard! It is!"

But Richard could not speak, could not even nod his head. Realizations rushed at him, those facts he'd inexplicably missed. The reason why the handwriting on Rifesnider's affidavits looked familiar, and Featherstone's signature, too. Where he had seen this house before, and this woman. They were all in his father's files, all labeled with his same meticulous hand. And so was the photograph that Richard now recognized, of young Leonard Perlmutter as a soldier in World War II.

He gazed into the frame as if it were a mirror, as though he could finally see himself in it as well. He did not laugh, Richard, and tried his best not to cry.

SIX

Night had fallen and with it another sprinkling of snow. But the silvery sparkles meant nothing to him—beauty, magic, were meaningless—and no cold could penetrate his coat. He walked, aware only of the steam coursing out of his nostrils and his galoshes' metered crunch. From his cottage to the dragons' teeth to the clearing and its crispy scrub—the same path he had always taken, ever since he was young. Many years had passed, but he still had his forest, his pincers and his oilskin sack. He had his secret, hidden. Nothing had changed, until now.

The Americans had returned. Not the same Americans he had known in the war, not the cocky young soldiers with their helmets askew and their pockets streaming with dollars. No officers offering diamonds and burying them deep in the ice. No, these Americans were tired, feeble and rubber-legged: they took all and offered nothing. They came and drank, came and gallivanted, and behind them they left a stone.

He could see it, an irregular presence at the far end of the field, by the ridge where the fighting had once been the heaviest. Nearing it, he bent and gazed at the strange, indecipherable letters, at the snake coiling slyly around a sword. He understood none of it and yet he knew what it meant, was no fool, in spite of what the villagers said. He knew what the Americans sought. He'd seen the man and the woman poking around his cottage. He saw the stone, angled in the direction of the cold house.

He had his power, stronger than ever; the pincers were ready to strike. No one could ever take it from him. His secret would never be told.

☆ ☆ ☆

The Bayonet Hall was scarcely recognizable. Streamers and balloons rained from the ceiling; tinsel glittered on the walls. A mirrored ball caught candlelight from the tables and scattered it over the floor above which music—old favorites: Tommy Dorsey, Glen Miller, Jo Stafford and the Andrew Sisters—floated. Miles manned the stereo and Yvonne a makeshift bar where the drinks were all on the house. Hermansdorfer presided over a buffet of freshly baked pastries, pilaf, and four different kinds of quiche. These were merely garnishes for the main dish, however, the *piece de resistance*: a whole roasted pig. The meat especially fresh, delivered by the local butcher—or so the hotelier bragged—directly to the door.

Yet none of this array, the decor or the ambience, could in any way compete with the ladies. Older women and young, dumpy and svelte, in long dark skirts and sequined, padded sweaters, their hair pulled taut by pins. The ladies: Legend had it that they'd been at it for 200 years, since Napoleon's time, entertaining soldiers on a voluntary basis, feeding them, making them feel at home, but mostly just dancing with them on the belief that dancing was what soldiers liked best, was the farthest thing from battle. Once, in less placid eras, the men would take considerable risks, crossing enemy lines to Houffalize, the tranquil village where the ladies lived, just for a waltz or two. But peace had come to the country, and the men were no longer robust. Today they stayed, warm and feted, snug in the Hotel Ardennes, while the ladies crammed into Kuhlmann's bus and motored over to them.

And they danced. Croker with a snaggle-haired housewife, half his age and twice his bulk, fox-trotted while Pringle lindyed with a button-nosed ingénue, nubile and feathery on her feet. Buddy and a not unattractive dowager, in a décolletté sweater and form-fitted skirt, danced, and Buddy felt nothing, no pain, only exhilaration. Nor did Kaye seem to mind as she watched them, tapping time with her cane. Even Spagnola was on his toes and jitterbugging, inscribing circles around not one but two of the ladies—twins, well into their seventies and indistinguishable still—while Crosby crooned.

Those not dancing—who couldn't—sat at the tables, their plates piled with food and faces dappled by candlelight. Billings and the Vicar leaned closer, and Stan Morgan closer still, as Pappy regaled them with facts.

"Did I get that right?" Stan asked Pappy again. "A bathtub?"

"He told me hisself."

"When? When did he tell you?" Billings pressed him.

"The day he disappeared. I was coming down from digging on the ridge, goin' to take a crap or something, and I run smack into him." He paused to partake of his Bloody Mary. "I say to him, 'Where the fuck are you goin', Featherstone?' And he looks at me with that pretty-boy Hollywood grin of his and says, 'An errand. Rifesnider's sent me on an errand.' Hell, I just laughed. 'Like, to the Five 'n' Dime to buy him some milk?' But Featherstone wasn't laughin'. He was dead serious. 'A bathtub,' he tells me, 'The colonel wishes his bath.'"

"And that's why he left for Saint-Vith?" the Vicar marveled. "That's why he never came back?"

"Good thing she don't know," said Billings, motioning toward Muriel on the floor. She was dancing with Hermansdorfer, two-stepping cheek-to-cheek and no longer crying—for once looking genuinely pleased.

"And she won't," snapped Pappy. "Ever."

Morgan shook his head. "To find a bath, I'll be doggoned."

"Take one's more like it."

They leered at him—Billings and Morgan, even the Vicar—not quite getting his drift.

"The last thing he says to me before he goes—I remember, he takes this comb out of his pocket and smooths back that bright red pompadour of his and says, 'I'd kind of like a dip myself, if you know what I mean.' And he winks at me."

"Jesus," first Billings gasped, then the Vicar: "No shit..."

"Which is probably how he bought it, taking that bath when the shelling started." Pappy tilted back and emptied the remains of his glass. "Cleanest corpse in town."

Pieter Martinson could hear the laughter from Pappy's table, but it never occurred to him to join it. It didn't dawn on him to help himself to some of the food or to bid one of the ladies to dance—a request that was never denied. He sat, rather, as he had the night before, alone and staring into his cocktail glass, at his own reflection superimposed on the ice. He barely looked up when someone inquired, "Is this seat taken?" and the chair next to his pulled out. Scarcely a mumble came out of him when Alma asked, "So what's been eatin' you, soldier?"

She placed her own glass on the table and framed it between her elbows. "Swell of you to have carved that stone, Sweet," Alma told him. "Swell of you to agree to make one for the Major, too. He'd be pleased, I'm sure."

She waited for Pieter to reply—he didn't—then tried another tack:

"I noticed you weren't there for the burial. You didn't come up on the ridge."

Pieter turned the glass in his hand. Candlelight gleamed in its cubes. "I had no right to be there. I wasn't *there* back then."

Alma sighed. She wanted to put an arm on his shoulder, to touch him in some compassionate way. Not since Vance, her late husband, had she met a man so permanently and irrevocably scarred.

"There's no shame in it, Sweet, what happened to you. Battle fatigue can be worse than getting shot, sometimes—lots worse, trust me. And it can happen to anybody, anytime."

"Please…" Pieter turned away.

"If you'd just look at it like any other wound, like Hollister's fingers. Like the Vicar."

Teeth bared, he shouted at her, "Please, I said!" so loudly that Pappy heard him and whispered something to the men at his table.

Alma folded her hands around her glass and stared into her lap. "Sorry…"

"No…it's me. *I'm* sorry," Pieter muttered. "It's just that I was so different before. I had life."

"A girl?"

Pieter nodded.

"Her name was Meg."

"Ah," Alma breathed, nose rising. "Meg."

"*Is* Meg, I should say. She's living still somewhere round Washington, though I haven't heard from her in—gosh, what is it?—fifty years."

"Well, maybe you should look her up."

He eyed her querulously, not quite sure she was serious. "Look…her…*up*?"

"Sure, why not? Drop her a line. Give her a phone call."

"I think you don't know who you're dealing with. Who I am."

"I think *you've* forgotten." Her chair scraped closer to his. "It ain't never too late and it ain't over till it's over—those are my two sayings in life. Hardly original, I know, but I live by 'em."

For once, Pieter didn't pull back, he leaned forward. "You really think so?" he asked Alma. "Call her, just like that? I wouldn't know what to say…"

"How about, 'Hiya, Meg. What d'ya say to you and me dancin' our socks off Saturday night? It's been a long, long, time.'"

Pieter might have seriously considered the idea, but before he could, a disturbance broke out on the floor.

"Stop! Stop the music!" someone was hollering. "Shut that fucking thing off!"

Miles looked for help, turning to Buddy who nodded consent. "The Boogie Woogie Bugle Boy" went dead. Neon blinked then blasted, illuminating the scuffed linoleum. What had seemed an idyllic ballroom was once again, blandly, Bayonet Hall. And standing in the middle of that hall, his eyes puffy and ponytail undone, swayed Richard Perlmutter, drunk and very disturbed.

"You!" He pointed a finger at Buddy first, then swerved it around the crowd. "All of you! You knew it all along…"

Spagnola asked, "Knew what?" He was wiping his face with a hanky. "What is it we're supposed to know?"

"About my father. You knew what he was doing here. In Saint-Vith."

"Clerking," Croker shrugged, "what else? He was Label."

Richard practically lunged at him. "Don't! Don't call him that. I hate that name."

"Richard," Buddy eased toward him, "I think you've…"

But Richard's hand shot up and he barked, "Stay away from me! You knew it too, Hill. Why my father came back here after the war."

"*After* the war?"

"With Rifesnider. The two of them. Supposedly looking for the bodies of your missing friends—Toth, Tully, Dean Featherstone—you remember them, I'm sure."

The mere mention of her brother's name sent Muriel sobbing again. Hermansdorfer tried to comfort her while Richard sought his own comfort, snatching a bottle from the bar. "Later," he told Yvonne as he swigged. "You know the room."

He dragged a leather sleeve across his mouth and said, "They found 'em, too. The bodies. GI bodies, but somehow those stiffs managed to change identities—*shazam*, just like that, they became Germans. So the GIs get buried as Krauts, as you called them, and the Krauts get away free, living the good life in North or South America."

"Let me understand this," Hollister cut in. "Rifesnider and your dad were burying Americans as Germans and helping the Germans to escape to America?"

"Congratulations, valedictorian!" Richard cheered.

"But who would want such a thing?"

"Right-wing politicians. The military establishment. Folks who saw the Nazis as natural allies against Communism, the *real* enemy."

Buddy scratched his head. "Sounds farfetched to me. But what's it got to do with us? Everyone here was either captured or wounded in the battle. Me, I crossed the Rhine. None of us came back to Saint-Vith."

Richard took another swig, gulped and scowled. "You knew all right Which is why you did in Rifesnider, in case the truth got out. To protect the unit's honor, and all that crap. All of you together, a conspiracy!"

Alma tried approaching him, reaching for the bottle. "Give it a rest, kid," she said.

But Richard only hissed at her, and hugged the bottle to his chest.

"Just like you knew about the girl…"

Alma turned to Buddy who, in turn, glanced around at the others. Their stares were as blank as his.

"That's it, try to look surprised," Richard chortled. "But you knew my father kept a girl here, and not one of your prime little ladies. And she didn't just dance…"

His gaze became distant, casting beyond the crowd to the door where Claire, looking worried, appeared.

"They had a child together. I suppose you didn't know that, either. Like you didn't know he kept supporting them for a while, sending money, no doubt promising them that someday he'd bring them both to the States. Only that day never came. My father became the professor, acquired a blueblood wife—a Belgian peasant and her bastard son, that just would not do now, would it? So the child grew up not far from here, in Houffalize, and then he had a kid of his own. A daughter…"

All eyes switched from Richard to Claire and then back again.

Buddy stammered, "We're sorry, son, believe us. We didn't know Label…"

"Don't call him that! You refer to my father by his real name. Professor Leonard G. Perlmutter, Emeritus."

Through the veterans, the wives and the ladies, Claire pushed her way. She stood opposite Richard on the dance floor. "We need to talk about this," she said. "Alone. Quietly."

"And you…my sister, my niece, whatever the fuck you are…you probably knew it, too."

"Richard, how can you…"

She moved toward him and he tried to push her off, flailing as Croker and McCloski stepped between them. As Phil Conforti burst into the hall and cried, "Help me! Everybody, help!"

"This is no time for a show, Phil," Croker said.

"No show…" the one-time entertainer puffed. Terror illuminated his face. "Mary…"

"But Mary was just here," Genie assured him.

"Was and now she's gone. *Gone*. She's not well…" Phil beseeched them, even Richard and Claire. "You've got to help me find her. *Please.*"

☆ ☆ ☆

Cold beams of light pierced the trees, probing them. A half-dozen flashlights, stockpiled by the hotel in the event of blackout, shone on the path, on the tracks, which were clear thanks to the newly flurrying snow. Pieter's, the strongest beam, led the pack, and the others followed—Hermansdorfer and Buddy, Alma, Phil and Croker, even Spagnola, who had managed to tag along. Gingerly, they felt their way through the blackened forest.

The going, hard enough during the day, was rougher and slower at night, the ground more slippery, canopied by snow-burdened branches. But there was no mistaking where Mary was headed; the triangle and dot imprints of her semi-high heels pointed indelibly.

They saw her at once. In the clearing, caught in a crossfire of light, she stood and admired the monument.

"No…don't," Phil importuned, and the rest of the posse waited while he joined her.

"So beautiful," she was saying. "So smooth," as she petted the stone with her fingertips.

Phil took off his coat and draped it around her, cupped her hands in his and blew on them. "It's freezing out here, hon. Wouldn't you feel better inside?"

"I'd like something like this for us. Someday. Do you think that nice man—what's his name—would make us one?"

"Sweet. Sure he will. Anything you want. You know that. But now, come, we wouldn't want you catching cold."

She allowed herself to be ushered back, finally, still commenting on the wonders of the stone, on the snowflakes glittering like diamonds.

"She just wanted to see it again," Phil explained, blinking into the flashlights. "She's very sensitive like that. Sentimental. But she's fine, just fine."

Buddy smiled at him and sighed. The crisis had passed, the last, he hoped, in this crisis-beleaguered reunion. Now they could go back to the hotel, back to the ladies dancing. Tomorrow they would each board their respective planes and return to wherever they came from—resume their lives, what remained of them.

They turned and pursued their own footprints now, their pace no less desperate because of the cold. Halfway down the path, though, Buddy sensed that something was different. Something was wrong. The bright and steady beam that had led them on the journey out was no longer in sight. He squinted ahead, wheeled and scanned behind him, but all he could see was darkness.

"Sweet's gone," Buddy announced. "He's up and vanished."

Croker groaned, "He stayed at the stone, the old fool. Looks like we'll have to go back and get him, too."

"No, you all carry on. I'll go. Tell Kaye I'll be there in a minute. Tell her not to worry."

Buddy shone his light on the path behind him. The exhaustion, the pain that had spared him during the dance had resurged with a singular vengeance. He wasn't sure he could make it five steps, much less to the clearing and back, yet he couldn't ask the others to go. The duty was once again his.

He trudged, a prisoner to his will, prodded by it. The flashlight shook in his hand. His vision grew blurry, and for a moment he thought he saw not one but two beams fencing in front of him. But then he felt someone drawing up beside him, someone wheezing and stumbling as he came.

"Couldn't let...you...alone," Francis Spagnola gasped. "No way, Lieutenant."

☆ ☆ ☆

Pieter had indeed stayed behind. Long after the others returned to the hotel with Mary Conforti, the old mason remained staring at the footprints in the snow.

Large footprints, they led away from the ridge, across the meadow, and back into the forest. They reminded him of the first night of the battle when, fleeing Saint-Vith, he had followed similar footprints, convinced they'd been made by an American. They brought him to a place he only vaguely remembered, a dark and cloistered place, firmly girded in ice.

Pieter followed them again, fixing them in his flashlight. He traced the footprints through the trees until suddenly he encountered strange, pyramidal forms. The dragons' teeth! He recalled passing this way during the battle, winding between the teeth and again through the forest, emerging into...a yard. Pieter staggered into it and was not at all surprised to find the footprints trailing around a cottage and down the banks of a snow-packed hollow. To a structure all but hidden by the night. The scene seemed thoroughly familiar to Pieter. Events were uncannily recurring.

The door to the structure was unlocked, and Pieter did not hesitate. Stooping as low as he could, a fist in each flank, he ducked beneath the lintel.

Inside, the darkness was so complete, so dense that even his flashlight seemed snuffed by it. An ancient, unholy cold. Pieter shivered, though less from the plunge in temperature than from the sense that he wasn't alone.

The flashlight lit on slabs of marbled flesh, on ribs and shanks and hams. *Yes, the meat,* he reminded himself. A sheep, a pig, a cow: each relinquished its identity, buttonholed by the light. Assorted joints and chops. A flabby man, naked and tallow-skinned, dangling.

Pieter felt the air rush out of his lungs, felt his legs go wobbly. But he didn't panic, didn't run. Instead, he worked the flashlight around the corpse. In addition to the thick iron hook sunk between the man's shoulder blades, Pieter noticed, there were large puncture wounds on both his temples. The face, illuminated, displayed not so much shock as relief, as if death had brought a solace of sorts, a long-anticipated reunion. To tell by his expression at least, Rifesnider had died contented.

The body, however, was not the presence Pieter felt. There was something else in the cold house, far older and deeper within. Through the carcasses he maneuvered, light shining ahead, into the smoky gray recesses of the room. Between the saddles of mutton, around a side of beef. In front of him, somewhere, a tiny sparkle gleamed—first one, then others, keenly bluish. Pieter stepped faster now, no longer caring about the ice underfoot or the creak of the door opening and closing behind him. He had to reach it, the terror that had caused him to shatter, that had tapped his inner fault.

Pieter advanced until the beam of his flashlight refracted against a glass-like surface, reflected into his face and blinded him. He dropped the flashlight, and bending to retrieve it, found himself seized by a monstrous force. It gripped him by the shoulders and lifted him off his feet. Through the meat, backward, he was dragged, thrashing, struggling to regain his balance. Until a starburst of pain exploded across his lower back. His body slackened and went limp.

The presence—snorting, stinking—loomed over him. The door was only a few feet away, but Pieter could not reach it, could not move. There was nothing to do but watch as the shadow of some giant tool, heavier than any on his workbench, rose in the air above him.

☆ ☆ ☆

"Pieter Martinson!"

"Pieter!"

The calls, urgent if not strong, echoed out of the forest. Pieter heard them as the tool—a two-handed affair, like garden shears—hovered over his head.

"Sweet!"

He wanted to call to them, warn them, but wasn't sure he had time. He wasn't sure he possessed the strength, but facing death anyway, he had nothing to lose by trying.

"In here! Quick!"

The power of his own shout, amplified by the chamber, startled him. It startled his assailant as well. The big man paused, lifted his massive jaw and narrowed his minuscule eyes. Then, abruptly, he stepped away, bowed low and burst out of the door.

They saw him at once. Nearing the peculiar stone house in the back of the yard, following Pieter's footprints, they had expected to see the mason himself emerging, and clicked their flashlights off. Spagnola managed a breathless "thank God, Sweet," before realizing his mistake. "Jesus," uttered Buddy.

He hardly had time to think as the hulk in the tattered greatcoat came charging. The most Buddy managed was the memory of an enormous tackle breaking through the defensive line and gunning for him. And like the running back Buddy had been, he lowered his head, hunkered his shoulders, and ran.

"Buddy…no!" he heard Spagnola cry, but it was too late. The ex-combat officer, the retired bank manager, had plunged, throwing all his weight into the attacker's midsection. But like a glass hitting rock, impacting, he shattered. Fists still flailing, he stumbled backward and fell.

In stiff lumbering steps, the giant man approached. In addition to the greatcoat, he was wearing galoshes, and clutched in his mitts was a large wrought-iron implement. Pincers. He stood and for a moment regarded the well-dressed intruder sprawled on the snow before him. Looked down on him with his face strangely screwed, a mixture of contempt and derangement.

So this is how it happens, Buddy thought, and thought of the irony of his death not by disease or even a surgeon's knife, but in hand-to-hand combat, defending his men on the ridge.

He heard the hiss, felt its deadly density fall, and without intending to, rolled away as the pincers smacked into the ground by his head. Rolling back again, he brought his elbow down hard on his attacker's forearms. The pincers dropped to the snow. The big man reeled, then straightened himself. He emitted a sound—half-grunt, half-howl—and pounced on Buddy barehanded.

Clutched, he could no longer roll. Couldn't call for help, either, for massive fingers were crushing his windpipe. Buddy struggled, but not fiercely. He was tired, terribly tired, and only hoped it wouldn't take long or cause him exceptional pain. He tried to fix a picture in his head—his last—of Kaye as a younger woman or of Robert, his son. But there, without being conjured, was a swarthy, thick-browed girl at once laughing at him and blowing a bubble. He clung to it as he gasped for air, and the night grew stunningly dark.

Ktchung. A crunchy-wet thudding sound, so distinctly did Buddy hear it that he wondered if it weren't his own neckbone cracking. But then other sounds followed—gagging, choking—and the pain of wintery air, ice-spiked, lacerating his lungs.

Buddy tried to sit up, fully expecting to be smashed again. But instead of being hit, instead of the giant dispatching him, he was treated to the sight of Spagnola. A look of abject shock was stamped on his face, his mouth ajar, and slung from his hands were the pincers. Before either of them could speak or even catch their breath, light beams crisscrossed the yard. "There they are!" someone called out, as first one then all of the beams found Spagnola, caging him. Rob and McCloski rushed over.

"You okay? You okay?" Rob asked nervously. "Christ, you had us worried."

McCloski pointed to the ground, "And who's that? *What's* that?"

Buddy pawed at his throat. "He tried...kill me..."

"Is he dead?"

Alma arrived, out of breath, cursing under it. She knelt to feel the unconscious man's pulse. "He'll live, probably," she pronounced. "And so will his headache."

"Will you look at the size of him," Croker remarked the moment he caught up. And Pringle: "The smell..."

They straggled in, Claire and Muriel, Greg Hollister and Stan Morgan. Roger and Phil sans spouses. The very last was Richard. He crouched next to Buddy and touched his upper arm. "You're going to be all right, aren't you?" he whispered, sounding as if he just might cry. "Aren't you?"

"Somebody—Alma—help Pieter," Buddy croaked, "Help Sweet. He's in there," and motioned toward the cold house.

More flashlights, more arrivals. Miles and Hermansdorfer and the two policemen whose names nobody had learned. All crowded around Buddy, helped him to his feet and dusted the snow from his coat.

"You did it. You really did it," Roger congratulated him. "Just like the old days."

"You're a hero, Lieutenant!" cheered Morgan.

Buddy collected his breath. "Not me, him…he did it."

All heads swerved to where Buddy was pointing—at the fat, trifocaled man in the Caterpillar cap and the bowling jacket, swaying slightly, the pincers still gripped in his hands.

"Spa-a-a-gnola!" the chant began, an anonymous solo and then a chorus as one by one everyone present joined in. "Spa-a-a-gnola!"

Cringing under a hail of back slaps, shrugging humbly, the former prisoner treated himself to a smile. "Whaddya know, I guess I did."

The celebration would have continued longer, back to the hotel and on through the night, if not for the scream.

An amalgamated scream composed, Buddy sensed, of equal parts of pain and sorrow and fear. Too high-pitched to be Alma's scream, too mature for Claire's, and very loud, the scream penetrated the walls of the cold house.

They hurried, all of them, crowding around the stunted doorway as first Buddy then the others squeezed through. The sight inside was disorienting. Alma on the ground tending to Pieter who, though frightfully pale, was conscious and pointing onward, inward through the macabre forest of meat.

Forward toward the light. A stunning, pulsating gleam brighter than all the flashlights shining, Buddy was drawn to it. He couldn't help himself, nor could the others behind him. They pressed on, threaded between the carcasses, dazed. The light grew stronger, absorbing all of their beams. Half-blinded, Buddy raised a hand over his brow and wincing, made out Muriel shivering pop-eyed in Hermansdorfer's arms. The proprietor held her, but he was gazing ahead, at whatever had made Muriel scream.

And Buddy might have screamed as well. Screamed as he hadn't throughout the entire war, on the ridge or crossing the Rhine, or at his only son's funeral. But he was too old for screaming, too sick and stupefied. All he could do was stand and wonder, stare and gasp, at the astonishing sight before him.

A niche. A grotto of sorts, carved from solid ice and studded with a multitude of shimmering crystals. Diamonds. Real diamonds for all Buddy knew, hundreds of them set faithfully in the ice. A shrine, a secret shrine. And in it, ensconced, was a man.

Seated on an icy shelf as if he had just paused there, he sat with an elbow perched on one knee. A young man whose uniform, battlefield drab, accentuated the sharp searing blue of his eyes, the hair so fiery it threatened to melt the surroundings. Ineffably young and beautiful, brimming with cockiness and ease, with the might of his own carnality. Not so much a man as a moment, a dream and a memory, splendidly preserved in time.

He smirked at them, Dean Featherstone, at their ogling old faces, their shoulders stooped and kneecaps wavering. Dean Featherstone frozen solid with an expression both pitying and glib. *This was once you,* it seemed to remind the old men, taunting them. Earnestly it asked them, *but would you trade places with me?*

SEVEN

The flight, said an announcement in English, was boarding.

"You think this is a good idea, flying so soon? Why not stay on for a week or so. Give yourself time to heal."

Pieter replied with what for Pieter passed as a smile, labored and fissure-thin. Even that minor gesture seemed to cost him, however, stiffening in his corset and sling. A Saint-Vith doctor had taped him together, realigning his back and setting his disjointed elbow so that he could catch his plane and survive the twelve-hour flight to Wisconsin.

"I think I've had enough healing time," Pieter told Buddy. "Fifty-five years, in fact. And I won't spend another day in Saint-Vith." He sighed and shook his head. "Frozen to death, you believe it? Frozen solid in that cold house he'd hidden in."

Buddy said, "Wouldn't take long, I hear. Not with his hair all wet from bathing, his clothes. He didn't feel a thing, probably."

"A merciful end," said Kaye, with only the subtlest glance at her husband.

"I followed his footprints in there, the first night of the battle. I saw him suddenly and then…I don't know. Something just snapped…" Pieter's eyes lowered, his shoulders hunched.

"It's over, Sweet," Buddy whispered. "Closed."

"Hey there, no disturbing the patient!"

The three of them looked up to see Alma tottering toward them on her high heels, struggling with Pieter's valise. "Don't you know regulations?"

"Sorry, nurse," Buddy apologized. "We were just wondering about Pieter. Maybe he should wait a day or two, strengthen up a bit."

Lowering the valise to the floor, Alma straightened her back and rubbed her sore hand. "The man's built like a forty-year-old," she attested. "A few dents and scratches, but otherwise in full running order."

"I want to get back to my work," the mason informed them. "I have to."

Alma explained, "There's the Major's stone to work on. And one for an old high school friend of his. Franks?"

"Shanks. Herbert Shanks."

"Killed in the Pacific. Anyway," Alma winked, "our Mr. Martinson's a very busy man."

"I'll say," said Kaye.

A gap of silence followed, filled only with the woman's voice on the PA system, once again announcing their flight.

Buddy rocked on his heels. "Well, that's it, then..."

"Yes...I guess it is," Pieter muttered. His head lowered but then suddenly it shot up again, and he sang, "Come visit me, sometime! Both of you!"

"Jeez, Pieter...I don't know..." Buddy was gibbering, rocking harder now, blushing. "I'm a real homebody, see. Bottle of brew, Game of the Week—the living room's far as I usually get. And Kaye's hip..."

"But maybe you'll come to Iowa," Kaye suggested, sincerely enough but with another glance at her husband. "That is, if your business brings you there."

"Yes. Of course. Count on it."

"Good."

"Good."

Buddy stuck his hand out to Pieter's left, his free hand.

"Lieutenant," Pieter said, taking it.

"Buddy, Pieter, please. Just Buddy."

Pieter laughed tersely. "Sweet," he said.

Kaye shook his hand as well, and Pieter parted from them, lumbering toward security and passport control.

But Alma lingered. She flexed her hands, sucked in air, and once again lifted the valise. "What's he got in here," she groaned, "samples?"

Kaye asked her, "Are you sure about this?"

"Sure?" Alma seemed puzzled by the question. "We got only one thing to be sure of at this stage, sister, and I prefer not dwelling on it." She leaned closer to them, conspiring. "Listen, the man wants to look up some old heartthrob of his, this Meg woman in D.C. Thinks I can nurse him up to it. And if I do, and if he goes—well, been nice, pal. But if he realizes that you can never bring back the past, that he kind of *likes* the nursing, who am I to talk him out of it?"

The Hills exchanged looks, then nodded.

"Either way," Alma grunted as she boosted the load, "I get to see Wisconsin in winter."

They watched her rushing to catch up with Pieter, watched as the two of them passed through security and disappeared down a corridor toward their flight. They were gone, and Buddy and Kaye were alone again amid the holiday swirl of passengers, the meager trimmings of Belgium's Christmas.

"You two day dreamin' or what?"

They turned back, Buddy and Kaye, to Spagnola and Pappy approaching them. The damnedest sight, the two old men practically arm-in-arm with one another, propping each other as they limped.

"Don't see much of this anymore, do you, Francis?" Pappy elbowed his partner. "Young people in love?"

"In love *and* different sexes."

Seeing them, the one grossly fat and the other emaciated, Buddy was unsure whether to laugh or cry, to feel sympathy or inklings of hope.

Kaye meanwhile inquired, "Both of you on the same plane?"

"Same plane, same destination," Spagnola said, and the Hills just looked at him perplexed. "My friend Papino here's seen Paris all right, but he ain't never seen Kearny, New Jersey."

"Francis has invited me," Pappy elaborated. "Gracious like."

"We'll have a bash," Spagnola assured them. "What with bowling on Tuesday and Thursday's the Knights of Columbus. And Wednesday, my ex-prisoners' support group. He'll meet all the members, and the leader,

Captain Carruthers—boy, are they gonna have what to talk about." He bumped his shoulder against Pappy's. "We're makin' him an honorary POW."

"And I'll make you a soldier yet. Inspections every morning, drills twice a day."

"Don't know that he'll need it," Buddy observed. "You saw the dent he put in that butcher's head."

Spagnola, reddening, studied the floor. "Guess I was afraid he wouldn't feel it otherwise, the guy was so big and crazy."

Pappy said, "Crazy is right, keeping a body frozen like that fifty years. Keepin' it secret."

"I think it was kind of a good luck piece," Buddy said. "Made him feel strong—that's what he told the police—indestructible. He was just a boy, you know, when his father was killed in the battle."

A crackle had slipped into his voice, as if he actually felt sorry for the butcher. But Kaye couldn't help needling him. "Not a bad idea, actually. I wonder if you'd fit in my fridge…"

Buddy pretended to ignore her. "And Rifesnider, the poor sonofabitch. What do you think he came back for, really—the diamonds or for Dean?"

"Whatever it was," Pappy concluded, "he got what he deserved," to which Spagnola snickered, "Yeah, a bath in Saint-Vith."

They shared a laugh, dry and sardonic, and sealed it with handshakes all around. There were more invitations for visits, for reunions that would never be held. Then, at last, they parted.

"Aren'tcha comin'?" Spagnola half-turned and asked as he guided Pappy toward security.

"Tomorrow," Buddy told him. "We have some business to settle."

He looked now at his wife and, clasping her forearm, turned her toward the exit. He wanted to get out as quickly as he could, wouldn't spend a moment more than necessary in any airport, even one as sedate and as tasteful as Brussels'.

The pair didn't get far, though, when a gut-wrenching alarm tore through the terminal. Buddy's first instinct was to hurry Kaye into one of the nearest stores—his heroic days were over—but his second was to hit his head with the butt of his palm and groan, "Not again…"

Spagnola was once more framed in the metal detector, mumbling with his hands in the air. Again there were soldiers converging on him from everywhere, with muzzles pointed at his gut. Only this time, Pappy was there to push his face into each of the guards' with a blast of tobacco-laced invective.

Soon the officer showed up—the same officer, runty and pale—but instead of confronting Pappy, he ordered the alarm to be silenced immediately, and barked at his men to back off. Then, turning to Spagnola and Pappy, the officer came to attention and saluted. For a second, the old soldiers could only gawk. They glanced at one another, exchanged a shrug, and finally saluted back at him, smartly.

Buddy observed for a few moments more, while Spagnola fended off kisses from his cheeks, before Kaye began tugging her husband's arm. This time he gave in to it. They walked toward the exit and the morning that sparkled through the glass doors, toward Kuhlmann, waiting just beyond them.

☆ ☆ ☆

Rocks. He hadn't remembered the rocks, slippery and round and black. Perhaps he was too busy hauling that boat that night to notice, too preoccupied staying alive. Or maybe he was thinking of the distance he had yet to cross, the unspeakable ordeals ahead.

But there were rocks now and gingerly Buddy negotiated them, maintaining his balance while Kaye poked her cane along the shore. He was grateful for the cold that numbed his old and now familiar pain, and for the conversation that lashed his mind to the present, against the pull of the past.

"I'm surprised at Muriel," Kaye was saying. "You would have thought she'd be an emotional wreck, but there she was this morning, like magic, completely recovered."

"That's how it is with loved ones—you're always better off knowing what happened to them than not knowing. And Hermansdorfer helped, too. The way he agreed to handle everything, the burial and all, and donating the diamonds to charity."

"And I'd have wagered he'd kept them all. Kept that cold house, too, charging admission."

"Just goes to show you," Buddy observed as he helped her over an icy patch.

"Just goes to show."

They were nearing the bank now. He could feel the colossal thrust of the water as it glided darkly between its shoals. Smelled the cold-stone river smell that threatened to lure him back to that night and its many lingering horrors. But fortunately Kaye continued:

"And that business about Rifesnider, collecting bodies, helping Nazis escape." She made a show of shivering. "Can you really believe it?"

"After all I saw in the war, at the bank. In life…" He tottered slightly and Kaye reached out to help him, but he managed to regain his footing. "We'll know eventually, I suppose. That Richard Perlmutter is researching the whole thing. The least he could do, he said, in view of his personal connection."

"Poor Richard," Kaye sighed. "Imagine, learning those things about your own father. And that nice young journalist he met."

"Claire? Oh, I think they'll stay friends at least. They've decided to go off and search for *her* father—his brother or half-brother or whatever. They're going to write a book together, they told me, *The Secret of Sandpit Ridge*. A bestseller."

They had gone as far as they could, inching down a muddy incline to the point where frozen land became churning water. A vast expanse of water—Buddy, seeing it for the first time in daylight, had never pictured it so wide.

He stood alone for a moment—Kaye purposefully hung back—straightening his shoulders against the cold, his face raised to the wind. Water raced through pebbles, tinkling like tiny bells. Squinting hard at the opposite bank, Buddy searched for any sign of the house where he'd gone to take shelter from the guns, where he fell asleep on a silken bed and vowed never again to wake up. He looked for the house in which a child had hidden, waiting to tug his sleeve, but found nothing, only a roadside diner.

The Rhine was just a river. Gray water and sooty chunks of ice. Neither frightening nor murderous nor even evocative of the past. Just a river, like countless others he had crossed.

"He was so beautiful," Kaye said suddenly, not really to Buddy, but thinking out loud about Dean.

Buddy nevertheless responded, "We all were."

Then he turned toward her, the woman with whom he had spent nearly three quarters of his life, the lion's share of a century with its myriad little victories and losses.

"Enough, Edwin," she said. "Let's go."

But instead of leaving, he hesitated again, looking back over the water. "I want to fly tonight if we can. Standby to New York. I want to spend Christmas with Allison and Paul, with my granddaughter."

"But your condition…"

"And then we head home, quick, so I can see that sonofabitch Sorgenson."

Kaye glared at him. Crying in this wind, at this temperature, could prove painful, she knew, and mightily she tried not to. "It's not too late?"

Buddy shrugged. "Could be. But, hell, I think we could give it a shot. That's if…" He bent slightly, as if to reach for a stone, reconsidered and stood. "I might have to be, you know, cared for."

"Imagine that, Buddy Hill depending on others." A single tear escaped her eye—she couldn't stop it. "It won't kill you."

She extended her hand to him, a cold, crooked hand, but firm enough to draw him from the bank. He turned now and took it.

"You were right about one thing," Kaye conceded as together they picked through the rocks. "Travel *is* nothing but trouble."

"Nothing but trouble," Buddy repeated. "Period."